COUNTERPOINT

TWISTED WISHES
BOOK 2

ANNA ZABO

Counterpoint

Second Edition

First edition published by Carina Press, 2018-2025

Copyright © 2018, 2025 by Anna Zabo

Edited by Mackenzie Walton

Cover design by L. C. Chase

Print ISBN: 978-1-947550-21-6

CONTENT NOTES

To all those who feel fractured. You are whole and wonderful.

CHAPTER
ONE

THERE WASN'T ANYTHING BETTER THAN FINE WINE AND MAC AND cheese made with some hipster, high-end, small-batch, aged-and-smoked cheddar, Dominic Bradley decided. Especially when it came with bacon.

God bless New York City. Or more specifically, Brooklyn.

Dom had found that the aptly named little bar, Poet and Whiskey, in his neighborhood was ideal to sit in on a late Saturday afternoon. Not crowded yet, so he could eat and drink and read in peace, and the food was really damn good, even if slightly pretentious.

Then again, so was he, with his bowtie, button-down, suspenders, and *jeans*.

He'd rapidly become something of a regular. The staff knew him by name now, and often just brought him a glass of merlot with his water, and let him stay and read as long as he wanted. For the most part, he was just another body in the city, but here, he'd become part of the familiar scenery.

Granted, the experience of being out and around in public and—for the most part—completely ignored was a strange one. Sure, he got the occasional appreciative glance and some-times even enough banter for a hookup, but generally, he was just another guy in the city. No one remarkable. A dude eating a late lunch or early dinner, with a glass of wine and a copy of *The Sins of the Cities of the Plain* as a companion. Lately, he'd been working through all the gay erotic classics he could.

What he wasn't at all was Domino Grinder, the most recognized and easy to spot member of the rock band Twisted Wishes. Even though that's also exactly who he was. He often got an illicit thrill when one of their songs played in the bar and he caught the bartender singing along under his breath.

So close—so anonymous, thank god!

He'd been so damn lucky people were oblivious and hadn't figured out he and Domino kind of sounded alike, though Dom was far more brash onstage. The whole hiding-in-plain-sight kept his nerves from becoming too damn frazzled.

One of the great things about having a persona he could shed at will was that he didn't have to be as cautious when he left his home, unlike the rest of the band. For the most part, the fans didn't bother his other bandmates, Ray, Zavier, and Mish. Some requests for selfies once and a while, but on the whole, they were respected.

For the *most* part. Ray and Zavier got photographed a lot. Mish had it worse—some of the fans tended to think that because she was a woman they could have more access to her time and space.

Dom took a sip of his wine. So far, nothing had come of that, but he didn't know how Mish handled it. He couldn't deal with that kind of stress—that was part of the reason Domino Grinder existed in the first place.

When his best friend, Ray Van Zeller, had first asked him to play guitar in the band he was forming, all Dom wanted to do was hide under his bed. Yes, he'd absolutely wanted to play in Ray's band—as long as they never ever left Ray's garage. The thought of getting up onstage had been too much for shy young Dominic. Hell, even playing at the talent show their senior year in high school had nearly done Dom in, and all he'd done was stand out of the spotlight and play guitar. Ray had been the sole focus then.

So, to survive climbing on that stage, he imagined what someone unlike the nerd he was might look like. He'd gelled up his hair, changed from button-downs to tight, ripped tank tops, faux leather pants, huge boots, spiked collars, and a bunch of makeup. An outrageous costume, something only someone with brass balls might wear. Dominic didn't have the guts...but Domino did.

That had made all the difference. He could play like he wanted to as Domino. Dance and scream and say whatever the fuck came into his mind. And when they were done, when they weren't touring, he could peel Domino off and be Dominic again. The nerd. The guy no one expected to be able to be a rock star. No one laughed at Domino.

As a bonus, he'd managed to keep himself—his true self—out of the limelight. Just as well, too. Because in the years that Twisted Wishes had risen to the top, Domino Grinder had become an unapproachable force of nature. A sex god no one could touch.

Which didn't suit Dom at all. He *liked* being touched. Enjoyed the company of other men. Was even happier if they preferred Dom on his knees, under their bodies, or riding their cock.

Which was exactly the opposite of what everyone thought Domino wanted.

Then again, being able to take Domino off at will meant Dom got his fill of one-night stands with the kind of men he did enjoy. Artists. Writers. Professors. Dancers. Any man interested in art or literature or history who wanted a nice roll in bed with someone who'd beg to be fucked.

Hey, it was a living. And a good one, too. Rock star most of the time, but a twink in bed.

Except now that they weren't touring, Dom had settled back into being his nerdy self one hundred percent of the time. Felt so fucking good—including the fucking part.

Though he hadn't had any of that for a while, not with moving into his new place and getting a feel for his neighborhood and the scene here.

So instead he sipped wine, ate mac and cheese, and read tales of a rentboy in London in the nineteenth century while some baseball game flickered on the TV above the bar.

Dom had gotten so into the recounting—which was pretty lewd despite the time in which it was written—that the world around him had vanished. Probably why he didn't notice the guy who'd sat down at the table next to him until a velvet voice had murmured, "Jack Saul. That's quite an *interesting* book."

Dom looked up and into the richest brown eyes he'd ever encountered. Depth and color. Flecks of gold. They were framed by stunning cheekbones, and auburn hair. And that grin... Dom's bones melted even as his dick did the opposite.

They weren't more than an arm's length apart at the tightly arranged tables, and shared the bench that ran all the way along the wall.

"It's fascinating," Dom managed.

"That's one way to put it." The smile deepened. "Pretty explicit from the get-go, in its own way."

Dom slipped in his bookmark and nodded. He let his gaze drift over the man's torso. Broad shoulders. Trim frame. And he was nicely put together, even dressed down a bit. Crisp pastel-green shirt that had probably held a tie earlier on in the day. Dark brown trousers that might have been paired with a suit coat. Belt looked well-made. Not a cheap thing.

Nice. Very nice. Especially those lips, which quirked up. Yes, the gentleman knew Dom was checking him out. And Dom was being sized up in return, given the lingering looks and the interest in Dom's chest and hands and crotch.

"Do you like it?" The guy nodded to the book.

What a leading question—did he like the vintage porn? Dom picked up his wineglass, swirled, and smiled. "Engrossing enough that I didn't notice you at all, so yes, I'm enjoying it immensely."

"And now?" That sly grin now showed teeth.

"This view's nice, too," Dom said, and didn't look away from those lovely eyes.

Laughter and a wink, but any more banter was interrupted by the waitress coming to take the newcomer's order. A pretentious panini of pot roast, caramelized shallots and Roquefort cheese—and a nice Shiraz. "And another glass of whatever my friend here is drinking."

Ah. *Friend.* Good. This might turn into an evening that would be far more interesting than merely reading about buggery. Dom shifted on the bench. Was the man from the neighborhood? Maybe. There was a trace of New York in his accent, though not much. They did get folks from other parts of the city here, and even the occasional tourist, but not that many. Did he want to get involved with someone he might see again? Dom found the owner of those lovely brown eyes checking him out again.

Yes. He probably shouldn't. But yes.

"I'm Adrian," the man said, and offered his hand. "Adrian Doran."

Dom took it. Firm grip with warm fingers that lingered a little too long. "Dominic Bradley."

"Dominic," Adrian repeated, as if rolling the sounds around in his mouth like one might wine. "Quite a pleasing name."

That's what made Dom shiver. Not Adrian's hooded look or the wine that appeared or how Adrian sipped his drink and swallowed. Nope, what hardened Dom's cock was the thought of his name—all three syllables—*pleasing* Adrian. "Most people call me Dom."

"Hmm." Adrian set down his glass. "Would you mind if I called you Dominic?"

Not if he kept saying the name like *that*. "No, not at all." And damn if his voice hadn't gone husky. Dom took a gulp of his own wine.

Adrian chuckled. "So, Dominic Bradley, who enjoys nineteenth century homoerotic tales, what brings you here?"

"I live here," Dom said. "Got a place and moved in about a month and a half ago."

Adrian chewed on that. "Live here *here*, or elsewhere in Brooklyn?"

That was a question a local asked. Hell. Because he really should back off now. "Few blocks away." Might as well ask the obvious. "You local?"

Oh, the humor in those eyes. "Yes, though not as local as you." He shrugged. "I like this place, though. The food is good, the wine excellent, and sometimes you meet a real gem of a person."

Just then, the waitress brought Adrian his meal. She glanced at Adrian and gave Dom a little grin, too.

Great. Encouragement. Didn't know if he wanted that or not. There was already a little buzz from the Merlot and the stimulating reading, and now there was Adrian, who was far better than fiction.

Adrian picked up his panini. "Like tonight."

It was, Dom thought, rude to watch someone else eat. But he couldn't help it. Adrian bit into that sandwich, and his eyes flickered closed. His grunt was downright sexy, as was that sigh of contentment as he tasted and swallowed. Long, elegant fingers. A pink tongue that flicked out to catch the remnants of cheese.

"Shit, they've outdone themselves," Adrian murmured. He focused on Dom again. "Would you like a bite?"

After that display? "Sure."

Dom had expected Adrian to cut a hunk off the uneaten

half of the panini, which he did. He hadn't expected that he'd hold out his fork for Dom to eat off of. That was intimate and sexy and...

"Come on, Dominic, don't be shy *now*."

Like fingers up his spine. Dom leaned in and took the bite from Adrian's fork.

"That's it," Adrian said. "Very nice."

Oh god. The panini. Adrian's words. Both were heaven. The meat and cheese combination was a delight for the taste buds, while that voice slithered down Dom's nerves and tightened his balls. He couldn't help the little moan that escaped.

"Now, see how good that is?"

Dom got the distinct impression Adrian wasn't talking about the food. He blinked back the pleasure in his veins. "I wouldn't mind some more."

Amusement colored Adrian's chuckle, then he stroked Dom's cheek with the back of his fingers. "If you're willing to stay and talk, perhaps we can share dessert?"

Dom shifted closer. "I still have three quarters of a glass of wine. I'm not going anywhere for a while."

That flash of teeth again. "Good."

Yep, he was all in, for whatever Adrian had in mind. Might not be the brightest idea, but Dom would figure out the ramifications of having a fling with a neighbor later. Right now? He really wanted to know what else Adrian Doran might suggest they do.

OH, HOW ADRIAN WANTED TO UNDO THE BOWTIE AROUND Dominic's neck and use it to pull the man closer to him. Those lips begged to be kissed and tamed, and he wanted to hear that sweet moan again.

But there was a difference between flirting in your own

neighborhood bar and some club in Manhattan. Things you could get away with and things you couldn't, and he was already pushing a bit of the envelope with feeding lovely, shivering Dominic bites of his sandwich. He'd push it more with dessert, and then perhaps they'd see where that went.

Granted, it wasn't exactly *his* neighborhood. He lived over in Park Slope, but the bar was close enough that he found his way here often enough to be known as a regular. The only reason he hadn't made the trip recently had been work—first loading him down with so many deadlines he'd been working twelve-hour days and weekends, then sending him out of town for two weeks.

But that was over with for a while, and here he was with a brand-new regular. Dapper and bespectacled, with that lovely mix of sexy and shy that turned Adrian on so much.

Dominic was now at half a glass of wine—and his cheeks held a little bit of color.

"So, Dominic, what brings you to New York?" There was a student look to the man, but his clothes were a tad too nice, and while his face was youthful enough, there was something in his manner that seemed a little more worldly than early twenties.

That blush deepened. "Oh." Dominic toyed with his wine. "I'm a musician."

Interesting. Certainly not a starving one. "Which instrument?"

"Guitar." He fidgeted and looked toward the door. "I'm in a band, you know, like everyone." Finally Dominic met Adrian's gaze again. "What about you?"

"Far less interesting. I'm a software engineer for a financial services company." In other words, a corporate office drone. But it paid the rent. Well, it would have, had he been renting.

Dominic gave a little shrug. "But do you like it?" He sipped his wine and peered at Adrian through thick eyelashes. His dark brown eyes that seemed to widen when Adrian peered back.

Oh, honey, you really want something I can give, don't you? But what? A quick suck? A hot fuck? One night? He was so tired of the quick Grindr hookups. Something more, something longer would be a nice change of pace. Getting off was fine, but longer-term, there was so much more you could do with a man.

He finished his panini before answering. "It's a fine job. Challenging in places. Boring in others." He mused over the top of his own wineglass. "I suppose I like it well enough."

Something in Dominic's expression shifted, but was gone before Adrian could pin a name on the look. "And outside of work?"

He set his glass down. "Mmm. You mean besides feeding bits of panini to handsome young men in bars?"

Oh, that got him a nice blush. "I'm not *that* young."

But quite handsome. And so obviously in need of a nice long fuck, given those plump lips and blushing cheeks. "How old are you, then?"

Dominic sat up straight. "I'm twenty-seven."

Yeah, he could see that, even with the little bit of roundness to Dominic's face. "Since I know you'll ask, I'm thirty-six."

Dominic dwelled on that for a moment, then smiled. "You never did answer my question. What do you do for fun?"

Men like you. Except—that wasn't entirely true. Dominic did pique his interest sexually, yes. But also in other ways. Maybe it was the book, or perhaps the bowtie. Or the fact that a *musician* was living in a neighborhood few could afford now. Even he'd be hard-pressed to buy into this market.

The server saved him from having to answer right away by swooping in to take his plate. "Dessert?"

"Yes, please." In more ways than one.

Next to him, Dominic practically squirmed.

As she picked up the debris from dinner, she gave them the lowdown on dessert. "We have cheesecake that can be topped with either fresh strawberries or chocolate syrup or both, a lemon meringue pie, and a flourless chocolate cake with raspberries."

Adrian eyed Dominic. What would a young man with such *discerning* taste in literature prefer?

Those dark eyes stared back at Adrian.

"Lemon meringue, I think," Adrian murmured.

Shock colored Dominic's face. "How did you—"

"Two forks?" the waitress asked.

"No," Adrian said. "One will be enough."

And maybe he was laying it on a little thick, because even she blushed. When she left, he studied Dominic again. He took a breath, as if to steady himself. "Lemon meringue's my favorite. Like—absolute favorite."

"I'd make some joke about being a little tart—but that's not why you like it, right?" Because Dominic had layers. Adrian wanted to peel them all off and find out what lay beneath. How did those lips feel against his? What would his moans taste like? Just the thought made him ache.

"It's—I love lemon. And yes, because they're tart. But no, that's not all. They're—They taste like summer and sun and freedom." Dominic's gaze drifted to the doorway again—to look outside, Adrian realized. "They're happiness in fruit form."

Yes, layers. And no, not a one-night stand. Not this one. "You write lyrics, too?"

Dominic seemed to startle out of his skin. "What? No. I—" He laughed, but it was strained. "I just play guitar. Help a little with the songs. Other people are so much better with words than me." He patted the book beside him.

"And what kind of music do you play?"

Dominic raised an eyebrow, and there was a little spark of

fire there. Very nice indeed. "What do you do outside work, Adrian?"

That was fair. Entirely fair. And he *did* like the sound of his name on Dominic's lips.

Their waitress came and dropped off a sizable piece of pie—with one fork. It was a beautiful thing, lovely shade of yellow with snow-white meringue curled and browned a tiny bit on top.

"Oh." Dominic's voice was almost reverent. "That's sublime."

So was the look on that sweet face. Right there and then—if this went further than today—Adrian would make it his mission to have Dominic sigh like that again, preferably while Adrian's cock was inside him. Wouldn't that be magnificent?

Adrian cut off the tip of the pie with the side of the fork, and watched Dominic bite his lip. "Sometimes I go to clubs and dance." He speared the piece with the tines and lifted. "Throw myself into a crowd of people and...let go."

Dominic's gaze slipped from the fork and met Adrian's. "Love to see that."

"I'm sure you would." He held out the morsel of pie to Dominic.

Oh, those wide eyes. He scooted closer and took what Adrian offered so gently. Wet lips. Pink tongue. And when the pie slid into Dominic's mouth, his eyes fluttered shut—and that was utterly sublime, too, down to the little whimper.

"God, it's so good." A whisper of words.

Adrian needed this man in his bed. More than once. More than twice. As many times as possible. Someone who moved like that, ate like that, *submitted* like that—Adrian's head whirled. He took a bite of the pie himself—and yes, it was quite lovely. The custard was perfect, and somehow it did taste like a sunny summer day.

"I also like walks in the park. Museums. The orchestra. History." Adrian sliced off another piece for Dominic. "And reading." This time he held the piece closer, and patted the space between them. "Are you willing?"

The answer must have been yes, because Dominic closed that gap and their legs brushed against each other. Laughter in that sweet face.

With his free hand, he touched Dominic's thigh lightly. "This okay?"

"More than. Thank you for asking."

Well, he wasn't about to feel up a man without consent. That was just rude.

When he fed the pie to Dominic this time, Adrian slid his hand up until he met the hard ridge of an erect cock.

The groan was deeper this time.

"Summer memories?" Adrian left his hand exactly where it was, but moved his finger enough to rub so slightly against that length.

Watching Dominic swallow was a treat. His chuckle was unexpectedly deep. "I practically grew up at the Jersey Shore. Lots of memories of lemon and sunscreen and—" He blushed.

"Sucking guys off under the boardwalk?"

The blush deepened. "Well, yes—and other things, too."

Adrian took his bite of pie and shifted his hand up, cupping Dominic's hard dick. He felt more than heard the inhale of breath. When he held out Dominic's piece, he slid fingers around the ridge. "You're a fascinating man, Dominic. What do *you* do for fun?"

This time, the bite was sensual, as was the way Dominic licked the custard off the fork. "Me?" His smile was wicked, and he pressed his shaft into Adrian's hand and leaned in close to whisper, "I seduce men and let them fuck me."

Yes. That was blindingly obvious. Adrian couldn't help the smile. "And how do you think you're doing?"

"I'm hard as a rock from being fed lemon pie. You tell me."

Right. That was enough of that. He set down the fork,

cupped the side of Dominic's lovely face, and drew him into a kiss.

The tart of the lemon mixed with the richness of wine and the sweet, sweet taste of unashamed need. Dominic kissed with a lovely mix of desperation and determination, and no, this wasn't his first rodeo. Not by a long shot. Adrian tightened his grip on Dominic's cock and kissed back with just enough force to impart one simple fact: he—not Dominic—would be in control.

And like perfection, Dominic *melted* and opened to him, giving way to lips and tongue. After a few more moments enjoying that little taste of submission, Adrian relented. "There's still more pie." And they were still sitting in a bar, one that had a few patrons trickling in. He wasn't about to go any further than that.

A shudder ran through Dominic. "That might undo me."

"Good." Adrian sat back. He slid his hand from Dominic's package. "Something tells me you need to be undone."

An almost knowing chuckle. "Probably."

He broke the remaining portion in two, eating his half before scooping up what was left. "Do you want more than this?"

Dominic eyed the pie. "We're not talking about lemon meringue anymore, are we?"

Perceptive. Adrian did like that in men—especially ones he wanted more than one night from. "No." He studied the pie, then Dominic. "I'm enjoying this—enjoying you—immensely. And I think I'd be rather disappointed if this night ended with a quick fuck and a goodbye. I'd like to get to know you, Dominic. Know you better than one evening permits."

Dominic didn't even look at the pie. "To be honest with you, I haven't tried anything more than one night with anyone in a very long time."

"That's somewhat of a shame."

"Is it?" Dominic's raised eyebrow and fire were back.

Oh, to draw that out and then quench it in turn. "Well, I find that learning about what a partner wants and needs takes time. You're a musician—you know what they say about practicing... How are you supposed to perfect pleasure if you only ever get one shot at it?"

Dominic's smile was replaced with something more profound.

"And I'm also quite interested in what's behind those pretty eyes of yours. You're an intelligent man and I suspect there's a lot more you do for fun besides being fucked."

"You're the first person who's ever thought I had pretty eyes." He flicked his gaze to the pie. "Maybe we should save that last bite for later, then."

"Be a shame to waste it. How about you finish the pie and meet me here next Wednesday at six if you want something a little longer than one night?"

Dominic cocked his head ever so slightly, then nodded. "Deal."

Adrian slipped the last of the pie into that luscious mouth, and the sight was just as spectacular as the first bite.

When they were done, the waitress cleared their tables and brought them their checks.

"I feel like I should pay for half of yours," Dominic murmured, his cheeks once again a little red.

"Oh, you treated me in the sharing."

A chuckle. "I do try."

They rose and made their way out to the sidewalk, and Dominic fidgeted for a second. "Look. I think I do want more than a quick—" He waved his hand and swallowed. "Sometimes my schedule is...erratic. Can I get your number, just in case I need to reschedule or—something?"

Poor Dominic, so flustered at not being dragged off for a nice uncomplicated hookup. "Of course."

They exchanged numbers, then Adrian drew that blushing

man in for a kiss. Once more it took only a hint of control to soften Dominic in his arms. And yes, poor thing was still all nice and hard.

Adrian broke the kiss. "If you end up liking the Saul book, I can recommend some others to you."

Oh, the lust and interest in Dominic's eyes—and not just for sex. "Can you?"

"Mmmhmm. Wednesday. Dinner and book recommendations."

"And more?"

Dominic was breathless, so Adrian drew him close again, cupping that nice hard cock again. "I promise that part of more will be worth the wait."

A laugh, as if Dominic couldn't believe what he was doing. "I'm gonna hold you to that."

Good. Very, very, very good.

CHAPTER
TWO

Sunday morning, and Dom was in hell. Well, he was actually just south of Hell's Kitchen, in Chelsea, in a practice and recording studio trying desperately to get into the groove of playing. The weight of his guitar felt foreign against his shoulder, the strings too rough against his fingers, and his head still rotated around and around images of Adrian Doran.

He'd been so hot and horny and still fucking hard when he'd gotten home on Saturday night. Spent a good part of that night jacking off to memories of Adrian's voice and smile. And that should have been enough, should have burnt the man out of his system.

But it hadn't. Not with his number in Dom's phone. Not with plans for Wednesday.

He was most definitely not Domino Grinder today, and that was a huge problem.

It was no wonder he flubbed the chords in "Finding Light" each time they tried to run through the song. It was a tricky transition, but one he was normally up for. After all, he'd played harder songs. Hell, he could play freaking guitar concertos on the instrument in his hands. But not at the moment. Might as well be a newbie plucking at the strings for the first time.

The song skidded to a halt mid-chorus, and silence descended on the studio.

"Dom, what the hell?" Ray slapped his hand against his thigh, his frustration so evident. "What's going on with you?"

Shit, yeah, he'd really fucked that up. His head wasn't in the right place. Too much Dominic and not enough Domino, all because Adrian's voice still echoed in his ear. "Sorry—I—Sorry." He turned away and plucked a chord, ostensibly tuning, though he'd done that several times already.

He heard rather than saw Ray's sigh and curse.

Mish caught Dom's eye, her arms cradling her upright bass. "Hon, it's okay. We all have off days."

This wasn't an off day, this was—he didn't even know what this was. He didn't feel like himself. Well, he did, just the wrong version. Dominic Bradley wasn't a rock star, but he couldn't get out of that skin and into Domino, the persona who was.

Zav thumped a little roll on the high tom. "Why don't we take a little break?"

"Yeah, maybe that's for the best," Ray said. When Dom turned back, Ray was watching him. "We need you here, Dom. *I* need you here."

His oldest friend. His *best* friend. And he was letting the whole band down. "I know. Let me get some coffee in me and get my head back on." He unshouldered his guitar and set it in its stand. Fresh air—he needed that, too. So he poured a cup of coffee from the carafe that had been delivered with the snacks and headed to the open window.

He wasn't even surprised when Zavier joined him. Pretty common, really, during breaks. They both liked air and contemplation.

But that wasn't in the queue for today, it seemed.

"Do you want to talk about it?" Zavier leaned against the

wall, his black tank top still pristine. Not even a drop of sweat. They hadn't been playing long enough to warrant a break.

"There's nothing to talk about. I'm just—" Dom waved his arm. "I'm fine."

A wry chuckle. "Dom..."

Damn Zavier, because he knew. Somehow, the man knew something was up. Zav had this way of reading people and was so damn fucking sensible most of the time. Then again, he had married Ray, who wore his heart on his sleeve and buried his problems behind fear, so one of those two had to be the grounded one.

Zavier was so grounded, it was a wonder he didn't grow roots with each step.

Dom glanced back at their leader. Ray was a hell of a lot better emotionally and temper-wise, which was good, since Dom had never been this shitty of a guitarist before. A year and a half ago, a flub like that from Dom would have caused chaos in the band. They'd been under such pressure, between a band manager out to get them, a horrible label, and a grueling tour as the opening act for one of the best bands in the country. They'd all learned how to rely on one another during those months, and Zavier, their new drummer, had become family and Ray's greatest ally.

Now he was Ray's husband.

Dom took a drink of coffee and pondered how much to say. Finally, he let it slip. "I met someone yesterday."

Zavier's eyebrows lifted, but his expression didn't change. "A professor in tweed?"

Dom grunted. Yeah, that was his normal candy. Maybe that's why Adrian threw him so much. "No, a computer engineer who'd taken off a tie and a suit jacket."

"Oh." Amusement crept into Zavier's voice. "Did you have fun?"

Yes, but he'd had more than that. He'd been excited and

turned on and...curious. Who was Adrian? What had he thought of the book Dom'd been reading? Which museums did he like? Dom wanted more of Adrian, and that was rare. Maybe it was because they hadn't fucked.

You know it's not.

Zavier was quiet and watchful, and his smile had fallen into seriousness.

More coffee didn't do a damn thing for Dom's nerves. Likely made things worse. "He fed me lemon meringue pie, felt me up, kissed me, then asked me to dinner this Wednesday."

"A date?" Zavier's brow crinkled. "That's unusual."

Yeah, it was for Dom. He pretty much only did one-night stands. He rolled his shoulders, and found his cheeks heating. "Domino Grinder doesn't go on dates."

"Domino doesn't whip out his dick at all," Zavier said. "That's not the image you take out when you go hunting while on tour. Domino isn't a thirst-trap for toppy intellectuals." He crossed his arms and tilted his head. "But *you* are. And you like this man. Enough to see him again."

Fucking perceptive Zavier Demos. "I hardly know the guy. I just—" Couldn't stop thinking about Adrian. That voice, the touch. His approval. What it would feel like when those hands were finally on his naked skin. "I have to focus on this." He gestured at their instruments. "Ray's right. I need to be *here*." Not daydreaming about Adrian bending him over or his *book recommendations*.

A nod. "Yeah, I get it. How can we help?"

See, now that was exactly why Zavier had been the right drummer for Twisted Wishes and the right man for volatile Ray Van Zeller. He *cared*. Tried to find solutions. Didn't get riled up easily.

Dom snorted. "You have a way to get my head into Domino? 'Cause that's where I need to be." Not stuck in an endless loop of twink Dominic. He needed that edge, that chaos.

Zavier got that damn grin of his, the fucking bastard. "I might." He pushed off the wall. "Hey, Ray? Mish?"

It was always a little amazing to watch Ray turn and see Zavier. The two had been married more than a year now, and though they weren't particularly outgoing with their affection, every time Ray met Zavier's gaze, there was this little catch of breath, a little hint of happy surprise.

"Yeah?" Ray said. His gaze lingered on Zavier, shifted to Dom, then swung back. Mish cocked her head.

"Do you think we could warm up with 'Dark Dreams' or 'Lightning' or one of the older songs before working on the new ones?" Zavier said.

Oh. A little jolt ran through Dom. Yeah, that might work. He knew those, knew how to be Domino when playing those. Hell, even thinking about the rhythms and the notes and how the stage felt on tour, how he'd held his guitar in his hands, that had him shifting and straightening his back. Muscle memory, and more. The knowledge of who he was when he played those songs. Domino was part of that music—and Dom *was* Domino.

Ray eyed Dom again. "Would that help?"

"Yeah." He drank down the rest of the coffee, then tossed the cup in the nearest trash can. "Yeah, it would. You mind?"

"Whatever you need, hon," Mish said.

"Shit, dude. What Mish said." Ray ran a hand through his hair. "I guess it has been a while."

A couple weeks since they'd last played together, partly because Dom had finally found a place to buy. He'd had to get all his shit out of storage and move it up to New York, sort through it, chuck half of the stuff, and buy all new crap that actually matched the place.

Then there'd been all the meetings with their new label and all the legal wrangling to settle on a contract that wouldn't screw them over. They'd ended up hiring a band manager with a legal background, and after that, Ray had wanted to get started on the new album, so here they were. They'd just started on the new songs during their tiny makeup tour to cover the cities they'd missed when the end of their original tour had been canceled.

Maybe it wasn't entirely Adrian that was throwing Dom off. A lot had happened, and he'd had to be more Dominic than Domino lately in every other part of his life, too.

They settled on "Lightning" and fuck, that was what Dom needed. He slid into the song like Domino always had, and by the end of it, his head was clear. The edge was back, along with that feeling of wild energy and sheer freedom, like he could take on the world and win. Because that was Domino. "Fuck yeah, that's better. Let's try 'Finding Light' again."

They didn't nail it perfectly, of course, but it sounded a damn sight better than before. Dom managed the tricky bits just fine, and each repeat sounded better as they found their groove, their synergy with one another. Domino was back, and he could work, fix the notes and timing with the rest of the band. Be there, be part of Twisted Wishes with them.

Strange thing was, the thoughts of Adrian didn't exactly *leave* Dom. In between songs or when Mish was working with Ray on a particular sequence on the upright, he found himself wondering what Adrian would make of *this*. Yeah, he'd said he'd been in a band. But Twisted Wishes wasn't just any band —not anymore. Not after their tumultuous rise to the top. Not with the scandal of their former band manager trying to roofie Ray and nearly killing him in the process.

They were well-known. In the news. A hot ticket with even hotter members.

Dom grunted at himself, tasting the bitterness of that, too. He doubted Domino Grinder was the kind of man Adrian Doran would pick up in a bar. Or ask out on a date. And if Dom explained who he was to Adrian, the jig would be up.

He couldn't be both—not at the same time. Not with anyone but the three people in this room.

Even on tour, he stayed mostly in persona, though he was a little amazed no one in the crew had ratted him out. Then again, he hadn't let any of them get particularly close, either.

When Ray called for them all to practice again, Dom pushed those thoughts aside. It was just a date, just a fuck. Chances were the whole thing wouldn't go further than a couple of rounds of sex. No need to worry about a future that wouldn't happen.

He slung his guitar over his shoulder again, and slipped into Domino.

CHAPTER
THREE

MONDAY MORNING ADRIAN FOUND THAT GETTING BACK TO THE gym was *almost* as good as feeding a panini to a blushing man. Hopefully, it would also put Dominic out of Adrian's mind for a while.

He threw his bag into a locker, and headed out to stretch and warm up. As always, Adrian's coworker Jackson was already there, raring to go in blue shorts and a white tank that stood out against his deep brown skin. They'd become fast friends. Jackson was fucking *brilliant*. Smarter and more talented at coding than Adrian—and he was no slouch—plus Jackson looked like a god in a suit and tie and moved like the devil on the dance floor.

"'Bout time, Adi," Jackson said.

Adrian hated nicknames from everyone else, but not from Jackson and not that one, because they had a deal that had been negotiated over time. "Jack," he said, drawing out the vowel.

Jackson's lips twisted in amusement. "I was wondering if you'd skip today. Didn't know when you got in over the weekend."

"Got home just before dinner on Saturday." And had

promptly gone out to eat, and that took Adrian straight back to Dominic. He shook his head. "And I fucking *need* the workout today." He stopped short of asking Jackson to push them both hard. Jackson wasn't exactly his trainer, even if that was the role he'd stepped into the first time he'd ever laid eyes on Adrian at the gym, mostly to keep Adrian from hurting himself, he'd said.

Dark eyes met his, and Jackson grunted, his gaze shrewd. They'd known each other for years, meeting first at the office, then running into each other here—then very unexceptionally while they were both out hunting for men at the same dance club.

They were so alike and so different, but their tastes in quickies ran similarly, so that night at the club, they'd fucked a lovely, built man into oblivion together in the bathroom. The next day, they'd worked out harder than ever, then finished an obnoxious project at work in record time.

Meeting Jackson when Adrian had moved back from California had washed the West Coast off him and grounded Adrian firmly back in New York after a month of floundering to find his feet in his own hometown.

Thank god.

This city's in your blood, man. Same as mine, Jackson had said the second time they'd had lunch. But that fast, hard friendship had opened him up more than usual, and Jackson could read him like a fucking street sign.

"Shit on my mind that shouldn't be," Adrian said.

"Mmmhmm." Jackson pointed to the floor. "Get your stretches done, Irish boy. We're gonna run."

Adrian hated running, especially around the tiny indoor track at the gym. Still, he started his routine of stretches.

"Now," Jackson said. "Is this work-related shit or personal shit? Because if that trip of yours turned bad..."

Adrian spent a little longer stretching his legs than usual and tried to be as nonchalant as possible. "The trip was fine.

Overall. The project's still a nightmare, but the site visits and installs went fine." They'd both been working on this system rollout forever. "I'd have given you a heads-up if that was the issue."

"So it's personal." Jackson crossed his arms. "You telling me, or am I working it out of you with sweat?"

Adrian rose and shook his arms out. "There's nothing to tell, Jack. Not yet."

A deep laugh. "Bullshit. But you can tell yourself that if you want." He grinned. "You ready?"

"To run? Never." Adrian gestured at the track, though, and Jackson loped out into the outer lane. Adrian followed, and they looped a few times at a nice, gentle jog before Jackson smirked at him and took off. Adrian groaned and followed, picking up speed to match his friend's pace.

They ran and ran and ran some more, beyond when Adrian wanted to stop and faster than he liked. At the end, when Jackson finally had pity on him, Adrian was drenched with sweat, exhausted—and the thoughts of Dominic and the dinner date he'd pried from the man still lingered in his mind.

"Fuck," he muttered. "Shit."

He didn't get hung up on dates.

Adrian grabbed his water bottle and drank down half in one gulp.

"You hook up with someone on the trip that has you rattled?" Jackson toweled his face off and took a swig of water from his own bottle.

Adrian blew out a breath and shook his head. Jackson wasn't even winded, which used to bother him, but when he'd started to see the results of all these runs and squats and the weight lifting Jackson put him through, he figured he didn't get to whine, not even in his head.

"No." He wiped his face with the bottom of his T-shirt. "Guy I met last night at Poet and Whiskey."

Jackson raised an eyebrow, then nodded toward the weight room. "Time to lift."

God, this workout was gonna kill him. But he made his way to the weights and let Jackson put him through a torturous routine until his muscles were just about to protest loudly.

And still Dominic was there in his head. That blush, the shyness mixed with the snappy comebacks and flirting. Contradictions. Intelligence. He nearly dropped the fifty-pound free weights on the way to putting them back in the rack.

"Hell, Adi. This guy have a magic cock or something? I've never seen you strung out over a piece of ass before."

Adrian leaned back on the weight rack to catch his breath. "Haven't fucked him yet. Just had dinner next to him. Flirted. Made a date for this Wednesday."

Oh, he'd shocked Jackson, given the wide eyes and skeptical look. "A *date*?" His voice pitched higher.

"Yeah, you know. That thing people do sometimes when they think maybe they want more than a fling?"

Jackson rolled his eyes. "How do you feel about burpees?"

He fucking hated every single moment of them, and the damn word, too. "You know how I feel."

Oh, that wicked, wide smile. "Give me three sets of twenty, then tell me about this *date*."

Adrian bit back the groan and did as told, his body burning in that way he actually enjoyed but would never, ever tell Jackson. Working out was horrible and wonderful, and he was stronger and more toned at thirty-six than he'd been at twenty-five.

Dominic was twenty-seven. Fuck. He pushed through the rest of the damn reps until he finished then collapsed onto the mat. "I hate you."

Above him, Jackson smiled down, a dark-eyed angel of

pain. "That's not what you said the last time I was buried in you."

No, those hadn't been the words. Hell, he probably hadn't been able to form words at that moment. They'd fucked on and off through their entire friendship, but ultimately they were decidedly not a match. Jackson wanted to find a husband and have kids. Adrian had never wanted kids, and was a bit too kinky for Jackson's tastes in the long run. Jackson didn't do bondage or submission, and that wasn't something Adrian could simply throw away.

But after the last time they'd fucked, Adrian had run his hands through the short curls of Jackson's hair and murmured, "You know, you're my best friend."

Jackson had pushed him away, but there'd been affection in his retort. "Don't get sappy on me, Irish boy."

Adrian sighed but didn't move from the puddle he'd formed on the mat. "He's a local, Jack. Cute. Wears glasses and a bowtie. Plays guitar. Reads nineteenth century gay erotica while eating dinner."

Laughter poured out of Jackson, and he offered Adrian a hand up. "You sure someone's not setting you up? 'Cause if there ever were a person who would make your head snap around, it would be a bowtie-wearing artist with a penchant for gay lit. Like someone read out a line from the 'Adrian Doran Dream Fucks' catalog."

He grunted as Jackson pulled him to standing. "I really do hate you." His cheeks were red, but that description? Yeah. On the fucking nose. "He's also twenty-seven."

That got him a roll of the eyes. "So? That's never been an issue for you. Older. Younger. Whatever gender. You like what you like."

Yeah, he did. And no, age hadn't been an issue before. "What's next?"

Besides the twinkling of Jackson's eyes, next turned out to

be balance work on the Bosu and then planks. All kinds of goddamned planks. Then a cool-down jog.

When they hit the locker room, Jackson leaned against the lockers and leveled a look Adrian couldn't turn from. "So what's really bothering you about this guy, Adrian? Because it's not his age, it's certainly not his taste in books or food, but you are *bothered*, my friend."

Adrian extracted his shower kit and a towel, then stripped off his soaked T-shirt and tossed it into the locker. "He's...fuck if I know." Layered. More than a pretty smile. He shook his head slowly, piecing together his thoughts. "He's wicked smart, I think. And there's a shyness there, but also such audacity."

"Lord, a man who's Adrian's catnip." Jackson got his kit and a towel, and they both headed to the showers.

Maybe. All right, yes. Adrian faced Jackson. "He let me feed him half a piece of pie, and the way he looked when I did—Jack. I can't even describe it."

A smile formed on Jackson's lips. "You don't have to. Written all over you. And if you had him literally eating out of your hand, he probably likes the other things you have to offer." The smile slid to something more serious. "Adi, boy, there's nothing wrong with wanting something longer. For all that we both play the field, you know my thoughts on that matter."

Yeah, he did, especially lately. Jackson had bemoaned the hookup scene as a source for something longer-term than a couple hours. *I want a man who can move, sure, and scream, but also one who wants to remember my name. Stick around. Get breakfast.*

And there was truth to what Jackson had said. "There's a lot more I could enjoy if it's more than one night." Adrian said the words almost to himself, then laughed. "I'm getting tired of hookups, too."

Jackson clapped him on the back, then shoved him toward

a stall. "You never really liked the music at the clubs anyway."

"I never went to the clubs for the *music*, Jack." Because when he went clubbing, it was *exactly* for a couple hours of fun and no names.

Jackson waved that away, and vanished into a shower stall of his own.

Adrian hadn't been at a club the other night. Dominic was more than a pickup—and that was okay. Maybe it was voicing his thoughts about Dominic or maybe the endorphins from the workout, but he was feeling a hell of a lot better by the time they both cleared the showers and dressed in their suits and ties and headed to the office. Thoughts of Dominic were still there, but they weren't throwing him like they had been.

Dinner was a start. They'd see where that went.

"Thanks for kicking my ass this morning." He grinned at Jackson as they carded themselves past security.

"You won't be thanking me later, but you're welcome." Jackson hit the elevator button. "And I'm glad it wasn't the trip that had you all freaked, 'cause shit's already too fucked in the department."

"Oh god, what did I miss?"

The elevator dinged, and Jackson gave a dark, bitter chuckle before stepping inside the car.

Adrian followed. Well, guess he'd find out soon enough.

By lunchtime, a dull ache had spread over Adrian's body from the workout Jackson had put him through, and a much sharper throbbing ran through his brain. Though his business trip had gone reasonably well and he'd completed all of his tasks, there was still a huge pile of work waiting for him when he got to his desk.

His boss, Russ, had swung by. "There were quite a few bugs in the code you're responsible for, Adrian. Your areas are usually rock-solid. What happened?"

He didn't know, because he hadn't touched that area of the software in two weeks. And no one else should've—it wasn't part of any of the features being worked on currently. "I'll take a look. Nothing should have changed at all."

He had his suspicions, of course, and a quick look at the change log bore those out. He IM'd Jackson.

> What the hell has William been doing in my code?

> Same thing he's been doing in everyone's code: "improving" it.

Oh, for fuck's sake. He'd be the first to admit he wasn't the tightest coder, but he wasn't sloppy and he was fairly economical. He ran the unit tests and Jackson regularly looked over his lines before he pushed them to production.

> I've only been gone two weeks. How could he have screwed up so damn much? Doesn't he have his own stuff to do?

> He claims he needs to fix stuff in our lines to make things work. I've been fighting with him and management all last week, but for some reason, they'd rather listen to William than me.

Adrian flinched. He knew the reason, as did Jackson. Despite the degrees and Jackson's brilliance as a computer scientist and engineer, William's white skin and Midwest accent always impressed the bosses. Guy could get away with murder—not to mention really shitty coding—and still get promoted.

Jackson had to fight—carefully—for every inch he got. It wasn't fair and it wasn't right, and it killed Adrian a little inside that he couldn't fix that. He'd gotten the side-eye, too, the first time he'd mentioned an ex-boyfriend, but it was nothing like the stonewalling Jackson got.

He spent the day cleaning up William's mistakes and debriefing his bosses on his trip. By quitting time, his mailbox was still a dumpster fire and his head a pounding mess. An hour later, Jackson leaned against the frame of his cube wall. "You staying here all night, or you wanna get a beer and bitch?"

He really should go home. He hadn't had a chance to catch up on his personal email yet. Thank god he'd gotten all the freelance website work for clients done before he'd gone on that business trip. Given the workload in front of him at the day job, he wasn't going to be picking up any freelance work for some time.

Adrian blew out a breath and scanned the horror that was the three displays of work he still had to do, then glanced at the clock. "Fuck."

"Come on, Adi. Let's get out of here. That'll be right where you left it bright and early tomorrow."

Jackson had a point. And he did need a beer. "I'm gonna need another run tomorrow to chill me out before I tackle all that, I think." Adrian locked his screen and grabbed his phone and his gym bag.

"Hell. Is it that bad?"

"You know exactly how bad it is." When they got into the empty elevator car and the doors slid shut, Adrian murmured, "I don't know how you put up with it."

Jackson grunted. "How do you put up with them making those sly comments about you being gay?"

Adrian gritted his teeth and kept his mouth shut. "You know what really annoys me about those?"

Jackson's lips twitched upward. "Yeah, I do."

He'd ranted about it often enough to Jackson. He wasn't gay. He was pansexual, even if his preferences did lean masculine. But explaining the nuances of orientation to rigidly straight men was a lost cause, so Adrian had given up.

The elevator door opened, and they headed out into the lobby and then into the city they both loved. In the back of his mind, he heard that question Dominic had asked on Saturday. Did he like his job?

Today, the answer wasn't yes, or even well enough. Shit. "This gig pays really well."

It was as if Jackson wasn't at all surprised by his shift in conversation—or maybe it was because there wasn't really one. "Other gigs pay well, too."

The way he said that... Adrian's heart flipped and his steps faltered. "Jack..." Because he didn't want to be left alone at the bank. Because he needed a friend at work.

Jackson glanced his way and huffed. "Beer, Adi. And I'll tell you."

They ended up back in Brooklyn, closer to Jackson's home in Far Rockaway than Adrian's. The bar was closer to an old neighborhood type, given that gentrification hadn't quite set in this part of Brooklyn—no hipster menu, no gleaming metal, and distressed wood. All the wear and tear of the place was genuine, from years of use, not from special paints or whatnot.

Adrian felt at home here, too. He'd grown up in Brooklyn during the '80s, back when his neighborhood wasn't *the* place to live. His parents both worked and their house—the one he now owned—had been neat, but as run-down as this bar.

When the bartender set beers down for both Jackson and him, Adrian turned and waited.

"Don't give me that look, Adi."

"What look is that?"

Jackson smiled and looked into his beer, a rare blush on his dark, chiseled cheeks. "The lost puppy look."

Adrian sat up. "I'm not—"

"Yeah, you are." Jackson took a swig, then leveled his gaze at Adrian. "For all that you're connected and have community, you don't make friends that easily."

That wasn't—okay, maybe that was true. He had his kink community and the LGBTQIA group he volunteered with, and he knew some of the other folks at the gym. There was the freelance work that kept his hand in social media and website design, but friendships...? He could count those on one hand.

"I never understood that about you, 'cause you're a good guy. What're you so afraid of?"

Losing. Adrian laughed into his beer and avoided the answer, because it would strip too much off. "So you've got another job lined up, then?"

Jackson shook his head, but it wasn't in answer to Adrian's question. "I've been interviewing. I'm close to an offer at this place uptown. Startup type, near Columbia." He paused. "Minority owned. They're putting together this great social media app."

"Chancy." Adrian couldn't help it. Startups came and went. Hell, he'd been on that roller coaster in California, enough to hate it. Yeah, so while he might not like the bank, while there might be a whole hell of a lot of prejudice, it was *stable.*

"Yeah, yeah, I know. But they're doing shit I believe in. And I've got enough saved up if things go south. And if they go north..."

Jackson would be fine then. This was a good thing. Hell, Adrian loved social media, so he got why Jackson would jump after a new thing that looked great. Part of Adrian was happy, but the other part...

"And if you think I'm letting your white ass off of working out three times a week, you've got another thing coming." Jackson sipped his beer. "Besides, if you settle down with this book boy of yours, you're not gonna be up for dancing at night."

So many emotions clashed in Adrian that he choked on his beer and laughed. "I haven't even had dinner with the man yet." If Jackson left work, they'd still be friends. It was a damn stupid thing to think that they wouldn't be, but he'd also experienced that in California. "And Jack, if you want to find someone long-term, I'm not sure those clubs we went to are the right place."

"You got a better option?"

A slow nod. "Maybe. You like art and music and all."

Jackson rolled his eyes. "I also like young and fresh."

Adrian held up his hands. "All I'm saying is maybe check out places that hold your other interests." Besides the quick hot sex they both liked. "There's a jazz place that opened up recently in Washington Heights."

That gave Jackson pause, it seemed, because he grunted and drank more beer. "Some folks I know have mentioned it, too, so I'm not going to be offended by your Irish ass recommending it."

Adrian gave an apologetic shrug. "I did their website. And it's a nice place. The music was top-notch. You never know who you might meet."

Jackson snorted. "Matchmaker Adi. At least you do know your jazz, thanks to me." Those shrewd eyes caught Adrian's. "What about you? I know work's grating on you. And you know they're gonna promote William right over you."

He couldn't help the flinch. "It's a paycheck, it's steady, and I don't hate it."

"But you don't love it," Jackson said, an echo of what had been in Dominic's face on Saturday night.

"There are very few things I love," Adrian said.

"Bullshit, Adi. Bull-fucking-shit."

Yeah, yeah. But if he told himself that, it made his work life a lot easier to deal with.

CHAPTER
FOUR

ADRIAN CURSED UNDER HIS BREATH AS HE STOOD ON THE SUBWAY platform. He'd never make the restaurant to meet Dominic by 6 PM. Not with the way the trains were running. He should have known, should have left early, but with the chaos at work—well, obviously that hadn't happened. Thankfully, he did have a cell signal for once, so he fired off a quick text.

> Trains are fucked. Going to be late.

Dominic's reply came fairly fast.

> S'ok. I have a book. I'll get a glass of wine and wait.

> Which book?

Couldn't help it. Perhaps it was on the list he had tucked into his suit pocket.

> Just some Whitman poetry. I like lingering over the lines.

Adrian inhaled a breath that smelled too much like humanity and not enough fresh air. Still, Dominic's words sent little sparks down his limbs.

> You sure you're not a lyricist?

> Ha. No, I'm really not. Just an admirer. The world is beautiful. Words are beautiful.

Adrian's fingers flew over the screen, and he sent the text before he could even think about it.

> You're beautiful.

The rumble of a train made Adrian look up. Thank god it was one of the ones he'd been waiting for. Yeah, it was gonna be packed, but he'd rather be crammed in and to Dominic sooner than later. His cell vibrated as he made his way onto the stuffed car and found a tiny bit of standing space. He reached up to grab the bar, and checked the reply.

> Thank you. No one's ever said that to me before.

The train lurched forward, and the tenuous cell signal vanished. Adrian stared at the message. Pretty damn obvious no lover had ever treated Dominic right. Maybe they'd been kind and hot. Maybe the sex had been exceptional, but for no one to tell that lovely man he was beautiful?

Fools. The lot of them. All of them. Adrian tucked his phone into his inner jacket pocket. Even if this flirting and date didn't lead to anything more, he'd be the person who showed Dominic what it was like to be *appreciated*.

By the time the train got to Brooklyn and his stop, he was

a good ten minutes late. He fired off another text as soon as he had a signal again.

> You're lovely, Dominic. And I'll be there in a few minutes.

Then he'd prove it to the man. Words. Actions. At least for one night. Perhaps more.

Took another several minutes to cover the distance from the subway to the bar. When he was close, Adrian slowed his steps and tugged at his clothing. No time to go home and change. Hopefully he wasn't too rumpled from the commute. He'd chosen a gray plaid paired with a purple shirt and a tie full of pinks and reds and blues. One of his *yes, I'm hella queer, but so much better dressed than you* looks. It was always interesting to note whose heads he turned as he travelled.

Several people gave him the once-over when he entered Poet and Whiskey, but he paid them no mind. He only had interest in one man tonight.

Took exactly one glance to find Dominic. He was tucked against the far wall in a corner, sitting on that long bench in front of a table for two, and yes, he had his glass of wine. But he wasn't reading his poetry—no. He was staring at Adrian like a man in a desert who'd just spied water. Moist lips. Wide eyes. He swallowed, and the smile that lit his face warmed every part of Adrian.

Hell, this was going to be fun.

Adrian crossed the bar and ignored the chair on the other side of the table. Instead, he sat next to Dominic on the bench, their legs brushing. "I'm sorry I got hung up."

"It's all right." Dominic leaned toward him, closing what little space there was between them. "I'm good at waiting."

"Are you?" He reached to cup Dominic's neck—but hesitated. "May I?" A simple thing, to seek permission. But so important if he were going to do everything as right as he could.

A lovely blush and a nod. "Yes." A breathless answer.

So Adrian caught his neck and pulled him close enough that their lips nearly touched. "A kiss?"

"Please." Almost a moan, that.

Took nothing to move that fraction of space, delve into that needy and tantalizing mouth. Dominic tasted of red wine and so much want.

Oh yes, he'd have his man in his bed tonight. No doubts about that. "I'm glad you waited for me, Dominic." He spoke against those sweet lips, then sat back.

A nice flush had spread down Dominic's neck. "So am I." He met Adrian's gaze. "You look amazing, by the way, in that suit."

Adrian touched Dominic's bowtie. This one was silk, with blue and green jewel tones and hints of gold, paired with a pale yellow shirt. "Thank you. You're quite the dapper man, yourself." Once more, he'd worn jeans, and this pair was so tight his arousal was almost indecently apparent. "And utterly beautiful."

There was that swallow again, but right before Dominic spoke, a waiter coughed from the other side of the table.

Damn. But they were getting ahead of themselves. They both turned, and Adrian gave the gentleman a smile. His nametag read Greg and he was blushing a little himself.

Greg cleared his throat again. "Can I get you something to drink?" He handed Adrian a menu.

Wine would be nice. He eyed Dominic's half-empty glass. "Would you be up for sharing a bottle of something red?"

A sultry smile, and Dominic leaned back against the bench. "Sure."

He glanced over the list and picked out a mid-priced Spanish wine. When Greg left, Adrian returned his full attention to Dominic. "We should decide on meals before we get too lost in each other again."

That earned him a chuckle. "I already know what I want. But I suppose I should have some food, too." He raised an eyebrow. "You gonna sit in your chair?" Dominic nodded at the empty seat across from him.

"Do you want me to?"

A slow shake of his head.

"Then not on your life." Adrian nudged him farther into the corner, then rotated their table ninety degrees so they could more easily share it. "This is far more cozy."

"It's like you want me trapped," Dominic murmured. The blush was still there, but there was an energetic edge to his smile and his gaze. Like he was winning whatever game they were playing.

Which, perhaps, was true. Adrian had the feeling they were both winning tonight.

"You could still slip out." He gestured to the other end of the table. There was enough room to squeeze between it and the wall.

"So there is." Dominic slid farther up the bench and shoved the table tight against the wall.

Oh, now that was nice. He followed, crowded Dominic into the corner. "It's like you want me to trap you."

"Yes, please." No uncertainty. Just the whisper of someone who desperately needed to lose himself.

Adrian didn't know Dominic's story, but he knew that look, the way he moved his body, the desire twisted into every motion. Adrian tapped the menu. "Pick your dinner."

"Will you feed it to me again?"

Lord, this man. He hadn't even fucked him, and yet Adrian already wanted more. More nights, more words. "We'll drink wine, eat our meals, talk books, and perhaps have some dessert." He leaned in close. "But I do have other plans for that mouth of yours tonight."

There was steel in those brown eyes when they met Adrian's. "Good."

Dinner was top-notch, and the wine warming. Watching Dominic simultaneously unwind and also become a creature of fiery passion was exquisite. They discussed the Jack Saul book, and that left Dominic squirming on the bench while they waited to order dessert.

Adrian couldn't help laying his hand on Dominic's thigh. "This all right?"

A huff. "Was the last time."

"But this is now." Adrian stroked a finger over hard muscle under denim. "I'm not here to take advantage of you."

"What if I want to be taken advantage of?"

Those dark eyes were bottomless and wide, it seemed. "Then it's not being taken advantage of. It's surrender." Adrian hazarded the word. "Submission."

He didn't think Dominic's eyes could get larger, but he'd been wrong. "Oh." A lick of lips. "Okay."

"Just okay?" He drifted his fingers higher.

Dominic chuckled. "More than. Do whatever you want, you know, without getting us thrown out or arrested for public indecency."

Ah, yes. They would get along *very* well. With his free hand, he pulled Dominic in for a long kiss full of flavor and need. Once more, those lips parted and Dominic softened under Adrian's hands.

Well, not all of him. His dick was nice and thick as Adrian traced it with his hand.

When he backed off, Dominic's chest was heaving, his cheeks were flush with more than wine, and he looked about ready to beg.

"I brought you a list of books," Adrian whispered against those willing lips.

A tiny moan. "Fuck, Adrian," Dominic whispered. "You're gonna give me whiplash."

Yes, yes he was. With joy. "That's the plan." He sat back and dug the list out of his suit pocket and passed it along.

Dominic took it, his hands surprisingly steady given the rest of his body, unfolded it, and read. The flush remained, but a sharp, focused look took up where lust had been. "I've read some of these." His gaze met Adrian's, and it was everything at once. Intelligent, sexy, needy, impressed. "But not all of them."

Good. That meant Adrian could offer the books to Dominic to borrow. "Which ones have you read?"

Before Dominic could list them off, the waiter finally came to take their dessert order. Adrian didn't bother consulting Dominic this time. "That chocolate cake you have. One fork."

Greg's gaze flicked between them, and he nodded before retreating.

"No lemon this time?"

Adrian brushed a thumb over Dominic's lips. "I want to see what you taste like with chocolate tonight."

Another tremble. Good. He liked the needy edge on Dominic. It was going to be such a pleasure to take him home and tease the hell out of him before fucking him good and hard. "Now, which books?"

Dominic focused on the list. The ruddiness of his skin had spread down his neck. "Well, *Maurice*, for one, and the bio of Oscar Wilde." He pointed out a few others. "I've been wanting to read *City of Night* for ages."

"I have a copy."

"Do you?" Hook, line, and sinker. Dominic's smile said *everything*. Yes, there'd be other dates after this one.

When the cake came, Adrian fed it to Dominic, watching the way those lips and tongue took the heavy cake off the fork. A beautiful mouth, no doubt as talented as it was pretty. The fact that Dominic was articulate and interested in literature and fine food as well as fucking? Perfect.

So was that smile, the one that seemed to say that Dominic

thought he was just as in charge of the situation as Adrian. And perhaps he was.

The cake was delightful, and so was that little sound Dominic made when he swallowed down the last bite. Hell, Adrian was harder than he'd been in a long while, if he discounted his first encounter with Mr. Dominic Bradley.

As they waited for the waiter to collect their dishes, Adrian pointed to the book of poetry. "May I?"

"Of course." Dominic placed it in Adrian's hands.

He flipped it open at random. "'To a Stranger.' How apropos."

That earned him a smirk. "We are, aren't we? Strangers. Eating and drinking."

The lines were obviously familiar to Dominic. To Adrian, as well. *I ate with you and slept with you.*

But it was the last line that held Adrian's attention.

"I am to see to it that I do not lose you."

Well, if that ever were a sign that he should keep pursuing the interesting man before him. Not that he believed in fate or portents. Life was far too chaotic for that. He closed the book. "Would you like to come over, Dominic?"

"I thought you'd never ask." A quirk formed on those lips.

He wanted under Dominic's clothes, wanted to press fingertips against skin. Drag his tongue down that neck and devour full-throated moans.

When the check came, Dominic collected it before Adrian could reach for the folder. "This is nonnegotiable."

A flare in his speech and gaze had Adrian nodding in agreement. "Of course."

There was strength in this man, enough to bend, enough to let go. But also to stand his ground, which Adrian appreciated as much as all the other parts he'd glimpsed.

Check paid, they both rose and headed out of the bar. Adrian caught Dominic's hand and pulled him close. "I normally don't take anyone home on a weeknight."

Warm hand in his. An even warmer one slipped beneath Adrian's suit jacket. "Breaking your rules for me?"

"I suspect I'll have no regrets whatsoever." He slid his fingers into Dominic's hair and tugged him close. Lips met lips and thighs brushed. And yes, Dominic tasted superb with chocolate.

This time when he broke the kiss, Dominic clung to him, cock hard and body trembling. "Adrian."

"Hmm?"

"Please take me home and fuck me." Low, soft words, so sexy, like silk over skin.

Before he claimed another kiss, he whispered against Dominic's neck, "It'll be my pleasure."

WALKING HAND IN HAND WITH ADRIAN WAS SUCH A HEAD RUSH for Dom. He never got to be this way in public, be gay, be *with* someone. But on the walk to Adrian's place, he was out and open and so fucking turned on it was actually a wonder he could walk at all.

Adrian seemed to know the effect he was having, given his amused smile and the glint in his eyes. Didn't help when he yanked on Dom's hand and pulled him into a searing kiss that shook him to the bones. At this point in his life, Dom had been with countless men, but this guy—this guy turned him inside out like no other. Maybe it was the way he gripped Dom's hair. Maybe it was the gold in his eyes or just how smart he was, but whatever the cause, Dom couldn't catch his breath around Adrian.

Even more troubling, he didn't want to. Being swept away was exhilarating and terrifying. Like a roller coaster where you couldn't see the hills and valleys or even the end of the line. He moaned into Adrian's insistent kiss and let himself go. Wherever Adrian led, Dom would follow, at least for tonight.

"You're such a treat," Adrian murmured. "How are you here with me?"

That was easy to answer. "I'm here because you commented on my choice of literature."

Hot, soft fingers over his cheeks. "But you were sitting there all alone. I don't understand why you were alone. You're a gem of a man."

Except Dominic only existed in the cracks and crevices of Domino Grinder's life, which left no time for long-term lovers. "I'm not *that* interesting."

Adrian huffed a breath. "Yes, yes you are." He nudged him in the shoulder. "A few more blocks, and I'll show you."

Dom shivered, even though it was summer and he was wearing a long-sleeve shirt. Yeah, he wanted uncovered and unmasked. So he went and walked and tried not to focus on the tightness of his jeans or the rapid beating of his heart.

They ended their walk in front of a brownstone in the middle of a block. As Adrian had said earlier, not exactly the same neighborhood, but close. Close enough to be local. Close enough that they could become a thing. A serious thing.

The fear caught his throat and scrambled down into his heart. Unmasking himself meant unmasking Domino, which meant Dominic would be the one in the spotlight. The one onstage. And he *couldn't*. He just...couldn't.

Adrian must have noticed something, because he loosened his grip. "You don't have to come in." He spoke in such a gentle, reasonable tone. "We can simply say goodnight."

Dom shook his head. "It's not you." Utterly true. Because if Dominic were anyone else, he'd be thrilled—he was thrilled on a deep level. This felt like a beginning of one of those grand adventures. If not love, then at least a romping good time. But he was also the guitar player of Twisted Wishes, and there was no forgetting that. No abandoning it.

A one-night stand was easy. This...wasn't that. He didn't want it to be that.

Adrian took his other hand. "Dominic."

That voice brokered command and made Dom lift his gaze. Stare into those brown eyes.

"Do you want to come in?" Adrian gave his hands a little squeeze.

"Yes." More than anything in the world.

A nod. "Then what's stopping you?"

"The fact that I want to come in."

Adrian's shoulders dropped, as did his eyes. He rubbed Dom's fingers with his own, then let go. "Goodnight, Dominic," he whispered, the hurt too evident in his stance, his words. He turned to climb the stairs to his door.

"Adrian."

He didn't turn, but he did stop. Thank god.

"Please don't let me walk away." Because he'd hate himself for weeks and weeks. Because he'd regret everything, maybe for the rest of his life.

Adrian swung around slowly and watched. Eyes intent. Jaw working. Dom couldn't read the shifting emotions on his face. Not even when he spoke. "Give me your hand, then."

Dom did, reaching out like Adrian's fingers were a lifeline. When the grip closed and Adrian pulled him forward, he went, like he had before. Up one step, then another. Adrian didn't let go when he fished out his keys to unlock his door. Nor when he pulled him into the house and locked them in.

A hand under his chin forced Dom to look up. "Am I *that* terrifying?"

"No. It's not you. It's—" He couldn't put it into words, and that had him laughing. "See, this is why I don't do lyrics. I can't actually get the shit in my head out. But it's not you. I *want* you."

A slight smile at that. Adrian swept a thumb over Dom's

jaw. "Love 'em and leave 'em. And I'm not letting you do that, am I?"

"No, you're not." Dom leaned into Adrian's touch. "You're making me want to come back. Need to see what happens. Which—that's never happened."

Adrian's gaze flickered. "I'm honored to be the first, then. Especially since I'm not particularly special." He kissed Dom's forehead, then let go. "Would you like to see my library? I can lend you that book."

The resistance in Dominic, that awful hesitation, cracked, because Adrian was absolutely that special. And he never could say no to books. "Yeah. A library would be fine."

"So books and food are the way to your heart." Adrian laughed. "No wonder I like you." He nodded down the hall. "Come with me."

The hall opened up into a living room, well-appointed with wooden floors and a bright rug. And bookshelves galore, plus a huge TV. Despite the books, something told Dom this wasn't the room Adrian meant. This wasn't a *library*.

Given that Adrian kept going down another hall, Dom must have been correct. Adrian nodded off to the right. "Kitchen's that way. Dining room is straight ahead." To the left was a staircase, and they climbed. He paused when they got to the next floor. "Bedrooms. Bathrooms. My office."

A glimpse told him that Adrian seemed to enjoy greens and blues and golds, because those were the colors that caught Dom's eye through the open doors. Calming. Soothing. God, he liked this guy.

Adrian rounded the hallway to another set of stairs. "The movers hated me for the next bit. All those boxes of books."

Even though he steeled himself, when they reached the third floor, Dom exhaled in wonder. "Oh my god."

The whole third floor of the house had been converted into

a library. There was a comfortable reading bench that looked like it might double for a daybed, and a small desk with a chair on the far side, but other than that, there were only shelves and books. And not just along the walls, either. Half-bookcases were situated into little rows, and there were even books stacked on top. Some of the tomes looked old, others new. Dom took one step and then another into the space, and drank it all in.

"I had to have the floor reinforced, but I've always wanted a space like this. My own haven." There was a wistfulness to Adrian's voice. "Some of these are my great-grandfather's books."

"I could live here." The thought came out of Dom's lips, unbidden and unstoppable. "You have no idea."

And there was the laugh Dom was finding heated his bones like no other sound. "I do now," Adrian said.

Dom stared at Adrian, at the suit he wore so well, the cut, the color. The tiny smile he had. Yeah, he could fall so hard for this man. Hell, he was already zooming down the tracks, screaming his head off in terror, and they'd not even gotten anywhere near a bed.

That smile deepened. "Would it help if I told you I could cook?"

"Can you?"

Adrian nodded. "Though I've never tried to make lemon meringue pie."

Dom didn't know whether to laugh or cry. "If you're as good in bed as out of it, I'm doomed."

That smile turned sharp and Adrian stalked forward. "Then Dominic, my dear man..." He caught Dom's neck with both hands and stroked down to his shoulders. "You're so utterly doomed."

This time, Adrian's kiss was hard and deep and didn't stop. It devoured and claimed, and Dom could only hold on to those strong arms and groan. It was a kiss that would end one way—with Dom completely stripped and undone. With every inhibition removed and with his soul laid bare.

He wanted every single second of that.

Adrian's fingers pressed into his shoulders, his grip like iron. Not painful, but commanding. He spoke against Dom's lips. "I'm going to take every stitch of clothing off you, Dominic. Then you're going to kneel for me and wrap those beautiful lips of yours around my cock." Teeth scraped Dom's lower lip. "Yes?"

He couldn't breathe for how fucking turned on he was. Bones hot, mind whirling. Cock so hard in his jeans it was painful. "Please. Yes." The books. The sound of Adrian's voice. The color of those eyes burning into him.

The tie went first, of course, deftly undone by Adrian's fingers. Lips followed, grazing Dom's neck as each button of his shirt was undone. He swayed under Adrian's touch and mouth.

When his shirt was opened, a caress of breath blew across his shoulder. "Now, this I wasn't expecting. You're full of layers, Dominic."

His tattoos. Of course. He kind of forgot about them when he was buttoned up in his button-downs. "Yeah. I...have a lot of ink."

"So I see." Adrian tugged the shirt from the waist of Dom's jeans, then pushed it off his shoulders. It caught at the cuffs, trapping his hands. Adrian took a step back, his eyes roaming across Dom's chest and belly. There was still bare skin, but Dom knew what else Adrian saw—ink that dipped down past the waistband of his jeans.

He'd never felt more exposed, more naked, despite still wearing his pants. He'd gone shirtless onstage, of course, but rarely took off all his clothes for hookups. Didn't have to, not when it was meant to be a quick fuck and release before never seeing the dude again. And most of the guys he met found it hot to fuck without much thought about the other person.

Maybe that's why Adrian scared him so. He noticed things. Asked questions. Wanted to know about Dom. Thank god he wasn't much of a rock fan, though. There was no sense of recognition of Dom's tattoos in Adrian's appreciative and lust-filled appraisal. No sign that he'd seen them on another, very different man.

"They're masterful." Adrian feathered fingers down the cardinal wing that covered Dom's right pec. "Must have taken hour and hours."

Countless. The heat from Adrian's fingers on his skin only highlighted just how much of his flesh was covered in ink. "I started when I was eighteen and—I couldn't get enough." They were *his*, too. Dom's, not Domino's—despite them being one of Domino's better known features, and despite him covering them up when he went about his life as Dominic.

"I don't have any. Never could settle on a design." Adrian traced his hand up to Adrian's shoulder, where a circle of Celtic knot-work capped the end. "The Irish in me quite likes this one."

He brushed his lips against it, and Dom whimpered.

"Turn around, please," Adrian said.

Dom did, exposing his back and the ink that stretched across his flesh there, too.

"Oh, good god," Adrian whispered. "I want to devour you."

Dom shivered. Couldn't help it. No one had ever spoken to him like that, with that heat and passion. Usually it was merely some variant of "I want my cock in your hole." Or "Suck my dick." He didn't actually know how to process this kind of desire.

Didn't have time, either. Adrian's lips skimmed the back of his neck and Dom gasped, pulling the shirt that was still caught up in his hands taut against his lower back.

"How can anyone not think you're beautiful?" Another

murmur of words. "I want to show you so much. All the beauty you possess."

Dom bit his lip and his eyes watered unexpectedly. Maybe because he was so damn turned on he felt like he'd come right there and then. Maybe it was that Adrian seemed to care, and Dom had only ever found *that* emotion in his band-mates. The guys he hooked up with wanted one thing—a screaming twink on their cocks.

Caring and sex didn't go together in Dom's world. Kind of like how love, relationships, and Domino didn't mesh.

Adrian tugged at the shirt and freed Dom's hands. He didn't know what the hell to do with them, so he curled and uncurled his fingers and tried not to fall over as Adrian blazed hot kissed over his shoulders. Dom's breath came in huffs and moans, and his dick strained against his jeans.

"You're too used to getting off fast, aren't you?" Amuse-ment in those words. Adrian slid a hand around Dom's waist and undid the button and zipper. "Bet you'll come the moment I wrap my hand around you."

Dom bit back the moan. Or tried to. It came out anyway, a thin sound against closed lips.

"Love that sound." Adrian scraped his teeth against Dom's neck. "You fighting against yourself."

Too close to the truth. This wasn't a hookup at all. He'd be back. If Adrian stopped now, he'd still come back. To hear that voice, to see his smile. "Fuck."

"Soon." Adrian hooked fingers into the waistband of Dom's pants and pushed down until the fabric slid down his legs. Underwear followed, and Dom's knees nearly buckled.

Adrian steadied him, though, hand across his belly and that strong chest pressed to his back. "I have you."

And he did. He had Dom's body and the hooks were already into his heart and soul. He couldn't do this. He wanted to do this. Needed every moment of this like the parched earth needed rain.

He was so *very* screwed.

Adrian turned him around, and he was staring back into those brown-gold-blue eyes before Adrian took his mouth into a fierce kiss.

Dom moaned into it, his will to stand slipping away.

It vanished entirely when Adrian wrapped his hand around Dom's cock. True to his prediction, between the torture of Adrian's tongue against his and the tightness of his grip, Dom couldn't stop from coming hard and fast. He clung to Adrian's suit jacket, tears pricking at his eyes, and Adrian swallowed his shouts and moans.

Adrian caught him with his other arm, pressing them close as Dom spilled himself on him. Fuck. Oh god. He couldn't breathe or think as his vision hazed over. He was vaguely aware of being lowered to the ground. Hands met hardwood, and when he could focus again, he was staring at Adrian's leather shoes. They were brown, polished, and the winged stitching was fine and detailed.

Fingers stroked his hair. "I hope you enjoyed that as much as I did."

The words didn't make sense, and Dom struggled through the fog to answer. "I'm the one who came."

"Yes, but I *made* you."

The power in those words made Dom look up.

Adrian brushed hair from Dom's eyes. "I took you apart with words and kisses and a single stroke." It wasn't a smile on those lips—nothing so lurid. No, Adrian wore satisfaction and delight. "And I don't think you'll ever forget that I did, should you vanish from my life."

Dom shook his head. "I won't. Won't forget it."

"Good." That word was like a kiss to Dom's spine, and it stirred up the desire that hadn't been quenched by his orgasm.

Nothing about Adrian was anything like any other man Dom had ever met, and he couldn't get enough. He sat back on his heels. Dark splotches marred the perfection of the cloth of Adrian's trousers. Semen had even managed to get onto the jacket. Despite that—or maybe because—Adrian was still visibly thick and hard under the wool.

Dom licked his lips. "I've ruined your suit."

A laugh. "There are plenty of dry cleaners in New York, Dominic. And if I hadn't wanted you to come on me, I wouldn't have turned you around." Adrian smiled down. "I rather like the thought of knowing your jizz was all over this suit when I'm sitting at my job."

That thought lit through him like lightning.

Adrian caressed his cheek. "You're so fucking expressive. So moved by everything, aren't you? Books. Food. Art. I bet you've wept at paintings."

Dom nodded. "I don't like...people seeing that."

A raised eyebrow, but Adrian didn't say anything.

Yeah, that wasn't quite the truth, was it? "Okay, I like controlling what people see."

Except here, he wasn't. At all.

A smile tugged at Adrian's mouth. "Layers and layers." The smile drifted away. "I want to see more, Dominic, but only what you want to show." Fingers traced lines over Dom's cheeks.

God, did he want to open himself fully to Adrian. Tell him everything. Blurt out the truth about the band and himself—but terror chased behind that need. Once he did, he could never take it back—Adrian would know.

And maybe Dominic would vanish if that happened. After all, fucking a rock star was so much more than fucking a bookish twink.

Dom needed this side of himself as much as he needed the hard-rocking guitarist. Needed the privacy and the lack of expectations. Needed to be made to come and be manhandled.

Now a frown tugged at Adrian. "Are you all right?"

"I—" Dom shivered, more from thoughts than cold; despite the AC, the warmth of the summer pressed in from the roof. "I want to give you more. But—"

Adrian's expression softened. "Only what you can, when you can. I won't press. I'm not that kind of man."

"And here I thought you were the kind of man who'd fuck me into oblivion."

The sharpness returned, and Adrian stepped in close, tilting Dom's chin up until it was almost uncomfortable. "Oh, I am that man. And I plan to fuck you so hard that there won't be any other thought in your mind but my cock and no other word on your tongue but my name." He pressed his thumb against Dom's bottom lip. "Would you like that, Dominic?"

"Yes." He groaned the word out, the spark of need and lust spinning in him again. He wasn't hard—doubted he would be coaxed back so quickly—but the pain and pleasure of being fucked? He wanted that all the same.

Adrian's grin was wicked, and he pushed his thumb inside Dom's mouth.

Fuck yeah. Dom sucked and licked it, relishing the hitch in Adrian's breath and the way he cupped the back of Dom's head.

Adrian pulled his thumb free, then undid his belt and the fly on his already ruined pants. "I'm gonna fuck your face and come down your throat. And you're going to take every damn drop, Dominic. Then I'm going to take you downstairs, lay you out on my bed and trace every line of ink on your body with my tongue."

Okay, maybe Dom had been wrong about not being able to get it up again. Lust poured through him like a summer thunderstorm, all violence and torrent. "Please."

He barely got a look at Adrian's dick before the thick head was shoved between his lips and he was moaning around the hard, hot length of it. Fingers tightened in Dom's hair, nails scraping at his scalp. Dom clutched at Adrian's pants.

"No." Adrian's voice was deep and lust-filled, but like iron. "Put them behind your back."

Oh. *Damn.* Dom whimpered, but did as told. Yeah, he should have realized this was the way this relationship was going. So so *so* fucking hot.

"There you go." More breathless now, Adrian thrust with slow, steady strokes as Dom did his best to lick and suck and open his throat. "That's good, Dominic. But I know you can take all of me."

It had been a while since he'd sucked a guy off, and then he'd always controlled the depth and speed. This—it had never been like this. Adrian's hands held him in place and he had no say in any of it, and yet—no panic. Dom let go, breathed deep when Adrian pulled out, and opened his throat as much as he could.

Trust and need. Adrian would take care of him, give them both what they wanted.

When Adrian thrust forward again, Dom was rewarded with a low growl he felt in every bone. "Yes. You're so fucking good."

The grip in Dom's hair shifted, and that was enough warning. He closed his eyes, let go of everything and let Adrian fuck his mouth. Perfect. Harsh. Loving. Dom caught air when he could and moaned and gasped and whimpered through every stroke and press. Took in the salt and the musk and the brush of Adrian's wool suit pants.

Adrian's breath was sharp, and his moans enough to bring Dom's arousal back to life, especially when he ground out words in that deep voice. "Fuck, oh fuck!"

Salt hit Dom's tongue, and he sucked and did exactly as Adrian had ordered earlier, drank down every last drop of come, greedily, wantonly, moaning as he licked and mouthed that pulsing shaft, until Adrian pulled away.

Finger under his chin again. Dom opened his eyes to look up at Adrian's rattled face, cheeks red, large pupils, and sweat-dotted brow. "Goddamn, you do like when I feed that mouth of yours."

Dom couldn't help the chuckle. "Call it an oral fixation."

"I'll call it a lovely talent," Adrian said. His words were soft. "Now, get up."

Dom rose on shaky legs, not knowing what to expect next. It certainly wasn't Adrian wrapping him in his arms and taking his mouth in a mind-searing kiss. God, he'd drown in this lust, in this need. The fire Adrian ignited and the warmth he offered.

It was as if he were trying to find every bit of his own taste in Dom, but when he finally broke the kiss, his touch was gentle. "Now, let's go downstairs. I still have plans for you tonight."

Dom sighed happily into Adrian. "You're the boss."

A brush of his thumb against his cheek. "Dominant," Adrian said. "But yes, I am."

Oh. Yeah. That made sense. He looked into those eyes. "Never done this before."

Adrian raised an eyebrow. "Really? Never sucked a man off?"

"Thousands of times, but not like this." He felt so light, even when Adrian nudged him toward the stairs.

"Railing," Adrian muttered.

Dom grasped it automatically. "Yeah, I guess that would harsh my mellow, if I fell down the stairs."

Behind him, a chuckle. "Did you really just say *harsh my mellow*? Because you're not nearly old enough for that slang."

"I'm twenty-seven!" He stopped on the stairs, indignation flaring through the happy haze of his body.

A warm hand landed on his shoulder. "To the second floor, please."

Adrian's tone brooked no argument, and Dom's feet were

already moving, even as his mind grumbled. But the next words were light. "I remember your age, Dominic. Do you remember mine?"

Dom's bare feet hit the second floor, and he turned to face Adrian. He was still in his suit, though it was shoved all out of whack and there were dark patches where Dom had come. "Thirty-six." Which put him nearly ten years older. "You're not gonna make me call you Daddy, are you?"

This time, Adrian's laughter was loud. "I don't think either of us want that kind of relationship. Harsh your mellow, indeed." But then Adrian's grip was on his chin again, and those eyes were boring into his. "But you do seem to like submitting to me."

"And you like telling me what to do." Dom swallowed. "Is this where you make me talk about limits and safewords and all that weird shit?"

Adrian blinked, and his expression was caught between amusement and something else. Maybe horror. "Weird shit?" He let go and nudged Dom down the hall.

Dom moved—and remembered which room Adrian had pointed to as the master bedroom. That seemed the obvious destination. "You still planning on using your tongue on my tats, right?"

A grunt. "Are you naturally a brat, or are you nervous?"

Not nervous. It hit him what he was, though. "I'm buzzed." Dom shook his head. "I shouldn't be buzzed." Not on a glass of wine an hour ago.

Adrian pressed his body against Dom. Closed him in his arms. "That's subspace. Some of that *weird shit* you don't want to talk about."

"Oh," he breathed. "So *that's* what they meant in those books."

Adrian kissed his neck, then nipped at the skin, hard enough to make Dom gasp and writhe. "Of course," he muttered, his hot breath gliding over Dom's shoulder. "Of *course* you've read about it in books."

Through the haze of pleasure, he couldn't tell if Adrian was amused or upset or what. "Is that condemnation?"

"Condemnation?" Adrian huffed a laugh. "Dominic, you are amazing." Another push. "Bedroom. Now."

So he moved and entered, and it was all the colors he loved. Soft blue walls, like the color of the ocean. Green accents with pops of gold. Rich brown furniture. The hues were so Adrian, too. Dom made it halfway into the room when he spotted something hanging from the solid wood bedframe. "Are those *manacles* on your bed?"

Adrian gave him a less subtle shove toward said bed. "They're leather cuffs. And yes, they're used for exactly what you think they're there for."

"Tying guys up."

"Tying people up."

Dom turned to meet Adrian's gaze. "You're bi?"

Not even a blink. "Pansexual. Is that an issue?"

"No, it's just—" He saw the flicker of hurt and annoyance in Adrian's face. "No. It's not an issue at all."

Confusion lay in Adrian, and he crossed his arms.

Shit, shit. His big clunky mouth when he was out of it. "You've been entirely focused on me," Dom said. "Like, completely. Whenever I've been with someone else, they notice other people. But you—"

Adrian bore down on Dom, his smile back in part, but the lines on his face so fucking intense. "You need better lovers, Dominic Bradley."

Dom's thighs hit the bed, and his ass a moment later. A second after that, Adrian's mouth on his neck, and Dom's back was pressed against the mattress. A hand skimmed his thigh, as that masterful tongue and mouth moved over Dom's jaw before claiming his mouth.

His mind was a reeling pile of mush when Adrian drew

back. "How could anyone look anywhere else when you're in the room?"

"You're such a fucking flatterer," Dom said, "I'm nothing special."

"Mmm. I'm gonna disagree with you there." Adrian took his mouth again, and under Dom went until Adrian finally relented and stood. "I need out of the fucking suit."

"Yeah, you do," Dom said.

Adrian grunted. "Don't give me lip."

"And this is probably where I shouldn't say 'yes, Daddy.'"

That got Dom a huge laugh. "Fuck, you're mouthy. Ever been gagged, Dominic? Because I can totally give your mouth something other than my cock or pie to suck on." There was just a hint of warning in those words, though.

Dom shivered from the weight of Adrian's gaze. "Never been gagged." He paused. "I'll be good." But then the other thought crossed his mind. "Wouldn't mind trying being gagged."

Adrian let out a huff of air and worked at his tie. "Of course you wouldn't. But for now, lie back and watch."

Dom did. Adrian didn't put on a show or anything, but watching him undress was something else. The tie went first, and it landed on a nearby chair. Stained suit jacket followed, with the casual ease of someone who'd been wearing them for years. Cufflinks—pretty silver ones that flashed in the light—came next, and Adrian turned to put them on his dresser.

His ass was spectacular, and Dom let out a grunt. The leer Adrian threw over his shoulder burned straight through Dom, and despite his instant orgasm earlier, his cock hardened at the sight.

Adrian turned as he unbuttoned his shirt, opening it to reveal what looked suspiciously like really well-defined abs, and when he shrugged it off, Dom murmured his appreciation.

Not just abs. Adrian was built. Not in a bulky way, but his frame was covered in lean, chiseled muscles and dusted with the same red-brown hair that graced his head. A thicker trail led from his stomach down into his semen-spotted dress slacks.

"You've already seen my cock," Adrian said.

Dom shook his head. "Just swallowed it. Didn't get to admire the look."

Something flickered in Adrian's face. Surprise? Maybe.

Dom remembered the earlier spoken words. "You lied to me," he said. "You *are* something special." He met those light-dark eyes. "Maybe you need to know you're beautiful, too."

Adrian took a breath, and Dom could nearly feel the flame of his need from ten feet across the room. Those pants and his boxer briefs came off and got kicked to the side, and yeah. Yes. Adrian Doran was something special indeed. Dom knew the length and thickness of that dick, but seeing it against the chestnut curls of Adrian's pubic hair and with the weight of his balls behind, and those damn powerful thighs? Fuck if that wasn't the icing on the cake Adrian had fed him.

Dom let his gaze roam all over that powerful body. "Hell, you gotta work out to get a body like that." He licked his lips.

Adrian lifted one foot to snatch off a sock, and then the other. "I do. Couple times a week." A smile graced his face. "And you just made every awful second of that worthwhile."

Dom sank back on the bed a little and kicked his legs. "You gonna come over here and keep all your promises?"

"Damn straight I will." It took no time for Adrian to cross the bedroom, knee Dom's legs apart, and stand between them. And then Dom was pressed into that bed by the weight of that hard, hot body against his own.

"Oh fuck," Dom moaned.

"Not yet." Adrian bit a trail across Dom's pecs, licking and nibbling at the swirls of ink he had there. When that rough tongue rasped across his nipple, he arched his back and groaned loud.

A rumble of appreciation, then Adrian was sucking and licking and biting at the nub and Dom just about lost his mind. He scrambled for purchase on the bed and twisted against the sheets, curses spilling out of his mouth until Adrian relented.

He pinned Dom down with those wicked, strong arms. "A little sensitive?"

Dom huffed a laugh. "Maybe."

"Mmm," came the reply, and Adrian headed for the other nipple.

When Dom tried to buck and thrash under Adrian, he couldn't and that had him moaning out in a voice he didn't recognize. "Oh fuck, yeah. Please!" Warmth flowed through every limb, and even as he struggled he flew high.

Their cocks ground together and Dom gasped for air. Holy shit, he was gonna come again after all. And before Adrian even fucked him. "I'm gonna...gonna..."

Adrian backed off, and Dom didn't know whether to be happy or utterly frustrated. What the hell?

Adrian had a little knowing smile, one Dom didn't understand. "I don't think I have the patience to lick all your tattoos tonight."

Dom let out a breath. "Don't think I would last." He was painfully hard again, his head swirling around. This big, strong man pinning him down. He felt—safe. Turned on to all hell and back. Completely at Adrian's mercy.

But safe.

He looked up at Adrian. "Please fuck me. Hold me down and destroy me."

Something feral leapt across Adrian's expression, then was tempered into razor-sharp control. "Hands and knees, Dominic. And you might want to take off those glasses of yours."

Adrian rose, and Dom scrambled to obey—and he was obeying. Submitting and he—oh shit. He liked it. At least with Adrian. And that made him laugh breathlessly, because it was exactly the opposite of hard-assed Domino.

"Enjoying yourself?" Adrian pulled lube and condoms from his bedside table. His expression was still sharp, but he wore an amused grin. He took Dom's glasses and set them down.

"You have no idea." Tonight, he was truly getting to be Dominic—the man Adrian was getting to know. He liked Adrian. Trusted him. And really wanted to feel the man moving inside him. Dom closed his eyes and let his head hang.

A warm hand smoothing over his ass made him snap those eyes back open.

"No ink here." Fingers glided and pressed and massaged his cheeks. Then Adrian's lips followed the same path, and Dom forgot how to breathe for a moment. In the very next, he moaned and collapsed onto his elbows.

"That's it," Adrian said. "I like that." Fingers skimmed between his crack and against his taint, and Dom could only grip the bedspread beneath him and rock back as Adrian's hands and mouth touched every part of his ass. When Adrian's tongue slid across, then into, his hole, Dom's world nearly broke apart.

"I can't," he gasped. Couldn't keep experiencing this kind of pleasure. His brain would melt. He was so lost in it, he didn't know which way was up.

"Yes, you can." The words were a silky caress. "Because I want you to. You're only gonna come around my cock when I say."

"Adrian, please."

"Shh. Listen to me. Trust me."

He did, and fuck if it didn't turn his head inside out. Cool, slick fingers replaced Adrian's tongue, breached him and slipped inside. He moaned and panted as Adrian fucked him slowly, probing and stretching, occasionally brushing over his prostate and sending him whimpering, flying, and begging.

A gentle chuckle. "Oh, Dominic..."

The sound of a condom wrapper, then the press of Adrian's thick cock against his hole.

"Yeah." Dom ground the words into the bedspread and rocked back. "Please. I need—"

Adrian thrust in, and the sensation stole Dom's breath and words. That sharp instant, then the overwhelming pleasure of being full, being warm. He gripped the mattress, and strong hands came down over his.

"Adrian," he whispered.

Lips pressed against his back, and Adrian pushed in deep. "You feel so damn good."

Dom could barely think straight for the pleasure coursing through him. The words, that mouth, and the hard, thick length of Adrian moving inside him. "Adrian," he repeated.

"That's it. Just like that." Adrian withdrew and rammed in hard. "I want to hear you."

He moaned and cried out as Adrian thrust over and over, stretching him, filling him with unbelievable light and heat. He was so close to coming again. Shuddered every time Adrian rammed against his sweet spot. Couldn't hold on much longer.

Lips and teeth on his back. "You're so fucking gorgeous. That mouth of yours. Your mind." Adrian shifted, curling his fingers into Dom's and tugging. "Let me have you, Dominic." He slowed his thrusts.

Dom didn't know exactly what Adrian meant to do, but he loosened his arms and found them carefully drawn back until his wrists were crossed at the small of his back and his shoulders and face were pressed into the bed. "Adrian!" The name came out like sparks and fire, like a cry and a moan all wrapped together.

Adrian replied with a deep rumble. "Like that?"

"Fuck yes." He did. He always liked when men manhandled him, drove into him relentlessly, but there was something about the strength of Adrian, the way his hands circled Dom's wrists, the sensual way he slowly rocked in and out of Dom that split his mind open.

"So do I. You beneath me. You're so tight and hot and mine for the taking. Fast or slow." Adrian thrust in hard. "Beautiful Dominic."

Dom could only moan and shout and yell when Adrian picked up speed until he was fucking him with hard, deep strokes that seemed to spear into Dom's soul each time he ground in. It was harsh and loving and perfect. And Dom was Adrian's. Helpless under him. Being held in check by muscle and words and those hands around his wrist.

Fire burned inside Dom, and he couldn't hold back as it left him higher and higher and the world narrowed down to Adrian fucking him down into the mattress.

Those thrusts became erratic, and Adrian cursed and moaned. He shifted his grip on Dom's wrists, and a hand wrapped around Dom's aching cock. "Come for me, Dominic."

A stroke later, Dom did, screaming Adrian's name as he broke into a thousand flaming pieces and burned while Adrian fucked him harder and harder until he too came with a groan that wracked Dom's heart.

Sex had always been good. But this—this was nothing like he'd ever experienced. Not in his head or body. And when Dom collapsed onto the bed, when Adrian released his arms and slid next to him, when those same strong hands pulled him into an embrace, only then did he realize he was crying.

"Shh. I have you." Adrian's kisses were gentle against his cheeks and forehead.

"Didn't hurt," Dom pushed out. Last thing he wanted was

for Adrian to believe he'd gone too far—because he hadn't—this was just so fucking overwhelming.

"I know." Another kiss, this one to his mouth, and slow and as tender. "It's okay to feel."

Dom sighed against Adrian and let those arms and hands and mouth soothe and comfort him as he fell back down to earth from the best orgasm in his entire life. Part of him wanted to apologize for being such a mess—but Adrian didn't seem to mind. "I guess I did ask to be shattered."

"Yes, you did." Fingers traced Dom's cheeks. "I truly hope you enjoyed that as much as I did."

Dom huffed a laugh and stole a kiss of his own from Adrian's lips. "It's never been better than that."

The spark in Adrian's eyes and that grin were utterly perfect. They softened, and he stroked a hand down Dom's side. "I have to work tomorrow, but please stay the night? Here with me?"

"Yeah." Dom breathed out the word. "Okay." Because there was really no place he'd rather be.

He was still pretty out of it when Adrian helped him to the bathroom to clean up. A glass of water later, his head spun a lot less and he watched while Adrian splashed water on his face, then toweled off.

"You know, I figured you looked hot under that suit the first night, but shit." Dom admired Adrian's body all over again, then shivered. Because that same body had controlled his so well.

Adrian grinned, a little flush on his cheeks. "It's been a work in progress." He raised an eyebrow. "You're pretty ripped yourself."

Dom glanced at his reflection and the vertigo came back for a moment, because with his hair all askew, naked, with his tattoos showing, he looked a lot more like Domino than Dominic. Except no one had ever fucked Domino so well he'd cried from it.

"Work out?"

He didn't, not really. Except that playing onstage, dancing with his guitar, and the hectic schedule of touring gave him enough of a workout to tone his body to almost too lean sometimes. He was still gaining back some of what he'd lost last tour. "I walk a lot," he said. "And my metabolism is annoyingly good."

Adrian laughed. "Well, whatever the reason, I still can't believe no one has ever told you how stunningly beautiful you are."

Dom ducked his head. He wasn't. That was the thing. Ray and Zavier? They were the beautiful ones. Especially Zavier, who had been born with astoundingly good looks. Next to them, Dom was plain. Domino only got attention because of the ink and his larger-than-life personality.

Fingers lifted Dom's chin, and Adrian's gold-flecked eyes peered into his own. "I'm not lying."

"I know you're not." He obviously saw something in Dom, but that didn't mean Adrian was right. You could be wrong without lying.

A huff, and Adrian kissed his forehead. "Do you wanna borrow a toothbrush? I have those spares the dentist gives you."

In the end, he did borrow a toothbrush, and a washcloth too before they crawled into Adrian's bed—sans bedspread. That had been semen-stained and unceremoniously stripped off.

Dom snuggled up next to Adrian's warm body. "Thanks for not making me sleep in the wet spot."

"I would never do that." Adrian played with Dom's hair, which felt so so *so* good. He shivered with the touch.

"And thanks for holding me down and fucking me," Dom whispered. "Feel free to do that again."

Fingers tightened in his hair, and Adrian's chuckle was deep and wicked. "Oh, good."

Dom closed his eyes and let Adrian's touches, murmurs, and kisses lull him to sleep.

THE FIRST WARM RAYS OF SUNLIGHT FILTERED IN THROUGH THE edge of the window shade, nudging Adrian from the edge of sleep. The warm, heavy presence next to him was a comfort and a thrill.

Dominic, in all his lovely, sultry, tattooed glory slept next to him. God, what a joy last night had been. Those moans, that tight heat, and the way he'd shattered around Adrian—so fucking hot. Submissive, yet so full of fire, and with an open hungry curiosity for the cuffs that still dangled from Adrian's headboard.

No jealousy that Adrian had tied up other lovers in this bed—just a natural and justified desire to know where he stood in Adrian's life. Of course, that was shifting every minute they spent together, at least for Adrian.

What was he to Dominic? A fling? Maybe—but then again, he was still in Adrian's bed. There were secrets Dominic held, answers he wouldn't share that shaped his wants and his fears. That was only fair, though. Trust was a tenuous thing, built on moments and decisions and care. Adrian had no doubt that when Dominic was ready, he'd offer explanations.

Until then, it wasn't really Adrian's place to demand those.

He glanced at the clock and suppressed a groan. He had to get up soon if he wanted any chance of making it to work at his normal hour. He did reach over and flick the alarm off, though.

The movement must have been enough to wake Dominic, because the warmth of breath and lips ghosted over the back of his shoulder. "Morning." That sexy, gravelly voice sounded so perfect.

Adrian turned over and gathered Dominic into his arms. "A very good morning."

That sleepy smile was something else. Endearing, charming, captivating.

You've got it bad.

Rather than words, he spoke in kisses, until Dominic was tight against him.

"I need to get up soon," he whispered against Dominic's lips.

An unhappy grunt. "Do you?" Dominic shifted, his warm hand tightening on Adrian's hip. Dominic's hard length pressed against Adrian's belly.

"Yeah, if I want to get to work on time." He stroked Dom's cheek. "I should have made you wait until Friday. Then I could have spent the morning taking you apart again."

A smile like the sun. "Nothing stopping us from dinner on Friday, too."

Adrian's heart flipped. Maybe this wasn't just a fling for Dominic. "I'd love that."

Such beautiful lips on Dom, especially when his face and eyes were still edged with sleep. "Me, too."

Well, another kiss wouldn't hurt, and that led to another languid, deep taste, then another, until they were grinding together and breathless, Dominic on top.

Dominic sat up, and wrapped his hand around both their cocks, his thrusts sensuous and slow when he canted his hips. "Can you be late today?"

God, it was hard to think when Dominic looked at him like that, when he moved and slid so perfectly against him. Fuck. It was Thursday, so Adrian didn't have any meeting until the eleven o'clock scrum. Sure, everyone knew he was usually in by eight-thirty, but he worked long enough hours that one late start wouldn't matter.

"I—yeah. I can. For you."

Oh, that grin. It was wide and wonderful, and suddenly

Dominic wasn't quite the shy twink he'd unwrapped the night before. Not with the way his gaze slid over Adrian's body, nor the way he slowly stroked both their dicks. "I wanna ask for something."

"Yes?" He caught Dominic's thighs and tried to speed up the tempo a bit.

That got him a laugh, and those slow movements got even slower. Fuck. "You wouldn't happen to be versatile?" There was a little quirk to the smile that followed.

"You want to fuck me?" Adrian's body warmed, his nerves tingling. "Figured you preferred bottoming."

Dominic released their cocks and leaned forward until his lips were so very close to Adrian's. "I do. But yeah, I wanna be inside you. Feel you come. Don't know why, but I do."

Adrian shivered under that stare. Fire and control, so unexpected, so welcome. "Then make me late for work, Dominic."

He caught the edge of the joyous grin before Dominic kissed him. Wasn't the brutal, punishing kisses Adrian had laid down the night before. No, this was intensely *tender*. Slow, sensuous, and delightful. He moaned into Dominic and felt him chuckle in response.

Adrian found himself at a complete loss for words when Dominic licked and bit his way down his body. Rough fingertips were followed by velvet kisses. Chest. Nipples. Stomach. He twitched and groaned under the onslaught, too aware of Dominic's weight.

Strange and wonderful. Been a while since he'd been this turned on and not actively the one engaging. Nothing Dominic did seemed dominant, but his grip and his mouth seemed to demand Adrian's stillness, his compliance. So he gave up control with hardly a thought.

Desire flared through Adrian. He wanted Dominic inside him, too.

The torturously wonderful heat of Dominic's mouth

vanished as he knelt between Adrian's legs, and when he looked up, the intensity of his gaze tore through Adrian.

"Please." The word was out of his mouth before he even realized.

Dominic sucked the tip of Adrian's dick between his lips and for a moment, the world vanished.

"Oh god, babe!" Dominic's mouth felt so fucking good. Even better than last night. Adrian arched against the bed, but no amount of thrusting seemed to slide him in any farther.

Then that hot, slick heat was gone and Dominic's quiet chuckle made goose bumps rise all over Adrian. "Call me that again."

"Babe?" Adrian was breathless and so fucking turned on, every inch ached for Dominic. Last night, he'd have flipped the man over and taken him hard and fast. But right now? He could only tremble under him.

"Yeah." This time Dominic was crawling up rather than down, determination on his face. "I wanna hear it again."

Adrian so rarely called any of his lovers anything other than their names. He wasn't even sure why that word had slipped from his lips. Except a tiny voice in the back of his mind whispered, *you know why*.

Yeah, there was something about this man, with all his interests and layers and complexity that drove right into the heart of Adrian's soul. He was hardly in love, but all the pieces were there, so that given time, given return interest— he could be.

He could seriously fall so damn hard for Dominic. It was *terrifying*.

And maybe that's why Adrian was a shivering mess of need by the time Dominic rolled the condom on, or why he moaned so loudly when Dominic's fingers slicked and loosened his asshole. God, it had been a while since he'd bottomed, and man, why hadn't he? Because this—this felt too damn good.

Dominic's grin was so fucking hot and the twink was gone, replaced with a tattooed god above him, the head of his hard cock pressed against Adrian's hole. "Want this?"

"Babe, yeah." Adrian hardly recognized his own voice. "Fuck me."

A laugh, then Dominic was pressing in, opening Adrian wide, and he burned with pleasure and pain and surrender. Every moment was gold, from the sound of his own cries to Dominic's throaty moan to his weight as he seated himself deep inside Adrian. Warm morning light burnished those dark brown eyes, and that's all Adrian could see, all he wanted to see.

He expected Dominic to fuck him rough and hard, mirroring how they'd come together the night before, had prepared for that. Instead, Dominic kissed him and moved slowly—tenderly, even—sliding in and out with each taste of lip and tongue. So close, they might as well have been one body.

Somehow Dominic managed to press in so deep with each thrust, and Adrian gasped and moaned into those languid, torturous kisses. God, every second was too much, from the stretch to the way Dominic's cock slid just right with every thrust. The heat and weight of his body, the friction between them stroking Adrian's cock. Delight flew through him and tension, too. Slowly stretching out until he was strung tight, vibrating and ready to break.

"Like that?" A murmur, full of joy and light. "I think you do."

"Babe." He practically moaned the word. "Please, please."

A caress of lips against his. "Please what?"

"Make me come." He never wanted this to end, but he couldn't contemplate climbing any higher into pleasure. It was too much, too soon. No lover had done this before.

He didn't know how Dominic could sound so together, not how they were fucking, but his words were as smooth as his strokes. "I am making you come, Adrian. Just the way I want. Just the way I like it."

Adrian ran out of words. Had he honestly thought he was completely in control of this situation? Heat blazed through him when Dominic thrust deep and ground in even more.

"In fact, you're close, aren't you? Right there."

Yeah, he was. On the edge. His breath came in pants and he dug his fingers into Dominic's arms. "Babe..."

"That's it, Adrian," Dominic murmured. He ground in hard. "I want to lick the come off you. Give it to me."

Hearing those words out of the mouth of the same man who'd blushed his way through dinner was too much—the world turned as gilded as the sunlight in Dominic's hair and broke into a thousand pieces, and he came hard. He couldn't even shout—the pleasure took him too fast.

"Fuck yeah." Dominic's thrusts came sharp and fast as he spent himself. Not with the cry of abandon from the previous night, but a growl of contentment that chased down Adrian's spine, mingling with the aftershocks of pleasure.

And true to his dirty talk, once Dominic had pulled out and ditched the condom, he came right back and licked every drop of semen from Adrian's skin. Adrian tangled trembling fingers into Dominic's locks. "You're unreal." It came out as a croak.

"You're not complaining," came the smug, snarky reply.

Adrian could only laugh. "Babe, you can make me late for work any day of the week."

Dominic quieted and spread his fingers over Adrian's chest. "I think I'd like that." Soft, wondrous words.

He propped himself up on his elbows to get a better read on Dominic's expression. Surprise, and maybe a hint of worry there. "So would I."

Their gazes met. Still that soft voice. "It's not like me."

So he'd said before. "Love 'em and leave 'em kind of guy?"

A snort, but it wasn't one of humor. "Makes me sound heartless."

Adrian shrugged. "There's no shame in one-night stands." He'd had plenty of them himself. Hookups. Hell, he'd had some amazing sex in the bathrooms of clubs. "Sometimes life just isn't right for more than that." He paused. "You're far from heartless."

Dominic traced patterns on Adrian's skin, warm fingers over flesh. "Thank you."

No more than that. His dark eyes were focused on his moving fingers, and there was that little hint of fear again. Adrian had no idea what the frown might be from, what churned behind the brow of the unexpectedly stunning and strong man in his bed. But he wanted to find out.

"So, dinner Friday, still? If you like, we could try the cuffs after."

Dominic's fingers slowed and stopped. "On me or you?"

Now, that was an interesting question. "Whichever you prefer, but I do think you might enjoy being tied up, Dominic." He brushed a hand over Dominic's cheek.

A little shudder. "Yeah, probably." He grinned. "Absolutely yes to Friday."

Again, Adrian claimed a kiss from those delicious lips. This one tasted faintly of musk and salt and a little like the beginning of something new.

Adrian walked into work a little past ten and to a few raised eyebrows, but the taste of himself on Dominic's lips had been so well worth it. Not even a hellish meeting and a pile of angry emails about broken code could dampen his spirits.

CHAPTER
FIVE

Dom had absolutely no issue falling into Domino for the next practice. The music came like lightning, with all the crash and edge and burn that he was known for onstage and in songs. Felt so damn good, too, that strength, that poise. Though he didn't always like being Domino 24/7 on the road, he did miss the no-fucks attitude that came with assuming the role. The righteousness.

It was *fun* being Domino. So he played like he could rule the world.

Ray was more than pleased. And the energy must have been infectious, because he danced around the studio, singing his heart out like they were back onstage at some sold-out arena. Mish was on top of her game, strutting across the floor, and Zavier was his absolute astounding self.

And the songs, oh god, Ray had outdone himself. Sure, they all added bits and pieces, but Ray's heart and soul had been poured out into this album. Every note, every word.

Dom loved it all, too.

When they broke for a rest, it was Ray who joined Dom by the window. The AC was on now, so this time the window was shut, but there was still something about peering out into the world after being surrounded by the motion and rhythm of their songs. A reset of sorts, to remind Dom that this wasn't a dream even when it felt like it.

"You're in a better mood today." Ray tried to sound casual.

He eyed Ray, who couldn't pull off innocent if his life depended on it. "You're fishing for info."

That earned Dom a laugh. "Yeah, but not really. I'm grateful to see you happy, whether you wanna share the reason or not."

Dom leaned up against the wall. He was still a tiny bit bruised from being well-fucked and fucking well, and he so enjoyed that, but there was more, too. "I have a date."

"Same guy as before?"

"Wait, you know about that?"

Ray's cheeks reddened. "Zavier mentioned it. After practice."

Okay, that made sense. Dom nodded. "Yeah, same guy. I...like him. Quite a lot."

Ray got a look like he couldn't understand what was coming out of Dom's mouth. "Well, you better if you're doing more than a hookup!"

And there was what elated and frightened Dom. "Yeah, it's more than that." He paused. "But I don't know if it should be."

Ray looked confused. "Why the fuck not?"

"Because of this." He gestured to the studio and their instruments.

From across the room, Zavier looked up from his conversation with Mish. Dom must have spoken loudly enough, because the next words were out of Zavier's mouth. "Because of this what?"

Of course, Mish looked over, too. Dom sighed.

"Sorry," Ray murmured.

Dom knew better. "You are so not." He punched Ray in

the arm and strode over to the table Zavier'd been sitting at. "It's that guy I met. I like him, but I'm not sure I should be dating him."

Zavier cocked his head. "Because of the band?"

Mish beat him to replying. "It's because of Domino, isn't it?"

Ray gave Dom a look like he'd grown rabbit ears or alien antenna on his head, but Zavier nodded.

Dom sank down into one of the folding metal chairs. "Yeah. Because of Domino."

"I don't—" Ray shook his head and seemed to chew on his thoughts. "Are you saying, if you got serious with this dude, you wouldn't *tell* him who you are?"

"I *have* told him who I am," Dom said. "He's seen who I am. I'm Dominic Bradley."

"Sweetheart," Mish said. "This is you, too."

He ran a hand through his hair. "I know. But who I am here, who Domino is, is so different from the guy Adrian met at a bar."

"So the gentleman has a name," Zavier said. "You *like* him."

Couldn't help the heat that rose to his cheeks. Dom shrugged, but he met Zavier's gaze.

There was amusement in those eyes. "Friendship's a good thing, Dom. I know you're not asking for advice—"

"But you're gonna give me some anyway."

"He always does." Ray looked up at Zavier and got that little dopey grin he always got when he looked at his husband. For his part, Zavier merely touched Ray's hair. But that seemed to be all the connection they needed, because Ray laughed.

Zavier snorted and returned his focus to Dom. "Enjoy your gentleman friend. He seems to make you happy."

Mish said what Dom had been thinking: "But..."

"But friendship is built on trust."

Dom knew that. But having the words spoken gave them weight. "Yeah, and that's why I don't know if it should go further."

Adrian might not like Domino. Hell, he'd said he barely paid attention to modern music—couldn't get into it. How the heck was he going to enjoy or even understand what Dom did for a living? And if it didn't go well...then his secret was out, and his privacy along with it.

He needed Domino to survive onstage, because Dominic Bradley sure as shit couldn't be a rock god.

"Eh, I'll figure it out." He wasn't sure if he was talking to himself or the rest of the band, but it really didn't matter. Right now, there were songs to play.

Tomorrow night, there was a dinner to eat and Adrian's promise to use those leather cuffs on him. If that night went like the last—it would be fucking spectacular.

He'd worry about what to do with Domino if he and Adrian kept seeing each other. Until then, it didn't really matter.

DURING THEIR AFTERNOON BREAK IN PRACTICE, DOM BIT THE bullet and texted Adrian, his heart in his throat.

> You still interested in dinner tomorrow?

He didn't actually know which answer he preferred. Sex on Wednesday had been something else, beyond every expectation, and it had rattled him to the core. Adrian was wicked and wonderful and kind and...everything Dom wanted. The promise of those cuffs lit every bit of his insides, but there was still the question in his head of where the hell this was going. Because what Dom wanted and what was the best for the band were two different things.

He'd left the studio, despite the heat, a long-sleeve button-down covering up all his tats. That was a downside to wearing nothing but pants onstage—everyone knew Domino's tattoos. And since they were also his, Dom hid them when he went out as himself. During a hot summer in New York? Sometimes that decision was a little brutal. But there was a breeze today, and he'd found a shady spot to sit and eat along the Highline, lost in a sea of people.

It was a good fifteen minutes before a reply came.

> Of course I'm still interested, Dominic. Dare I
> hope you are, too?

Dom stared at the text, and he could almost hear Adrian's soft, deep voice speaking those words, including the caress around Dom's full name.

Yeah. Yes. He was gonna do this.

> Sure. Just need to know where and when.

The reply came a little quicker this time.

> I took the liberty of making reservations at
> Glass Garden for 7 PM. It's a newer place in
> the Financial District. Not casual, but the
> food is exquisite and I think you'll enjoy it.

Dominic knew the restaurant. He'd been there with the band recently, but as Domino. And yes, it wasn't casual at all, but of course he'd gotten away with what passed as formal-wear for Domino Grinder.

It had actually taken quite a bit of self-restraint to play it cool every time the staff referred to him as Mr. Grinder. He swore they were doing it on purpose.

"I should have picked a better stage name," he'd murmured to Ray.

"I think it's perfect." Ray's smile had been large and full of teeth. It was so often lately. The melancholy and anxious version of Ray Van Zeller still appeared sometimes, but less and less often. No doubt due to the influences of Zavier.

Mish had patted him on the knee. "How'd you know Grindr would become a hookup app?"

Zavier chuckled. "Hell, Dom, Ray's right. It is kind of perfect."

Maybe it was—for Domino.

Dominic would rather be dating a built computer programmer with a huge library and hands that could put him on his knees. Still didn't mean he should do that, though.

His phone buzzed.

> If you'd prefer somewhere else, I can change the reservation.

Dom blinked at the text and realized he hadn't sent one in response to the last.

> No, that's fine. I can dress appropriately, even. I've heard great things.

Domino wasn't going to Glass Garden, Dominic was, and the staff would call him Mr. Bradley and be none the wiser to who they served. And he could be *himself* for once at a place like that.

> Might I ask you to wear one of your bowties? I do like seeing you in them.

That teased a smile from Dom's lips and his mood brightened like sunlight breaking through clouds.

> Yes, of course.

Something colorful, like you.

Are you trying to sweet-talk me?

Is it working?

Maybe. Depends on what you want.

What I want is you on my cock. I'll settle for holding your hand and watching your eyes roll back into your head as you eat.

Instant hard-on. Fuck.

Maybe we can skip dinner.

No. Part of the pleasure is making you wait, Dominic.

Another text came, but this one wasn't from Adrian, but from Ray.

Yo. We're ready to go again. Where the hell are you?

He blew out a breath and clicked over to Ray's thread.

Not far. Be right thoro.

A swipe got him back to Adrian's texts.

I gotta get back to practice. I'll see you tomorrow. He sent the text, then typed up another quickly. I love it when you make me wait.

Because he did. There was something utterly mind-numbing when he was in Adrian's hands and under his control.

Good. Until tomorrow, beautiful Dominic.

Heat to his face. And maybe it was still there by the time he got back to the studio, because Ray smirked, Zav had his know-it-all smile, and Mish patted him on the back. "You'd be a lot more comfortable in a tank, honey."

And a lot more Domino with all that skin showing. He stripped off his shirt and got back to work. Felt good, too, the burn in his arms as the day wore on and in his legs as he hopped around the studio, unable to stand still. The songs Ray had written—fuck, they were good. Better than the last album, and with the rhythms Zav dropped and the energy Mish put into the baseline, the album was shaping up to be something spectacular.

Playing these onstage? Oh fuck, that would be a delight. The screams, the vibe, the thunder of sound. He fucking loved being Domino then. Dom twirled around, flourishing the cord he was playing.

"Hey, wait," Ray said, breaking across Dom's thought. "What did you do there? I loved that."

Dom found his footing and caught his breath. The amp cord was lazily wrapped around him on the floor—thank god he always used one that was long, or he'd trip himself up. "You mean this?" He played the embellishment again.

Ray let out a soft sigh. "Yeah. That's it. Can we roll back and do that section again, without me singing?"

They all nodded, and Zavier twirled his stick and tapped out the beats before they plunged in again. Ray stood riveted to the floor, eyes closed, breath steady as he listened. When Dom hit the cord again, Ray's shoulders dropped and his smile deepened.

When Ray's whiskey eyes opened again, he met Dom's gaze, teeth flashed in a huge grin. "That's utterly perfect. You're amazing, Dom. Best guitarist ever."

Dom laughed. "Man, there's a ton of others ahead of me on that list!" Though he appreciated his best friend's words.

Ray shrugged. "Not to me."

Buoyed—and a little embarrassed—by the praise, Dom worked even harder at being Domino, the guitarist Ray and the band needed.

And it worked, too. They pounded out another song, adding to it, embellishing it, getting it into their blood. "Fuck, I can't wait to play these live."

Ray grinned, and there was this little edge to it, one that meant he was hiding something. Dom whipped his gaze to Zavier and raised an eyebrow.

Zavier laughed loud and long. "You might as well tell them, Ray."

"So, I've been working with Marcella to put together a little something."

Marcella Crane, their new manager and an attorney. One that had gotten them a stellar new contract. Dom crossed his arms. "Oh?"

"We do sound the best live," Ray said. "I was thinking of taking the album—most of the songs, anyway—on a trial run here in New York. A small surprise concert. Limited seating. Popup kind of thing."

Wow. Dom's breath caught. A chance to play these live?

Mish voiced Dom's next thought. "Before recording the album?"

Ray nodded. "Work out all the kinks, wouldn't it?"

She laughed. "Honey, the only kinks here are the ones between you and Zav."

And at that, Ray blushed to high heaven but laughed, too. Zavier just looked incredibly smug.

Dom's heart tripped over, though. Because, in an instant,

his mind was back on Adrian and his eyes, mouth, and words. And that tempting pair of leather cuffs.

"Are you okay, Dom?" Zavier peered over the kit at him.

"Yeah." He blew out a breath. "Just thinking."

Zavier studied him a little longer, until Ray rolled his shoulders. "We should probably take a break."

Dom stripped off his guitar and set it on a stand, grabbed a bottle of water, and headed for the window. He was completely *not* surprised when Zavier ended up there, too, water bottle in hand. A glance told Dom that Zavier hadn't finished his little game of mind-reading.

But Zavier didn't say a word, just leaned against the wall by the window.

Dom turned his attention that way, too. "The show idea is fucking fantastic. These songs should be heard live."

From the corner of his eyes, he caught Zavier shifting and drinking a gulp of water. "You should invite your gentleman friend."

The thought of Adrian there, seeing him—Domino—onstage raked through Dom like knives. He whipped his gaze to Zavier. "How do you even know I'm gonna keep seeing him?"

"Because you're happy. And because you have some lovely bruises on your back. Bites, I'm guessing."

"Zav!" Dom pressed a hand to his forehead. "Why do you always point these things out?"

A chuckle. "Because you're my friend. And because you're not *nearly* as innocent as you act."

Well, that was true. Still, the whole thought of Zavier noticing his bruises brought heat to his face. "I mean, there's the stuff I do, sure. But I don't need to *talk* about it."

Zavier took a sip of his water. "So why not ask him?"

"Because he's not into rock music."

Zavier made a humph sound and turned his attention to the window. "And you're Domino Grinder."

"Fuck, I can't tell him that, Zav!" Even the thought squeezed his heart and lungs. "Domino is—he's not me."

"Funny, I kind of thought it was you who worked out that wicked guitar rift just now."

Dom winced. "You know what I mean."

Zavier's shoulders fell. "That's the thing... I actually don't." He put his back to the wall. "I mean, there are a lot of things in this world I don't understand. But this...bothers me. Because you're *happy* with this Adrian of yours, more so than I've ever seen you before."

Dom sighed and took a long drink of water. "You're always you."

"I assure you, that's not true." Zavier's voice dropped. "We all hide things, Dom. Every single one of us, sometimes even from the people we most trust."

"You and Ray..."

"Don't hide anything from each other. Not anymore."

"Did you ever?"

A humorless grunt. "Of course we did. You were there."

Their last tour, where Ray and Zavier had danced around their feelings for so freaking long they'd driven Mish and Dom nuts.

Then Ray had almost died when their hellish former manager had tried to drug him to start rumors. Turned out Ray'd been so allergic to the roofie, he'd gone into anaphylaxis. Two days later, Zavier had asked Ray to marry him—probably out of fear of losing someone he cared for more than anything else in the world.

There'd been no great declaration of love, no fairytale wedding, just the absolute certainty that Ray and Zavier needed to be together forever.

Zavier laid a gentle hand on his shoulder. "Ray worries about you, too, you know. You've been off-kilter since the accident."

They all had been. The case and publicity had been brutal.

"He hasn't said anything." Dom gazed back across the studio to his best friend and Zavier's husband.

"He will, in his own time."

And it would likely be not nearly as forthright or as gentle as Zavier. Ray built things up. Held them in until, like his songs, they came pouring forth in loud, awesome glory. But sometimes you really didn't want to be in the way of Ray Van Zeller and that.

"I'll keep that in mind." His gaze snagged on Mish. "I'm actually kind of surprised Mish isn't prying info out of me."

Zavier laughed, and Ray glanced up, smiling. "Not yet." He sauntered across the studio to join Ray. While they were never sappy, there was no doubting the connection between them, the love in Ray's eyes or the fire in Zavier's.

Dom joined the rest of the band, and Mish pointed her chin at Zavier. "He teasing you about your new man?"

His man. More the other way around. "Not really."

"He should be. We want to meet him."

"I've only gone out on one date!"

She laughed. "But that's one more than any other guy you've fucked, honey. And I bet you already have another set, don't you?"

He eyed his cell phone, which lay over on the table on the far side of the room. "Maybe."

Mish ruffled his hair. "Tell me one thing that's wonderful about this guy, and I'll leave you alone."

Fuck. There were so many things—and that realization left Dom blushing and hot. "He's—he's got this library in his attic that's to die for."

She clapped him on the back. "Sounds like your guy to me."

He was. Adrian was every inch the kind of man Dominic Bradley could fall for. Just one problem...

His gaze landed on his guitar—on Domino Grinder's guitar.

More and more, Dom wondered whose life he was really living, and whose life was the lie.

Ray cleared his throat. "I'm working on another song, but something's not right. Wanna listen?"

Of course they all said yes, and that's what they spent the rest of the afternoon and evening teasing apart.

CHAPTER
SIX

ADRIAN COULDN'T HELP THE TRILL OF PLEASURE THAT RAN DOWN his spine when he spotted Dominic walking toward Glass Garden. He was wearing a suit that fit that taut, built body as if it had been tailored to it, and even from a distance, Dominic's bowtie was brilliant, like the summer day around them. Adrian caught yellows and blues and maybe a hint of red.

He couldn't wait to see it closer, watch Dominic feast, then strip everything off that body and claim the man as his own. And perhaps be claimed, as well.

Both prospects made him shiver.

Dominic must have spotted him, because his gaze became riveted and his smile one part happy, the other part lust-filled. When Dominic was close enough, Adrian took his elbow, then his chin, and gave him a not-so-chaste kiss right there on the street.

Dominic moaned and gripped Adrian's arm. When he relented, there was surprise in his eyes and that lovely flush on those cheeks. "Hi," he said, his voice breathless and hoarse.

"Hello." Adrian dropped his fingers to Dominic's bowtie

and yes, it was beautiful close up, a yellow base with blue-and-red paisley designs. From the feel, it was silk. "You look spectacular."

People flowed past them on the sidewalk and Dominic's eyes were bright. "So do you."

Adrian had worn one of his better charcoal-gray suits to work—which Jackson had commented on that morning at the gym because nothing got past him—and paired it the a pale yellow shirt and a tie that was an homage to his roots, Celtic knot-work in greens and yellow and browns. He'd even dug out his gold cufflinks, the ones with his initials.

Watching Dominic's hungry gaze drift over his body now, he was glad he'd taken the time to dress to impress this interesting, contradictory man. "Shall we go in?" He slipped his hand into Dominic's.

That sweet voice was still breathless. "Yeah. Or your place." His blush deepened. "Whichever."

Adrian gave the fingers entwined with his a squeeze. "Patience." Then he led Dominic into the restaurant.

The staff was cordial, punctual, and perfectly mannered as they led them to a small table in the dining room, all arranged so that diners wouldn't be crowded by others, would feel the intimacy of the low light, glass, and dark wood that mimicked art deco trees. It was ideal for taunting and teasing Dominic in the ways Adrian so wanted.

Dominic unbuttoned his suit jacket like he'd worn them often enough, and a glimpse of the interior fabric plus the way it hung on his frame made Adrian reassess his earlier thought. It wasn't just a good fit—this suit *had* been tailored for Dominic. Custom-made, likely. The fabric, though not showy, was high quality and the lining uniquely patterned.

A place in Brooklyn. A bespoke suit. A musician. Not quite an equation that added up, but Adrian set it aside.

They received menus and their server described the specials in detail. Adrian half-listened to her and half-watched Dominic's reactions. Yes, this was a man moved by food. Or at least by taste and experiences.

In the end Adrian chose the filet mignon while Dominic chose short-rib ravioli in truffle sauce, and they split a pricey bottle of red Bordeaux. It wouldn't break his budget, but it was more extravagant than he usually was on a date.

Then again, he usually just bought hookups a cheap drink at a club and pulled them into a darkened corner for some fun. This was completely different, down to the fine china. He sipped his expensive wine.

"Why are you smiling?" Dominic's voice was full of curiosity.

"Would you like to know a truth?"

Dominic's look got distant for a moment. "I prefer truths."

"Mmm. Me, too. But this—" he gestured between them "—is young yet. We all have cards we hold to our chests."

A nod and a very steady look.

"I said I wanted more than a one-night stand. But that's not my usual motive, either."

Dominic tipped his head back a little. "So you're a love 'em and leave 'em guy, too?"

Adrian shrugged. "I can be. It's certainly easier sometimes."

"But..." Dominic picked up his wineglass and swirled.

"You're worth more than one night. I knew that when I sat down next to you."

Dominic let the wine level out and stared at it for a moment before shifting his gaze to Adrian. He might be all of twenty-seven, but there was a great deal of experience and that same steel Adrian had glimpsed before. "Because I was reading about rentboys?"

Adrian laughed. He couldn't help it, and he caught a few other diners looking their way. But that was, in some respects, part of the truth. "Not just any book about rentboys. How many people do you know who read Jack Saul?"

A touch of red on his cheeks. "None. R—" Dominic froze and the blush was gone, replaced with something that looked a little like terror. He shook himself once. "One of my band-mates prefers history. The others like fiction, but not..." He let the comment die and didn't look up.

The mysterious band. And obviously a subject Dominic preferred to keep off the table.

"This is probably presumptuous, but I think perhaps we both prefer quick and easy from time to time because we don't make friends that readily."

The smile returned to Dominic, knowing and wry. "That *is* presumptuous, given we've met, what, three times."

And fucked so very much in one evening, but Adrian kept those thoughts behind his lips.

Still, Dominic's eyes danced. "But you're not wrong. I don't make friends easily. I don't like opening myself up."

"Yet here you are."

A slow nod. "But so are you."

Adrian so wanted to take this man apart. Instead, he reached across the table and offered his hand.

Dominic took it, and his lips hitched up. "For the record, it's kinda nice, this not being a one-time thing."

Good. So very good.

When their meals came, Adrian thoroughly enjoyed his steak and the soft, appreciative noises Dominic made while he ate. The flutter of his eyes, and the slow swallows. It wasn't a show at all—likely Dominic didn't even know how expressive he was.

The wine had mellowed his stare, though left it more heated. Dominic was emboldened, too, that solid core showing through the blush when he trailed his foot up the back of Adrian's leg.

Oh yes, this night was perfect so far. "How do you feel about dessert?"

A smirk. "Gonna feed it to me?"

"Yes." The reply was simple, straightforward, and made Dominic's eyes widen.

He sat up a little straighter. "Here?"

"Yes, here."

"You wouldn't!" He looked around the dining room and gestured. "I mean—"

Adrian tilted his head and let his smile widen. "It's not like I'm asking you to kneel down and suck my dick."

A visible shudder ran through Dominic. "Yes, it is." His voice was low and rough. "It's exactly like that, just—less obvious."

"Will you? Lick lemon tart from my fork?"

Dominic's cheeks were red, and he shifted in his seat. "Fuck yes. Do me."

This time Adrian clamped down on the laughter, but his face ached from grinning and his heart soared when Dominic smiled widely. If he had to guess, those very expensive dress pants of his were tenting nicely.

When the waiter came, he ordered a lemon tart. One fork.

Such a treat to have Dominic lean forward so much he had to lift his ass off the chair to claim what Adrian offered. And the blush, and the throaty little whimper, and the wide eyes. Dominic was a blushing, squirming, well-dressed mess by the time they finished dessert. And yes, it was very, very much like having Dominic on his knees before him.

Maybe even a little better, since the restaurant couldn't exactly throw them out for something het couples did all the time at eateries.

Adrian left a large tip on their large check, and led Dominic out of the place. His own cock had been hard as a rock during Dominic's show and still wasn't completely down again. "If I didn't know better," he murmured in Dominic's ear, "I'd think you were an exhibitionist."

Oh, the blush. "I'm not really. You just..." His eyes were a bit glassy. "I like how I feel when you do this to me."

Adrian shifted his hand from the top of Dominic's back to the small of it. "So do I."

He'd never quite done this kind of subtle domination before, since he'd never dated anyone remotely like Dominic before. Hardly dated at all.

Walking through Manhattan with Dominic Bradley all strung out and half into subspace? Pure bliss. Adrian led him down into the subway, and there he could tell Dominic was used enough to the city. Every motion was automatic and normal, like someone who'd ridden the trains for years.

There was also a spark in those eyes now, one that drove Adrian's pulse up, because there was the flame he glimpsed in Dominic sometimes.

While they waited on the platform for the train that would take them back to Brooklyn, Dominic slid close and ran a finger down Adrian's tie. "Thank you for dinner. And especially dessert." He angled his lips close and just brushed them over Adrian's. It would have been a gentle kiss, except that Dominic's palm slid low and pressed against Adrian, hard and right over his cock. "Though I wonder..." he murmured, his lips brushing Adrian's with every word. "What would have happened if you had asked me to suck your cock?"

"Knowing you," Adrian replied, trailing fingertips over Dominic's face, "you would have. You're not as shy as you let on, Mr. Bradley."

A surprised laugh. "I am, really, I am."

But he didn't kiss that way, and when Adrian grasped those hips and held them close together on the subway platform, the way Dominic ground and moved belied any ounce of shyness. Hell, Adrian probably could have jerked him off right there and then.

But there were other people on the platform, and this was near Wall Street, and it wasn't even midnight yet.

So he bit Dominic's lip, then said, "Behave."

The chuckled response was soft, and so sexy, Adrian

wanted to take him right then and there. "I'm just remembering your promise."

Leather around those wrists. Yes, that would happen in due time.

They necked like teens the entire ride to Brooklyn, and stumbled from the subway station like they'd had three bottles of wine rather than one. Dominic had been handsy, finding all the chinks in Adrian's armor and making him just as hot and bothered. Bratty, lovely. Perfect.

As soon as the front door locked behind them, Adrian took Dominic by the lapels of his beautifully cut suit and rammed him up against the wall, knee between those legs and all his body weight pressing him against unyielding plaster. There was the little moan in response, the heat of desire on Dominic's face and the glaze of lust in his eyes.

Adrian skimmed his mouth over Dominic's neck. "You're a fucking little tease, aren't you?"

The reply was a wicked chuckle Adrian felt against his chest. "You don't seem to mind."

Adrian pressed himself harder against Dominic and ran his teeth over the light stubble on that neck. "Just means I get to do all sorts of things to you in retribution." He claimed Dominic's mouth and swallowed whatever reply was about to come out from between those lips.

As always, Dominic melted into Adrian as they kissed. So hungry and blazing hot. Every inch of the lithe body squirming and grinding against Adrian begged to be tamed and teased and fucked.

And he would. Tonight he'd show Dominic how much their lovemaking on Wednesday had been an appetizer to the main course Adrian could provide.

If Dominic wanted more than a fling. Which it seemed like he did—just like Adrian.

When he broke the kiss, Dominic whimpered and leaned his head back against the wall, eyes closed, breathing fast.

"Want leather around those pretty wrists of yours?" He nipped at Dominic's chin. "Because I wanna tie you up and take you apart."

Dominic opened his eyes, and his pupils were huge. He met Adrian's gaze with fire and decisiveness. "Yeah. Been waiting all night. Put those cuffs of yours on me and break me into a million pieces."

Desire spun up Adrian, quickening his heart. He'd been hard off and on since they'd been seated for dinner. He was hard now, with Dominic against him, but this—this scratched another need besides getting his rocks off.

Control. Dominance. The ability to withhold or give pleasure as he saw fit. Sure, it stoked his fire, but just like feeding the tart to Dominic at dinner, that control also fed Adrian's mind and heart and soul.

"I'm not going to be gentle." He ground his thigh into Dominic's hard length.

Dominic tried to arch, but only managed to lengthen his neck. His moan was half a sigh of contentment and half a groan of lust. "Good. I want to feel you on me and in me for the next week."

Adrian closed his eyes and breathed in the smell of Dominic's skin and hair. The crisp linen of his shirt and the slight scent of pressed wool from his suit jacket. "We're going to my bedroom, and once we get there, you're going to do everything I say, unless you have some fundamental objection to my requests."

Though he was standing still, Dominic was shaking—vibrating—with excitement and tension. "And if I do have a fundamental objection?"

Adrian opened his eyes and looked straight into Dominic's. "You tell me." He paused. "Or you can pick a safeword."

Dominic huffed out a breath. "Would you feel better if I did?"

Interesting question. He kept his weight against Dominic, and still pressed his thigh against that hard cock Dominic tried to rut against him while he considered his answer. "I've played both ways. With a safeword and without."

"But which do you prefer?" That was a purr, a luscious whisper of words. "What turns you on most?"

Dominic turned him on the most. All of him. His mind and body and the unfulfilled needs Adrian had glimpsed Wednesday. That core of steel, the softness and shyness. His passion and openness. His exhibitionist streak.

He kissed Dominic's jaw, then met those deep brown eyes. "I want you to feel safe and secure."

This time, his chuckle was gentle. "I've felt safe with you since you sat down next to me that first night. And I'd feel absolutely ridiculous if I have to blurt out *kumquat* or *marzipan* or another word I'll never remember rather than just telling you I don't want something."

Adrian laughed. He couldn't help it. Then he kissed Dominic's neck until he heard that helpless moan before relenting. "All right." He released his hold on Dominic's suit and worked his tie loose. "Do you remember where the master bedroom is?"

"Yes." A breathless answer.

"Good. I want you to go up there, strip off every last bit of clothing you're wearing, and I want you kneeling with your hands behind your back before I join you. You're going to have about three minutes, and I don't want to be disappointed. Do you think you can do that?"

Dominic shuddered. His eyes were wide and clear, and he swallowed before answering, "Yeah."

"Good." Adrian let go of the tie and stepped away. "Go."

Dominic swayed for an instant, then moved quickly toward the stairs. He didn't run—nothing so frantic as that—he just moved at a very determined pace. He was out of sight and on the second floor in no time at all.

Adrian palmed himself through his pants. Oh, he would enjoy every second of this. Dominic responded beautifully to commands, and he had a feeling placing his cuffs around those wrists would turn Dominic inside out.

And if he indulged in the deep, deep satisfaction of being the first man to ever tie Dominic Bradley up, well, maybe that was only natural.

The only firsts he'd ever had the pleasure of being part of before were his own.

After pouring and drinking a glass of water in the kitchen, Adrian headed upstairs. He hadn't been timing Dominic—he hadn't even intended to. The creaking of the floorboards above his head did stop pretty rapidly nonetheless, and Adrian savored how Dominic might feel.

The nervousness. The anticipation. The desire to please.

Not unfamiliar emotions, since he had all of them as well, though he knew it couldn't be the same.

Still, when he entered his bedroom, nothing prepared him for the sight of Dominic naked and kneeling, hands at the small of his back, head slightly bowed. He'd positioned himself at the foot of the bed. Not too close, though—there was still enough space for Adrian to walk completely around Dominic.

The wood floors sounded as Adrian entered, and Dominic shivered, but didn't look over.

Adrian never spoke right away—part of it was to savor the quiver and shake of his submissive while they waited to see if there was praise or scolding.

Tonight, most of his lack of speech was due to Dominic taking his breath away.

Dominic was fucking gorgeous on his knees and *delightful* to watch. Flushed. Hard. Nearly panting as he tried to control his breathing. So turned on and wound tight. He was someone who needed release in the worse way.

A gift to Adrian—and he'd return that to Dominic, with interest.

He paused behind Dominic, watching but not touching. Silent and waiting. Some submissives spoke around now, to ask if Adrian was pleased. Dominic raised his head slightly, but didn't say a damn thing—and that alone nearly made Adrian groan in pleasure. He hadn't asked for silence, but he also hadn't given any other commands but strip and kneel. Yet Dominic waited. And waited. Controlled. Bound, even without leather. Without even knowing.

God, this would be a pleasure.

Dominic's clothing was folded into a pile on the dresser. Adrian continued past him and slipped off his own suit jacket, folded it, and set it next to Dominic's clothing. He turned and started in on his tie.

An ever-so-slight movement from Dominic. He didn't move his head, but he was obviously watching Adrian from the corners of his eyes.

Good. There was that heady mix of soft and hard in Dominic—the need to obey and the strength to do it.

Adrian took his time sliding off his tie, then worked the buttons of his shirt free before stripping that off, too. He left the suit pants on for now.

Dominic shook, and his lips were parted as he strove to take in enough air.

Adrian couldn't help the smile as he spoke. "You're magnificent, Dominic."

Instant flush. Dominic's head bowed and his mouth snapped shut. But some of the tension was gone, melting into pleasure.

"I find it hard to believe you've never knelt for anyone before."

Dominic straightened and looked at Adrian. "I've knelt plenty of times before, but never *for* anyone."

"But you're kneeling *for* me."

A slow nod, and Dominic's gaze turned inward. "For myself, too. But yeah, for you."

When he looked back Adrian's heart skipped a beat, because there was the vulnerability, the trust, the hope he so wanted to pull from Dominic. *Yes. Give me that.* Like water in a desert, he wanted to drink Dominic down, pull them both into pleasure and comfort and that perfect moment where the world holds still.

He held Dominic's gaze a moment longer, then turned to his bed, to where the leather cuffs still hung off the frame, trusting that Dominic would look, too—and yes. There was that hitch of breath.

He walked to the top of the bed and claimed the cuffs, and ran his fingers over the leather and metal. He'd used them on many partners, and it almost seemed like sacrilege to put them on Dominic, perhaps because there was more to this than merely claiming Dominic for the night. But he had no others that were this comfortable.

And, in the end, they were Adrian's cuffs, not anyone else's.

When he turned, Dominic met his gaze. His hands were still clasped behind his back, cock still hard and jutting, but that desperation was gone, replaced by a deeply rooted calm. "Please," he said, his voice low and soft. "I want to know what it feels like."

"And so you shall." As Adrian closed in on Dominic, two thoughts coalesced in his mind. The first was that claimings went both ways. The other was that after tonight, he'd never use these cuffs on any other person.

Adrian gripped the cuffs and stepped forward.

DOM HAD NEVER FELT SO LIBERATED, FREE, AND POWERFUL AS HE did kneeling on the floor of Adrian's bedroom, naked, and under Adrian's command. All the pornos he'd seen and books he'd read with submission and BDSM—they seemed to have gotten this part wrong. Or maybe he hadn't read the words right, because he probably ought to not feel like he could take over the world right now.

Then again, that's how he felt when he put Domino on and walked onstage.

Yeah, he was nervous and so fucking turned on that every breath ached his balls and cock, but even when Adrian stroked his cheek and he shivered into the touch, that sense of calm and poise and power remained.

He'd do whatever Adrian asked because he could and chose to.

"Dominic." His name was a caress on Adrian's tongue. "You've truly never played before? Never done anything like this?"

"No. I—I've read about it, though."

"Yes, so you said." Laughter there. Adrian slipped behind Dom. From the shift of fabric and the creek of the floor, Dom guessed that Adrian too had knelt.

Fingers at Dom's left wrist, somehow cool against his skin. "Loosen your arms for me." Adrian's breath was hot across the back of Dom's neck.

He'd worn leather cuffs as part of Domino's outfits. But he'd been the one to buckle them on himself. This—this was different. He was acutely aware of the smoothness and soft-ness of the padding inside and the cool touch as the cuff tight-ened around his wrist. The tug wasn't his own. Adrian's hands held him, his fingers traced up Dom's arms.

"I can't get over all this ink," Adrian murmured. "I want to taste every inch of you again."

The weight of those words circled him like the leather band, and Dom shuddered, tendrils of pleasure sliding down into his balls and up into his head.

Then Adrian put the other cuff on, and somehow it was

more intense this time. Still, that sense of power, but it was coupled with such a feeling of security. Of peace. That overlaid the desire and need and heightened every ounce of it.

He moaned. Couldn't help it.

"God," Adrian breathed. "You're so fucking beautiful." He brought Dom's wrists close together, and there was a little *click*. "There you are." Lips brushed the nape of Dom's neck. "In my leather, with your hands bound behind your back. For me."

"Yes." The word came straight from his soul, and it was Adrian who moaned.

The floorboards echoed Dom's groans as Adrian rose and came to stand in front of Dom.

Those strong fingers gripped Dominic's chin. "I think I know what to do with that mouth of yours."

God, yes. He wanted Adrian's dick so badly. Wanted the salt and taste of him. The groans. "Bet you do."

"I'm not going to be kind tonight, Dominic. I'll fuck you how I like, including that throat of yours."

It was a warning, but also a question, too, Dom realized. Still making sure this was fine, that Dom had no reservations. He smirked up at Adrian. "Bet I can take it."

Yes, fuck yes. He wanted to be used, wanted it to be hard and raw and rough. Dom wanted it, trusted Adrian, and knew he would take care of him.

Adrian's lips twitched, and he reached for his belt.

There was the glorious sound of the buckle opening. The slide of the tongue from the loops and the sensuous sound of a button and a zipper being undone. Adrian freed his thick shaft from his pants and underwear and stroked himself idly. "I suppose we'll find that out."

Adrian slid one hand into Dom's hair and pulled tight. The shock and flare of pain had Dom gasping just as Adrian stepped in and shoved the head of his cock into Dom's mouth.

He moaned around it, unable to move his head for the tightness of Adrian's grip. Tears sprang to the corners of his eyes. So fucking good. No one *ever* manhandled him like this.

"Suck it, Dominic. Now." An edge to Adrian's voice.

Dom shivered and did as told, with all his skill and passion, taking in as much of Adrian's length as he could. Working his tongue around the shaft. Over veins, around the glans, into the slit, then opening his throat even more when Adrian thrust in. He'd fucking make Adrian come if he could.

If he was allowed to. And *there* was the sense of freedom and euphoria. He didn't have to worry about that—he only needed to take Adrian's thrusts, open himself, and give the best blowjob he knew how.

He doubled down and was rewarded by a moan and Adrian's slurred words. "Fucking hell. Your mouth. Goddamn."

Dom strained against the cuffs and the link that held them together, wanting to feel the weight of Adrian's balls in his hands, the hard muscles of his ass, but he was bound and restrained, and for the first time, he ached at the loss of control.

Adrian chuckled. "I was wondering when you'd realize that." He gripped Dom's hair harder. "Means you can't stop me if I want to go deep."

That was all the warning Dom had before the gentle thrusts in and out of his mouth became harder and more demanding. "Open for me, Dominic. Fucking take every inch of my cock."

His moan sounded more like a whine, and he let Adrian slide in deep and long until he was almost sure he wouldn't pull out enough to let him breathe—but he did. Just enough before he thrust in again. Fast, deep. His nose in Adrian's pubes. Tears in his eyes. The slick sounds of grunts and choking and moans—his and Adrian's.

"That's it. Just like that. A good little cocksucker getting his face fucked like he deserves."

Yeah. He did deserve it. He fucking *wanted* it like this. He'd never known how much he'd needed this. It was hot and perfect and just brutal enough to leave him gasping and moaning and a total wreck. He was so fucking hard that if Adrian nudged Dom's dick with his shoe, he'd spill all over those nice, shiny leather shoes.

He nearly did without the nudge, but he couldn't quite reach that release. Heaven and hell. He'd never been suspended like that before.

Adrian's hold on his head loosened ever so slightly, and his breath was hard and ragged as he spoke. "You're gonna drink down every drop of my come, or I'll make you lick what you spill from the floor."

Oh god. Yes. He'd do either. Dom could only moan around Adrian's shaft, and it thickened and thrust in and out of Dom's throat until Adrian bit back a wordless curse and came hot and hard on Dominic's tongue.

Dom sucked and swallowed and mouthed Adrian as he groaned and thrust with a hell of a lot less control than before, until he was utterly spent and Dom was left shaking and wanting with tears in his eyes. He looked up, and Adrian's eyes weren't dry either—his expression was almost one of shock.

Fingers traced his chin and caressed his lips. "Fucking hell, babe," Adrian murmured.

Dom knew from experience that this wasn't the end of the night. He didn't expect Adrian to drop down to his knees, though, to take Dom's face between his hands and kiss him like he was the only man in existence.

But that's what Adrian did, and Dom moaned into him, every nerve on fire.

Adrian wiped away the wetness on Dom's face. "I love tasting me on your tongue."

"Fuck my face more often, then." His words were whispered and hoarse.

A deep rumble of amusement and a pat on the cheek. "We've only had two nights."

Felt like so much more. Everything with Adrian was hot and fast, and yet somehow so slow and perfect, too. Like now, when Adrian pulled him up from the floor and took him to the bed.

Adrian unclasped the cuffs from each other. "Lie down on your back. I'm going to tie you to the headboard for a little while. See what you think of that."

Dom exhaled, a strange heat running through his body that had nothing to do with the ache of his cock. "Yeah, okay."

Adrian took each arm and swung it up, murmuring how Dom should move, how he needed to position his body. Gentle voice, gentle touch. He was still in all his clothing, too.

"Wanna see you naked," Dom said. Everything was heady and light again.

Adrian smiled and touched his face. "Do you?"

"Yeah. I mean, if you want? 'Cause I guess I'm not supposed to demand anything, am I?"

He couldn't even name the emotions that flickered over Adrian's features, but there was such a weight to them, and in his gravelly voice. "You, Dominic, can always ask me for anything you wish."

What he wished. He wanted everything. This moment. Wednesday. Whatever happened tomorrow. He wanted the band and Domino. He wanted Adrian to make the world go away so only Dom existed. Dom and Adrian.

"I'm in way over my head."

"Shh." Adrian's brow furrowed. "So am I."

Dom closed his eyes. Oh fucking hell. He was gonna fall in love with Adrian. After two damn dates. That wasn't safe and it wasn't fair at all.

A touch on his arm had Dom opening his eyes again. "You'll miss the show," Adrian said, and pulled off his tie.

He stripped the rest of his clothing off, watching Dom the entire time. Soon that amazing body was exposed once more, in every mouthwatering detail. It was everything Dom remembered, and so much more. "You're fucking hot."

"Why thank you." Adrian got his quirky, wicked grin and picked up a bundle of rope. "And as a reward, I'm going to tie you up. If it's too much, tell me and I'll cut you free."

"It's not gonna be too much."

Adrian shook his head. "You don't know that yet."

But he did. Because ropes didn't scare him. The thought of being bound only made his blood hot and his mind relax. What terrified him was the looming future, his guitar, and how much he'd have to give up to have everything he wanted.

Adrian tied his right wrist first, stretching his arm in the process, and it felt so damn good he arched his back. "Fuck, babe, you do like this, don't you?"

Dom met Adrian's stare. "Yeah it's..." He huffed out a breath. "It's like soaring." Or being onstage. The thrill, the heat and charge, and the utter security. "I'm safe." He relaxed into the bed. "I'm safe here."

Adrian stroked his arms. "Makes me want to tie your legs down, too."

Oh hell, that sent a bolt of lightning down his body. "Yeah, please."

"Not tonight. Partly to tease you—because I love that—but mostly because I think you can hold yourself still for me."

A different heat flowed and settled in his balls and dick. The cuffs might calm him, but a hit of Adrian's command sent lust racing into every part. "Fuck."

For that he got a smirk, and Adrian stroked himself a few times. "Not quite there yet. But I bet once you're tied down and listening to me... I will be."

"I'm listening."

Fingers danced up his left arm, and that too was tied to the headboard. Same warm touch swept over Dom's lips. "You're *talking*, not listening."

He couldn't resist opening his mouth and sucking those fingers in. Adrian hissed, then grunted. "Your mouth is always trouble."

Dom hummed around Adrian's fingers, which slid in and out between his lips. He couldn't help thrusting his hips in time with the motion.

"God, I could watch you like this all day," Adrian murmured. "In fact..." He withdrew his fingers and slipped down to the end of the bed. He cascaded both hands up Dom's legs, tightened, and pulled him down the bed until his arms were taut and stretched to either side of his head.

Oh fuck, that felt fantastic, and he couldn't help squirming and bucking.

"Dominic." Adrian's voice was sharp. "I want you still."

Fire rained down along his body, and he fought to control himself, even as every instinct said to keep moving, keep searching for purchase and pleasure. He was panting by the time he managed to stop the squirms and the thrusts.

"Better," Adrian said. Sure enough, Adrian's flagging dick was thicker now. He patted Dom's legs, then spread them apart, bending them at the knees and arranging them wide, making Dom's thighs ache ever so slightly. "Now, I want you to stay like that for me."

"What are you gonna do?"

"Touch you anywhere I want." Adrian ran fingers over the instep of Dom's foot. "And you're not going to move, are you?"

Dom pressed his head into the mattress and fought every twitch. He whimpered and then groaned when Adrian chuckled darkly.

That sound didn't nearly prepare Dom for what followed.

Adrian stalked around the bed, touching and teasing with his hands and his mouth until Dom was a moaning, twitching mess. Those minutes or hours—he honestly couldn't tell— were the most amazing, wonderful, sensual, and painful moments of his life. Like walking onstage to screams and cheers, only magnified a thousand times. He was brighter than the sun and he'd melt away and die if Adrian didn't fuck him soon.

"Please," he moaned. "Please!"

Adrian's own breathing was raspy and rough. This time he trailed a finger against Dom's taint, and it took everything not to buck up. Dom pulled on the cuffs at his wrists, needing the security and strength there. "Adrian!"

"You want me inside you, Dominic?" Gravel voice, dripping with desire.

"Need you!"

Another laugh, but this one wasn't dark. No, it was sweet and full of warm honey. "Good. Because I need you, too, babe. Want your heat and your tears." He grabbed a condom and the lube from the bedside table.

Finally he had Dom move, enough to allow Adrian to prep his entrance with lubed fingers. Then he had Dom wrap his legs around him as he slowly—fucking hell, so slowly— slid in. That was torture, sheer pleasure coursing up Dom's body, into his brain. He shook against the rope that tied him to the bedframe and screamed.

"God," Adrian breathed. "You're perfect." Then he thrust hard and deep, and any hope Dom had of remaining still flew away.

He thrashed and gasped, as much as he could with leather at his wrists and Adrian's strong hands gripping his hips. He'd probably have bruises tomorrow. Lovely, wonderful marks to remind him of this wondrous torture. Of Adrian plowing into him like he could take all of Dom, like they were built to be together. He'd been on edge for so long, body aching for release, that he flew and soared and cried Adrian's name over and over until that heat and light became too much and all he could do was babble.

"Dominic," Adrian called, his voice surprisingly soft, given how hard he was ramming into Dom. He took Dom's cock in his warm hand and stroked it in time with their motions. "Let go. Let me take you where you want to be."

Out of his head. Out of the world. He was nearly there. Trembling and crying, Dom let go of everything and trusted Adrian would sweep up what was left. His orgasm broke over him, hard and fast, blinding him and steeling his breath. Heat melted his bones and his brain clicked off for one glorious moment.

"Yeah, babe, just like that." Adrian rode him through the peak and came himself, moaning and shuddering into Dom.

He didn't know how long Adrian held him, remained inside him, just felt the horrible absence when he pulled out.

"Shh." Fingers on Dom's wet face again. "It's okay."

"Fuck." He couldn't think straight. "How do you do this to me every time?"

Adrian lowered Dom's legs, then crawled up enough on the bed to kiss his forehead. "Only two points of data. Need more to see if it's every time."

Dom's laugh was half a sob of pleasure.

Lips brushed his. "You're okay, right?"

Dom met Adrian's gaze. Would have smoothed out that creased brow if he could have moved—if he hadn't been tied down. "Oh yeah. Better than okay." He was well fucked and still trembling. His pulse pounded, and the man whose voice and touch made him want to do that all over again was hovering above him. "Please kiss me, Adrian."

He did, and it was the best damn kiss Dom had ever experienced. When Adrian untied him, cleaned him up, and poured him under the covers, after he'd taken Dom into his arms, he kissed him a second time, and that was nearly as good. "I quite like you, Dominic Bradley."

Dom huffed a laugh. "Good. 'Cause I wanna keep seeing you, Adrian Doran."

Adrian's grin was like moonlight and stars, so beautiful. Dom traced a finger over that fine chin and held on to that image, that thought, even as Adrian pulled him close and fell into sleep beside him.

Dominic Bradley kinda wanted Adrian forever. That should have been terrifying, but it felt as secure as the cuffs had around his wrists.

The only problem was, he had no idea what to do with Domino or Twisted Wishes if that happened. Dominic—Adrian's Dominic—didn't live in the rock-and-roll world.

But Dom did.

CHAPTER
SEVEN

ADRIAN LEFT DOMINIC SOUNDLY SLEEPING WHEN HE CREPT OUT of bed just past eight in the morning. He'd have loved to remain curled up around that lovely man, but nature called and sleep wasn't going to come any more this morning. After the way he'd topped Dominic the previous night, he doubted Dominic would be moving much before ten. He'd barely fluttered his eyes when Adrian had kissed his brow.

Instead, Adrian had grabbed a pair of boxers, padded down to the kitchen, ground fresh beans, and started a pot of coffee—and tried to work out the kinks in his sore muscles.

Fuck, Dominic was something else. Adrian really couldn't get enough of him. Utterly satisfying in bed, beautiful to behold, and a mind that whirled like a machine behind those deep brown eyes. What he wanted more of today was that mind.

He'd probably have the body, too, but damned if they both needed a little time to recover from their escapades. While he still had plenty of energy, his stamina in his thirties wasn't what it had been in his teens or twenties. Plus, he'd put Dominic through the wringer, too, judging from his screams, the way he'd come, and the tears on his cheeks. Second time he'd made Dominic cry from sex.

Second time he'd made anyone cry like that. It was humbling and heartening and made Adrian's heart tumble over and over. He'd seen it at BDSM parties a few times, but that had been with pain play, flogging, that kind of thing. Not from fucking. Not from merely tying someone up.

A voice murmured in the back of his head, one that sounded very much like Janelle, the woman who'd taught him most of what he knew about bondage. *There's nothing* merely *about tying anyone up, Adrian.*

That was true.

The coffeemaker's gurgling marked the end of the brewing and the beginning of Adrian clearing out the fuzziness of his head. He pulled the little carton of heavy whipping cream out of the fridge, gave it a hearty shake, and poured a smidge in.

Yeah, it was decadent as hell, and Jackson would have rolled his eyes at the fat content, but he only ever took his coffee like this at home on the weekend. Besides, the body still needed a little fat. Might as well grace his coffee with luxury.

Adrian sipped and savored, then sipped again. This part of Brooklyn might have been rapidly becoming hipster central, but at least he could get small-batch beans that made his eyes roll back into his head.

God. Brooklyn. Here. Home. He'd tied Dominic up. Fucked him. Topped him, even. No negotiation, not formally. Even though Dominic had consented, they were a bit in the woods when it came to this strange Dominant/submissive bondage arrangement they seemed to be developing. Adrian wasn't sure that really bothered him, though. After a second sip, he decided it didn't. Yes, he would always probe for consent, but something else Janelle had said was that lovers were like jewels. All were unique. All had their flaws. All required different settings.

And that the wrong kind of pressure only cracked the stone.

He didn't want to crack Dominic. Shatter his world in bed, sure. But not *hurt* him. He wanted Dominic safe and secure in...whatever this was they were developing.

He let out a sigh, poured himself a little more coffee, then headed upstairs. It had been a while since he'd been at a party, but the contacts were all still there. He and Janelle still saw each other on occasion. Coffee. Lunch. He'd made a point to rekindle the few friendships he'd had when he'd returned to New York.

And this was not a topic he could share with Jackson, even if he were far closer to him. Jackson had tagged along to one party—"To see what it was all about," he'd said. Afterward, he'd looked at Adrian with that shrewd gaze and shrugged. "Not my scene. Interesting, but not my scene."

No scorn, just facts. Nothing between them changed, other than Adrian rarely bringing his kink up to Jackson after that.

Once Adrian dropped into the desk chair in his office, he sent a short note to Janelle. A friendly greeting. A suggestion to meet for lunch. He needed advice—assurances, really— that how he was handling kink with Dominic was fine, especially since he wasn't following any path he'd taken before.

Yeah, yeah, he knew in all the fiction about BDSM, the Dominant was supposed to be this godlike know-it-all. Even on the internet, in blogs and shit, they were these over-the-top personalities. Adrian wasn't—not all the time. So yes, he worried that he'd fuck up. Especially since Dominic—

He let out a breath and closed his eyes. Especially since he could fall very, very hard for Dominic if he let himself. He'd wanted more than a one-night stand, more than the occasional quick fuck at a club. Maybe he wasn't looking for the husband and kids Jackson was after, but he wanted a partner.

Someone to share his passions with. Learn about other passions from.

Something other than the job that was slowly taking over his life.

Adrian peeled his eyes open again and blinked at his inbox. Janelle had answered already.

Of course we can do lunch, Adrian. Name the time and place.

Simple, easy. He suggested midweek at a cafe close to his work. Moments later, she answered with an affirmative.

So, that was done.

He let his gaze roam around the office to all the mundane tasks he needed to do this weekend. Bills to pay. Shit to shred and recycle. Some magazines he wanted to read.

Well, with lovely Dominic out like a light, he might as well clear his plate of some of those tasks. Extra time to focus on learning more about the beautiful man in his bed, once he woke up. He reached for the piles of bills and logged onto his bank's website.

DOM WOKE TO AN EMPTY BED, THE FAINT SCENT OF COFFEE IN THE air, and an aching body. The pain, though, felt good, and every move as he burrowed deeper into the sheets on Adrian's bed reminded him just how well fucked he'd been the night before. Commanded. Used. Tied up. *Holy shit.*

Throughout it all, Adrian had been kind and respectful. Forceful, too. Full of dirty talk and searing kisses. But also tender. And Dom had soared and floated and been so blissed out he'd cried and screamed.

Was this what it was like to date? He didn't think so. It had been *years* since he'd had any sexual relationship that had lasted more than a couple hours and hadn't ended with Dom deleting the guy's number. But he remembered the laughter and the joy of discovery and the unfolding of likes and dislikes.

But not the passionate, heated, *incredible* sex. He didn't just ache from the poundings he'd endured last night—he ached for more than that. To crawl not just into Adrian's bed, but into his life, too. What else besides sex and books did the man like? What music, what art? Which movies were in his collection? How long had he lived here?

There were traces of an authentic New York accent there, but also bits of a smooth all-American one going on, the voice broadcasters had. Or interviewers.

Dom shivered. And there it was, the fear, the anxiety gnawing its way up his spine. Because for all he wanted Adrian to share his life—there were parts of Dom's he couldn't share. Not right now, anyway. What if Adrian rejected Domino? Worse, what if he *told* someone?

It was that apprehension that had him crawling out of bed and grabbing his glasses. After he found his underwear and jeans, he used the bathroom and splashed water on his face.

The face that reflected back looked a combination of happy and sleepy and scared, but none the worse for wear. Adrian face-fucking him with a vengeance hadn't left him looking any different.

Though he couldn't say the same for the rest of his body. The ink hid a lot of it, but there were bruises on his hips and shoulders from hands and teeth, and Adrian's hot-as-fuck mouth.

Sparks ran up his back and he wiped his face with his hand. *Down, boy.* Yeah, he wanted another round, but he needed to know where they stood—what Adrian thought—and where this was going.

It wasn't casual. It wasn't a fling. It was beyond a one-night stand. But *what* was it?

And what could he let it be? Dom glanced at his hair. Once more, it was more or less a judicious glob of super-hold hair gel shy of being Domino's unruly locks. He flattened that shit down as best he could. Last thing he needed was the rock star looking back at him.

He'd planned on heading down to the kitchen, but gentle clicking drew him to a room on the same floor, one down the hall and next to the door that led to that exquisite library. Inside a room of blues and browns, with light streaming in from the window, sat Adrian in a leather desk chair, naked but for boxers, a pen in his mouth and papers—bills—spread out on his desk.

Dom held his breath and watched because this—this moment was Adrian Doran. Truly him. Something he probably did every weekend. And god, was he gorgeous like this, too. Brow furrowed, lips twitching around the pen that bobbed up and down. His chestnut hair flopped in every direction, redder in the morning light, and his pale skin was lightly freckled on his shoulders, a detail Dom hadn't noticed before, despite two nights with the man.

Muscles moved as Adrian typed in numbers and clicked the mouse. Damn, those arms. The ones that had held him down and also held him sweetly. Dom exhaled, then whispered, "Adrian."

The pen fell from Adrian's mouth and he jumped a bit, but when he turned, his whole being seemed to light up. "Dominic."

The deep rumble in that voice made Dom's knees weak, and he leaned on the doorframe, smiling back. "I smelled coffee."

Adrian bent to retrieve his pen from the floor, then righted himself. "I made a pot. It's down in the kitchen. I'd have cooked breakfast, too, but I didn't know how long you'd sleep."

"Right. You said you cooked." And as if on cue, Dom's stomach growled.

Laughter from the other man, and the sound was magic and as bright as the sunlight burnishing that auburn hair. "Well, I think someone likes the idea of food, so let's feed that stomach of yours, shall we?"

Adrian stood, and every part of Dom wanted to kneel down before him. "Wow."

"Wow?" Amusement and confusion in that one word.

"You—do things to me." Dom clutched the doorframe. "My mind goes all kinds of places when I see you."

"And where did your mind go now?" Adrian tilted his head, but didn't move any closer.

Should he actually tell the truth? That seemed—dangerous. But also the right thing. "The floor." He met Adrian's stare. "I wanted to kneel for you again." He shook his head. "I don't know why."

Adrian let out a small breath, and his fingers twitched. "If you'd like, you can do that. Come here and kneel for a moment."

That same strange buzz of headiness that had engulfed him last night rose and filled his head. "You don't mind?"

"Oh, Dominic." Soft, velvet voice. So full of emotions. "No, no, I don't mind at all." He held out his hand.

But rather than take it, Dom crossed the room, fell to his knees, and wrapped his arms around Adrian's legs. Calm enveloped him. Joy. Things he didn't understand. He wasn't hard, wasn't in a state of lust. Hell, he hadn't even had coffee yet.

A touch on his head, fingers caressing, smoothing his hair. "What is it you want?"

"I have no fucking clue." He pressed his cheek against Adrian's thigh. "I don't even know what I'm doing."

Adrian made a strangled sound. A laugh? A sigh? Dom

pressed his forehead against skin and breathed in the decadent smell of Adrian. "I know I sound foolish."

"No, you don't. Not at all." Fingers tipped his chin up until he met Adrian's downward gaze. "You're a highly intelligent man. You've just found yourself somewhere unexpected."

In Adrian's office, kneeling before him because he desperately wanted to. "This isn't like me," he murmured.

"Maybe it is." Adrian stroked his cheek. "I did want to talk to you about this today—about you and me and what you want—but I do think you need some coffee and food in that belly of yours."

Yeah, that sounded good. "Do you know what I really want?" He gave Adrian's legs another hug.

"I have a feeling you're about to tell me." Dom heard the smile in those words. Didn't even have to look up.

He chuckled. "French toast. With a ton of syrup." He raised his head and found Adrian laughing quietly. "And maybe some bacon."

"I have bacon, and everything I need to make you French toast that's the best in the city." Adrian patted his cheek. "But you do have to let go of my legs and follow me downstairs to get it."

Dom did, and Adrian helped him up. "Thank you." Heat rose to Dom's cheeks. "I feel better. I—needed that."

Adrian cupped the back of his neck and drew him in for a gentle kiss before speaking against his lips. "You're welcome." Then he let him go and gestured to the door. "Breakfast?"

"God, yes." Dom blew out a breath and followed Adrian downstairs. Everything was either very right in the world, or sideways entirely.

All he knew was that he was warm here, and calm, and Adrian was fucking amazing. Maybe that was a good start to figuring out all the rest.

ADRIAN DIDN'T FEED DOMINIC THE FRENCH TOAST, BUT watching him eat was pleasure enough. The happy sigh, the content noises. The way he tapped his bare feet against the breakfast bar stool. So many questions flew through Adrian's mind, and many were tinged with fear. That he would screw this—whatever *this* was—up. That he wasn't the man Dominic needed.

Though everything that had happened in the office had felt right and natural. Slipping into the role Dominic needed at that fragile moment had been pure instinct, and he'd come out the other side. Happy. Content. Joyful as he ate his breakfast and sipped his coffee.

Adrian toyed with his bacon, moving it about in the syrup, and finally voiced the question at the forefront of his mind. "Do you want to date me, Dominic?"

Dominic's body stilled, and his eyes turned inward for a moment. Considering, calculating.

God, Adrian wished he knew how that mind worked.

Finally, Dominic nodded. "Yeah. I do. I just—don't know what dating you entails. I mean—I haven't actually dated anyone since college. And I kinda doubt 'let's study together, then fuck' is exactly what I'm supposed to do now."

It was those quips that flipped Adrian's heart around and around and made him want to haul Dominic in for kisses. The honesty, the absurdity. "Five years? You've been just hooking up—for five years?" He paused and laughed. "Mind you, I have no room to talk. Plus, there's nothing wrong with casual."

Dominic raised an eyebrow and pointed his fork at Adrian. "So, when did you last date, then?"

"California," Adrian said automatically. "Nearly the same timeframe. A little over six years ago. When I moved back to New York... I needed time to settle in."

There was a thoughtful look in Dominic's eyes, but he didn't ask anything more. "And what about the whole tying up and kneeling thing?" Color touched his cheeks.

Adrian shrugged and ate his bacon. "You tell me. Do you enjoy it?"

A deeper blush now, and that was so fucking nice. Dominic even squirmed on the stool. "Yeah. I do. I've just never...done anything like that before."

That was an answer Adrian didn't quite buy. "Hard to believe you've never been held down and fucked. I know you've been on your knees and sucked a man off before."

Even Dominic's neck was red now, and his mouth open. He looked down at his plate. Then up. "Uh. Okay. I've done *that*. Lots of times. But no cuffs or rope or anything like that." His gaze turned inward again and his voice wavered. "And I've never wanted to kneel like I did this morning for anyone. Ever."

Too much emotion there. Adrian rose and rounded the bar to Dominic's side so he could brush the locks off his forehead and plant a kiss there. "I should tell you that I was utterly honored."

"It's like my life is still when I'm here with you. Like it's *mine*."

He combed his fingers through Dominic's unruly locks. "What's it like when you're not here?"

A huff of a laugh. "I can't even describe it. Sometimes it's my own. Other times it's—a roller coaster. I'm—playing a part and holding on and enjoying the ride. Then I land back here, and I'm myself." He leaned his head against Adrian's chest. "I know you want to know more than that."

He did. However, he wouldn't demand it. Not now. Not later. "We've been on two dates. In that time, you've trusted me tremendously with your body, Dominic. And yes, I'm kinky. And I think you are, too." He stroked Dominic's neck. "But trust isn't something you give all at once—different parts take time, and maybe there are things you never want to share with another."

Dominic exhaled and found Adrian's hand. Held it. Kissed his fingertips.

Oh god, the need that burned through Adrian from that one simple act. "Give me what you can, when you can. Tell me if you need me to slow down. Ask whatever questions you want."

"Aren't you supposed to be the boss?" Bright brown eyes met his. "Tell me what to do?"

"Yes...and no." Adrian chuckled. "It's complicated."

"It's been easy so far."

Yes, it had been. "The books you've read about BDSM...fiction or non?"

"Oh, fiction. Um. Erotic, mostly." Adrian felt the heat of Dominic's skin against his own.

"Then I should lend you some nonfiction ones. Maybe that'll help."

Dominic snorted a laugh, which Adrian didn't expect, but his smile was perfect and Adrian drank that in.

"You know, in all the sexy librarian romances, it's usually the librarian who's the shy, timid one." Dominic gestured at himself. "He's usually not the ripped, worldly hero who sweeps the other off his feet."

Adrian couldn't breathe for a moment, because his lungs were too tight. Dominic was warm and solid and a joy next to him. Finally, he caught a breath. "Did I sweep you off your feet?"

"Yeah, I think. Maybe that's why I keep ending up on my knees."

No doubt he'd end up there again, before the day was through. Adrian stroked a finger over Dominic's mouth. "I think we should get dressed. Go for a walk. Talk. I'd love to hear more about what you've been reading, my dear bookish man. And you can ask me whatever you like."

"Even about California?" He spoke around Adrian's finger.

Dominic must have felt Adrian flinch, because apprehension filled his eyes. That vanished the moment Adrian pressed his finger between those silky lips. He savored Dominic's throaty moan. "Even about California. They weren't the best years of my life."

Though there had been moments of utter brilliance. But in the end, he'd been alone and bereft.

Dominic sucked gently on Adrian's finger, licking and nipping, and every warmth filled Adrian now. "If you keep that up, I'm going to take you upstairs, bend you over my bed, and fuck you so hard, you'll regret it later."

As he hoped and, honestly, expected, Dominic only sucked harder. Adrian laughed and hauled the man up into his arms so he could claim that mouth again. Then he did exactly as he had promised, much to Dominic's delight, judging by his cries and screams of pleasure.

CHAPTER
EIGHT

DESPITE THEIR DETOUR TO THE BEDROOM, THEY STILL ENDED UP on their walk. They both wore jeans and Adrian wore a T-shirt. He would have gladly lent one to Dominic as well, but he'd asked for a button-down with sleeves.

"I don't always like showing off my tattoos."

"They were for you." Adrian traced the colors and lines of his favorite, the Dara knot Dominic sported on his shoulder.

After a sensuous little shudder, Dominic nodded. "Yeah. They all mean something to me."

"This one?" He knew the meaning and wondered if Dominic did.

"Strength. Security. It's an oak knot. Supposed to represent roots."

"Inner strength," Adrian murmured. "Power and wisdom. It's perfect for you."

Dominic's eyes were wide.

"I'm Irish-American, remember?" Adrian gestured at himself. "It's somewhat obvious."

While Dominic stood slack-jawed, Adrian pulled out one of his tighter button-downs. It was loose on Dominic's frame. The fabric was pale yellow, and Adrian couldn't help kiss that inked skin again before Dominic covered it up. "Thank you for sharing your tattoos with me."

"Kinda hard to have sex with clothing on."

"Not really."

Dominic got a look, then laughed. "Okay, you're right there. For hookups I usually didn't take my top off."

But Dom had for Adrian. He savored that knowledge. He'd seen all of Dominic, every line, every inch of flesh. Tasted just about all of it, as well.

They headed out into the summer sun and tried to stay in the shade of buildings and trees as they rambled around the area.

"You said you wanted to know about California."

Dominic nodded. "If you're fine with that."

More or less. "I was born here. I grew up in that house." He gestured in the direction of his home. "And back in the '80s, this wasn't the neighborhood it is now."

"Yeah, I've heard. And I guess the gentrification pushed a lot of people out."

It had, and that grated on Adrian, even though he was, in part, also part of that process. "My granda bought the place in the '50s, and my folks held on to it, but it needed so much upkeep and so many repairs. It wasn't in the greatest of shape when me and my siblings lived there."

Dom stopped. "You have siblings?"

Adrian turned toward Dom. "Two brothers and a sister. I'm actually the youngest. And the one who stayed—well, came back." He held out his hand, and Dominic took it.

"I'm an only child." His voice was soft. "Do you get along?"

"We did. Things are strained now. I'm hoping they'll ease up in the future."

"This is a longer story than just why you went to California and came back, isn't it?"

Adrian laughed. "Oh yes." Years and years in the making.

"Money. Religion. Wealth. A prodigal son. It's practically biblical."

"Jesus."

"Him, too."

Dominic swallowed a laugh.

Adrian gave his hand a squeeze and contemplated where to begin, because like the knot-work on Dominic's arm, the story looped and tangled in on itself. "As you might imagine, my parents were Catholic and devout, and we were raised as such."

"Oh shit. And you're queer."

Oh shit, indeed. "Yes, that's part of it. Didn't help that my second oldest brother, Patrick, went off to become a priest." The light of his parents' lives, or so he'd thought. "I idolized him when I was young. Thought about going into seminary myself."

"You didn't!"

"Well, no. I didn't. Especially when I realized what the Church said about people like me." He waved a hand. "Yes, they dress it up pretty, and yes, there's a faction that doesn't believe queers are sinners, but doctrine is doctrine, and you can read that we're *disordered* right on the Vatican website, so..."

"I probably shouldn't interrupt, or you'll never get it out."

Now *that* was true. "It's a mess, Dominic. I'm not sure I can explain it all, but I'll try to take the most direct route."

He launched into it. His eldest brother, Sean, had gone into the military, Patrick had become a priest, and Moira married a rather well-off investment banker, all before Adrian had gone to college.

"I was essentially an 'oops' baby."

"So you kind of grew up alone, too."

"I suppose in a way. They were around for my early years, but were gone for the later ones. Mainly, I was my mother's baby boy. My father's, too, for a while. He worked in construction, on the white-collar end. Management. Finances. Still, with four kids, he also worked a job at a diner as a cook —one of those twenty-four-hour types."

"City that never sleeps."

Adrian gave Dominic's hand a little squeeze. "It meant that I didn't see Dad as much as Mom, and thing were always a little strained between us." Awkward and tense, as if his father hadn't known what to do with the quiet child he'd sired. The one who devoured books, was good with computers, and tied up every single one of his GI Joes.

"Patrick and Sean had both been into sports. I was a nerd. Dad didn't know what to do with me on weekends, since his go-to activities were things I only tolerated."

They passed one of the many coffee shops that had sprung up in Brooklyn, though this one wasn't as pretentious as some of the others. Dominic slowed. "Can we stop in? I think I need some more caffeine. And strangely, I'm a little sore this morning."

Adrian pulled Dominic close and kissed him, right outside the door. "I can't *imagine* why that would be. And yes, let's fuel you up."

There was an industrial and secondhand feel to the place. Exposed beams and pipes. Wood and brick. Mismatched tables and chairs. The customers were a mix. Ages and ethnicities. Sexualities and genders, too. Adrian made a mental note to come back. This was a place he could frequent. Support.

Dominic ordered a large raspberry latte, then bumped Adrian's hip when he snorted. "I can't make this at home, so shut up."

"I didn't say a word." Adrian caressed the back of his neck, then ordered a regular coffee with a mound of whipped cream.

Dominic hip-checked him again, and Adrian laughed.

Someone wanted to be even more sore before the day was out.

"So," Dominic said as they sat down together on an old love seat. "High school."

Adrian took a sip and considered both the coffee and how to tell his story. The coffee was damn good—another reason to return. He set the mug down. "I knew I was interested in more than just women by the time I was a freshman. And I realized very quickly that I was a little more interested in masculine than anything else, regardless of gender. But I didn't come out to my parents until I was a junior—when my senior boyfriend asked me to the prom, and I said yes."

"Did they—Were they—" Dominic stopped. "Mine were fine with me. But I know not everyone—" Such concern. Such honest worry. Adrian patted his thigh.

"It took them by complete surprise, and that played into their first reactions. But they did love me, so they came around, especially Mom. She was more worried about how I might struggle through life. They'd been very aware of the AIDS crisis, even though by the mid-to late-'90s, things were much better."

There'd been tears and worries and long conversations about safety and love and not jumping into *anything* too fast. Some of the conversations he knew they'd had with his other siblings when they'd started dating.

"Thankfully, they did get the whole thing about teens having sex, so I didn't get a sanctimonious lecture about fucking—or not fucking. At least not from them."

"Oh shit. Your brother."

His brother, the priest. "Father Patrick Doran. Sanctimonious out the ass." He sighed and the spike of pain made him reach for his mug of coffee. "He was livid. Absolutely livid. I didn't know why, really. Still don't. We stopped talking. But I know it wasn't just about Church doctrine."

Dominic took Adrian's free hand. "Oh hell, I'm sorry."

The warmth in Dominic's voice and in his hand tightened Adrian's chest and tumbled his heart. "Sean was fine with it, but not what came later." He took another swallow of coffee. "Moira still talks to me. She and her husband figured out what I'd done, so while they were horrible shits after Mom died, they both apologized later."

Dominic held on to his hand more tightly. "Yeah, you're right, this is complex. I'll be quiet. You talk."

Adrian's bark of laughter had no mirth. He leaned back on the love seat, fortified by coffee and Dominic's hand, and launched into the tangled and woven tale.

He'd come out, gone to his boyfriend's prom, and dealt with the fallout from *that*—including Patrick's spiritual "counseling" that had done more to drive him out of Catholicism than anything else. For his own prom, he'd gone with a very cute trans guy his own age—one who'd allowed Adrian to tie him up with scarves and shit. The latter, of course, he'd never confessed to his parents.

Some things he never shared.

For college, he'd ended up at SUNY in Buffalo and gotten his BA in computer science in three years. Then, like every other tech person at the time, he'd headed out to California and hopped from start-up to start-up.

"I made a decent pile of cash despite the dot-com burst. Focused on equipment companies and financial ones. Stuff that was still making money. Which was good, because my father died and I learned my mom was about to lose the house."

The funeral had been hellish. Patrick had presided over the Mass, of course, which meant Adrian had been locked out of just about every part of that. His mother, in her grief, hadn't noticed that he'd been the only one of her children not to have a part. Not a reading. Not a psalm. Not even bringing up the gifts before Communion. Shut out completely.

So he'd stood next to his mother and been her support, her

pillar. The arms that had held her up even as he wanted to dive deep into his own complex grief for his father—a man he loved and didn't understand and wished he could have.

In the days that followed, he remained close to his mother, helping her with everything his father had taken care of—or hadn't, as it turned out. Their finances were a mess. Yes, his father had his pension, and yes, there was some life insurance, but the cost of raising four kids and sending them to college—even with Sean's ROTC scholarship—*then* sending Patrick to seminary had led his dad to mortgage the brownstone twice. And there wasn't enough to cover everything and provide for his mother to live on.

So Adrian had quietly cashed out as much of his stock options as he could, and taken over paying the mortgage. He would not see his mother lose the family home. Not the house his grandfather—her father—had worked so hard to obtain. Both he and his mother had decided it would be best if his siblings didn't know. Sean was on active duty. Moira was struggling to start a family of her own, and both she and her husband had their own burdens. And Patrick—well. He couldn't help. Not on a priest's salary. All the finery that surrounded him was none of his own.

Adrian had headed back to California to work, found a smaller place, and worked as many hours as he could to keep earning what he'd needed to for both himself and his mom. Did freelance work on the side to earn a little extra.

And because he'd managed to pull a decent amount out of the market, he'd done okay in the end. Yes, he'd lost his job a couple times, and scrambled and scraped to grab a new one, but he'd come out on top. In the end, he'd paid off one of his parents' mortgages and the other had a sizable dent in it. His mom was safe and learning to live again, surrounding herself with friends and knitting and books and volunteer work.

In California, Adrian had dated all over the spectrum and

learned quite a lot about himself, his love of bondage and domination, but also his apathy toward much of pain play. "I *can* flog someone," he murmured, dropping his voice. "It just doesn't *do* anything for me."

"I like what we've done so far," Dominic replied.

Both their cups were empty, so Adrian took the opportunity to sling an arm around Dominic and pull him close. "Good. If there's any aspect you don't like—"

"Believe me, I'll tell you. I've got a mouth."

"Yes, yes you do." Adrian tipped Dominic's chin up and took those lips into a sweet kiss. Not a long one, though, because they were in public—and he needed to finish his story.

Dominic settled against him, and he fell back into it. "For all that I made money, had decent jobs, and found myself in California, I wasn't happy there. I missed New York with every bone in my body. The scant time I'd been back had only increased that ache. I'd already lost large portions of my family and I felt like I was losing touch with all my roots, too."

The disdain some of his West Coast acquaintances—even the few people he'd dated—had shown to the city of his birth rankled every time. Especially since most of those people were transplants like him. The traffic, the car culture, and the lack of actual seasons also got on all his nerves. He'd glimpse the skyline of New York on TV and the reaction, the deep longing, had been so visceral every time.

"I would occasionally float my résumé out in New York, but the economy wasn't great at the time, so I either got no nibbles or ones that wouldn't bring in the income I needed to help mom."

"But you did come back, eventually."

Adrian nodded. "Six years ago, my mom died."

Dominic took a breath. "Oh."

Adrian closed his eyes for a bit. He'd mourned her the way he never could for his dad. Patrick had still said the Mass and he'd still been locked out, but he'd been there for her when his other siblings hadn't.

"She was sick leading up to it. Didn't tell anyone right away. Finally told me. I had vacation stored up, so I pretty much dropped everything and ran home." He grunted. "She was—well. A week later, she died. I was there, holding her hand in the hospital."

"I'm so sorry." Whispered words.

Adrian stroked Dominic's hair. "Thank you." He coughed to clear out the sudden tightness in his throat.

"What changed everything was Mom's will. She left me the house. Me. No one else. Everything else had been divided equally between the four of us, but the house was mine."

Dominic sat up. "Makes sense. You were paying it off."

He nodded. "I'd actually completely paid it off by then. But my siblings didn't know that. Patrick—good, loving priest that he is, so open to forgiveness and all that shit—was convinced that I'd somehow taken advantage of Mom and had her change the will. Even though it had been that way for a pile of years."

"I think I hate your brother."

Adrian's chuckle was dark. "Every last one of my friends does." He sobered. "I can't even blame the Church entirely, because not everyone's like that. He just...clings to the most conservative parts that he can without actually being in schism."

His own feelings were so much more complex. Patrick had been kind to him when he'd been a boy and he couldn't quite forget that, even if Patrick had shut the door completely as an adult.

"The other problem was that the gentrification of Brooklyn had begun and the housing prices shot up. That house is worth quite a bundle now."

"Yeah, I know." Dominic laughed. "All too well."

Because he'd bought in Brooklyn. On a musician's salary. Adrian turned that over in his head again, then set it aside.

"My siblings contested the will. All of them. Took forever for it to get resolved, but it was, and the judge ruled in my favor. Sean was disgusted that I was so—money-grubbing, he said. Moira didn't talk to me until about a year later. Her husband dug into the house and figured out Mom couldn't have been paying the mortgage, and realized I had. They called and apologized. Said she'd speak to the others, but...no word from Sean." Adrian shrugged. "So six years ago, I quit my job on the West Coast and moved home. Lived on savings until I got a job here, renovated the house, and moved in."

He stroked a hand down Dominic's thigh. "That's my story."

"That's a lot of story." Dominic sat on the edge of the sofa and put his head in his hands. "Wow."

Adrian looked around the coffee shop again. Yes, he'd come back here. But right now? "I think I'd like to walk some more."

"Yeah. Me, too."

They gathered up the dishes and placed them in the bin near the front, then headed back out into the warm summer day.

It was, Adrian realized, slightly unfair of him to drop all of that into Dominic's lap. But another part of him was utterly curious to see what he might share in return.

Because there was so much behind those brown eyes and that sometimes shy, sometimes wicked smile, and Adrian longed for it the same way he'd longed for the very streets they now walked.

He could wait, though. He was very good at waiting.

THE WALK WITH ADRIAN HAD BEEN ENLIGHTENING AND humbling, and had set Dom's head spinning. They spent some time watching a pickup basketball game, found a spot neither of them had eaten at before for lunch, and on the way home had even bought a pie from a place Adrian claimed was the best pie shop in all of New York.

All the while, Dom marveled at the man next to him, the one with the huge heart and stunning eyes. The one with old pain in his past, and a touch that could be tender or commanding.

He still wanted to kneel beside him, wrap his arms around him, and give him as much of himself as he could.

But he didn't know how *much* that was. He talked a little about his childhood in New Jersey, how supportive his parents had been when he'd come out in high school and real-ized that his infatuation with boys wasn't at *all* a phase. He talked about his friendship with Ray, though he didn't name him. Trips to the shore. His love of music and history, gradu-ating with a bachelor's in the latter and a minor in the former. How he'd waited tables while at Montclair State University. His trips into New York with his classmates. Clubbing. Listening to the buskers whenever he saw one.

"Did you ever busk?"

Dom shifted on the stool by Adrian's breakfast counter. They were in his kitchen again, with Adrian at the stove working on dinner. Lamb chops and stir-fried vegetables. Seasoned rice. The place smelled fantastic.

"No. I...get stage fright a lot, especially performing solo. It's not so bad in groups." Thrilling even, now that he had Domino to put on. Much better than the wreck he used to be in public. He looked down at his nails. Most of the time on tour he painted them random colors that would chip as soon as he played, even when he used a pick. He hadn't worn polish in months.

"Hence being in a band."

Dom heard the question in Adrian's voice...and ignored it. "Exactly."

Adrian shook the skillet of vegetables on the stove and mixed them again. "You have a passion for more than history I think, given your interests in literature."

"I haven't met a book I didn't like."

At that, Adrian turned around completely and raised an eyebrow in utter disbelief.

Dom couldn't help laughing. "Okay, yes I have. There's a lot of books I can't stand. But I'll start pretty much anything you put in my hands, and read until I can't."

"I do hope you have a good level of *can't* because there's so many books in this world..."

And so many two floors above his head in that lovely attic of Adrian's. "When I was young, I used to read everything to completion, but now? Yeah, *can't* comes a lot faster than it used it. A lot."

Adrian's lips twitched a bit. Subtle, but Dom still caught the smirk he was trying to hold back. It was rather like the ones both Ray and Zavier got sometimes. "What?"

Adrian glanced over his shoulder, eyes a mockery of innocence. "Oh, nothing."

Dom slipped off the stool and joined Adrian at the stove. He placed his hand at the small of Adrian's back. "Nothing?" He nuzzled at that tempting neck. "I don't think so."

Adrian hissed. "Don't you know it's dangerous to distract the cook?"

"It's nothing," Dom said.

Adrian turned off the gas on the burner, set down the wooden spatula. The next thing Dom knew, his arms were pinned behind his back and Adrian had him up against the fridge, scattering magnets and papers to the floor, thigh between Dom's legs and mouth inches from his own. "Not nothing at all."

"You first." Dom licked at Adrian's mouth, and that

earned him a groan. Adrian's thigh pressed against Dom's swelling cock.

"You're not at all old." Adrian kissed the side of his mouth. "And you're delectable. After we eat, I think I want to savor more of your ink."

That didn't help the state of Dom's dick. Or did. Depended on which way he wanted this to go.

"Your turn." Adrian sucked on Dom's neck.

"Fuck."

That only earned him a chuckle and a nip to his earlobe, which made him unable to think at all. He squirmed against the refrigerator and Adrian's hard body, his limbs on fire. Felt so good, so real, so right.

"Want me to make you come, babe?" Adrian's hot breath tickled his face and his teeth scraped against Dom's stubble. "An appetizer before dinner?"

God, Adrian could make him hard and hot in an instant. "What...whatever you want." Because he couldn't decide. Waiting was its own pain and pleasure. But this—oh god, he would die from this, too.

Adrian let out a breath that was pure bliss. "Ah, thank you for that."

In the next moment, Adrian had trapped both Dom's wrists in his hand, taken his mouth, and had his other hand in Dom's jeans.

Holy shit. Dom moaned and fought as Adrian jacked him off and feasted on his mouth. The only thing that existed was Adrian's hard body, the hum of the fridge vibrating into his back, and the feel of that hand fisting his cock hard and fast. There was no way he'd last, but he fought anyway until he came, light blinding his vision and Adrian drinking down his screams.

When Dom came down from his high, he was sagging in Adrian's arms. "How—how do you do that?"

"How can I not?" Adrian nuzzled his temple. "You look so amazing when you come."

He hitched a breath. "I'm a mess." He was falling in love. He shouldn't be falling in love. Mind-blowing sex wasn't enough to hang a relationship on.

Except it wasn't just that. It was everything in between.

Adrian pressed another kiss, this one to Dom's cheek. "Go clean yourself up, and I'll finish dinner."

Dom raised his gaze and found himself looking into those flecked brown eyes. "If this is the appetizer, what's for dessert?"

Laughter washed over Dom like light and joy, and Adrian's smile was a spotlight shining on Dom. "Pie. And anything you'd like."

Oh. Oh god. Dom swallowed, his mind whirling at what that meant. "Anything?"

"Yes."

"I should go clean up, then." Dom found his footing and straightened.

Adrian tapped him on the ass. "I'll be waiting."

Dom went, cleaned himself up as best he could, then came back downstairs. Dinner was amazing, and yes, between this and the French toast in the morning, Adrian had proved he could cook just as good as he'd implied he could.

They shared a slice of pie—after Adrian had retrieved his cuffs and a blindfold from his bedroom. Hands restrained, eyes covered, Dom ate from Adrian's fork, and his mind and body exploded with each bite. The pie, bourbon chocolate pecan, was the best he'd ever had of that flavor, but the experience of eating it turned his head inside out and melted his bones.

He was so damn hard again by the end, it wasn't at all fair. "You're gonna kill me."

Adrian kissed him before removing the blindfold and

unlatching the cuffs from each other. "Strangely, that doesn't sound like a complaint."

"It's not," Dom said. He rotated one of the cuffs. "I'm gonna guess you don't get off on being tied up."

"No, I don't." Adrian's lips quirked. "Opposite, in fact."

Yeah, he figured. "How about being fucked by someone wearing your cuffs?"

That hit—and hard. Adrian's breath caught and he shivered. "Yes." His answer was full of rumble and gravel. "That would get me off nicely."

Dom smiled, stole a kiss from that shocked face, dragged Adrian upstairs and did just that, making it last as long as he possibly could.

Sunday, they cleaned the kitchen, went out for bagels and coffee, and spent the rest of the time in Adrian's library, reading one another interesting snippets of texts until they succumbed to each other.

"I've never made love to anyone up here," Adrian murmured, his mouth skimming over Dom's now naked back.

"There's always a first time."

That earned him a laugh. Adrian also laid Dom out on the daybed in the reading nook and took his sweet time making them both come.

Sex and books. Dom could get used to that. So fast. So much.

But when evening ticked around, they both knew what was coming—the end of the weekend and a return to their own lives. This time, they ordered pizza, drank it with wine, and watched episodes of *White Collar* on Netflix until the sunlight slipped away into the night. Dom's heart dropped. "I should go home," he whispered.

Adrian chuckled and kissed his brow, then his mouth. "Probably. I have work in the morning, and I am not twenty-seven."

"Thirty-six."

That earned him a longer kiss. "And I can keep up with you, babe. Don't you forget it."

God, he loved hearing Adrian call him *babe*. Almost as much as the silky caress of *Dominic*. "I won't."

"But it does mean I need to sleep tonight if I want to have any hope of being coherent for my nine o'clock meeting."

"Oh, fuck that. Some days I'm glad I'm a musician."

"Some days?" It was a quiet question, but one with a lot of weight. Adrian hadn't probed, hadn't pushed for more about that part of his life. But Dom had left the door open.

He cupped Adrian's face and traced his cheeks with his fingers, memorizing the texture, the bone structure. "Honestly? Every day. I'm grateful every day."

Adrian closed his eyes and smiled. "Good. You deserve all the happiness, Dominic."

Fuck, that hurt, but in a deeply good way. His chest tightened and he blinked a couple times, clearing his vision. "Adrian—so do you."

Those eyes flicked open, and Adrian's smile turned sad at the edges. "Maybe."

"You do," Dom repeated. "And maybe I can be a part of that."

A huff of laughter. "So we are dating, then?"

"Well, I found myself thinking that next weekend, I probably ought to bring a change of clothes...so...yeah. I think we are."

"Next weekend sounds lovely." Adrian's voice was so quiet, so perfect, Dom kissed him again.

It was many more kisses before Dom made it to the front door with the books Adrian had pulled from his library earlier in the day, and then at least another dozen more before he found himself walking down Adrian's steps, out his gate and into the summer night alone.

He turned and looked back up at Adrian, framed in the doorway. "Good night, Adrian."

"Night, babe. I hope you have a good week."

As Dom walked home, he realized it didn't matter what kind of week he had—it wouldn't be better than the two astounding days he'd just lived through.

He was in deep, deep trouble when it came to Adrian Doran.

CHAPTER
NINE

THE WEEKEND WITH ADRIAN HAD KNOCKED DOM SO OFF-KILTER that he nearly forgot Twisted Wishes had an interview with a journalist from *RockPass Magazine*. Thank god the photo shoot would be later, because he had more bruises from the manhandling Adrian had subjected him to than he wanted to admit.

A manhandling he'd begged for.

But out in public with the band meant pulling Domino out of the closet—and that was hard. Playing the guitar? Well, mostly it was him doing that, using Domino to cover for his overwhelming stage fright and the singular fact that no one wanted to see a nerd prancing around stage with the likes of Ray and Mish. But the publicity stuff?

Oh god, that's when he acted the most like Domino. He could be brash and flippant and they wouldn't ask him too many personal questions, which left the ones about music, and Dom never minded answering those.

But he really wasn't ready to be Domino, not after this weekend. Two days and two nights of...everything. Amazing sex. Some of the best food he'd ever eaten. Cuddles in front of the TV. Long walks through Brooklyn. Learning about Adrian and who he was...outside of being a computer programmer for a bank and a guy who adored putting his lovers on their knees and tying them up. His heart ached at Adrian's story, at the loss of his parents, then the estrangement from his siblings.

Dom wanted to make the world bright for him, especially since Adrian's day-to-day job was...*well enough*. And he'd seen the look in those eyes when he'd mentioned returning to work and 9 AM meetings.

Dom was so lucky he got to live his fucking dream, even if he had to do it as Domino, and even if it did require the occasional interview.

Dom checked his phone and reread the text from Ray. They needed to be at the magazine's office by noon, which meant that he needed to be over at Ray and Zavier's by ten-thirty so he could transform into Domino. They'd go by limo from there, like the rock stars they were.

Fuck. He needed an outfit. He pulled out one of his white ripped tanks artistically held together with safety pins. It would show off enough ink and keep him cool—the opposite of what he normally wore as Dominic.

A pair of tight black jeans followed. A studded belt. His boots with their heels and their bling. Thankfully, Domino was one walking wrinkled outfit, so he could shove all of it into a duffel and not worry one bit.

From his dresser, he pulled out Domino's makeup kit and took a quick look inside to make sure he had everything. Yup. All the essentials, sans gel. He grabbed the bottle of hair goop and turned it over in his hand. In an instant, he was taken back to Adrian's bathroom and his own reflection, how he'd looked Saturday morning, mussed with sleep and sex and the slow realization that he—Dominic—was having a life.

Dom blew out a breath. He really wanted to rewind the

day to his walks with Adrian, to those intimate moments that weren't about sex. He'd learned so much and even shared what he'd felt comfortable giving. Couldn't he even have one day to dwell on that? Turn it over in his head? Enjoy the thought of being Dominic before he was thrust back into Domino?

He rammed the drawer on his dresser closed, rattling the items on top. Photo frames. A bottle of cologne. Some anime figurines.

Get a grip. It's not like you've been Domino at all this summer. True. Mostly they'd been practicing at the studio. And since the building housed other businesses, no one even gave him a second glance when he wandered in for practice. He walked right by fans in his button-downs, glasses, and bowties.

Today, he threw on a thicker white T-shirt to cover his tats, and a training jacket, pants, and a ball cap to match. It kinda looked like a uniform...and hopefully that would be enough to allow him to waltz up to Ray and Zav's place and enter without anyone being the wiser.

There weren't always fans there, of course, but they were there often enough.

Dom had a key to Ray and Zavier's place, and Mish's, just like they all had a key to his. They'd been through too much not to have each other's backs, not to be family. Getting to Ray and Zav's was tricky, but getting in without notice was harder. Thankfully, their place had a doorman who'd been given a heads-up about Dom as a friend of the Van Zeller-Demos household, so he often slipped in the front door. Most people thought he was some kind of employee. He'd even been asked if he could take notes in from fans.

He'd just kept his head down and mumbled something about losing his job if he did that, and they left him alone.

But someday, someone was gonna figure it out. Terror lurked behind that thought, 'cause he had no idea what he'd do on that day. None. Maybe hang up his guitar. Or never leave his house again. He didn't have the strength or resolve the others had.

He slung the bag that contained Domino over his shoulder and headed out to catch a train into Manhattan again. They lived in the Upper East Side, in a spacious apartment. Both Ray and Zavier loved the pulse and beat of the city, and never seemed to mind the fans and photographers that sometimes trailed them.

Dom had opted for something a little less expensive, with a little more space and a little more anonymity. A house next to a bunch of others, not an expensive apartment in Manhattan.

Then again, the *fans* had never been a problem. Not yet anyway.

Getting across town at rush hour? That was a problem. The trains were packed, but he managed. On the inevitable delay as they sat on the Manhattan Bridge, he stared out at the water, then caught the reflection of a businessman next to him.

Shit.

He hadn't considered that. He and Adrian lived close enough together that they might end up on the same train at the same time at some point. And how would he explain where he was going? If he said *to practice*, would Adrian want to tag along? He'd seemed honestly curious about Dom's music, even if rock was totally not his thing.

Their musical paths did cross a little. Jazz. Classical. Some Spanish guitar schools. "I just like to listen," Adrian had said. Dom had been lying in his arms listening to a compilation of 1940s jazz, and Adrian had trailed his fingers over the musical notes tattooed on the outside of Dom's right arm. "I have no talent for playing, or even singing."

Also no interest in current rock music. "I just can't get into it," he'd said. "Hard to find the soul."

The dismissal hurt a bit. A lot. And he guessed Adrian had noticed that, because he'd shifted and turned Dom's face so they looked each other in the eyes. "I'm sorry, that was heartless of me. The fault is likely mine. Sometimes I'm too set in my ways."

"Maybe I can find something you'd like."

Adrian had smiled and kissed him. They'd ended up making love on the couch, this time Dom topping Adrian because that, it turned out, was something Adrian wanted, as well.

"I like when you fuck me," Adrian had said later. "It's—"

"Sweet?"

That had gotten him a laugh. "No. It's very much you."

"And I'm not sweet?"

"Oh, you are, but you're so much more as well, Dominic."

The train jerked forward, and Dom gripped the poll to keep from tumbling into other passengers. Shit. Mind in the clouds. Or with Adrian, which was where he wanted to be.

Except Adrian was likely at work. They'd already set up to meet again on Friday—both their weeks were too busy for any evening meet-ups. Not with the way they tended to spend so much of it screwing each other. Or talking.

They needed more hours for both.

By the time Dom got to Ray and Zav's, he was hot and sweaty and cranky beyond belief. Thankfully, there weren't any fans or pap that he could see, so he made it into the building and past security with no issue, but he was still in a mood by the time he got into their apartment, and it obviously showed, because unflappable Zavier raised both eyebrows and backed away. "He's all yours, Ray."

"What?" Dom snapped.

"You're, um. Not happy," Ray said.

No, he wasn't. "I just spent far too long crammed in a train car in this getup." He gestured at himself. "And you expect me to be happy?" And even he could hear the crack of annoyance in his voice.

After a very pregnant silence, Dom closed his eyes. "Shit." He set the duffel down and dropped the ball cap on top of it. "Can I catch a shower?"

Ray nodded. "Dude, of course."

He high-tailed it for the guest room and took a nice cool one, and then slipped some of Domino's clothes on. Odd to see those two halves of him again. When he was dressed enough, he headed back out to find Ray and Zav.

They were talking in the kitchen, coffee in hand. Zavier was casually holding a wooden spoon, though there wasn't a damn thing cooking on the stove. Ray had one of his dopey sexy smiles he only ever got for Zavier.

Did Dom look like that with Adrian? He cleared his throat, and they both turned. Zavier placed the spoon on the counter. "Feel better?"

"Yeah, and I'm sorry I was hellish when I got here. I'm... It was a long weekend."

Ray's face fell. "Your date didn't go well?"

That...what? Then Dom pieced together why Ray thought that and started laughing. He crossed the room and plunked himself down on a chair at the kitchen table. "Oh my god, no. The date was amazing. I spent almost the entire weekend with Adrian."

"Ah." Zavier had this wicked little grin. "You're pissed off that it's not the weekend anymore."

Yup. That was it exactly. Dom's humor fled and he scrubbed a hand through his wet hair. "Got it in one."

"That explains the bruises," Zavier murmured.

Ray punched him in the arm—not hard. "You're not supposed to say shit like that, Zav. It's rude!"

Zavier's smile sharpened, and he turned to his husband. "Really?"

"I mean." Ray waved his arms. "It's personal."

"Guys..." Dom said. "I...don't actually mind. I mean, it's Zav. He says that shit all the damn time. Wouldn't be him if he didn't."

Zavier shrugged and gestured at Dom.

"Wait." Ray pinched the bridge of his nose. "You're taking his side? I'm your best friend!" But there was a smile on both their faces, and Dom felt a hell of a lot better.

Dom raised his hands in surrender. "I'm just saying." He pushed himself out of the chair. "I better go deal with this before it dries." He gestured to his hair.

"I should get better dressed than this." Ray tugged at his T-shirt.

Zavier looked perfect. But then, he always did.

Dom headed back into the bathroom and gooped up his hair into the perfect spiked Domino mess and even sprinkled a bit of glitter in it.

"You know, every time you come here, it takes six months to get rid of the glitter. It even ends up in my office." Zavier leaned against the bathroom doorframe.

Dom flipped him off and Zavier snorted.

He got to work on Domino's makeup next, under Zavier's watchful eyes. "Does your Adrian have a last name?"

He stared at Zavier in the mirror for a second before resuming work with his eye pencil. "Gonna do a background check on him or something?"

"Would you be mad if I said yes?"

No. 'Cause that was Zav, too. Watching out for the band. "Well, it's either you or Mish. One of you is gonna check up on him."

Zavier chuckled. "You like him."

"He's—" Dom put down the pencil and studied his own eyes. Makeup on point. "Zav, he makes me feel like I haven't felt before. I have absolutely no idea what I'm doing."

"You *like* him," Zavier repeated.

"I like him. A lot. Maybe more than I should."

"Is there such a thing?"

Dom grabbed eyeshadow next. "Yeah, maybe? I don't know."

Zavier crossed his arms and levered his foot up on the opposite doorframe. It was a pose that should have been in a magazine, but those came so natural to Zav. "What was the best moment of your weekend?"

Breath caught in Dom's throat. That moment in Adrian's office when he fell on his knees and had held on to Zavier's legs. "I...uh. Don't know if I could explain it to you."

Zavier looked at the toe of the leather shoe he had up on the doorframe, pursed his lips, and met Dom's stare in the mirror. "Try me."

It was, Dom realized, said in the same tone Adrian sometimes used. He straightened and turned around. "So the morning after he fucked me into oblivion, I woke up and found him in his office. In boxers. Paying his bills. He was just...himself. And we talked and...all I wanted to do was kneel at his feet."

Zavier's foot slid off the doorframe and he straightened, his eyes a little wide. "Did you?"

"Yeah, I told him and he let me."

"And?"

"And that's it. I held on to him and he played with my hair, and I don't think I ever felt more calm than in that moment."

Zavier let out a breath. "I think you should give me his last name, Dom."

A little spike of panic raced through him. "Was that wrong? What we did?"

Zavier blinked a few times. "No. Not at all. From what you've said, it was absolutely *right*."

"Oh." The panic subsided and Dom turned back to the mirror, his heart still pounding. "Then why..."

"Because you're my *friend*. And Ray's, and Mish's, and I'm

an overprotective asshole who looks out for his own. Your gentleman sounds fine. But our...interests overlap a bit, I think. And you have me curious."

Dom looked into a reflection that was mostly Domino Grinder. "He's Adrian Doran. And I think I might fall in love with him."

Zavier grunted. "I can't help you there."

Dom laughed. "I don't think anyone can." Because *fall* was an apt description.

He rooted through the kit and pulled out a blood-red shade of lipstick and put the finishing touches onto Domino Grinder's face.

———

ADRIAN MADE IT INTO THE LOCKER ROOM BEFORE JACKSON, BUT he hadn't managed to change completely before his friend joined him. Jackson took one look at his torso and whistled. "Someone had fun this weekend."

While Jackson changed, Adrian gave his friend a once-over. There were telltale bruises on his hips and back, too. "Looks like I'm not the only one."

That flash of smile was bright, if a bit weary.

"Club conquest or..."

Jackson waved the question away. "Club. You know my routine."

Except he also knew what Jackson craved—and it wasn't just a young buck. "This one interesting?"

Jackson made a dismissive noise. "Too young. He's a player." He closed the locker and leaned against it. "Don't give me that look, Adi."

Adrian held up both hands and held his tongue. He'd given the advice often enough—Jackson should get out of the clubs if he wanted more than Mr. Right Now.

Jackson eyed Adrian. "What about you?"

"Spent the weekend with my catnip, as you so generously called him."

That earned him a laugh. "And?"

"We fucked and ate and I told him my life story."

At that last bit the smile fell from Jackson's lips. "Damn. You *are* serious about this one."

He was. Quite. And it seemed like Dominic was, too. Adrian shoved his duffel in the locker, grabbed his water bottle, and nodded toward the exit. "Shall we?"

Jackson rolled his eyes, and they headed out to cycle through whatever routine was in store for today.

As it turned out, Jackson went easy on him—and Adrian wanted to thank whoever Mr. Right Now had been for taking the edge off their workout. He didn't want to admit how sore —and tired—he was from his weekend with Dominic. But the workout soothed the part of him that was roaring in circles as he processed what had happened.

He'd given much of himself. Gotten back quite a lot, too— including Dominic's almost natural submission. That need to give in, to kneel, to give himself over. Adrian had also gotten a taste of another part of Dominic, one that blazed with strength and power. He was very much like the intricate knot-work on his shoulder—beautiful and complex. One moment, Dominic would moan and cry as Adrian took everything, and the next he could kiss and fuck Adrian with such passion and conviction.

A jewel indeed.

He turned all these thoughts over in his head, even as they headed into the office.

"He's gotten to you." Jackson adjusted his tie in the mirrored surface of the elevator bank. "Your catnip."

"He has." He met Jackson's gaze. "And his name is Dominic."

The elevator dinged, and Jackson clapped him on the back and murmured, "Good."

They entered, and Adrian rode up to his well-enough job in a cube. Not quite nine. He wondered if Dominic was even awake yet.

Adrian woke his computer and sighed. Friday seemed very far away indeed.

MIDDAY WEDNESDAY WAS ONE OF THE HOTTEST OF THE YEAR. Before heading out to lunch, Adrian stripped off his suit jacket and tie, and rolled up his sleeves—and was utterly remorseful he hadn't thought to bring shorts and a tank to work when the wall of humid, sticky air hit him when he strode out of his office building.

Thank goodness he'd settled on lunch with Janelle close by. Hopefully she wouldn't want to sit outside, because he would both bake and burn—his Irish heritage was no match for sunlight like this, even if the brightness lifted his mood.

Unfortunately, she was waiting for him at a table on the patio. Thankfully, it was in the shade and there was a current of air that swept around them—fans, he realized. She offered her hand, and he took it, leaning down to kiss her cheek. "You look lovely."

She did, too. He never flattered unnecessarily, and she knew it. A stylish sundress of reds and yellow complemented her rich brown skin and thick black hair. Every bit of her looked perfect and elegant and cool, despite the heat.

"Adrian," she murmured as he sat opposite. "How are you?"

"Doing well, actually."

"Mmm. Then what do I owe the pleasure of your company to, if not for consolation?"

He laughed. Yes, he did tend to seek her out when he needed advice or a sounding board about topics that made

Jackson uncomfortable. More personal things. Family. Kink. "How about consultation?"

She raised an eyebrow.

Just then, the server came to take their orders. They both opted for salads and ice water—it was too hot for anything else. After the server left, Janelle's eyebrow went right back up. "Consultation?"

He folded his hands on the table and studied them before looking up. "I've met someone."

"My dear Adrian, I know you. You meet *someones* all the time. You've never asked me to lunch to consult about one of your flings."

"He's not a fling."

That got her interest. "Are you getting serious, Adrian? Settling down?"

Ouch. "I've always been serious." Even his couple-hour conquests had been done with thought and care.

"Not about sex. But this isn't just about getting your rocks off, is it?"

There, to the heart of the matter. "No, it's not. And I don't want to fuck it up."

Their waters came first, and he was glad for something to hold. He liked Janelle quite a bit, but she was perceptive and cut through bullshit, and that always intimidated him, though he knew he needed that, too.

Stay humble. Feet on the ground.

"He's never had any experience with bondage or submission."

"Ah." She picked up her glass. "And you want advice on how to broach the subject?" She sipped her water.

"No. I've already tied him to my bed and fucked him."

Janelle choked on her water and Adrian almost laughed. Instead he continued, "And he knelt for me for no other reason than he wanted to."

That had her swallowing delicately and placing the glass back on the table. "Well, that *is* interesting."

"I'm in the weeds here." He spread his hands helplessly.

"No, Adrian. I don't think you are." She studied him, her dark eyes meeting his. "Is he running scared? Backing away?"

No. They'd even exchanged more text messages than he wanted to admit since the first one landed on his phone Monday afternoon. That evening, he finally figured out how good sexting could be. "Quite the opposite."

"Then you're not in the weeds. Or the woods. Or any other metaphor you might care to use."

"It's like it comes naturally to him."

"What, the desire to please you? To enjoy what you offer?" Janelle laughed. "Oh, Adrian, that's what lovers do!"

Of course, that was when their server arrived, somewhat ruddy-cheeked, to deliver their salads.

Janelle gave Adrian a look once they were alone again. "Please tip that poor thing well."

"Oh, I will." He drizzled dressing over his salad. "I've had more lovers than I really should enumerate."

"You've had numerous fucks, but precious few lovers. Only one since you returned to New York." She paused. "Well, one before your current lover."

One? "Who?"

The look she leveled him was every part *are you fucking kidding me*, and the day became unbearably hot.

"I—who?"

"Jackson."

Jackson? "We didn't date."

"You did date. Both of you refused to call it that, and you also both figured out quickly enough that you weren't compatible for the long run. But you still loved and cared and worked to please each other—as lovers should."

He could only study the pile of greens in front of him.

"And you're still good friends."

Adrian lifted his gaze. "Dominic is nothing like Jackson."

"No doubt, if he's kneeling for you."

He gave her that, completely. "And I actually am dating Dominic."

She laughed. "Of course you are."

He spread his hands again. "Janelle."

She'd perfected her long-suffering sigh, and it made him smile that little bit. A smile graced her lips, too. "Adrian, here's my advice—Continue to do as you're doing. You're a good soul and it's about damn time you found someone to share yourself with. If this man is coming to you, returning to you, kneeling for you, then he needs you, too. Needs what you have to offer him."

She stabbed her fork into her salad. "Or to put it more simply, stop overthinking."

His own sigh was less long-suffering and more of a huff.

"And yes, I realize not overthinking is asking the *world* of you, Adrian." She smiled at him. "But I believe in you."

Stop thinking too much. Enjoy Dominic. "Let the kink come as it may?"

"Exactly."

He could do that. Tension dripped away, much like the sweat on his brow, and he worked on his own salad while silence fell between them.

Their conversation drifted off Dominic and to Janelle's life. Local parties. Some gossip. But it was no one he knew—some timpanist turned rock star who'd been active in the scene once upon a time. Apparently he was back in New York and the scene was abuzz about if he'd return.

"You met him once—the Juilliard student."

That would have been on one of his last trips back from California. "I honestly don't remember."

He let Janelle's commentary swirl around them, soaking in her presence and calm.

Don't overthink.

He deserved someone to share his life with. Was that where this was heading? Maybe. Too early to tell.

When the check came, he paid and left a sizable tip, and then saw Janelle out. He kissed her cheek again when they parted company. "Thank you. Lunch did help." At least to put some of his mind at ease.

His heart was another matter. That ran off into those self-same weeds and woods, even as his mind tried to corral it, lest his heart become entirely lost.

CHAPTER
TEN

D OM HAD SPENT MORE OF THE WEEK DRESSED AS D OMINO THAN he had in a while. Ray suggested it might be smart if the brash, loud rocker actually showed up at the studio once in a while, since the press and fans had figured out where they were practicing.

That made sense. He could get away with slipping in as himself, but it was a bit conspicuous that Domino never walked in. Eventually, people would catch on that Domino was practicing—just not as Domino. The fear that had raked up his back at that prospect had made Mish ruffle his hair and kiss him on the forehead.

"Put on your makeup and those kick-ass boots of yours, and come play with us, honey."

He dropped his head and muttered into her shoulder, "I think you have boot envy."

Mish patted his cheek. "I do, but those things would kill my legs in concert. No fucking clue how you move in them."

Practice. And—he'd never admit this—for the first couple shows on tour, his calves ached to high heaven.

So Tuesday he'd marched into the studio to flashes of camera phones and shouts, fully his rock-god self—and it felt good. Really fucking good. The energy, the courage. The strength. He rubbed his Celtic knot tattoo and thought of Adrian, of his mouth and hands. That smile.

The next moment, his stomach had tangled like the lines of his ink. Because what—who—Dom was now was not the man who wanted to kneel down at Adrian's side in that cozy office. Or cuddle up with him on the couch. Or be taken apart by mouth and cock and hands.

Yeah. No way Adrian would want Domino.

"Little weird, huh?" Ray bumped his shoulder. "Back in the saddle."

Dom pushed thoughts of Adrian aside. "What? We've been practicing for weeks!"

"Yeah, but not like this." Ray grinned at him. "With you as rock-star you."

As Domino. A strange vertigo filled Dom. "I'm me. I'm always me." But was that true? Had it ever been?

In the end, those practices were some of the best they'd played. Near live-performance quality. And there was more about that, too. The venue was nailed down, and the time and date—six weeks from now. They were set.

Thursday was the photo shoot for the article that was going into *RockPass Magazine*, and the marks Adrian had left were gone, so Dom put on his low-slung leather pants and not much else, and posed for the cameras. Sexy, snarling Domino Grinder. And once more, it felt so damn real and *right* that it hurt—and gave Dom whiplash.

Ray and Zavier were still talking with Marcella and the photographer when Mish and Dom entered the dressing room to change into something a little less full-on rock star and to pack up. Mish leaned against her makeup station, crossed her arms, and leveled that look at him. "You okay, hon?"

He should have expected her to ask eventually, but it caught him off-guard anyway. "Yeah, I'm fine." Not exactly a lie. Not quite the truth. He caught a glimpse of himself in the mirror, the man Adrian never saw. The rock star. The persona that gave him the ability to walk onstage.

She got that look she always got when one of them was bullshitting her. "Tell me for real, Dom."

He dropped his shoulders. "I love this." He gestured to himself. "I feel a thousand feet tall when I'm Domino and onstage."

She cocked her head. "And you feel safe."

His laugh was strangled. "Yeah. You should have seen me when I was younger. I was a wreck."

"You're not that old, honey. People grow."

True. But the strangling fear still lurked deep inside him. The voice that told him he wasn't good enough to be onstage with Ray. "Yeah, I know that."

"And your man?"

God, Adrian. He closed his eyes briefly. "I feel safe with him, too. But not as Domino."

"If this guy is worthy of you, you should be comfortable with him all the damn time, no matter what." She pushed herself off the station and opened her arms. An invitation.

He took it, stepping forward and letting her wrap him into a hug. Mish gave the best hugs, probably because she towered over him by several inches, even when he wore his boots. "But Domino is so different," he murmured. "And what if he tells someone else who I am?"

Mish pulled back. "Sweetheart, someday your cover's gonna be busted. You've been damn lucky it hasn't been yet."

His heart stuttered and a cold wash flew up his back. "I know." He hated thinking about it. "But it'll happen faster if I tell someone."

"Even the man you trust?"

That was the question, wasn't it? "Maybe?"

Her sigh was heartfelt, and cut straight through Dom. "You need to be true to you, hon."

"I know."

They broke apart and got to packing when Ray and Zavier entered the room.

If Domino was his true self, who was the man who wanted to spend time with Adrian? The one who playfully texted him, the one who'd stroked himself off to Adrian's voice on the other end of the phone whispering just how hard he should come. He'd skimmed through the books on BDSM Adrian had lent him, and there Dominic was, too, in some of those paragraphs and explanations. Adrian was on those pages, as well. His control and care.

In the dark of his room Thursday night, he stared up at his ceiling, thin lines of light cutting across the painted white surface, and tried to piece all of it together. Domino. Dominic. The music and the stage. The burning need to play and perform. The fear and panic. Bowties and button-downs. Kneeling. Being tied up. The way Adrian made him feel so good and complete with words and touches. With laughter and sweets fed on the end of a fork. The light in Adrian's eyes when Dominic turned around and fucked him instead.

He wanted every single piece of it all. But one was a lie, a sham, and the other was real. And in the end, he couldn't be both. He could never be both.

What happened when there were two dreams, and holding one meant losing the other? Dom closed his eyes and tried not to think about that.

IF THE WEEK AS DOMINO HAD THROWN HIM, HIS WEEKEND WITH Adrian twisted him around, tossed him up in the air, and set him gently back down on his feet. Two weekends, that's all it had taken to upend everything he'd planned. All he knew about himself.

Friday during one of their breaks at practice—he'd slipped

into the studio sans Domino again—Zavier joined him by the window. "Your gentleman friend is, by all accounts, a very decent man."

Dom chuckled and stared out the window. "I could have told you that."

Zavier gripped him on the shoulder, and Dom turned to meet his gaze. "You did. But you're also somewhat biased."

Dom swallowed, the previous night's musings rushing back in. "I don't even know if I should be seeing the dude."

The comforting hand shook his shoulder. "Dom. You're allowed to be happy. And I think you are. This dude—he gives you something you aren't getting here." Zavier nodded at their instruments and the studio. "Even as happy as the band makes you, too."

Dom pulled away. "I don't think Adrian would be interested in Domino Grinder. And more often than not, that's who I am."

Zavier was quiet for a time, then sighed. "I have no head for romantic entanglement, but I know people and I know connections and I know kink." He tipped his head and studied Dom. "I'd be willing to bet just about any amount of money that the man Adrian Doran wants is the same one standing in front of me."

That was absurd. "You'd lose."

"I'd win." Zavier's grin fell away. "Life's short, Dom. And fragile and unexpected. Don't throw this away without thought."

Dom studied Zavier and those serious blue eyes, then his gaze drifted across the studio to Ray. Zavier—and he and Mish—had nearly lost Ray last year. Sometimes the images of Ray struggling to breathe, of the chaos of the work to save his life, still haunted Dom, and he wondered if Zavier had nightmares, too.

Yeah. He probably did. Of all of them besides Ray, that night had impacted Zavier the most.

"I'm not going to lose." Zavier's eyes flickered, and he patted Dom's shoulder before heading back toward his drum kit.

Dom wouldn't throw anything away without thought, even if he wasn't sure which *this* Zav had referred to. But he was gonna have to throw something in the end, once he figured out who the hell he really was.

That was the thought that stayed with him, even as he headed toward Wall Street and the building where Adrian worked on Friday, a duffel of clothes and toiletries slung over his shoulder. He'd always been able to balance the two disparate halves of his life, mostly by hiding Dominic and letting Domino take the stage, literally. The man he was now, wearing a button-down and bowtie? That was for little snippets of time when he wanted to snag a fuck—or just be left alone. That's probably why no one had ever figured out who Domino was—Dominic wasn't around all that much. But now he was.

Adrian wasn't a fuck, though, and Dom didn't want to be alone. Not now, not this weekend. He wanted to forget all about Domino Grinder and just be the man Adrian wanted. But who was that guy? Maybe that's what he needed to find out.

Because Dominic Bradley hadn't really been himself since college, and even then, Domino had existed, had cried out for his time, for the stage and the lights and the music.

Yeah, he was *fucked*. Dom stopped walking. This wasn't going to work. He should—

"Dominic!"

Adrian's bright voice slammed into Dom, and he turned toward it, wanting, needed to see. Oh, and yes. He wanted the relationship, too. *Shit.*

Adrian wore a light gray suit and a light pink shirt. His tie was purple and charcoal, and his hair shone red in the summer sun, as if the light had stripped away the brown to reveal the ginger beneath. He was fucking gorgeous. And that smile—it was for Dominic. For *him*.

The duffel slid off Dom's shoulder when Adrian drew close, and he couldn't help wrapping his arms around him. Adrian stiffened momentarily, then moved to tip Dom's head up.

The kiss was blinding. It wasn't erotic or lurid or even that long. Just a sweet touch of lips, a hint of tongue, and the happiest damn sigh Dom had ever heard.

"And here I was wondering if you'd missed me," Adrian murmured. He pulled back, opening a more appropriate amount of space between them.

"Yeah, I did." That was the only truthful reply. "A lot."

Such a bright grin. "Let's go home."

And they did go, straight to Adrian's house. More kisses, and this time, in private, they were intense and breathtaking. Adrian's mouth found Dom's with a fierceness of purpose, as if each swipe of his tongue could mold their bodies closer together. Dom moaned when those hands grabbed his ass and ground their cocks together.

"Dinner first, Dominic?" Adrian asked between nips and sucks and bites. "Or do you want to scream for me?"

And fuck did that melt Dom's bones and enflame his cock. "Scream, Adrian. Make me scream." He wanted to forget who he was. Remember that, too.

Adrian fucked him over the back of the couch in the living room, hard and fast, holding Dom by the hands he'd clasped at the small of his back. Dom's feet lifted off the ground with every hard thrust and he did exactly what both of them wanted: writhed and moaned and screamed in pleasure.

"Pictured this all week," Adrian growled. "Your ass in the air. Your tight hole."

"God, Adrian, please!" He needed every second of this, every inch of Adrian in him, every bite. "Fuck!" The roar of his blood, the way Adrian hit him inside so perfectly. "Can't. Gonna."

"Good," Adrian bit Dom's shoulder through his shirt. "I want to feel you come, Dominic. You fucking beautiful man."

Everything hazed and he screamed Adrian's name, spilling all over the couch cushions underneath him. And for the first time in his life, he thought maybe being Dominic was better than Domino.

When Adrian pulled him upright, there was that loving concern that always made Dom's heart ache. "Hey, you okay?" Adrian seemed to be searching his face, his hand so gentle against Dom's cheek. "Babe?"

"Yeah," Dom croaked. "That was just so fucking—" Perfect. He laughed as his heart and mind tumbled over and over. "I'm fine."

"All right." A peck on the nose, and Dom closed his eyes. "Let's go get cleaned up, and I'll cook dinner."

The rest of Friday was spent laughing and eating, then snuggling on the same couch—though they avoided the cushions that were damp from Adrian's cleaning.

"I stain-proofed them, but I have no idea if that stuff actually works against jizz."

Dom laughed. "I guess that's not something they're gonna put on the can."

Adrian pulled him close. "Might be good marketing, though."

"You just call up the company and tell 'em. I'm sure they'll love it."

The laughter that poured from Adrian was contagious, as was the warmth, and Dom's head spun again. He wanted *this*, this companionship. What he'd glimpsed that Ray and Zavier had. Someone who understood him and needed him just as much. But living this meant no more band, no more touring. No more Domino.

Fingers touched his cheeks. "What can I do to chase away that sadness?" Adrian's voice was thick.

Dom shook his head. "Take me upstairs and teach me joy."

Adrian shivered, and there was that feather touch again, and those eyes so full of light, and something Dom didn't want to name because it felt too deep.

"Dominic." Adrian breathed his name, and it was a brand and a promise. He seemed to want to say more, but then drew Dom off the couch. "Let's go."

CHAPTER
ELEVEN

SATURDAY, THEY HEADED INTO MANHATTAN. DOM WAS pleasantly sore from yet another round of Adrian fucking him deep into the mattress, and each step reminded him of that odd juxtaposition of fierceness and tenderness Adrian possessed. The orders and control and the soft questions that asked for consent.

Zavier was right about Adrian being a good man. And Dom had been right when, in Zavier and Ray's house, he'd said he might fall in love. There was nothing for him to catch, no way to stop the plummeting fall he felt in his stomach every time Adrian smiled, or when Adrian had read clips of interesting news from his tablet while they'd shared home-made pancakes that morning.

"There's a photography exhibition a friend told me about. Said some of her work was in it." There was something sly about the way Adrian said that, about his smile that made Dom's blood heat. They ended up in Chelsea at a gallery that was eerily close to the photography studio the band had marched into from the recording studio on Thursday.

Which seemed so very far away now. A dream, even.

Domino's snarls and smirks. Giving the camera the finger. All of it.

They had to let their eyes adjust when they entered the gallery. Even with powerful lights illuminating the photographs hanging on the walls, the brilliant summer sun and clear blue day had been brighter by far. And when Dom blinked away the sun, he was struck blind again—mentally.

The photographs, the whole exhibition, were pictures of skin and rope and leather. None explicit. All erotic. Adrian handed him a postcard with that same damned smile.

Strength in Submission, the glossy page read, with details of the photographer, Det Newhar, plus two of their works. "You know the photographer?"

"This is the first time I've seen their work," Adrian said. "Though I did design a website for them."

That was interesting. "You design websites?"

"Freelance, for the right people. Started doing that in California for extra cash. And I like the creativity." Adrian pulled Dom to a wall of photographs, sepia in tone. Dark skin—a masculine chest—with leather across it and a sheen of sweat. Another with a cuffed hand, the side of a face, eyes hidden by fingers, but lips parted, almost as with a sigh.

Beautiful. Heart-stopping. Dom wanted to see those eyes. Hear if that was a moan or a breath. Know what the person captured—both on camera and by leather—had felt. His heart hammered against his chest. At the same time, he knew exactly the emotion. Felt them so viscerally, he trembled.

Adrian put his arm over Dom's shoulder, pulled him closer, and the shaking stopped.

"Do I..."

"Yes," Adrian said, answering the unasked question.

Yes, Dom looked like that when cuffed. He swallowed. "Oh."

Adrian's arm slipped off Dom's shoulder and his hand touched the small of his back. "Come see my friend's work."

He was drawn deeper into the gallery. The photos showed more here, out of the view of the street. Breasts, nipples, the hint of pussy and cock. Heat burned through Dom slowly, not in his balls or dick, but deeper. In his gut and soul. His mind.

All the men and women in these photographs were tied with rope. Lengths and lengths. Cords over flesh, pressing in. Restraining. Beautiful designs of knots and lengths, of arms and legs and torsos.

Dom could barely breathe. The beauty, the serenity. The strength, too, in those closed and opened eyes and mouths, those haunting faces, caught for a moment in something so profound Dom's body itched as his mind cried out.

This. *This.* He wanted this. His skin under those knots. Bound. Caught. Safe.

"My friend Janelle's work." Adrian's voice was reverent.

"Not the photos." Dom could barely get the words out through his tight throat.

A nod. "The rope."

"It's...exquisite." Dom moved closer to the photographs. They drew him like a magnet turned toward the north. Oh god, he ached and buzzed and needed.

Adrian followed, his hand still on Dom's back, fingers brushing against where his shirt and jeans met. "I thought you might like them."

That Dom might like the concept. This was—an offer.

"Can you do this?" Dom kept his voice low, a mere murmur.

Adrian heard anyway. "Not like she can. She knows bodies so well, she can suspend a submissive in the air by their bonds."

Holy fuck. Dom tried to imagine that—being tied so tight and hanging above the ground—but his brain overloaded and he could only swallow a moan.

Those hot fingers caressed his back. "It's something I want to learn. But I do know how to tie someone up." Adrian skimmed a hand up to Dom's neck. "I'd like to try something else first, because this—" He gestured at the photos. "This is a lot to process at once."

Yeah, it had to be. "That's...yes. I want this. But yes. I trust you."

Adrian turned his face and kissed him with that heady mix of hard and soft. Control and giving. When he opened space between them, he smiled. "Is there any one of these you want?"

It took Dom a moment to realize what Adrian meant. "You don't have to buy me one of these."

A shrug and a grin. "But I want to. And they're not *that* expensive."

They weren't, really. Not for what they were. Heck, he'd dropped far more than two hundred on single pieces of art for his house. Still. "Adrian."

"Dominic," he countered. "I can afford it." His finger shot up to tap Dom's lips. "And I'm guessing you can, too. If there's one you want, let me do this."

In the end, Dom chose one of a man's legs, bound by a web of rope, his stomach and a hint of his swollen dick visible. A swirl of ink, just a few lines, swept over his hip. Adrian paid, a little red dot was placed by the placard, and they were told when they could come claim their purchase.

As they shook hands with the gallery owner, the door opened and a smooth, lilting voice called out Adrian's name. A woman entered, elegant and tall and stunning. Black hair, dark eyes, and deep brown skin.

Adrian started when he saw her, and a smile broke out on his face, one that was comfortable, but not the sunshine Dom saw when Adrian smiled for him. He was grateful for that and also itchy at how much he was grateful.

Relief that he didn't have to be jealous was overshadowed by the fact that he would have been. He was head over heels in love with Adrian.

"Janelle." Adrian took her hand and kissed her on the cheek. "I had no idea you'd be here."

Janelle. The woman who could suspend people in nothing but rope. Excitement, desire, and embarrassment flared. Dom's cheeks warmed and he hoped he wasn't blushing too badly.

"Same, though it's always a pleasure to see you." They parted, and Janelle peered at Dom. "And this is...?"

"Dominic," Dom said, voice shaking slightly. And yeah, he was blushing. "I'm Adrian's—" Boyfriend? Lover? Submissive? What was he to Adrian?

Thankfully, Adrian filled in the gap. "This is the gentleman I've been seeing."

Gentleman. That was a far cry from Domino. And yet, also not. Perfect. It was kind of perfect. Adrian's gentleman.

His face heated even more. "We bought one of your photographs," he blurted out. "Well, I guess not your photographs, but..." Dom waved his hand and closed his mouth. God, he was babbling.

Adrian's hand slid to the small of Dom's back, warm and soothing. "Your rope work is masterful, as always."

"Flattery. Det's artistry always makes mine look better." Her smile was warm, and directed at Dom. "But I am glad you appreciate it." She returned her gaze to Adrian. "And if you ever wish to learn more, my door is always open for you and your gentleman."

Fire up Dom's spine. His cheeks must be glowing by now. Maybe his whole face. He kept his mouth closed, because who knew what would come out of his brain now?

Again, Adrian took the lead. He nodded deferentially. "Thank you for the offer."

She touched Adrian on the arm. "Good to see you, Adrian." She held out her hand for Dom to take, which he did. "And a pleasure to meet you, Dominic. But I don't wish to keep either of you from your day." She gave him a gentle squeeze, then let go before slipping past them into the other room of the gallery.

When they stepped back out into the bright day, Dom's world had rearranged itself again. "That—did she really mean that?"

"Janelle doesn't offer to teach to just anyone." Adrian glanced at the gallery door for a moment. "Yes, she meant that."

"Wow. Do you—? Would you—?" Dom shivered, despite the warmth of the day.

"Janelle is an excellent teacher, and yes, I would, if you were willing. But I think we should wait on that, until you're sure you are."

He was pretty damn sure he wanted that. The rope, the binding. To hang in the air. "The whole exhibit was amazing."

"I'm glad you think so." Adrian's grin was nearly as bright as the sun.

Yeah, and there was that hint of devil in the glint of Adrian's eyes. "What do you have planned for me?"

"Something for tomorrow. To settle you before you return to your week."

Before he stepped back into his life and out of Adrian's. Dom glanced down the street toward that other studio, the one that smelled of makeup and people and lights. Where Ray had laughed, Zavier had smiled, and Mish had danced on heels that had been pencil-thin.

He couldn't even envision Domino tied up like the men and women in those photos. How could he have both these things?

Adrian touched his cheek, his smile dimming. "I wish you would tell me."

Dom's whole being snapped back, and he looked into Adrian's eyes. "You said there were secrets we could keep."

Adrian nodded and rubbed a thumb over Dom's chin. "I did. I meant it."

"I can't yet." Might not be able to in the long run.

Another nod. "Let's go get some ice cream, then."

Adrian didn't bring it up again. Just held Dom's hand as they bought cones and walked the streets and sat on the giant boulders in Central Park. Kissed his neck and mouth when they rode the subway back to Brooklyn, fed him another amazing meal, then made love to him in the bed Dom was rapidly starting to think of as *theirs*.

"I think we really are dating," he whispered into the darkened room once they'd finally slipped under the sheets to sleep.

Adrian's chuckle vibrated against Dom's back. Hands slid over Dom's arms. "I was hoping you'd say that."

"Me, too." A far cry from wanting to turn and run. He had absolutely no idea what he was doing at all.

IT WASN'T UNTIL THE AFTERNOON ON SUNDAY THAT ADRIAN followed up on his "something" comment, and it came after a long walk around Brooklyn after a breakfast out.

By the time they'd returned, they were both hot and sticky and had climbed the stairs to Adrian's master bath for a shower—ostensibly to cool down—which did nothing of the sort due to Adrian's hands and mouth and hard body sliding against Dom's.

Dom was breathless and hard by the time they were through. "I need another shower after that one."

Adrian shut off the water. "I think you're fine for what comes next."

Like lightning through him, like the feel of his calluses running up guitar strings before the sound of a thousand people. "Yeah? And what comes next?"

"A little something I want to try—to see if you enjoy it." Adrian grabbed a towel and tossed another at Dom.

"You have me curious." He dried off and followed Adrian into the bedroom.

Adrian had already pulled on a pair of boxers and jeans. "I'd like you naked, if you wouldn't mind."

Naked while Adrian was dressed. This was sounding better and better. "I'm fine with that."

When he looked over, Adrian's gaze was fire-hot. "You are absolutely fine." He grabbed a simple white tee and donned it, then rooted in a drawer Dom had not seen him open before. From it he pulled bundles of rope and a black sash. He looked in again, but grunted and kneed the drawer shut. "These will do."

Dom couldn't stop staring at the rope. "I thought you said..."

"Oh, I intend to tie you up, Dominic. Just not as completely as you saw in those photos." Adrian paused and smiled, hot and wicked. "Not yet, anyway."

Dom shivered then heated then shivered again. "I—okay."

Adrian nodded at the door. "Follow me."

They returned downstairs to the living room, and Dom glanced at the spot where they'd started this weekend. Couch looked none the worse for wear. Score one for that stain guard.

Adrian dumped his handful of rope bundles and the sash onto the couch. "Would you like me to tell you exactly what I'm going to do, or would you rather just experience it?"

"Is it gonna end with your cock down my throat?"

Adrian snorted and shook his head. "No, not this time."

Dom stuck out his lip in a mock pout, then considered. "I think—just do it. Whatever you intend. I—trust you. And you're really not into that whole pain thing, as far as you've said."

"No, I'm not a sadist, really. And, tattoos aside, I don't think you're all that masochistic."

"I mean, I like when you fuck me hard."

"Well, so do I, but that comes from a different place than, say, you wanting me to flog you until you have welts. Or vice versa."

Dom knew people enjoyed that and didn't have a problem with the concept, in theory. He just didn't want to be on the practice end of it. "Yeah, that doesn't really excite me."

"But rope..." Adrian picked up a bundle. It was black and looked soft and strong. "The thought of rope over that lovely skin of yours makes you moan in galleries."

"Just one," Dom murmured. "You only took me to one."

Adrian closed in and sipped a slow kiss that felt like a cool breeze. "Turn around, Dominic."

He did, and Adrian arranged his arms in a particular manner, behind his back and stacked but not uncomfortably so, then started coiling rope around them. The first touch of the soft fiber had him sucking in a breath. When he felt the pressure of it against his skin, he stifled a moan.

Adrian kissed the nape of his neck. "I'd rather hear you, Dominic. I want to know what this is doing to you."

"It's—oh god, Adrian." He couldn't even describe how his heart was racing or his mind tumbling. He was hard, but he didn't want to be fucked, not now. He wanted—more. "Please keep going."

A deep rumble of pleasure, and then there was more looping and tugging and that amazing sensation of his arms being tied together. He couldn't see what Adrian was doing, but oh god, did he feel it. And since Adrian wanted to hear— Dom moaned and gasped and shivered and swayed.

"You're going to kneel soon, but this is a little easier from this angle."

Dom didn't care. He'd stay upright if he had to, or fall to the floor if that worked. It was like alcohol. Or the stage. Only quiet and close and so, so safe. "Adrian," he whispered. "Yes."

A huff of breath at his back, then another kiss. "Kneel for me, Dominic."

He did, and once more, Adrian positioned his body, shifting him so he knelt sideways against the couch, his ass on his heels. "Just in case you need to tip over."

His whole body was a live wire. "I thought this was supposed to calm me down before I go?"

Adrian peered down and ran a finger under his chin. "Oh ye of little faith." Then he was on the floor, too, kneeling behind Dom, and there was rope around Dom's ankle. *Oh god.*

This—was better than the stage. Fuck. "Adrian!" He heard the panic in his voice.

Everything halted. "I'm here, babe. You need me to stop? Cut you free?"

"No, no. Don't cut." He sucked in a breath, then another. "It's just..." This was gonna change him. Like Domino changed him. Like when he picked up a guitar for the first time. When the first chord he played had echoed through the air.

"Talk to me, babe." Concern. Caring. All the things he wanted, wrapped in Adrian's shaking voice.

"It's a lot." He swallowed, and his chest loosened. "You were right. I just want this so much."

A kiss to his shoulders, then another and another. "Let me know if you need me to pause."

When the tugging and pulling started again, that same headiness came, the sense life was turning and shifting and repositioning, even as the bonds drew tighter. Then his arms were tugged down slightly.

To his ankles. His arms were tied to his ankles. The realization was like ice water flowing over him—then there was calm and quiet, but for Adrian's breathing and a faint buzzing in Dom's blood. He tugged a little. Squirmed. But no —he really was tied down. "Oh."

"That's all the bonds, all the rope, for tonight," Adrian said.

Yeah, Dom didn't know if he could take more—not at first —because his mind was still caught and circling and full of light and heat, even if his body was relaxing and melting.

"There's one more thing I'd like to try." Adrian held out the sash. "I'd like you to focus on feeling. I want to cover your eyes."

A blindfold. Dom shifted, and was reminded that he was bound and kneeling before Adrian—and there wasn't a way he could free himself. He looked up into those hazel eyes and nodded.

Adrian took off Dom's glasses, then once more stepped behind him. Darkness descended as the cloth stole his sight. Two tugs, and the blindfold was tight around his head.

Bound, blindfolded. But not gagged.

"If you need out, say the word." Adrian's touch skimmed over Dom's shoulders, raising goose bumps. The couch next to him moved and groaned—Adrian must have sat. Fingers in Dom's hair. Smoothing, brushing. "You look exquisite, Dominic."

He felt—he felt like he was floating. Swimming. Swinging through air. It was heaven, without a touch of hell. Adrian's touch was a lifeline, keeping him safe and secure. He nodded his head forward—and yes, there was Adrian's warm thigh. He sighed and sagged against it.

A warm hand cupped the back of his neck. "Babe."

Yeah. He was that, too.

He had no idea how long they remained like that, him bound and blindfolded, resting against Adrian, who sat quietly, occasionally running his fingers through Dom's hair. Murmuring words of encouragement and support that trickled off Dom like water from an umbrella. Everything was sweetness and light.

He loved this. And strangely, Domino might love this, too.

This—yeah. He could see himself, see Domino like this. Maybe even at Adrian's feet.

A yawning chasm opened up—hope and despair—but he didn't fall. He just...floated above it. Watching. Until it slid closed again.

All the while, Adrian touched and soothed and crooned.

Dom knew, though, the instant the end of the night began.

Adrian sighed, and it was resigned. Then he shifted, his weight pitching toward Dom. "It's time," he whispered.

And—that was okay. Dom had expected loss or sadness or —something. But the calm remained, even when Adrian lifted the blindfold free.

"How was that?" He cupped Dom's face.

Dom leaned into the touch, but didn't close his eyes. Adrian's were too full of hope and wonder to turn away from. "Perfect. I never knew..." He huffed a laugh. "You were right about calming me down."

He wasn't hard anymore, and though his body ached from the past weekend's activities, his soul felt rested. Clear of the anxiety that usually plagued it whenever he wasn't onstage in the middle of a show or in a bed in the middle of orgasm.

"There are ways I could excite you, too. But I think we both needed this."

"You—you liked it, too?" It hadn't occurred to him, but of course. The books had said—

Such a profound flicker of emotion over Adrian's face. "I loved it," he said, and his voice was deep. "More than anything, this trust is—a gift."

Dom's heart shuddered and swelled, because he'd heard the words Adrian hadn't spoken. Maybe he hadn't even thought them yet, but they were there nonetheless. *Oh, oh god.*

But he still floated, right over *that* pit and safely to the other side before the panic could even touch him. "I'm—yeah. That's really good. Because I shouldn't be the only one getting something out of this."

"You're not, believe me." Adrian seemed to search for words, then shook his head. "Thank you." Lips skimmed his. "Thank you for every moment together."

"For all the ones to come." Dom meant that, because he wanted those moments, too.

Adrian untied him and helped him to his feet, then handed him his glasses. Dom slid back into his clothes and his life. But this weekend's kisses by the door weren't full of worry or longing. "You free next weekend?"

Adrian took his mouth again, then after another sweet taste of lips answered. "Yes. For all the foreseeable weekends, too. But for some of them I'd like you to pick what we do. Where we go."

"I can do that." And would soon. Show Adrian what he could of the man he was.

The summer evening was warm and perfect, and Dom hummed one of their new songs as he headed back to his place, head high and heart soaring even higher.

Maybe he could be both the men he wanted to be.

CHAPTER
TWELVE

As they climbed the steps to the Metropolitan Museum of Art, Adrian tried to remember the last time he'd been here. It'd been a while. Maybe a year or two. Certainly he'd been since he moved back into the city after he'd inherited the house and gotten his banking job.

Such a change of pace, from sunny California to weather-temperamental New York City. Though today? Today was practically postcard-worthy. Clear blue sky. Warm summer sun, but a dry, cool breeze that kept the temperatures mellow and the humidity low.

Wouldn't have mattered if it had been pouring rain, though. He was still so fucking glad to be back where he belonged. Didn't regret *that* decision at all, even if taking over the house had estranged him from most of his family.

But if he hadn't come back, hadn't moved into the brownstone, he'd never have met Dominic at Poet and Whiskey.

And now, with Dominic tugging him up the steps of the Met, there was no place on Earth he'd rather be.

When Dominic had suggested going to the Met this weekend, Adrian'd been a little disappointed, since he wanted more than just looking at art. He'd wanted a glimpse behind some of those walls Dominic threw up.

Then Dominic had said the magic words: "There's a tour today where they're bringing out some of the stringed instruments for a demo, including a seventeenth century guitar." His eyes had shone with excitement and delight. "I've heard recordings—there's even stuff on the website—but to experience that in person?"

Adrian recognized the shiver of delight, and that had cinched it. He could touch Dominic like that—he wanted to know what else did. And this was music-related, something Dominic tended to push away.

As it happened, the galleries that housed the Met's musical instrument collection had apparently been undergoing some major renovations over the last couple of years and they were finally in the process of being reopened. As part of that, there'd been some special tours, including performances with instruments from their extensive collection.

Normally, this was the type of thing Adrian would have passed up—tours were tourist traps or designed for school groups—but the way Dominic's face lit up each time he thought of hearing some instrument from a couple hundred years ago played live...

Yes, he'd seen Dominic in the throes of passion, but that didn't nearly measure up to the intense need in every fiber of Dominic's frame. The man was a musician, indeed. He might not talk about his career or his band for whatever reason, but this—*this* Dominic was willing to share, so Adrian followed, and gladly.

He also adored the feel of Dominic's hand in his and how utterly unashamed Dominic was to hold his. For someone who could be so shy at times, Dominic was utterly free about expressing his sexuality. Though sometimes, when he looked at Adrian, there was still that haunting sadness or worry. Less and less, though.

They were *dating*.

And Adrian was grateful for that. He'd rather have Dominic's smiles and sexy little glances, and not have to worry about whether this was a very long casual thing. Plus, he wanted more, too. More throaty cries, more cuffs and rope, more lazy talks after sex, more of Dominic paging through books and snuggling next to him to read poetry.

As they walked through the Met's Great Hall, Adrian had that quickening of breath he got whenever he visited a museum. This one topped his list. The Met had art and history—and he was here holding the hand of Dominic Bradley, with his flushed cheeks and a smile Adrian wanted to kiss forever.

This moment, right here, was giddy and full. The seed of deep love. Tantalizing. But calm and sweet. It took everything Adrian had not to get his hopes up yet.

They'd seen each other every weekend since that first one, and a few weeknights, too. More and more, Adrian learned about Dominic, and his childhood in New Jersey. He'd gotten a degree in history with a minor in music from Montclair State University, which explained his familiarity with New York City.

In return, Adrian shared pieces of his own life, beyond the tangled mess of his return to New York. Pieces of his childhood in Brooklyn. His parents' reaction to his interest in more than just women. His running with his neighborhood crew until college in Buffalo. How hard it'd been to move to a place where he'd needed to learn to drive and own a car. And hadn't that blown Dominic's mind, that Adrian hadn't bothered to get his license until well after he turned eighteen.

Being at the university had also been less diverse in many ways.

Adrian glanced around as they stood in line to get entrance tickets. Not so true here. Many different skin tones. So many languages. Sure, some were tourists, but not everyone. It felt more like home than anywhere else had. And people had the gall to say New Yorkers lived in a bubble?

"Are you staying?" The question came unbidden to Adrian's lips. "Here in New York? For good?"

There was a hint of confusion in Dominic's face as he replied, "Yeah. I bought a house here. I mean, I'm gonna travel some." He got that faraway look again. "Sometimes the band—" He shrugged, and the brilliant smile returned. "*This* is my home. I love it here."

That was one of the other things Dominic never touched on—how a *guitarist* for this band he was in could afford to buy a place in Brooklyn. But Adrian let the thought slide away. Dominic would tell him in time, would open those doors to whatever it was he wasn't sharing. After all, Adrian had said that was fine, that some secrets could be kept.

He would live with that. Or it would grate on him too much eventually—and they'd go their separate ways. Though right now it pained him horribly to consider it, there was still that option.

He needed a partner who trusted him, and suspected Dominic needed that, as well. That took time, but at some point, it also meant Dominic opening the doors to the secrets about his career, the one he loved so much.

Dominic gave his hand a squeeze. "I'm not going anywhere for a while."

Adrian brought the back of Dominic's hand to his lips and kissed it. "Good. I like having you here."

And he fucking loved that smile and the light in those eyes.

When they reached the front of the line, they showed their New York IDs, but paid a little more than the recommended donation amount for the entrance fee anyway, since they could both afford it. Dominic handed over his card before Adrian could. When he started to complain, Dominic held up his hands. "Hey, this is me dragging you to see old instruments. I'll pay. I know this isn't really your thing."

"Well, I do get to see you obsess all over something you love. I'd be happy to pay for that privilege. Plus, there's the rest of the museum, and plenty of things I'd love to see again, too." There were tons of galleries Adrian had loved as a child, and no trip was ever complete without a stop to see the Egyptian temple in the Sackler Wing.

"Whatever you say." Dominic winked, then took his card back from the cashier and got their stickers for admission. They paused long enough to put the stickers on, then headed to the tour sign to wait for the guide.

"I've never done one of these tours," Adrian said. "Not since I was a kid. And those were mandatory pains in the ass."

"I loved going to museums as a kid, especially the ones here in the city." Dominic almost looked heartbroken at Adrian's words. "Field trips were the *best*."

"Oh, I loved them, too, but I wanted to explore and go to my favorite exhibits, not be dragged around for educational purposes. I suppose I've never been very good at being a follower."

Dominic's lips twitched, but he said nothing.

"What?" He nudged Dominic. "Out with it."

Dominic looked up at the vaulted ceilings, his mouth still curved into that quirky smile. "Well, on the one hand, you can be passionately domineering, challenging, and you often forge ahead..."

There was definitely another part to that. "But on the other hand?"

Dominic dropped his gaze from the ceiling to stare at Adrian. "You work as a computer programmer for a bank."

Touché. And for some reason, one of the very first questions Dominic had ever asked Adrian tumbled through his mind again. Did he *like* his job? *Well enough* had been his answer. That was still true...and Dominic had pegged it for exactly what it was: a passive and safe position. "It's computer engineer, and technically, it's a financial services institution."

Dominic's lips lost their upward curve, and he looked down.

No, no, that wouldn't do. Not for the truth. He raised Dominic's hand again and pressed his lips to it once more. "But you're right. In some things I'm fine with following. And it is a bank, and I do program."

The smile didn't return, but Dominic did meet his gaze. "You're so passionate about everything else. Your house, your books. I think you're passionate about your programming, too. It's just that when you do talk about your job, other than the people you enjoy and the challenges you overcome..."

"It's not with the same intensity?"

Dominic nodded.

Well, he'd wanted truth. Adrian scrubbed a hand through his hair. "I like it well enough." The words tasted a little dry, though he said it with humor.

There was something sad about Dominic's smile, so Adrian bumped his hip. "I have other outlets for my passion."

This time Dominic laughed and that lovely flush returned, so Adrian pulled him close and wrapped his arms around him until the tour guide appeared to lead them to the galleries with the musical instruments.

The tour, it turned out, was incredibly interesting. Each instrument type was explained and the subject was wrapped in history and musicology, though that was aimed more at Adrian's level of understanding than Dominic's, obviously. There must have been a few other musicians in their group, because some of them asked questions with terms Adrian didn't know and the answers that followed, though in

English, made no sense to him. From Dominic's subtle nods, he understood perfectly, though.

This must have been what it was like for a non-programmer to stand in a sea of software engineers talking shop and code. Next holiday party, Adrian was going to take pains to converse about other topics with some of the non-techheads.

Or he needed to learn a thing or two about music—not just listen to it.

The best part, as he predicted, was Dominic's joy. The way his eyes lit up when he studied the various guitars and mandolins and violins and...well, all the other stringed instrument names Adrian didn't catch.

Dominic pulled him close to one case. "God, look at the inlay around the sound hole on this gittern. And the wood. This must have sounded glorious in its day." He reached out and his fingers hovered just shy of the glass. "I once held one of Bo Diddley's cigar-box guitars and that was a trip, but I'd saw off my right arm to play one of these, if there was one still in working condition."

Adrian blinked a few times. "Wouldn't you have a hard time playing it if you sawed off your arm?"

Dominic huffed a laugh and his eyes fucking twinkled. Adrian wanted to kiss him right then and there. "Well, there *is* that. I guess it stays on for now."

"Probably for the best."

Dominic stepped over to the next case. "I wonder if they ever let anyone play the ones in good condition. I mean, aside from on a tour like this."

Someone coughed behind them, and they both turned. Their tour guide, Luke, a stunning black man with an easy professional smile, stood with his hands behind his back. "We do. Most often on these tours we have musicians who play as part of the demonstrations, but we do also invite professional musicians to record pieces with some of our less fragile instruments."

Dominic practically vibrated. They'd been holding hands the entire time, and his grip on Adrian's held the same intensity as the other lines of his body. "How do you choose? I mean, that has to be such an honor."

"Well, *I* don't personally choose." Luke placed a hand on his chest, and that smile became less professional and more flirtatious for a moment. "But I can give you the card to the curator's office and you can inquire with them. Tell them I sent you."

Adrian gave Dominic's hand a little squeeze. Encouragement—at least for the getting the card part. He certainly admired the figure the tour guide cut, but Dominic was *his* date. His boyfriend.

A thrill like sparks ran through Adrian. He still couldn't get over that fact. He shouldn't feel this giddy, but he couldn't help it.

"Yeah, that would be fantastic," Dominic said, and the tour guide slipped him a card, beamed a little too brightly, touched Dominic a little too long, then moved on.

And on the heels of giddiness, jealousy struck. Strange to have that tumble through him—he *rarely* felt that kind of spike of covetousness. Or anger.

"He likes you," Adrian murmured.

"Yeah, I know." Dominic had this wry look. "But I'm seeing someone."

Adrian's heart flipped over in his chest. "Oh? Must be quite the guy if you're passing up a museum guide who can get you an in with a rare instruments curator."

Dominic pulled him close. "Are you fishing for compliments?"

"Who, me? Never."

Dominic grinned and kissed his nose. "My guy's quite the gentleman, yes."

Another cough from Luke redirected them, and the tour moved on to the next section.

When they reached a more open gallery, there was a cloth-covered table with four instruments related to the modern guitar, and a woman waiting by it. She was dressed in all black, and her dark, wavy hair was piled up into a bun on her head.

Luke nodded to her. "Adelaida Mellado is here from Juilliard to demonstrate some of the instruments we discussed."

As she picked each one up, the guide gave a little speech about the particular piece's history, the maker, who owned it, where it had been played—all the interesting tidbits—then talked about the music that would be played.

Then a sweet melody swept over the room, and everyone hushed as she played. Her eyes were hooded and her body flowed with the same controlled movements he saw in every orchestra performer he'd ever seen in concert. Next to Adrian, Dominic watched, gaze fixed, mouth open. Such intensity. His fingers twitched in Adrian's.

Oh yes—Dominic wanted to play. Wanted his fingers where this woman's were. His desire was entirely for what she held in her hands, for the sound that echoed across the room.

And that was only the first of four instruments.

By the time the demo and the tour were over, Dominic's eyes were a little glazed and his fingers very twitchy. He approached the table with the reverence of a pilgrim looking at relics. Adrian trailed, savoring this rare view of Dominic's world.

Adelaida looked up at Dominic. "Do you play? You have that look..."

He laughed, his cheeks reddening. "Yeah. Mostly modern, you know? But I studied classical in college, and the history..." He shook his head slightly. "They're beautiful. They sound—" He gave a little sigh.

"Would you like to—" She turned to the guide. "Could he—?"

Luke glanced at Dominic and then Adrian, and resignation flickered there before smoothing into a smile. "For a moment, yes. I think that would be okay."

Dominic made a noise that was half a wheeze and half a sigh. Adelaida handed him a late-Renaissance-era guitar, and he ducked under the strap and cradled it in his arms, setting his left fingers on the strings. He tapped the body gently with a fingernail on his right hand. "Wow. God. The resonance."

He took a breath and strummed the strings gently, playing chords, his expression so profound, so utterly open and clear.

Adrian held his breath, listened to Dominic play, and drank in every flicker of his eyes, twitch of mouth, and curl of those amazing fingers.

After a few minutes, he quieted the strings, took the strap off and handed the guitar back to Adelaida. "Thank you," he said. "That was amazing."

She smiled at him. "You're very good! Do you play for a quartet or orchestra, or...?"

He shrugged. "I'm in a band. It's—rock. Nothing like this." He gestured at the instruments. "I just love music and history. The sound. That someone hundreds of years ago made and then played this. That I can."

She nodded. "Yeah, it's really amazing, isn't it?"

Dominic thanked her again, shook hands with Luke, and backed up until Adrian pressed a hand against his spine. "You okay, babe?"

Dominic's smile was blinding. "You called me *babe* in public."

Adrian noticed that Luke rolled his eyes but had a small smile as he packed up the instruments. "Well, yes?" He couldn't help but grin back at Dominic.

Laughter followed, and that was more beautiful a sound

to Adrian than what had come from the three-hundred-plus-year-old guitar. "I'm fine."

"Why don't we go get some lunch and then figure out what else you want to see?" Adrian put his arm around Dominic and they headed out of the gallery, back toward the main part of the museum. "Cafe here or food carts outside?" It was a nice day, after all.

"You know," Dominic said, "there's supposed to be a rooftop bar in here somewhere..."

"Really?" Adrian's voice pitched up. "That place is a tourist trap."

"Well, yes." That flirty, cock-tightening grin was back. "Let's play tourist. See how the other half live."

Adrian shook his head—but this was Dominic's day, so they went searching. It took a little bit to find it, since they had to head back down to the first floor to take the elevator to the fifth, but they emerged into the perfect summer day and a stunning view of the city.

"Okay," Dominic said. "Now see? This view is worth it."

It really was, actually. Million-buck vista of the skyline. "Lunch? Drinks?"

"You gonna get me tipsy at the Met?" Dominic bumped his hip.

"This was your idea." Adrian slid an arm around him again, and pulled their bodies close. "And I don't have to— you're already tipsy." Drunk on old instruments and sound.

A huff of a laugh. "I'll give you that."

They opted to split a sandwich and get two glasses of wine. It was still early enough that the bar wasn't horribly crowded, which was good, since there wasn't anywhere to sit, so they leaned on the railing.

Dominic ate his half of lunch in silence, peering out over Central Park. He cleared his throat, then sipped his wine. "I don't know if I can explain what it means to be able to touch an instrument like that, to play it, to be connected to all that history." He shook his head.

"You don't have to explain." Adrian turned from the stellar view of the city to take in an even better one—Dominic's soft smile. "I saw what it meant when you played. What it means to you now."

Dominic's eyes were lovely and full of thanks. "I'm glad we're here."

So was he. Adrian was so very grateful he was standing on the roof of the Met and that Dominic Bradley was in his life.

———

FOR DOM, ONE OF THE BEST PARTS ABOUT SUNDAY WAS WHEN Adrian cooked breakfast. Anything Dom asked for. Waffles. Pancakes. Bacon. Today, he'd asked for an omelet and Adrian had crafted this brilliant one of onions, bacon, tomatoes, and some very sharp cheddar.

Perfect. Utterly. And the look on Adrian's face when Dom groaned at the taste only made the moment better. When he could talk without a full mouth, he spoke. "You kinda get off on cooking and feeding me, don't you?"

Adrian's grin was lopsided and matched his messy hair. He wore a pair of shorts low on his hips and nothing else. "I enjoy taking care of you in *many* ways."

Including holding him down and fucking him until he couldn't think. Dom squirmed on the breakfast bar stool. "I wish there was something I could give back to you."

Adrian stilled, and Dom got the distinct impression that he almost said something before a tight smile returned. "You give me enough."

"What? What were you going to say?"

A touch of color on those cheeks. "Not something I should ask for."

That baffled Dom. Because honestly, he couldn't think of anything Adrian could ask for that he wouldn't give. Well, maybe not a gangbang or something like that. But he didn't think that was Adrian's thing anyway. "Tell me. I mean, if I'm not willing, I'll let you know."

Adrian turned away to grab the pan off the stove and take it to the sink. The lines of his body were sharp and tense. "Hearing you play that old guitar yesterday was amazing. I'd very much like to hear you play again." He turned, and there was sadness in his eyes. "But I know it's off the table."

God, the conflict in Dom's head and heart hurt. He wanted to share that with Adrian, but the moment he outed Domino, what he had with Adrian might end. Or Domino would. He let out a breath.

Adrian's shoulders dropped, and sorrow moved from his eyes to his smile. "That's why I didn't want to ask."

Dom pressed a hand to his chest. He hated when his heart beat like this, flopping and hard. It made his lungs tight and his mind race. Fucking hell. Maybe, maybe there was a way to play for Adrian without bringing in Domino. After all, he had played at the Met. "We can get my acoustic." He managed to push the words out.

A play of emotions crossed Adrian's face before settling into concern. "Are you sure, Dominic? I don't want to make you uncomfortable."

It wasn't Adrian doing that, it was Dom's own life. The voice that told him Adrian could never love a rocker like Domino. But acoustic and classical pieces, he could play those. Tension drained from his back and the voice quieted. "Yeah. We just have to go to my place to get it."

A soft smile replaced the frown. "Thank you."

They finished breakfast, and though they were both quiet, it was still warm and tender. Adrian skimmed fingers over Dom's bare back, and pressed a kiss to his shoulder before grabbing their dishes.

They showered and dressed and headed out into the over-cast day. Warm and humid, one of those sticky summer days when you hoped it would rain. Nearly matched Dom's mood. He caught Adrian's hand in his. "My place isn't as nice as yours on the inside. It's still kind of sterile. Would you mind if we came back here after I grab my guitar?"

"Not at all," Adrian murmured.

Dom led them toward his place, down streets and through Prospect Park. He really didn't think of the brick town house as *home* that much. Was his on paper, but not really in his soul. Classic on the outside. Modern inside. Kind of the oppo-site of Dom, really.

Throughout the walk, Dom knew Adrian had questions. Wanted answers. He watched those eyes and that face and the restraint.

He fucking didn't deserve this man. At all. He never wanted to let him go.

When they made it to his place, Adrian tilted his head. "Shall I wait here?"

Dom nodded, his throat tight. Adrian knew where he lived now. But inviting him inside would expose too much of Domino. "Do you mind? It's kind of a disaster inside. I haven't picked up recently." Not entirely the truth, but not really a lie, either. There was so much of his rock-star life scat-tered around the house at the moment, anyone stepping inside would know instantly who Dom was.

There was that sad smile again. But Adrian drew him in and kissed him on the forehead. "Go. I'll wait here."

Dom went, heart in his throat. Up the steps, into his house and to the living room, where he kept his favorite acoustic guitar. He slipped it into its case, and was back out the door as fast as he could manage, heart slamming in his chest. He could do this. Bring a tiny bit of his musical life to Adrian.

Adrian kissed him when he returned. "Better?"

It was. The fear was there, the thought that this was a

mistake, but not so horrible now. "Yeah. Thanks for understanding."

Fingers brushed the hair from his forehead. "Privacy is important."

So was trust. He *should* trust Adrian. But a knot kept forming in his soul at the thought of unraveling his life that much. If Adrian rejected Domino, where would that leave Dominic? And if Adrian *didn't*—how soon would the world know about Dom's real name?

The walk back was relaxed, and like the sun peeping though the clouds, Adrian's smile broke through the gloom in Dom's soul.

He didn't take the guitar out right away. They relaxed in the library, reading snippets of books to each other until Adrian's sensual poetry reading got the better of Dom, and he plucked the book from Adrian's hands and kissed him until they were both breathless and hard.

"Downstairs. Now." Adrian's voice was both commanding and guttural. Dom did as told, with pleasure.

Clothing ended up everywhere in their wake. On the stairs, in the hallway when Adrian rammed Dom up against the wall and jacked him off until he was moaning and struggling against that hard body. "Gonna come," he gasped between kisses.

"Not yet, you aren't." But Adrian didn't stop stroking, not until Dom was trembling and incoherent.

Wasn't fair. Was absolutely everything Dom loved.

When they finally ended up in bed, there was only skin and mouths and teeth. Lubed fingers and moans. Cocks grinding together. Then Adrian entered him and everything was right in Dom's world. He was full and home and Adrian had him.

He loved the way Adrian fucked him, somehow brutal and tender at the same time. Dom came hard and fast, too stunned to even cry out.

Adrian followed, Dom's name—all three syllables—on his lips. In the aftermath, when they were tangled in each other's arms under the sheets, Dom whispered, "Can I play for you?"

He felt Adrian's shudder. His answer was full of gravel and almost begging. "Please, Dominic. Please."

The air in the house was cool and the trip down to the living room to collect his guitar felt like a dream. But then, everything in Adrian's house was that way.

When Dom returned, he sank down on the bed next to Adrian, guitar in hand, and touched the strings to tune them.

Then he played.

The calm was breathtaking. Just like always. Music was the life he'd chosen, the one he'd loved. With or without Domino, in the still and quiet, he could stroke the strings, feel the vibration against his skin and hear the notes. So many notes. Snippets of classical pieces. Jazz. Modern. He even played a few lines from one of the band's new songs.

When he finished, he found Adrian's gaze and it was full of admiration and awe, and that both broke and healed Dom's heart.

"Babe," Adrian whispered. "That was beautiful. Thank you so much."

"You're welcome." He rose and set the guitar back in its case.

When he returned to bed, Adrian pulled him into his arms. "You're a gift."

He didn't know about that, only that his soul ached as much as his heart and he so desperately wanted to climb over the fear that held him from telling Adrian about Domino.

But that wall seemed too high and the fall on the other side so great. Instead, he lay in Adrian's arms and drank in his warmth, touch, and kisses.

CHAPTER
THIRTEEN

DOM WAS GETTING USED TO THE WHIPLASH EFFECT OF MOVING IN and out of his two lives. Weekdays, more often now than not, he was Domino, even dressing the part to go into the studio.

Part of it was a marketing ploy—their show was coming up. He even headed out on the town with the rest of the band a few times. Camera and cell phone flashes. Autographs. People screaming their names. *His* name.

God, he loved it. As much as the stage and the center of attention scared Dominic, Domino thrived in that environment. Dom could be as brash and cocky and brave as he wanted to be in this, his other life.

And he had another life now, not just moments as Dominic, but during the weekends and a few weeknights, he *was* Dominic and *with* Adrian, thoroughly enjoying every aspect of what it meant to be dating him, from the lovely food to the stimulating conversation, to the sex that left him wrecked and panting and wanting more, even when he topped.

Thursday had been a full-out Twisted Wishes fun fest. He'd started the day as Domino, sneaking out of his house in the very early mornings, hoodie pulled over his head and slouching through the subway. Once in Manhattan, he'd relaxed and let people see a little more—and soon he'd caught some kids staring and trying surreptitiously to take photos of him.

Dom raised his head, held up his middle finger to his lips, then broke into a smile when the kids gasped and laughed. Then he let them take selfies with him and signed one girl's arm.

At the next stop, he got off because he was close enough to walk to the studio without too much trouble. He stepped out into the bright day, tossed his hoodie back, and strode through the city on his way to their studio.

When he got there, Ray gave him a look. "Having a little fun?" He waved his phone with Instagram opened and photos of him and the kids on the subway displayed.

Dom shrugged. "Eh, it's been a while."

Mish snorted. "For someone who claims to hate the spotlight, you have such an odd fucking way of showing it."

Zavier was silently fiddling with his drum kit, but he had the damn smile on his face.

"Look," Dom said. "I kinda miss being Domino sometimes. And I can *be* in the spotlight as him." He certainly couldn't as Dominic.

"Actually, I'm glad for this." Ray waved his phone again. "'Cause it's good they're seeing you out, too. There were some really weird rumors you'd been booted from the band."

Dom laughed. He couldn't help it. But once the absurdity had worn off, sobriety slipped in—the humbling kind. "Yeah, I guess I could see how people might think that."

"But the more they see you—coming to the studio, going out with us, out on your own—the more those will go away. They'll know you're a part of the band."

"I've been here the entire time!"

Zavier stood. "But not as Domino. And you've been enjoying your other life."

Dom swung around, fear twisting up his spine. "What are you saying, Zav?"

He held up his hands. "Nothing in particular. Just that you haven't melded these two sides of you."

"I don't intend to." The words were out of his mouth before he realized what he'd said and what that meant—keeping Adrian out of the loop permanently. Which wasn't sustainable. He was going to lose Adrian in the end.

But the thought of the spotlight shining down on the Dominic that Adrian knew—and that light being trained on Adrian himself—tied Dom's stomach into knots and had his heart pounding. It was as if he'd been transported back to that first time onstage behind Ray—as himself, not Domino. Ray could take the spotlight, the crowds, and the scrutiny. But could Adrian? Was it even fair to ask him to endure what he couldn't without a disguise?

Dom couldn't do it, not as Dominic. He thought he could, but he'd been wrong.

Zavier's shoulders dropped. "Dom."

"Don't you start." He rounded on them all. "Don't *any* of you start. It's my life and my decision." Even if a voice in the back of his head screamed that it was perhaps the most foolish one he'd ever made in his life.

"I can't be Dominic and Domino at the same time." He spoke softly, and peered at Ray, his oldest friend. The one that had been there in high school after that talent show, when he'd puked his nerves up into porcelain. "I *can't*. I'm not—" he gestured at himself "—built for rock-and-roll when you take all this shit off."

Ray opened his mouth as if to say something, then must have thought better of it. But after another moment, he did speak. "You're the best damn guitarist I know, Dom."

The anger was ebbing, but the horror, the creeping along his veins at the thought of leaving Adrian started working up his body. "Can we just play? That's what we're here for, right?"

Mish clapped him on the back. "Get your guitar, sweetheart, and let's get to work."

Took a few songs to get out of his head and into the music, but once he did, Dom felt so much better. Didn't matter if it was his electric or some three-hundred-year-old instrument—when there were strings under his fingers and notes in the air, everything in the world faded away.

It was like being onstage. Or in Adrian's bed.

He didn't fumble the next chord, or any of the ones after, even though his heart was in his throat and tears lurked behind his eyes.

Domino Grinder didn't cry, and there was a saving grace to that.

HE DIDN'T GO TO ADRIAN'S FRIDAY NIGHT—THAT HE SPENT AS Domino, too. Dinner out with the band, then hitting Broadway for a show. He'd let Adrian know earlier in the week that he'd have to break their streak of Friday dinners. "It's...um...work-related."

"Ah," Adrian had said, his voice thin over the phone. "I see. Well, I will miss you, certainly, but I know you do have a life outside of the one you share with me."

It was, as digs go, very gentle. Still, it hurt. "You free Saturday?"

The reply came instantly, and was warm and smooth. "Of course. You're welcome here anytime, Dominic. Any evening, any day." He paused. "Though, if it's during the week, I'm likely killing brain cells from stress in a cube."

Dom laughed. "Is it really that bad?"

"Sometimes." Ruefulness played out in his voice. "When should I expect you Saturday?"

Dom dropped his voice low. "Early. Don't bother getting dressed, 'cause I'll just drag you back to your bed."

"Sounds lovely." The cheer was back in Adrian's voice. "I can't wait."

Now it was six-thirty in the morning, Dom hadn't had any coffee, and he was standing on Adrian's steps, wondering if this was, indeed, too early. He rang the bell and waited. When he was about to ring it a second time, the distinct click of locks being thrown sounded, and the door cracked open to reveal Adrian, muss-haired, bleary-eyed, and blinking, and wearing nothing but a pair of boxers that were way too low-slung.

Damn, Dom would never get enough of seeing that body. "Hi."

Adrian's smile was the best thing in the universe. He opened the door wider and reached for Dom. "Come here." A whisper, slurred with exhaustion.

He went, and wrapped his arms around this man he cared so damn much for. Kissed the junction where his neck met his shoulder.

Adrian drew him inside, kicked the door closed, and threw the locks. "Upstairs," he murmured against Dom's hair.

Dom let the duffel slip off his shoulder, let Adrian lead him up those stairs, strip every last piece of clothing off of him, and pull him down into his bed.

Felt like home. Dom closed his eyes against kisses and touches. Adrian's hands—his whole body—were warm. He'd lost the boxers along the way, and their bodies meshed perfectly, molding and sliding until there was very little space between them. When Adrian took his mouth, Dom moaned and tried desperately to beg for what he wanted without using words.

Speaking would mean Adrian's mouth wouldn't be on his —and he needed to be lost in that kiss.

Maybe Adrian figured it out, or maybe he wanted the same thing, but it only took a little bit of time for Adrian to get the lube and a condom, and then he was pressing in, opening up Dom. Minimum prep, which was fine, because he needed the sharpness, the fullness, to grunt and cry as Adrian took him.

But it wasn't the fast fucking he'd been expecting—no. It was something far more profound. Deep, long, slow strokes. Teasing kisses, smiles, and murmurs of endearments. His name. *Babe.*

He came with tears in his eyes and Adrian swallowing his own name on Dom's lips. Those long strokes turned shorter and harder, until he, too, had fallen over the edge into bliss.

Perfect. Too much. Never enough.

I'm screwed.

Even more so when, after disposing of the condom and the tissues Dom had used to clean his chest, Adrian slid in next to him, wrapped his arms around him, and muttered three words.

"I love you."

They were so soft, and Adrian fell asleep a moment later, so Dom didn't even know if Adrian had realized he'd voiced them.

But Dom had heard them, and his whole world tumbled down, along with his heart.

SUNDAY MORNING, A WEEK AND A DAY AFTER THEIR TRIP TO THE Met, was just as lazy as Saturday, and once again, Adrian had made love to Dom, a contrast from the previous evening that had left bruises on his hips and scratches on Adrian's back. Adrian had taken him dancing, and the club had been out of this world. Gay. Loud. Full of beautiful people.

Not a single soul recognized him as Domino. It was so

damn liberating that he bumped and ground and teased Adrian—who everyone seemed to have known—without mercy.

They'd very nearly fucked in the bathroom because of that, though Adrian got close to bringing Dom off and had left him hard and panting. "That's what bad boys get when they're cock teases," Adrian had growled into his ear.

When they'd gotten back, Adrian had wrapped those leather cuffs around his wrists again, tied him to the bedframe, and fucked him so hard, Dom must have woken the neighbors with his screams of pleasure.

Now they lounged on the couch, books in hand, claimed from the library two floors up. Over near the entrance to Adrian's brownstone, the photograph he'd bought for Dom was all wrapped up and ready to go home with him. He had no idea where he'd put it in his big but empty house. And seeing the photo before the gallery workers had wrapped it for him had flipped his heart and mind over and over. To be tied like that. Held like that. His body craved knowing, especially since the experiment that other weekend had turned him inside out in so many ways.

They'd picked the photo up Saturday, after they'd gone to a production of *The Tempest* in Bryant Park, then stumbled upon an interesting lecture about immigration in the New York Public Library.

It was, as Adrian said before taking him clubbing, another great day of playing tourist in their own city.

Dom had seen some posters about the Twisted Wishes concert, too, at the club and while they'd wandered all over the city. Weird to walk right by a poster blaring the name of his band. Adrian didn't even give them a second glance, which was fine. Less complex. Less complicated.

Except for the gnawing feeling in the back of Dom's head and the voice that told him he was living a lie. Eventually he'd have to confess and trust Adrian with his secret—or walk away.

He had no idea what Adrian would think. What he would do.

And that was the musing on his mind as he sat with Adrian on the couch, their legs entwined as they read. Dom had a book of poetry on his lap and Adrian had been paging through a pamphlet about the makings of the borders of New York State. There were more books strewn on the coffee table.

When he glanced over, the pamphlet was closed on Adrian's lap, and his gaze was locked on Dom like a spotlight.

Heat flared in Dom's veins, because he'd come to know that calculated expression and that wicked smile—and welcomed it.

"Would you like to try something a little more interesting with rope?"

Dom closed the book of poetry he hadn't really been reading. "Yes." Didn't even have to know what *more interesting* meant.

Adrian chuckled, then nudged him with his foot. "Up then. Let's head to the bedroom."

There was this subtle change in Adrian when he was giving orders, a deeper voice, a more exact pronunciation. Even the way he held his body was different, despite being relaxed.

Power. Control. Dom had read a little about what it was like to be a Dominant. Didn't really get it all, but obviously it really was a thing for Adrian, and he had all those signs now. That shift in being ticked Dom's heart up and shook out his soul and mind.

The submission thing? Yeah, he got *that*. Loved that feeling. Didn't know why, despite reading those books Adrian had lent him. Didn't care, because some part of him felt so damn good when he followed what Adrian said—even if it was the simplest of orders, like go upstairs. That would lead to more commands, and surrendering himself, and being lost and safe in whatever Adrian chose for today.

He could forget about the future. Forget the other half of his life. Forget the words he'd voiced out loud to the band.

He paused when they reached and entered the bedroom, and Adrian circled him from behind, pulling their bodies close and brushing his lips over what Dom suspected was one of Adrian's favorite spots—the back of Dom's neck.

Made him whimper every time.

"Love that sound," Adrian murmured. "Take all of your clothes off. I want you naked for this."

Dom exhaled. "Yeah. Okay." Naked was always a good start. But Adrian didn't let go.

He spoke, deep and dark against that sensitive spot on Dom's neck. "I'm going to tie you more fully today. Arms. Torso. Legs. See if you like it."

Dom trembled, needing, wanting to tell Adrian he wanted what was being offered. "I've been dreaming about that. Like the photo."

"Yes, like the photo. All that skin and rope. Except my rope, and your flesh, body, and mind, Dominic."

Adrian's arms might have been the only things holding him up. He leaned back into his heat. "Perfect."

"Mmmhmm. And if you like the experience and are comfortable..." Adrian nipped Dom's neck. "I'm gonna fuck you nice and hard in those ropes, too."

It was like Adrian flipped a switch in Dom. In an instant, he'd gone from mildly aroused to hard as hell and needing every inch of Adrian possessing him. "Oh fuck. Yes, please."

"We'll see." Another kiss ghosted over Dom's neck, and Adrian let go. "Clothes off, Dominic."

He didn't waste any time undressing, but rather than throw his shirt and jeans all over the place, he folded them somewhat haphazardly and dropped them onto a bench on the side of the room. Everything went, down to his socks and his watch.

Adrian's admiration was obvious, from the heat in his stare to the hard bulge of his dick in his jeans. "Onto the bed, please, on your back."

Dom loved this bed more than his own. His was inherently lonely. This one? Large and full of life and company. He positioned himself in the middle, arms at his sides.

"Hmm, no. Arms up above your head."

He swallowed and raised both toward the headboard. Wasn't uncomfortable, but it did leave him feeling more open, more exposed. His breathing hitched up a notch.

Adrian must have noticed, because he raised an eyebrow. "Everything all right?"

"Just fucking turned on."

A wicked, wicked quirk to those lips, but no reply. From his dresser drawer of goodies, Adrian pulled out several bundles of the black rope he'd used before—but far more bundles. He placed them on the bench by the bed, then scanned Dom's body, that same burning desire in his eyes as before.

It wasn't entirely sexual, Dom realized. Sure, Adrian was hard, but the way he flicked his eyes over Dom's flesh—it wasn't with the gaze of someone who wanted to devour.

Adrian wanted to possess. Tame. Have.

Dom couldn't help the shudder.

That gaze softened a little, and Adrian went back to the drawer to pull out another item—a pair of large scissors. He placed them on the bedside table. "At any time you need out, tell me, and I'll have you free as fast as possible."

Dom nodded. "Yeah, I can do that." He paused. "But I want this. You know I do."

"I do know. But wanting and handling can sometimes be different things." He patted Dom's calf. "Trust me on this."

He had no other choice, really.

Dom had expected Adrian to start at his wrists and work down, but that's not what happened. He started at the chest and worked up and down, shifted Dom this way and that. Looping, knotting, tying until rope crossed his body in weblike patterns and Dom felt the gentle pressure and friction with every breath. Arms were secured above his head, wrists tied together. Both arms bound down with rope. Adrian stroked and touched and murmured as he worked, and Dom's nerves zinged and shook. His skin felt tight, and he was light and strong and secure in the web Adrian created over his body.

Then he worked his way down, rope lying over Dom's hips and between his legs and—

Dom sucked in a breath and moaned when Adrian crossed the rope around the base of his cock. Lifted and separated his balls. Not tight, though. Just enough that he knew those bonds were there.

As if answering Dom's thoughts, Adrian spoke, his words low and husky. "Yes, I could make it tighter. But we really haven't discussed cock and ball torture. So we'll leave that for now."

Cock and—"I haven't gotten to that chapter yet."

Adrian laughed and set to work on his legs. Those were bound together, all the way down to his ankles. Adrian even wove rope between his toes.

The bed shifted beneath Dom when Adrian finished and stood. "There." Adrian had a quirk of a smile.

He didn't ask how Dom felt, which was good, since he didn't even know how to process the sensations over his body. Rope pulled when he shivered or breathed or flexed a muscle, sending spikes of awareness down his body. There was security here, but also terror because he really was completely tied up and at Adrian's mercy. He could move his arms a little more than the rest of his body—but not much.

Strangely, he was hard—but not aroused. At least not in

the way he normally thought of it; that driving need to fuck wasn't there.

Adrian drew his finger in a circle around Dom's bellybutton, and everything went hazy. He moaned against the touch. Ropes pulled. Skin responded.

And oh, that grin. "Yes. Very nice. You're a dream, Dominic."

This felt like one, like some strange, surreal moment where everything he'd ever desired coalesced into one thing —the ropes around his body. He tried for words, but that seemed like too much, so he just met Adrian's gaze.

A chuckle and more touches, and the same overwhelming flood of sensations. Adrian ghosted fingers and tongue over so much of Dom's body. Rope shifted. Skin sang. No idea how long it lasted, but in the end, he was whimpering.

He was exhausted. He wanted more. "Please." This time, he managed to get that word out.

Adrian bent down and kissed him. Not the devouring kiss he expected, but a sweet one that tasted of calm and quiet. He cupped Dom's face. "I'm gonna untie you."

Dom croaked. "But—sex?" Then again, the thought of Adrian flipping him over and plowing into him made him squeeze his eyes shut as waves of pleasure rippled over his body.

The hand remained. "Not tonight. You're a little too far gone. And this is new to you."

"Okay." Yeah, 'cause he was actually really out of it. Good god. This was like being drunk.

"Dominic, thank you for trusting me. It's been—a very long while for me."

Dom had no idea what that meant. "Welcome."

Adrian slowly unwound the rope from Dom's body, so carefully, so reverently, it felt like worship, and in the end, all Dom wanted to do was melt into the mattress. He wasn't even hard anymore.

"That was amazing," he whispered when Adrian covered him with a light blanket, then lay down next to him under it, naked, as well.

"Yes, it was." Adrian kissed the tip of Dom's nose. "I set an alarm for later. Enough time to make you dinner before you need to go home."

"Wish I didn't have to." The truth slipped out.

A small sigh. "But you do. You have a whole other life out there, and I know you love it. I'll never keep you from it."

Dom buried his face in the crook of Adrian's neck. He was in love with this man. He trusted this man.

He needed to tell Adrian about the band.

Not yet, his brain whispered. Not tonight. Later.

Yeah. Because if he opened his mouth now, he might ruin the night he'd just had—that they both had just had. But he could say *something*.

"I love you, too."

Adrian's breath caught, and he wrapped his arms around Dom—bonds that Dom loved more than rope. More than anything else.

He needed Adrian as much as he needed Twisted Wishes.

CHAPTER
FOURTEEN

DOM BROUGHT ALL THE CLOTHING AND MAKEUP TO BECOME Domino when he went to the studio on Monday. He should have gotten up early. Hell, he'd gone to bed as soon has he'd gotten home from Adrian's and slept through the night. He could have.

But his heart hadn't been in it. Because reality had come crashing back down on Dom the moment he'd cracked his eyes open in his empty room in his empty house.

He'd told Adrian that he loved him. He was in love with Adrian Doran.

That should have been a happy realization, but as he stared up at his white ceiling, all he could think about was stepping out onstage as Dominic, not Domino.

And that filled him with terror.

His heart pounded against his rib cage and he kept coming back to that vision of everyone discovering that Domino wasn't a rock god at all but a nerd under all that leather and makeup. Ray might think he was the best guitarist, but that couldn't be right.

Except Ray didn't lie about shit like that.

Dom buried his head under the pillow, and fought against the throbbing in his head and the bitter taste in his mouth.

He'd remained in bed far past when he should have gotten up to sneak out as Domino as he tried to talk his panicked mind out of the spinning and spinning it'd gotten itself into. Except that wasn't really working too well this morning. His brain wouldn't shut up.

So he'd thrown all of Domino's things in a duffel and slinked into the studio about a half hour late. He waited for Ray to give him crap, but his best friend's eyes only widened as he slumped down into his seat.

Zavier, as usual, said nothing, but very loudly.

"Hon, are you all right?" Mish took the duffel from his shoulder and pulled him into her arms.

Damn it, he was not going to cry, he was not going to— and then he was, weeping into Mish's shoulder.

She crooned at him. "It's okay, sweetheart."

"It's a panic attack," he murmured. "Just a panic attack. I need..." Air. He took a breath and let Mish guide him to a chair. His panic wormed its way through his body, setting his heart on triple time, shaking his hands.

Fuck, he needed this to stop. It had been a while, and there was no reason for it. None.

Except being caught between Domino and Dominic and needing to be both people at the same time. Wanting to bring Adrian into this side of his life, but being too terrified to do it.

A moment later, Ray crouched at his feet, a bottle of water in his hand, which he offered to Dom. "Hey, there's no one here who doesn't love you."

Dom hiccupped a laugh, the tears dried-up but his body still shaking and hot-cold. "I know. It's—nothing."

Ray sat on the floor and Dom met his gaze. "Dom, we've known each other since we were fourteen. This ain't nothing."

Rather than reply, Dom cracked open the water bottle and

drank. Mish was at his back, Ray at his front. That left one other bandmate. "Zav, where are you?"

"Here." He was over on Dom's left, leaning against a nearby table that held more water and some snacks. "Didn't know what help I could be."

"I used to get panic attacks before concerts, when we started playing live. Even when I was dressed as Domino, I'd need about an hour to get myself into a good enough space to step out onstage. I was always worried someone would find me out and realize I wasn't the rocker people thought." Not the kick-ass guitarist.

Zavier pushed off the table. "You're an incredibly talented musician, Dom." He came and stood near Ray. "And I don't say that lightly."

No, he didn't. Zavier was honest almost to a fault when it came to music and whether something worked and sounded good. He'd even call Ray out if songs weren't coming together right.

"I know. It's...not a lack of confidence."

"It's a change in your life," Ray said, almost to himself.

Zavier looked thoughtful.

"That boy toy of yours giving you trouble?" Mish rubbed Dom's shoulders, and man, that felt good.

He took another draw of water. "Just the opposite." He paused. "And he's like...nine years older? Not exactly a boy toy."

Ray's eyebrows shot up. "So it's serious?"

Zavier huffed. "It's been serious since day one, I think."

Interesting how embarrassment could pull him out of panic. This was the kind of stuff he knew, was used to. Loved about his bandmates. He pinched the bridge of his nose. "Look, I'm feeling better. Maybe we should practice?"

"Have you told him?" Zavier's question rammed a spike of terror right back into Dom's soul. He struggled to shrug it off, blinking a few times.

"Zav!" Ray looked up at his husband, then back to Dom. "Tell him what?"

"About the band," Dom said.

That got him a look of confusion. Then Ray kicked his foot and his voice pitched high. "You *still* haven't told him about the band?"

"I—No. I mean, if it turned out to be a fling, I didn't want him to run off and tell anyone."

Mish patted his shoulders again. "He that kinda guy?"

"No."

Zavier shifted, and Dom looked up at him. "I suspect even if you parted ways, he'd keep your secrets, Dom." The way Zavier said that made Ray look up again.

Oh yeah, Ray was gonna put two and two together and figure out what Dom had already figured out about him and Zav—there was more going on than just sex. There was submission and domination and giving yourself over to someone you needed to care for you.

And for Dom, at least, there was bone-deep love, too.

Zavier was right, though. "Yeah, I know he would. And yeah, I know I need to tell him. It's just—" Dom waved his hand. "Old fears."

That he wasn't good enough. That he'd never be good enough. He could hide that from the others by being Domino, but he could never hide from himself.

Zavier held his gaze. "Tell him, Dom. Trust is an important thing."

Ray's cheeks reddened. "Oh shit. You—" He caught himself. "We probably should get to practicing."

Mish sighed. "You boys and the secrets you think you're keeping."

Zavier laughed and helped Ray up.

Dom didn't bother with changing into Domino's clothes. Didn't need to, actually. He picked up his guitar and within fifteen minutes was lost in the throes of one of their new songs. Here, with the band, in the studio, he could be that blend of Domino and Dominic he longed to be everywhere.

But the terror still haunted in his mind, even if he knew much of it was unfounded.

During their next break, he texted Adrian.

> Dinner Friday?

> Of course! Would you mind a night out on the town?

> Chance to see you in a suit and for you to embarrass me? Never.

He could almost hear the laughter in Adrian's reply.

> Babe, I live for those moments.

So did he. This Friday, then. He'd tell Adrian this Friday, because Ray and Zavier were right. He needed to tell Adrian. Needed to trust. Then they could go have dinner and share dessert and maybe the future, too. Looking forward to it.

After practice, he slipped into Domino, makeup and all, and strode out of the studio. Tonight they had a radio interview, then a dinner in the city. Time to see and be seen.

ON THURSDAY AT THE GYM, JACKSON MADE A QUIP ABOUT THE bruise on Adrian's shoulder. It was pretty damn obvious. A result of a rather passionate but quick encounter with Dominic the previous evening.

"You've got yourself a biter."

Yes, he did. Not always, but Dominic had practically climbed his body as soon as he'd walked into Adrian's house.

He turned his back and showed Jackson the scratches there, then threw a grin over his shoulder.

His friend laughed. "Oh man, Adi, I haven't seen you looking like that in ages."

Not since he and Jackson had last fucked—and that had been quite a while. "He's quite something," Adrian said.

That got him a nod. "Don't let it go to your head, but this relationship shit looks good on you."

Adrian snorted and pulled on a tank top, covering up his back.

"I'm serious, man. This is the happiest I've seen you." No quips, no sly grin. No, this was Jackson being honest.

Heat raced to Adrian's cheeks. "Thanks. I—yeah, it's been real good."

Heartbreakingly good. Sensual, loving, hot, too. Last night, Dominic had shown up unexpectedly on his porch, freshly showered but so full of energy and need he'd practically burst through the door and into Adrian's arms. They hadn't even made it up to the bedroom—clothes had come off in the hallway, been scattered everywhere, and they'd bitten and scrabbled at each other until he'd lifted and carried the moaning, begging Dominic into the living room and fucked him hard and fast on the rug in front of the couch. Dominic had clawed and scratched and urged him on.

It had been fast, messy, and perfect.

"Is he the one?" There was something in Jackson's voice that Adrian, in all the years they'd been friends, hadn't heard before. It was both warm and sad.

He hip-checked Jackson, wanting the sadness to vanish and not wanting to answer his question. "Come on, Jack. Do your worst with me this morning."

Jackson chuckled. "Fine, Irish boy. Let's go run."

And they did, at a pace that was just a tad too fast to be comfortable for Adrian, as if Jackson was punishing him for not replying. When they finished, he was winded, and even Jackson looked a little tired.

Miracle of miracles. Adrian piled his hands on top of his head as they walked some cool-down laps. "I don't believe that there's one singular person who is an utter match or soul mate or whatever."

Jackson glanced at him. "That's cold."

Adrian lowered his arms, his breathing ticking down closer to normal. "Is it? I mean, under that theory, if you miss your chance, then you're shit out of luck."

This time, the gaze was more thoughtful. "Okay, there is that."

Silence for another lap.

"Dominic pushes pretty much all of my buttons, and hard. Intellectual. Sexual." Adrian shrugged. "If you're asking if this is serious... I think it could be."

"The man has a name!" They headed down to the weight room. "But 'could be'? Sounds like it is."

"For me." Adrian didn't want to admit, even to himself, that his heart was sitting on the line now. "But I'm not so sure for him."

"Why not?"

Because afterward, when he and Dominic had lain on the floor and caught their breath, Adrian had asked, "What brought that on?"

Dominic had huffed a laugh and bent one of his legs, eyes still closed. "Fucking awesome practice. When we play that good—"

And it had been like a switch had been thrown. Dominic opened his eyes wide and sucked in a breath, and then there'd been an awkward silence.

After a moment, Dominic had crawled to his feet and collected his clothing.

Adrian finished three reps of arm curls before answering

Jackson. "Because he doesn't trust me with the thing that's most important in his life. I've...been trying to be patient."

Jackson had him on swats next. Fucking squats. Fucking Bosu ball.

"Time to press the issue then. I would." Jackson shook his head. "Then again, what the fuck do I know about love?" He got that odd look again.

"Wait—Jack, are you seeing someone?"

Jackson's skin darkened, but his lips quirked up. "Maybe."

"Do tell!"

A shake of his head. "Not yet. If it turns to something more, I'll unload on you, but for now, it's time for your least favorite exercise."

Adrian closed his eyes and tried not to throttle his friend. If he hated the Bosu, he loathed burpees.

The rest of the talk swung toward work, and by the time they made it into the office, Jackson had updated him on his job search—he'd gone for a second interview at the company he'd been vying for. The whole thing, he said, looked promising.

That twisted Adrian's stomach, which turned even more when they'd compared notes on the glitches in the programming they'd both run into. "William," Adrian muttered.

Jackson grunted and smacked his badge against the pad to get into the office.

Adrian followed Jackson through the door. "Maybe I should talk to Russ about him." Their boss.

"Good luck with that," Jackson said, entering his cube. "You know how that'll turn out."

Yeah, he did. But what else could he do? Something had to give—they were losing time and energy to William's bad programming.

When he got to his own cube, he woke his computer up, logged in, and went to grab a cup of coffee.

When he got back, the screen on his phone had darkened, and he scrambled to check it. A text. From Dominic.

> Hey. Wanted to thank you again for last night. I know I was moody, but I really needed you.

Moody was one way of putting it. After sex and letting slip a tidbit about his mysterious band, Dominic had been on edge until Adrian had pulled him into his arms and just held him. It had taken a good ten minutes before either of them had spoken, and it had been Adrian. "Would you like something to eat?"

Dominic had pressed his forehead against Adrian's chest. "I'm sorry." It was a whisper, and it made Adrian's heart ache.

He ran his fingers through Dominic's hair—it had grown in the time they'd known each other, and there was an untamable aspect to it now. "That's not really an answer to the question of dinner."

A huff, and Dominic drew back. "I probably should eat. But I don't want to be a bother." Fear and sadness there. That internal conflict Adrian saw, but could never touch. Whatever the issue, it had Dominic in its iron grip.

So he'd drawn Dominic into a sweet kiss, then whispered against those lips, "You're never a bother."

And that was true. Dominic was tangled and entwined into Adrian's life now, and it hurt that he wouldn't share with Adrian the passion that mattered. But he was never a bother.

He texted back.

> I'm glad I can be here for you, Dominic.

He wanted to add more, wanted to say "Please trust me" or "I love you." But those seemed too pushy, too much for a text. So he set the phone down and started working through his inbox.

Dominic had said the words, an answer to his own whisper. Adrian had thought Dominic hadn't heard. But where he knew his own feelings, Dominic's had been voiced after being tied up for the first time, an emotional and overloading situation. The last thing Adrian wanted to do was take advantage of something Dominic might not have meant. He needed to hear those words when Dominic was clear-headed.

There weren't any more texts after that one, and Adrian pushed aside the worry about that. They'd had a pleasant dinner last night, and reaffirmed their date for Friday.

Besides, he really needed to focus on why he'd been copied on this chain of emails. The problem they were discussing wasn't in any of the features he was responsible for. He let out a frustrated sigh, scrolled to the bottom of the email chain, and started reading up. About halfway through it, he sat up straight, his blood boiling.

William had inserted code for one of the modules Adrian had developed for an entirely different project smack into the middle of this one with barely any changes.

Oh hell *no*. He was not being blamed for this fuckup. And he certainly wasn't going to clean up William's mess this time. He was all for reusing code, but this was ridiculous. You didn't just drop one function into another project without so much as *testing* the damn thing.

A glance told him Russ had been copied on the mail. Good. He rose and strode to his boss's office—and found William sitting on one end of it, in conversation with Russ.

Well, *fuck*. Adrian schooled his features and knocked gently on the frame. "Hey, Russ, when you get a moment, can I speak with you?"

Russ's smile was one of those managerial ones. Pleasant, but without honest emotion and warmth behind it. "Sure. I'll stop by."

"Nah." William stood. "I should get back to things." He pushed something that looked suspiciously like tickets to a Yankees game closer to Russ, then turned. "He's all yours, Adrian."

In contrast, William's grin was infused with feeling, but all the wrong ones. Spite. Malice. He slipped past Adrian without touching him.

Yeah, this was not going to go how he'd planned. Not with a buttered-up boss. Shit.

Russ gestured at his guest chair, and Adrian took it. "So, what's up?" Russ folded his hands in front of him.

Adrian chose straightforward. "Did you get a chance to read this morning's email from the Brada team yet?"

Russ nodded. "Looks like you have your work cut out for you."

"But it's not my code and I haven't been working on that system. I'm...not sure how I'm supposed to fix this for them." He paused. "Not when I'm also cleaning up code issues in our own products."

"William said you were struggling."

Adrian's head felt like it might explode, the rage so sudden, it momentarily stole his breath. He wrestled it back under control. "I'm not struggling. Not with my own code. Not with my developer responsibilities." He took another breath. "In fact, quite a lot of my work lately has been cleaning up William's coding changes. He broke bits and pieces of critical infrastructure."

Russ waved his hand. "He was improving speed and tightening the code. It was bound to expose weaknesses..."

There hadn't been any weaknesses. And no need for a rewrite. Adrian swallowed.

Russ leaned forward. "Look, Adrian, I know the customers love you. And your work on your trip was invaluable. But since you've been back, your quality's slipping. I don't think William should be picking up your slack."

"...picking up..." Adrian straightened. "How are the issues with Brada *my* slack? I'm not on that team."

Russ shrugged. "You are now. Run with it."

Fucking hell. Adrian stared at Russ.

"Anything else?"

"No," Adrian snapped, and rose. "Thanks for having my back, Russ."

Another fake smile, and Adrian was out the door. Shit fucking *hell*. He contemplated marching to William's cube and strangling the asshole—but murder would only complicate his life.

When he got back to his cube, he fired off an IM to Jackson.

> Guess who's putting out fires on Brada now?

> Ah hell, man. That joker do you, too?

Didn't have to ask who Jackson meant.

> Affirmative.

> Beers? 6 PM?

> Yes, please.

Would ruin the workout, but so did stress. Adrian ran a hand over his face and checked his phone. Another text from Dominic.

> I really appreciate it. You're the best, Adrian.

He stared at the text, then set his phone aside, the tangle in his stomach pulling tighter and burning deeper.

Because he didn't quite believe what Dominic had said. Felt more like placation than actual affection. Or his fucking job, his *well enough* job, was getting to him. Either or. Probably the job. God, he should take on some freelance job to have an outlet, but he had no *time* right now.

Beer tonight with Jackson sounded fantastic, though. He really needed to get his head screwed on better.

CHAPTER
FIFTEEN

AFTER A FRIDAY MORNING OF PUTTING OUT METAPHORICAL FIRES for very real customers, Adrian itched to get the hell out of the office for lunch. Seemed everyone had the same idea, because most of the cubes he passed were empty, their occupants already having fled into a summer day that wasn't hellishly hot for a change.

The weekend was nearly here, thank god. His work with the Brada team had been grueling and infuriating. The code was a disaster, and he'd worked late the previous night, even coming back to the office after snagging a beer with Jackson to get on top of it.

Today? He was gonna slack a little today.

He grabbed some kebabs from a nearby cart and ate while wandering up into Tribeca. While he preferred meandering through independent bookstores, he ended up in one of the big corporate types, along with a mix of tourists, students, and people who worked in the area. The new releases didn't hold too much interest, but the magazines caught his eye. Sometimes they had good literature journals. And maybe there was some kind of history magazine he could buy for Dominic.

Worth a look.

Of course, they lumped all the arts together on the bottom shelves, so he ended up on his knees, sorting through some popular movie and music magazines to find what he was wanted. He picked out a few poetry journals and found a magazine on archeology. Perfect.

Right before he rose, a swirl of color half-hidden behind some drumming magazine caught his attention. It was a tattooed arm, so like Dominic's he nearly dropped the magazines in his hand. But it couldn't be.

Except...the more Adrian stared, the more he realized the tattoo wasn't similar.

It *was* Dominic's arm, down to the knot-work on that shoulder. Had to be. Adrian knew every line and curve. Had traced them all with finger and tongue. He fished the magazine—one on rock music—out, and a band stared back at him.

Twisted Wishes. A group photo of the four members of the band, all of them in various poses.

And there were Dominic's tattoos on a guy who didn't look like the sweet, bookish man he talked about poetry with and took to museums and art galleries. Nor the man he'd fed cake and pie and ice cream. This man was shirtless and in leather pants. His dark eyes were surrounded by makeup, and that smirk was crimson red. But the designs on his skin—those were inked into the man Adrian fucked and loved and bound. The man who kept secrets and had fear in those same dark eyes when Adrian dug a little too deep.

Adrian's heart tumbled over and over and over. This was the answer, what he'd been waiting for Dominic to tell him, except now he *knew*.

He'd been dating a fucking *rock star* all this time and hadn't known it. Been ignorant and foolish.

Something like anger zinged through him, and then embarrassment. He didn't keep up with the music scene, hadn't in years, and Dominic had walked in and taken every advantage of that.

Adrian gathered the magazines he'd collected, plus the one with Dominic on the cover, and took them to the counter to pay. On the walk back to his office, numbness set in. Why hadn't Dominic told him? That tumbled around in his head, along with an image of Dominic from that rare moment the Sunday after their trip to the Met. Dom with his acoustic guitar, playing it inches from Adrian, after having tangled in the sheets. The gentle, beautiful sound, and that poised edge he'd had, eyes hooded, fingers moving like magic over the strings. The calm, centered look he'd had, the one that had melted into both joy and sadness when he'd smiled at Adrian.

There was more to this than deception. There *had* to be.

On the way back to his cube, he passed Jackson's, then backed up. "Hey, Jack?"

His friend started, hands poised on the keyboard. "Yeah? What's up?" His eyes were a little wider than normal, and there was a darker spot just under his collar—a bruise that hadn't been there this morning.

"You, uh, have a good lunch?"

A smile broke out that Adrian hadn't ever seen on Jackson before—at least not as wide and as sappy as this one. "Yeah. I did."

"Anyone special?"

Jackson laughed. "You know, I finally checked out that place you and everyone's been bugging me to try a couple of weeks ago. You were right."

"Good jazz?"

"Great jazz. And a very fine gentleman who is tired of the club scene, as well. And yes, same man from earlier, and yes, it's serious." Jackson's grin was brilliant.

"How about that." So, his best friend had finally found a guy worth seeing more than once. About time. Adrian chuckled, but it mixed with the jolt of pain in his stomach over the man he'd found. "I'm glad for you."

"You didn't just stop by to ask me about my hickey, Adi. What's up?"

"I wanted to ask you about a band—I figure you know music better than I do." He gestured to Jackson's phone. It wasn't on now, but half the time Jackson would be nodding along to some song or another. And his tastes went all across the board. Classical. R&B. Pop. Swing. Country. Rap. You named it, he'd probably listened to it—and had an opinion, one based on knowledge and taste.

Jackson swiveled in his chair. "Hit me up. Which band?"

"Twisted Wishes."

"Oh, them. Fuck, they're good. A little strange in places, like they can never decide if they want to be alternative or heavy metal or pop or punk, but man, really doesn't matter." Jackson scratched his chin, exposing more of his love bite. "They were in the news a ton recently. Sued their label to get out of their contract—and there was a whole police thing, too. Apparently their manager put the lead singer in the hospital with anaphylaxis by drugging him."

"Holy shit." Adrian gripped the side of the cube wall. This was in Dominic's past?

"Anyway, they signed with a new label and are supposed to be working on a new album right here in New York. There's been photos of them out on the town and everyone's trying to get into the studio where they're at."

Adrian nodded. A new album jived with Dominic talking about practices with his band. But why the subterfuge? Why not tell Adrian about this?

"What's your interest? I mean, they're an extraordinarily queer band, but you don't do rock, at least not anything from the last decade or two. You're not gonna be hearing Twisted Wishes at the clubs."

"Wait, what? Queer?"

Jackson stared at him, eyes a little wider. "You don't know anything about them, do you?" Adrian might as well have asked Jackson to program in COBOL or something—complete shock and disbelief were all over his face. Though, knowing Jack, give him a fifteen-minute primer on COBOL, and he'd be able to program in the language. Still.

Adrian knew he was blushing. Felt the heat of it. "No. I might have heard some songs in passing if they're that popular, but..." He leaned against the cube frame. "Do you mean queer as in..." He waved his hand between the two of them. That would also jive with Dominic.

"Yes, exactly. Their lead singer has been openly gay since day one, and he up and married their drummer. That dude's pansexual, according to the interviews. Everyone thinks the bass player is bi, since she's been seen with men and women. No one really knows anything about Domino, but I'm betting he's gay, too."

Felt like spiders were walking up his spine. "Who's Domino?" The words were out of his mouth even as he knew the answer.

"The guitarist. He's wicked talented—I mean, they all are, Adi—but Domino plays like he could rule the world. Dresses like he wants to give everyone the finger."

Dominic. His lovely bookish man. Not at all the image in his mind. Though...there'd always been that spark, that steel behind the shyness and blushing. And that meshed with the cover of the magazine.

"Why're you asking, anyway? Though, to be honest, you might like them."

Adrian's mind whirled, trying to slot in what he was learning with his reality. His limbs felt like lead. "I saw them on the cover of a magazine and they caught my eye." He shook his head. "I was looking for poetry." For Dominic. Only to find the man he knew was not the man he knew at all.

"Well, they are all beautiful people, yeah. But you ought to listen to their lyrics, given your interests. Ray Van Zeller writes some stunning words. And the music." Jackson let out a satisfied sigh. "I like 'em." He glanced as his smartphone. "Give 'em a shot."

"Yeah, I might." Adrian patted the cube wall. "Thanks."

"Hey, no problem."

He headed back to his own cube, dropped the bag of magazines on his desk, and sat down. Dominic had planned to come over tonight. A late dinner out, which also meant passionate sex and sleeping in with Dominic next to him— one of his very favorite things. But now? He rubbed his face as his stomach knotted. How was he going to do this?

Yes, secrets. But this—he looked at where the magazines lay in their plastic shopping bag—wasn't a secret. Dominic was a fucking well-known, gossiped-about rock star.

The rest of the day was pretty much a wash. He struggled to get his damn code to compile until he realized William had been mucking around in his lines again. Every time that man tried to "fix" a bug, he introduced six more. And now he was creeping around in two of Adrian's projects, one of which Adrian didn't even want.

It was fucking hell.

All the time, that cover photo of Twisted Wishes—and of Dominic—sat in the bag on his desk, taunting him, daring him to look to see what he didn't know and everyone else did. Finally, after yet another attempt to fix his damn code, he fired off an email to William, copied their boss, and sat back hard against his chair, rocking it in frustration. Any other day, he could probably untangle the mess William had made, but his own head was tattered and shredded.

He reached over and slid out the rock magazine, and there was his Dominic again, except not his Dominic at all. Leather and makeup and a freaking studded collar.

And he'd been so amazed when Adrian had wrapped leather around his wrists. Tied him down. Had that been a lie? Acting innocent to get what he wanted? Moisture pricked at Adrian's eyes again, along with a fury that stoked up a headache.

None of this made any sense!

He took a breath, then another, and pushed his emotions aside—as much as he could—and studied the other band members. Jackson had been right. They were all beautiful in their own way.

Their names were inscribed under their photos. Ray Van Zeller, dark blond hair with wide golden eyes, ripped blue jeans and a tank top that could easily be stripped off. He looked like he might walk right through the page into the room. Behind him must have been Ray's drummer husband, given the sticks in his hands. He, like Dominic, was covered in ink. Brown leather pants, no shirt. Muscular arms, black hair, and eyes that couldn't possibly be that blue. Zavier Demos.

Why did that name sound familiar? Looked a little familiar, too. Adrian shook his head, and turned his attention past Dominic to Mish, the red-haired woman on the far right. She stood taller than the guys and wore tight jeans and a top that clung to her perfectly. She had a smile that tingled Adrian's nerves, as if she could stare through the page and read his mind. God, the *presence* in that look.

At last, he came back to Dominic. The name read *Domino Grinder* and Adrian swallowed a chuckle. It sounded—well—made up. Which, obviously, it had been.

They all wore makeup to some degree, though Domino's was so much more evident than any of his bandmates. In this photo, he had black lips, and eyeliner, starkly different from the cover of the magazine. The eye shadow was gold and his hair had been spiked and teased up, rather than the soft feathery mess Adrian was used to.

No bowties. No button-downs.

Same eyes, though. Dark and strong. And that smirk—

he'd seen *that* a few dozen times. He touched Dominic's face on the magazine, then flipped it open to find the article.

The text swam in his vision. Right, so he wasn't going to be able to read it. Not yet. The photos, though, he could look at. Most were studio shots, obviously staged, and they all looked perfect and utterly untouchable. Still, there was something about Dominic that was fierce and full of energy, despite the white backdrop.

There were also some shots from concerts, and those Adrian stared at. Because they were real and visceral and he could almost feel, hear, and taste the crowd, the music.

And he wouldn't have known a Twisted Wishes song if it hit him in the head.

In the heat of the concert, they all looked magnificent. Drenched in sweat, but so full of passion and life that, either by movement or a trick of the camera, they were streaked at the edges.

There was Dominic in the center of it all, flesh and leather and metal, with a flame-red guitar, makeup still perfect despite the dots of perspiration on his face. His fingers were blurred on the guitar strings, and he looked like he'd been caught in a moment of dancing.

Despite the outfit and the hair and how different he looked at first glance, Adrian would have known that look of sheer bliss anywhere. Same grin he'd seen at the museum when playing that old instrument. Same blissed-out expression Adrian had seen in his bed—only ramped up about one thousand percent.

The utter joy and passion and fire. He'd seen those, too.

Adrian shivered, then closed the magazine. Here was Dominic's secret life, the one he hadn't been willing to share, not with the man he'd been sharing everything else with.

The hollow feeling in Adrian's gut turned to burning. He hadn't asked for every piece of Dominic. That would have been unfair and toxic. But this side—this Dominic had shared with the world. His utter passion, his life's work. And he'd kept it from Adrian, like a dirty, scandalous secret.

Or, a horrible voice whispered in the back of his mind, *maybe you're the secret he keeps from the world.* Adrian swallowed against that thought.

Well, one way or another, tonight the truth would come out.

He set the magazine aside again, and tried desperately to lose himself in coding.

FRIDAY ROCKED, LITERALLY. THE BAND WAS A FEW WEEKS AWAY from their concert and working up the set list, discussing which songs, new and old, they'd play. There were a couple different options, and they worked through a few combos to see how songs sounded, how they could transition and blend into the new ones.

Felt so fucking right, for all of them. Ray pranced around the studio, and Mish was a ball of energy. Even Zavier—often a rock—was full of grins and playfulness. He'd even drawn Ray close and whispered something into his ear before kissing him. A rare display of affection for Zavier, and one that seemed to push Ray even higher in energy levels.

When they played, the room filled with sound, vibrating through Dom, setting his soul right.

To add to all of that...tonight he'd tell Adrian about Twisted Wishes, about Domino, and he'd ask Adrian to come to a practice and maybe be there at the concert to watch Dom play. To be a part of this life, too—one that was public for everyone else, but secret to Adrian.

He'd worked hard to keep the resolve to open up to Adrian tonight, despite the fear and the voice in the back of his head telling him how foolish the idea was. Talking to Mish, Zavier, and Ray at their practices helped, too, even if he had fucked up on Wednesday. He could have said something then, but he hadn't been ready yet.

He was now. He hoped.

Yeah, they'd have to talk about how Dom kept the life Adrian knew out of the public eye, but like Zavier had implied, Dom could trust Adrian.

Had, and with more than his heart. Those times on his knees or tied up—Adrian never ever took advantage. Had always sought consent. Never pressured for *anything*, not even when Dom screwed up and said something about the band. Asked, sure. But never insisted.

His demands were always in what Dom realized were scenes—those moments when they both acted out roles for each other's pleasure and need. When Dom submitted and Adrian took control.

But they also existed outside that dynamic, too. Friends and lovers. Reading partners. Museum hoppers. Boyfriends.

He really hoped Adrian would be okay with dating someone whose public persona was nearly always in the limelight.

The hope was there, buoyed by Zavier's smile and his clap on the back, and Mish's and Ray's hugs.

"Hey," Ray said. "You know you can call me anytime with anything, right? Just like always."

Dom patted his best friend's—his near-brother's—cheek. "Yeah. I know, I just hate talking to you about the sex stuff."

Ray made a face. "Ditto."

They both laughed. As close as they were, there were a few lines they didn't cross.

Dom headed back to his place first, to shower and change into something a little nicer. Classy pastel-red button-down, paired with a blue jewel-tone bowtie. Tan slacks rather than jeans, and a pair of brick-red dress shoes he'd spotted the other day. They matched his shirt nicely. He picked out a bottle of wine from his collection—something to drink later in the weekend, for when they ate in.

He fucking loved when Adrian cooked for them.

During the walk to Adrian's, his heart was in his throat and his mind spun. He so wanted this to go well. He needed this to go well.

Ten minutes later, he climbed the steps and rang the bell.

As soon as Adrian answered the door, Dom knew something was horribly wrong. Yes, Adrian was dressed in one of his nicer dress shirts, sans tie, and his finer suit pants, but there was a remoteness that had never been in his expression before, not in all the weeks Dom had known Adrian. His gaze held no warmth, and his expression was masklike rather than full of joy and laughter. It was as if a wall had been built between them since Wednesday night, the last time they'd seen each other in person.

But there had been nothing remote in Adrian's voice last night on the phone. He'd been dirty and wonderful, whispering wicked thing until Dom had spilled himself all over his chest, then sweet and gentle when they'd finished their goodnights.

"Hello, Dominic." Cool words. No smile.

Oh shit. This was *bad*. Dom had no idea what it was, but something awful had happened. Or was about to. He replayed all their recent interactions, but aside from Wednesday, when he'd deflected conversation about the band, he came up empty. That couldn't be it, could it?

"Hey." Dom gripped the bag with the bottle of wine he'd brought. "Can I come in?"

Adrian nodded, and stepped away from the door. No hug, no kiss. He just—walked down the hall.

Dom's heart thudded against his ribs. So so *so* not good. Fear bit in hard. This—this was the motions of a breakup. Oh god. He closed the front door and latched it, then made his way to the living room. Adrian stood by one of the chairs, his hand resting on the cushioned back. He stared at Dom, sad eyes roaming over him for a moment before they focused on the coffee table.

Dom followed his gaze and recognized the magazine that lay there. His stomach lurched and the bag slipped from his hand, the wine bottle hitting the rug with a thunk. Everything in Dom's vision tunneled down to that cover.

Twisted Wishes. Domino. Adrian knew. He *knew*.

He'd found out before Dom had had a chance to tell him. Explain things. Ask for him to keep Dom's secret. Who knew who Adrian had told? Had he? *Fuck.* The press would have a field day. Be on his doorstep.

Oh god, he was gonna puke. Or have a heart attack. His chest heaved and it took every effort to rip his focus from the magazine to meet Adrian's eyes.

"So." Adrian spoke coolly and calmly, as one might talk to a stranger. "Who are you really?"

Shit. Dom really *was* going to throw up. He pressed a hand over his mouth and swallowed a bunch of times, trying to quell his stomach and heart. When the awful acid taste lessened, he lowered it and answered. "I'm who I said I was." Because that was the truth, too. "I'm Dominic Bradley."

"And yet..." Adrian nodded at the coffee table.

Yeah. "I'm him, too. Domino Grinder." The name sounded harsh and wrong in the mess Dom's voice had become.

Fire and itching crept along his skin, and he fought against the growing panic. But this was worse than he'd been in the studio. This wasn't unfounded fears—this was *real*.

Silence stretched between them for a very long time, and little cracks and fissures formed in Adrian's expression. The wavering stance, the way his lips quivered when he took a breath. Worst, though, was the hissing pain when he whispered, "Were you ever going to tell me? Or wasn't I good enough to trust?"

The irony struck Dom like a knife to the side. "Tonight."

He should have been crying, but no tears came, just that over-whelming sense of dread and fear. It built and built, cracking his bones and dissolving his organs. He blinked a few times and everything turned *wrong*. "That was the plan." He shook his head. "I'm so sorry. I should have said something sooner, but..."

God, he needed to hold it together. He hadn't wanted to be rejected by Adrian, and he'd needed to find a way to exist as both Dominic and Domino, which he still hadn't. Then he'd fallen in love. So foolish he'd been to wait. Trust went both ways, didn't it?

Or had it been completely reckless to believe he could have two lives he loved at the same time?

Maybe he could live without love. His heart wrenched in his chest and his lungs tried to flay themselves.

"But you didn't. You didn't say anything at all. Kept pushing me away." The tears that should have been in Dom's eyes were collecting in Adrian's. "I waited and waited, Dominic. How could you..." His voice shredded and broke.

Dom picked up the paper bag with the bottle of wine and set it on the coffee table, next to the magazine. "I don't get the chance to be me—really me—very often." Finally, the tears he felt pricked at his eyes. "I was just enjoying the time..."

It was then the whole realization caught up and his breath gave out. He was losing this. Losing Adrian. Losing a part of himself—because he could never go back to being Dominic, not like this.

And there was nothing keeping Adrian from telling anyone who he really was. He shook his head as his lungs squeezed shut and his pulse hammered up, a staccato beat that was too fast and too broken. "Fuck, Adrian. Please don't tell..."

If the public knew, then there'd be *nothing* left of Dominic anymore. Only Domino. Except, Domino? He wouldn't exist, either. No one would believe his nerdy ass was a tough-as-nails, sexy, flippant rocker.

Where would that leave the band? Or him? Who would he be without Twisted Wishes?

Fuck, everything was *done*. Over. His legs shook and melted, and his vision tunneled as blackness closed in and the coffee table suddenly became a lot closer than it should have been.

Strong arms wrapped around him and hauled him away from the table and he fell backward. When he could catch air a little again, he was sitting on the floor and was wrapped in Adrian's arms, but everything hurt, his pulse was sky-high, and his chest felt like it would seize up any minute.

He was going to pass out. Maybe that would be better. Yeah. Shit. Couldn't even do that right. His gut tried to rebel.

"Dominic, breathe." Adrian's strong voice. "Breathe."

He couldn't. Not now. Not ever. Oh god, what would he tell Ray? There should have been more tears, but he couldn't stop trembling.

This time, Adrian's voice cracked. "Babe, *please*. One deep breath. For me."

The distress in those words. *Babe*. Well, he could try. Dom sucked in a breath and exhaled.

"Can you do another?"

He could. And another and another. His vision cleared and the tightness in his chest loosened. Still ached all over, and his heart still threatened to burst from his chest.

"I'm sorry." Sorry he'd sat in that bar. Sorry he loved Adrian so much. Sorry he hadn't said anything sooner. Hadn't opened up and shared like Adrian had.

Fuck, Adrian's family had *abandoned* him. And now what the hell was Dom doing? Didn't even know. Nothing made sense in the jumbled mess of his head.

"It's okay. It's gonna be okay." Slowly, Adrian unwrapped himself from Dom.

Didn't feel right to be alone, though. He didn't want to be alone anymore. Dom closed his eyes.

Warm fingers brushed his cheeks. "Would you like a blanket? Water?"

Why was Adrian being so damn *nice*? Dom nodded because both of those sounded reasonable. And a quiet part of his mind whispered that he needed comfort. A safe place to recover.

He heard Adrian withdraw, and blinked open his eyes to stare at the rug.

Yeah, things were getting better. Shit. He hadn't had a panic attack this bad since high school. Oh wow. Still—his cover was blown. What the hell was he supposed to do now? What had Adrian done?

Adrian returned with a thick, soft fleece throw and draped it over Dom's shoulders. "Ice or no?"

Dom pulled the blanket tight around him, securing the world a little more. He'd always liked to be wrapped up. Covered. Bound.

Huh.

Strange what you realized sometimes when your mind was going in circles really fast. "Um. Can I have tea, maybe? Herbal or decaf or something." He looked up and met Adrian's gaze. "If that's okay?"

"Babe, I'll get you anything you need."

That didn't make sense. "I *lied* to you, Adrian."

A pinched expression crossed Adrian's face. "You didn't, actually. But let's shelve that conversation for a little while?"

Because Dom was sitting tightly wrapped in a blanket after nearly passing out, after wanting to throw up his heart and lungs and stomach onto the rug. That made sense.

He exhaled. "Fuck," he whispered, and pulled the fleece up over his head. "Shit."

"I'll make you something. Hang on." Adrian padded away, his footsteps light against the rug, then wood.

Dom didn't know which was worse, being in the middle of panicking, when he couldn't breathe and thought he might explode, or the trembling afterward when the shame and self-flagellation kicked in. Should probably find a counselor or someone, 'cause his coping mechanisms were like fifteen years out of date and he felt like a goddamned fool breaking apart like that.

Fucking tears finally came, and he was shaking and weeping by the time Adrian returned with a mug that smelled of mint and honey. He sat right down on the floor next to Dom.

"Hey, babe. Here you go."

The mug warmed his hand when he claimed it from Adrian, and a sip warmed his mouth and throat. Another loosened the knot in his chest a little. "I'm a mess."

"No. You're human."

Silence settled between them as Dom drank and blinked and let the tears dry up. Finally, he held the mug and asked the question he'd been dreading. "Who did you tell? About me being Domino?"

Adrian fiddled with the toe of his sock and raised both eyebrows. "No one. I didn't tell anyone."

A little chunk of panic fell away, to be replaced by a small pebble of shame. "Oh."

Adrian was still pulling at the material at his toes, bunching and twisting it. "It's not my secret to tell and—" His voiced dropped, and he nearly pulled the sock off his foot. "I shouldn't have gotten upset like that."

Dom rotated the mug in his hand. "Once I'm more coherent, I'll go."

Adrian stilled. "You don't have to."

Except he'd lied. He'd hidden who he was. "I broke your trust." There wasn't any coming back from that. He turned the mug in his hand again and sipped. "I—probably should have said no that first night." Kept apart. Enjoyed his solitude. Gone for a simple fuck with someone, rather than this complicated, perfect, wonderful, beautiful thing he'd completely fucked up.

A grunt from Adrian and an audible swallow, as if he were trying to keep something in. "Babe, don't. Can we—I don't want this to end. Especially not like this."

Dom hazarded raising his head. Looking at Adrian's face was nearly as painful as the thought of vanishing from his life. Because all the poise and calm Dom was so used to were gone. Yeah, the strength was still there, but so was the shattered soul of someone who loved very hard and so so *so* much.

Dom didn't deserve a moment of it, a voice in his head whispered. Another answered that maybe, maybe he did.

"Can I tell you why? Why Domino?"

A slow nod. "I'd be honored if you did."

Those words pierced and stung, but in a good way. Like the first swallow of ice water in a parched throat.

Maybe, maybe what Adrian had said was true. Maybe it would be all right.

ADRIAN RUBBED THE FABRIC OF HIS SOCKS BETWEEN HIS FINGERS and quelled his own panic. Dominic was more or less sounding like himself again. God, watching him fall, watching him struggle to breathe, to find the safety he needed...

Adrian's fault. Of *course* there'd been a reason behind Domino. The rational part of him should have guessed that, but the emotional, fragile side only felt betrayed. He'd been utterly unfair. Mean, even. Not the actions of a lover or a friend.

Dominic let the throw slip away from his head as he drank the tea. When he finished the mug, he set it down in front of himself, and lifted those beautiful eyes to stare at Adrian. "I met Ray Van Zeller in high school. He's got this brain that's full of words and music and—" Dominic shook his head. "He's wicked smart, but struggled a lot 'cause people saw a skinny kid wearing hand-me-downs who had a hard time with shit, so no one took the time to get to know him."

"You did, I bet."

Dom shrugged. "Not at first. We had a homeroom teacher who decided that rather than seating us alphabetically, to alternate. Bottom of the alphabet, then the top. So Ray ended up in front of me. Turned around and said hi. First kid *ever* to do that with nerdy me." He paused. "And I was a complete nerd, every stereotype, and I got picked on a lot. I don't even know why, but I could never dress cool. Even if I came in with the hottest T-shirt and perfect jeans, I'd get pushed around for *that*."

Kids were awful. Hell, adults were awful, but kids...they could be so damn cruel.

"But Ray? He's outgoing. Always was. Still is. You should see him onstage. He just...lives and breathes the music and the crowd and—" Dominic got this faraway look, one of deep passion and love. "He didn't care what people thought. Just was himself."

This was the piece of what Adrian had been missing. The spark in Dominic he'd seen but never quite understood. "You love him."

Dominic started, then laughed. It was a pure sound, and one that melted Adrian's heart a little, because it sounded like joy. "He's my best friend. Like a brother. So yeah, I do. But not like I—" Dominic's smile dropped away, and he looked down at the mug sitting before him.

Adrian waited and held his breath.

Slowly, Dominic looked up and locked gazes with him. "I don't love him like I love you, Adrian."

Adrian let go of his sock. "Babe." There were tears in Dominic's eyes. In his own, too.

A sad chuckle. "Not how I was supposed to tell you who I was and what I wanted."

They'd get through this. "It's okay."

"Yeah. Yeah, maybe it is." He blew out a breath. "Anyway, Ray and me? Became friends. Then he found out I could play guitar, 'cause my parents read this thing that said music was good for math and they thought I should be a scientist—" He broke off. "Fuck, I'm rambling."

Adrian resisted the urge to utter the words *it's okay* again, but it was. Fuck, it was just fine. Rambling, talkative Dominic. Who loved him.

"Anyway, he started trying to get me to play the songs in his head. And he'd write and write and write words and music in this odd shorthand he had." Dominic shook his head and laughed. "God, we were so *young* back then!"

"When did you first play music together?" Adrian absently gripped the toe of his other sock.

"Summer between freshman and sophomore years. We were fifteen and thought we were the hottest shit ever." Dominic gave a rueful laugh.

Adrian eyed the magazine. "Well, you weren't too far off the mark."

Dominic's gaze followed his, and he gestured at the coffee table. "Can I see it? I haven't read it."

Adrian grabbed the copy and handed it over. "I only flipped through the photos."

Another chuckle. "You and about a million other people." He thumbed through the copy. "Sometimes it's really surreal to see this. Like—I remember the photo shoot and the interview, but it's...far away. I mean, this one must have been months ago. We just did one, recently, too. They all kind of blend together." He touched a photograph of himself. "It feels like I'm someone else on these pages. Like it's a dream." His eyes were glassy when he looked at Adrian. "Or this, me now, is a dream. I never know which."

Oh. Understanding ripped through Adrian. Dominic was *hiding.* He was hiding both halves of himself from each other. Here was the heart of Dominic's terror and fear, that if one was the truth, the other was a lie.

He put his hand over Dominic's. "Maybe both are real."

He'd seen Dominic the musician. He'd seen the strength, the knots, and the twines that held him up, like the tattoo on his shoulder that Adrian loved so much. He fucking *knew* every part of Dominic was real.

"No. They can't be." Dominic's chuckle broke Adrian's heart. "Domino exists because when Ray asked me to get up onstage with him our sophomore year for the talent show, I spent the rest of the evening after puking and shaking and the rest of that week trying to will myself invisible. Everyone thought Ray was great and marveled at how a fucking *dork* like me could play the guitar. Didn't believe it."

Because kids *were* cruel. But Dominic was both shy and fearless. Both timid and strong. Adrian suspected all of it had been hard-won. His skills. His education. So much he didn't know about this man he could very well love forever. "So you made a persona."

Dominic nodded. "I could be *someone else* and get onstage. Someone not a dork or a nerd. A person no one would suspect was me because Dominic Bradley isn't a rock star." He paused. "Domino always knew he was one. From the moment he set foot onstage." His eyes fluttered shut and his breathing slowed. A memory, probably. Reliving the experience. "I'm Domino when I'm there."

Adrian squeezed Dominic's hand. No, he hadn't known Dominic that long. A month and a couple weeks, really. Enough to start passionately loving the man, to see the possibilities that lay down the line if things continued. He didn't know that much about Dominic's past or Twisted Wishes or any of it, but he was damn sure that Dominic and Domino weren't two different people, persona be damned. Because even in the photos, there were glimpses of the man he knew, and now he had a name for the steel and fire he saw in Dominic. The strength that lay at the base of him.

Adrian rubbed the bridge of his nose.

"You're not saying something," Dominic muttered. "What aren't you saying?"

Adrian shrugged. "I think Dominic Bradley *is* a rock star. I think he's also a scholar and incredibly intelligent. He's sexy and fun and utterly unexpected. He looks damn fine in my ropes, too." He twined Dominic's fingers in his own. "And I want to know more about him...about you. I want to know the whole you."

Dominic tossed the magazine between them, but didn't pull his hand away. "You were so mad at me for this."

That hit hard enough that Adrian flinched. "Yeah. I know. I shouldn't have been. It's—" He struggled to put his emotions into thoughts—he was a shitty poet, too. "It's your secret to tell. I knew there were aspects of your life you weren't sharing, and that was your right. I mean, I'm just a guy you met at a bar—"

"You're more than that." Dominic's voice was tight.

"Now, yes. But—no one has the right to demand everything from you. You weren't ready to tell me. And I shouldn't have gotten mad because you didn't. End of story." Even when he'd discovered Dominic's secret. After all, tonight he'd have found it all out anyway, and from the proper source. "I wish I could rewind to lunchtime and not bothered with the bookstore."

Dominic grunted. "I didn't know how to tell you earlier. Because the thing is—I don't want anyone to know. I mean, outside the band. They know."

And Adrian wasn't the band. "Is it...anxiety?"

"Kinda? That was the diagnosis way back when. My

parents dragged me to see someone after that talent show, and they wanted me to stop the whole 'band nonsense' as they called it. But I *wanted* to be in Ray's band." He laughed. "And the therapist agreed I should try. We worked on coping mechanisms and the like, and the panic attacks lessened. This was the first really bad one in years."

"Fuck, I'm sorry." Adrian shouldn't have been such a shit.

"But I should have told you. I mean, I trusted you enough to let you tie me up. After that weekend—" The throw slid off Dominic's shoulders. "I was so fucked up, because it was perfect and beautiful and you've given me so much of myself."

He turned and held out his other hand. Adrian took it.

"Fuck, Adrian. After the first time you put cuffs on me, I should have been able to tell you that I'm hiding from my big-name rock-star persona because if the world sees me like this, the twink in button-downs, I'm probably gonna pass out. And no one will ever look at Domino the same way again."

Except with the world the way it was...it would come out eventually. Secrets were hard to keep. But Adrian didn't voice that, not now. "I won't tell anyone."

Dominic nodded. "I know we were supposed to go to dinner—"

"I'll cancel the reservation."

"No," Dominic breathed out. "Maybe move it back a little? Still gotta eat and I want... I want to do something normal with you. Be your boyfriend. Be—myself."

Of course he agreed. He kissed Dominic's hand, then rose from the floor to call the restaurant. By the time he was done, Dominic was standing, too, the magazine in one hand, the blanket in the other. He stared at the cover, his brows furrowed, then tossed the blanket on the couch. "Are you gonna read this?"

"I'd like to, if that's okay."

One of Dominic's smiles cracked through all the worry

and pain. "Yeah. I think I'd like that. You're right. This is my life, too."

It was, and one Adrian desperately wanted to know more about.

Dominic handed him the magazine. "I should go piece myself back together well enough so we can eat."

The cover was slick under his fingers, and cool. Such a contrast between that and the warm, rough man before him. "My house is yours, Dominic. Always."

Dominic's eyes widened. "Do you mean that?"

"Yes. Absolutely." He opened his arms and Dominic folded into them, their cheeks brushing. "I adore you. I love you. I don't want you to hurt. You can always come here."

"Library and all?" The words were muffled into Adrian's sweater.

"Especially there." He stroked that lean back. It was glorious naked, and perfect clothed. He wondered what it looked like onstage.

Dominic pulled back, and that beautiful grin had returned. "I'm so glad you sat down next to me all those weeks ago."

"Me, too." Because that moment had changed Adrian's life. He didn't know exactly where he was headed, but he was excited to find out.

CHAPTER
SIXTEEN

Dom's body ached as he climbed the steps up to Adrian's master bathroom. He took off his shirt and bowtie before washing and drying his face. What he really wanted was a nice long shower that he could hide in, cry in, and come out feeling drenched and purified.

But he'd asked Adrian not to cancel the reservation, and honestly, he didn't know if a shower would even help at this point. Parts of him were flayed, cut open wide by his own actions. He shoved the desire to dwell, to replay the whole set of events over and over, to grasp onto the hurt he'd seen in Adrian and roll in that forever.

He leaned his palms against the edge of the marble countertop. Fucking hard not to. When he examined himself in the mirror, his eyes were still red. "You're such a fuckup," he whispered at himself. "You're not really good at anything, are you? Not music, not love."

"Babe." A soft reply from the doorway.

Dom dropped his head and groaned. "You weren't supposed to hear that." No one was. He only ever took himself down in private.

Adrian huffed. "Would you come here, please?" He stood

just outside the doorway of the bathroom, before turning to retreat to the bed.

Despite the hollowness in his gut—or maybe because of it—Dom went out to see what Adrian was doing. By the bench that sometimes lived at the foot of the bed, Adrian turned, met Dom's gaze and—sat.

Just sat down. On the bench. As if he was waiting for something.

Dom was halfway across the room before he realized it, and by Adrian's side when it occurred to him what Adrian was offering and what he—Dom—was doing. What he needed. He fell to his knees, and pressed his head against Adrian's thigh.

Felt right. Even more so when Adrian stroked fingers through his hair. Dom wrapped his arms around Adrian and held on, finding that center in Adrian's calm, and remembering where it was in himself.

He didn't know how long they sat like that, with Adrian stroking his hair, only that it was Adrian who spoke first.

"Dominic," he said in that voice that made Dom both melt and tremble. "I'd like you to listen to me now, because this is important."

Dom raised his head and met Adrian's warm, strong, gaze. The one that commanded. "Okay."

Adrian brushed fingers over his jaw. "Usually, when I demand something of you, it's for a moment, or a short time. During sex or bondage, or times like now."

Dom nodded. "Not full-time domination."

"Or submission," Adrian said. "Not your thing. Not mine, either."

"There's a 'but' coming, isn't there?"

"I'm going to demand something of you for long-term, open-ended, a command that I would like you to follow."

A hard edge to Adrian's words, to the way his fingers moved, too. He wasn't joking. This was real. "What?"

"Don't *ever* say anything like that to yourself ever again." A hint of outrage slipped into Adrian's smooth voice, making it crackle. "Don't undermine yourself like that."

For a moment, Dom couldn't breathe. Parts of him rejoiced, other parts yelled, and those fucking tears were back in his eyes.

Adrian's gaze softened, and he took Dom's face in his hands, his palms warm. "And yes, I know what I'm asking of you is hard. But yes, you can do it."

"But what if I can't?"

Adrian stroked his thumbs along Dom's cheeks. "You're strong and you have a heart of fire. You can."

Yeah, he didn't think that was true. Besides, the voice wasn't always wrong.

Except it kinda was wrong most of the time. Maybe all of it. *Shit.*

"How would you even know?"

This time, Adrian's smile was sly. "Because you'll tell me. And every time you do, I'm going to be compelled to prove that nasty little voice in your head is a fucking liar."

"I—Can you prove it to me, even if I don't beat myself up?"

A laugh. "I intend to do that, too." Adrian leaned down and took Dom's mouth into a kiss that was like air and light. Dom let himself be carried up and into Adrian's arm, into his lap, until they were tangled into each other.

When they broke the kiss, Adrian threaded his hands into Dom's hair. "I can't abide anyone breaking you down, not even you."

"You're not my therapist."

A small smile. "No. I'm your lover and your boyfriend, and sometimes the person who puts you on your knees and ties you up."

All of that sounded good. So good. "Yeah, okay. I'll do it." Because it would be nice to ignore that shitty little voice for a while. "And I should see about actually getting a therapist, 'cause this is on me, not you."

Adrian touched his forehead to Dom's and stroked his cheeks. "Agreed."

"Should we finish getting dressed? Or cancel dinner?" Just as Dom asked the question, his stomach growled.

"There's your answer." Adrian nudged Dom off his lap.

Yeah, now that he was calmer and more collected, hunger burned through him.

He finished cleaning up and put his shirt and bowtie back on while Adrian donned a tie and jacket that matched his pants. He looked crisp and finished, even with his hair slightly disheveled.

"Hey," Dom called, then beckoned Adrian over. A quick brush of Dom's fingers set Adrian's hair right. "There."

That got him a hand behind the neck and a sweet, slow kiss. Then Adrian straightened his bowtie. "I like the shoes," he murmured.

Dom shook his head. "*Now* you notice them."

They were both smiling when they left the house, hopped in the Uber Adrian had called, and headed to a nice place up by Columbia University.

"Hipster central," Dom said.

"Says the hipster." Adrian took his hand and tugged him into the restaurant.

The place? Nice. Really nice. If he weren't actually secretly a rock star, it would have been way-out-of-his-budget nice. "Um, this is..." He looked around as they were led into the dining room. "May I pay for this one, Adrian?"

"No." A very final answer, but delivered with a smile. "One nice benefit of my *well enough* job is that it pays far more than its enjoyment factor. And with no rent or mortgage..." Adrian shrugged.

Fuck. How many people would love to be that lucky? "Wow, okay." Dom paused. "You really don't like your job?"

Adrian gave a sigh, then looked up. "Hold that thought."

Next thing Dom knew, a server materialized at their table. She took their drink orders. Well, order—Adrian asked for a bottle of wine Dom knew better than to check the price of. Part of him still cringed at how much things cost. But another part liked that he could afford them. The third part gave quite a bit to LGBT charities because he *could* and he fucking well *ought* to support the community. He'd always feel a little weird about the wealth, he was pretty sure.

After the server left, Adrian tapped at his menu. "We should order, then we can talk."

Which could either be a diversion tactic, or a legitimate suggestion. Given his own exhaustion and emotional frailty, Dom leaned toward the latter, especially since he didn't have the energy to poke secrets from Adrian. And he didn't have the ground to stand on to do it, either.

But once the wine came and their food orders were taken, Adrian folded his hands in front of him on the table. "I don't *hate* my job," he said. "It pays quite well and it's a damn sight more stable than the ones I had out in California."

Dom considered that, picking up his wine and sipping. For a moment, he was lost in the complex tastes on his tongue, and he closed his eyes. "Fuck, this is a good bottle of wine."

Adrian chuckled. "Well, it better be, considering."

Yeah, the price had been high, then. Dom flicked his eyes open to see Adrian's cocky smile. He, however, still hadn't touched his glass, aside from when the server had offered a taste. Dom set his own glass down. "Not hating something isn't the same as liking something."

"No." Adrian's voice was dusty. He sat back, humor fading, and grabbed his wineglass. "It's not. But not liking a job isn't always a good reason to quit it." He finally drank.

"But what keeps you there?" Because everything about the way Adrian held himself said he was unhappy, and Dom was pretty sure that this wasn't about him. They'd already had their—fight? Spat? Whatever.

Another sip, then a sigh. "Right at the moment? Not much, to be honest. This week's been hell. My best friend's probably quitting, and I've been given a project that's been royally screwed up by an asshole who somehow keeps getting promoted."

"Um, Adrian? That kinda sounds a lot like hating your job."

His laugh was dark. "Maybe." He met Dom's gaze across the table. "It's been on my mind since that first night we met. My *well enough* job." He took a larger swallow of wine, then set the glass down.

Dom toyed with his own glass. "What do you want to be doing? I mean, if you could pick?"

Adrian looked out into the dining room, brow furrowed. "Something creative. Web design. I love the freelance work I've done. I'd really like to come up with a better social media platform." He looked back. "Honestly, anything's got to be more worthwhile than fixing broken code for a corporate bank."

Okay, so Dom did want to know more about Adrian, too. Learn what made him tick. But spiraling him into sadness was not exactly what Dom had planned. "Financial services institution," he murmured.

Adrian's eyes widened, and he laughed. "Right."

Dom grinned back. "What about your friend?"

"Jackson? He's probably going to take a massive pay cut to go work for a startup that's full of people of color and developing apps for queer kids." Adrian's face fell a little. "He has more integrity than me, to be honest."

Now look who was beating himself up. "Hon, it's okay to make a living."

Adrian arched an eyebrow. "Hon?"

Dom dropped his voice. "I guess Mish is wearing off on

me. She calls us all hon."

A smile. "The bassist."

He nodded, trying hard not to glance around, but failing. Wouldn't that be something? Domino Grinder, nerd extraordinaire, secretly out with his boyfriend.

Adrian reached his hand out across the table. "We're far enough away from everyone else. One good thing about some expensive places, they don't pack us in so you're sitting on your neighbor's lap."

Dom slipped his hand into Adrian's. "I know. It's just... I kinda live in fear."

The smile dropped away again. "Yeah, figured that out recently."

He tried not to flinch. Failed.

"Babe, it's okay. I get it now." Adrian squeezed his hand.

Maybe he did. "Tell me more about your job. Or, like, what's going wrong?"

Arched eyebrows. "You really want to hear about that?"

"Yeah, I kinda do." He ran his thumb over the back of Adrian's hand. "I want to talk like a normal couple. So...tell me about your week?"

Adrian laughed, loudly enough to turn a few heads momentarily, but once he quieted, the other diners looked away. "Dominic, are we getting *domestic*?"

Maybe Dom had been reading those BDSM books a little too much, because what came out of his mouth was, "Spanking isn't really my thing."

And, of course, that's when the server brought the food.

Adrian dissolved into another bought of laughter, while the server impeccably and unfazedly laid down their meals.

"Don't mind me, I'm just going to shrink into this chair." Dom's cheeks were hot.

There was a slight smile on the server's lips, but he didn't say anything except, *"Bon appétit."*

Across the table, Adrian sighed, but it was a happy sound. "This is exactly why I'm falling in love with you."

Heat and joy and embarrassment all blazed through Dom at the same time, and he looked into his wine.

Adrian clicked his tongue. "You're witty and wonderful and my world is so much brighter."

Was that what Adrian thought? Dom looked up—and there was nothing but love and admiration in those eyes. "I—Thanks."

A nod, and a different blaze of heat at Adrian's approval.

They both picked up their silverware. "So," Adrian said, "you really want to know about my week at work?"

"Yeah, I do." Dom stabbed a ravioli, slid it into his mouth slowly and carefully, well aware that Adrian was now fixated on his lips. Once he'd chewed and swallowed, he took a sip of wine. "Then when we get home, I'll tell you about mine."

An almost imperceptible shudder ran through Adrian. Had Dom not been watching him closely, he might have missed it. He didn't miss the slow smile that blossomed, or the way Adrian shifted in his chair. "All right," he said. "You have yourself a deal."

As they ate, Adrian talked about his software programing job. Sometimes the terms didn't make sense to Dom—wrong language—but the struggles Adrian had with management, the way he'd been used by his coworker, those Dom understood.

"I suspect Jackson will turn in his notice soon."

"Your best friend?"

"Yes, he's—" Adrian huffed a laugh, and color touched his cheeks. "We've been friends for a while. We met at a club."

"I still think it's weird that you go clubbing, given how much you hate modern music."

"I don't *hate* modern music, I just don't listen to it much." Adrian took a sip of wine and grinned over the rim. "And I wasn't going for the music. I was going to get laid."

"Did you?"

"All the damn time." He paused. "Sometimes with Jackson. Friends with benefits on occasion. But not recently. Hell, except for that time with you, I haven't even been to a club in ages."

And not, Dom suspected, because of him—this felt like a before-Adrian-had-met-him kind of thing. "Any reason why not?"

"Same reason I didn't hook up with you that first night. I wanted something longer." Adrian shrugged. "Jackson's also my personal trainer, more or less."

That explained the toned body. "He does good work."

That got a chuckle out of Adrian. "I'll be sure to mention that next time. Maybe he'll fuck off with those damn burpees."

"Or make you do more."

"Shut your mouth, Dominic Bradley." Adrian grinned. That expression mellowed a bit. "I'm going to guess it's not the gym that keeps you in shape."

Dom laughed. "No. It's touring and playing and running around onstage. I usually lose weight on tour if I'm not careful because it's just so physical."

He kept peppering Adrian with questions about his job. What he did like: solving complex problems. Fixing shit. Cleaning up designs.

"I wasn't kidding when I said website design. There's a lot of thought that could be put into how to navigate someone through content."

Dom shook his head. "You're looking at someone who just uses templates on a build-it-yourself site."

Adrian cringed. "Babe, don't say such things."

Dom couldn't help laughing. Okay, for starting out nearly the worst way it might have, this night was shaping up to be a good one after all. When they finished their meal and their wine, Dom glanced at Adrian. "Dessert?"

"At home." The look in Adrian's eyes sent a bolt of lust across all of Dom's veins and his dick responded.

Home meant Adrian's. It also probably meant rope. And maybe a chair. "Let's go."

They behaved for the Uber driver. Mostly. Adrian's hand was high on Dom's thigh, touching and teasing, and his smile was just shy of leering.

When they entered the house, Adrian gave Dom a gentle shove forward. "To the living room, please."

The air changed, or maybe it was Dom's brain, because by the time he stepped into that space he was a little high and a lot turned on. Didn't help that Adrian placed both hands on his shoulders, halting him.

"Here's fine." Hands smoothed down Dom's arms, then fell away. "Turn around, please."

He faced Adrian and stared up into those gold-flecked eyes.

"Dominic." Adrian breathed his name like it was a chant. "I love you. I want to give you everything I can."

"You—I—"

Adrian framed Dom's face with his hands. "We didn't have a very good start to the evening, and that was my mistake and my fault. Before we do anything more tonight, I want to give you some time to make sure this is what you want from me."

Dom exhaled and fell back to earth with a grunt, but he couldn't look away from Adrian's sad and hopeful eyes. "I know what I want from you." Right now *and* later. "And I'm not gonna let you take all the blame for earlier."

A small smile, then Adrian let go and stepped back. "Humor me. Sit for a little bit while I change." He worked the knot loose on his tie. "It's important to me not to overstep your bounds. Give me only what you want, Dominic. No more. And certainly not anything you don't want to share."

Dom nodded, because he did understand. Adrian was

seeking Dom's comfort and consent—which said a lot, especially given their earlier spat and Dom's breakdown. He wanted touch and reassurance. But if it made *Adrian* feel safer and more secure...well, he could wait a little, too.

It was all about give and take and each other, after all.

"Okay," he said. "But I'm pretty damn sure I want to be tied up tonight, so maybe—" He waved in the direction of the stairs. "Bring something down for that?"

The look Adrian gave Dom was worth everything. A cross between shock and lust, until intense control took over. He nodded once, then headed down the hall to the stairs.

Dom sank down on the couch. The vestiges of his panic attack lingered, as did the anxiety that brought it on. Showing both sides of his life to someone who wasn't in the band was hard. He'd kinda had to do it with Zavier when he joined them on tour—but Zavier had known the old Dom in high school, at least in passing.

Adrian only had ever known Dominic. Showing him Domino was gonna be interesting. Sure, there were the songs and the videos, but existing in the same space as Adrian— that would be different.

He expected a jolt of worry, but none came. Excitement did, though—same as he'd felt when he'd dragged Adrian to the Met. He was something he could share. Give over. And those aspects of himself? Adrian fucking cherished them. Worshiped them.

Kind of like how Adrian worshiped Dom in his own way. Yeah, Dom might be the one on his knees, but Adrian took care of him, and that took Dom's breath away. He turned the thought over and over in his head. Let it heat his blood and melt away the lingering stress and worry.

When he heard the creak of the steps, he turned toward the hall to see Adrian return. He still wore his dress slacks and belt. Socks and shoes. The jacket and tie were gone, but the white shirt remained. The top two buttons had been undone to expose his throat and his pale freckled skin. Dom focused on that spot before raising his gaze to those lips. He slid off the couch and onto his knees.

Adrian's stare burned through him. "You really do know what you want."

Those words alone made Dom's mouth water. But what Adrian carried in his hands made his bones melt and dick harden. Several bundles of rope in one hand and a leather collar in the other. With rings attached.

"Yeah, I do." Dom met Adrian's hot stare. "And I love you, too. Trust you. Want to share myself with you."

Those eyes flickered like a fire, and Adrian nodded. He strode to Dom and placed the items in his hands on the couch before stroking the side of Dom's jaw with his fingers. "Are you fine with wearing a collar for me?"

"Yeah. I like 'em. I mean, when I wear them onstage."

"So I saw in this photos. But this one's mine, and will serve a different purpose."

Dom's cock pressed against the zipper of his pants. "Figured, given the loops." He licked his lips. "I want to be yours tonight."

Adrian stepped closer and tipped Dom's chin up. "Good. Because every inch of you is going to be."

Dom shivered. Couldn't help it.

Adrian stepped back. "Up to your feet, please. Take those pretty shoes and your socks off."

Somehow, Dom managed to rise without falling. He toed off the shoes and removed the socks, then waited, heart in his throat.

"You're so very good at this." Adrian cupped his face. "Giving yourself to me." His lips brushed Dom's in the barest of kisses.

Dom couldn't help the moan the came from his soul. "I fucking love you," he whispered.

Adrian bushed his thumb over Dom's lips. "Shhh. Feel."

Oh god, he felt. Every touch, every move of Adrian's hands on his. All his nerves firing when that gold-flecked gaze slid down to Dom's bowtie and nimble fingers pulled at the ends and untied the knot.

The tie landed on the couch next to the rope.

Fingers worked at the top button on Adrian's shirt. "Everything about you is—" Breath skimmed over his neck before Adrian's lips and tongue branded him there, kissing and sucking below his ear. "Delectable."

He would have fallen over, if it hadn't been for Adrian's grip on his shirt.

Adrian worked buttons over and kissed his way down Dom's neck until the shirt was open. Then it was sliding off his shoulders, and Adrian's teeth nipped at Dom's collarbone.

"I could spend years kissing every inch of you."

"Please." Dom groaned the word out.

A huff of amusement, and with a tug and yank, Adrian freed Dom's hands from his shirt. That landed on top of the bowtie. He caressed his hands over Dom's arms and pecs, skimming against nipples. "I love all this ink." He gripped the knot-work on Dom's shoulder. "This one most of all. Strong, like you."

Dom lolled his head back when Adrian's hands dipped lower to pull at his belt. Lost in the sensations of lips and breath. The sound of Adrian's voice. The firm way he undid Dom's belt and pants.

Adrian slid his hand down into Dom's boxers and wrapped his warmth around Dom's cock. "You're always so fucking hard for me." A few strokes stole Dom's breath and threatened to take his legs out from under him until Adrian pulled their bodies together.

Adrian didn't stop working Dom's cock. "Never takes much to make you come for me, does it, Dominic?"

"No." He breathed out the word. "You always make me

hard. Make me wanna come so fast. But I'd rather wait." He gripped Adrian's shirt. "But only if that's what you want."

"You're so very good," Adrian said again. "I adore making you wait. Stringing you out. Watching you squirm and pant and buck for me."

Finally, Adrian relented, which was for the best because Dom was so close to release, he didn't know if he could have staved it off much longer. He was humming like a struck chord that went on forever and ever.

Adrian pushed Dom's pants and underwear off, then opened space between them. "Step out of those." He beckoned Dom forward.

Moving was like walking in a dream, all floating and light. "You make my head spin."

A raised eyebrow. "Good spin or bad spin?"

"Good. Always so good." Dom really wanted to kneel again, but that wasn't what Adrian had asked for.

From the couch, Adrian claimed the collar and held it up. "May I?"

Of course Adrian would ask. Dom's heart melted even more, even as his whole body lit. "Yes. Please."

A smile, then there was leather around Dom's neck, being tightened until it was snug. "There."

So fucking good. The only thing on his body—Adrian's collar. Fuck, he wanted more. Hands, tongue, body. He moaned.

"Babe." Adrian's lips brushed his again, then picked the rope up from the couch. "Kitchen, please."

Not quite sure how he managed to cross the distance, but he did. Adrian nodded to the chairs at the breakfast bar—metallic, tall, and with reasonably high backs. "Sit, please. Hands on your thighs."

Dom did as told, the chair cool against his flesh. He couldn't help wondering if Adrian had picked these chairs for this reason—slick and hard against naked skin and with enough places to hook rope around.

This time, Adrian slid his hands over Dom's shoulder, drifting fingertips down biceps. "So open and so hidden," he murmured before meeting Dom's gaze. "Would you mind if I listened to your songs? Watched your videos?"

A shock of heat ran through Dom. The thought of Adrian seeing and hearing the other part of his life beyond the magazine was like slowly ripping off a Band-Aid. It itched and burned, though he knew it had to be done. "I—Yeah. I mean, you should. Watch them. Listen to the albums."

That earned him a kiss to his forehead. "I won't when you're here, I promise."

Which meant, at some point, Dom would need to leave. Probably before the weekend was over. "I love you," he whispered, because he hadn't said it enough.

"Sweet, sweet Dominic." Adrian planted another kiss on his forehead, then took a long sip from his mouth, one that left Dom breathless. "You are my heart." He stepped back and pulled at one of the bundles of rope, unfurling it.

Dom's whimper was swallowed up by Adrian's chuckle. "Shall I take that as consent to tie you up, Dominic?"

"Fuck. Please, please, please tie me up already, Adrian."

He did, crossing rope over limbs and torso and around the metal of the chair. Through the loops on the collar around Dom's neck, adding to the wonderful sensation of being caught, being bound and held and helpless.

Kind of amazing how just a little pressure around his neck could send him skyward. Make him so hard he wanted to rock and buck and beg Adrian to get him off. In short order, he couldn't have moved if he wanted to—and he didn't want to. Not with Adrian so close, so flushed, and his pants tented like that. The way Adrian drank the sight of him made Dom dizzy.

Adrian fingered Dom's nipple. Not hard, but playfully.

The gentle tugging went straight to his balls, though, and he tried to rock his hips. Failed, then moaned at the conflict between pleasure and need and—wherever the hell he went whenever Adrian tied him up.

"In the clouds, aren't you?" Adrian tipped his chin up. Looked down at him with those beautiful eyes.

"You make me fly." The words were out before Dom even registered them. But that was true. He flew and soared. Different from a concert. So safe, too.

A smile, then Adrian stepped away. "I have a treat for you." Then he vanished from view—heading for the fridge, from the direction. Dom couldn't crane his body, nor turn his head enough to watch. But the sounds were of the fridge opening and closing. A knife cutting something. A dish. The clink of metal on ceramic.

Dessert. Adrian had said he had dessert. Dom hoped it was pie.

And yes, when Adrian returned, he held a plate with one of the most amazing slices of lemon meringue Dom had ever seen. "Oh fuck, Adrian." He didn't think he could want this man more. Now. Forever.

"Sunlight in your eyes and on your tongue." Adrian set the pie down on the breakfast bar, pulled over the other chair, and perched on it.

"And you say you're not a poet." Dom swallowed. His skin was alive with sensations. The hard unyielding chair against his back, ass, and thighs. The soft, powerful rope pressing across his skin from his shoulders to his ankles. The strip of warm leather at his neck that he could feel with every breath and syllable and swallow.

Adrian didn't reply. He just cut a piece of pie off with his fork and held it out to Dom.

He couldn't do more than open his mouth—the way his collar was tied down didn't permit him to move his head forward. Adrian slipped the piece of pie into his mouth, sending tingles down Dom's spine, even before he closed his lips over the tines of the fork.

Tart and sweet exploded onto his tongue. Flakey crust. Perfect cloud-like meringue. Liquid lemon. The hard tines slid out over his lips and he moaned in ecstasy, every bit of his being overwhelmed by touch and taste. The citrus smell of the pie, the woodsy scent of Adrian. He closed his eyes because sight was too much to handle.

After he swallowed, Adrian's mouth claimed his, tongue forcing past his lips. He moaned and squirmed and fought against the ropes, but couldn't move.

Adrian could, though. Hands caressed thighs before one wrapped around Dom's cock and stroked slowly.

Dom whimpered into Adrian's mouth. This would do him in. There'd be a headline on some gossip site: *DOMINO GRINDER SUCCUMBS TO ROPE BONDAGE, PIE, AND A KISS.*

Adrian relented with a chuckle. "You taste so good."

"You're gonna kill me."

"Oh no." Adrian sat back and took his own bite of pie. "Not kill. Tease. Fuck. Make you cry out so loud the neighbors hear you again."

Too much. Dom's whole being was on fire. Body, mind, soul.

"Adrian." There was an edge to his voice.

Adrian heard it. "Too much?"

"No." Dom was swirling in pleasure, head so high, cock so hard. He didn't know he could even exist in this state for this long. "Might come without you touching me."

"Now wouldn't that be a treat?" That fucking smile was light and heat, and Dom shivered in his ropes, the tugs and pulls cascading waves of pleasure over his heightened senses. "More pie?"

Dom opened his mouth. Each astounding bite was followed by more kisses and touches, until the pie was gone and Dom was a mess of moans and pleading. For freedom, for captivity. To be fucked so hard.

Adrian untied him from the chair and Dom nearly fell out of it. It wasn't that his limbs were numb—his entire body was so turned on he couldn't think straight. Like too many glasses of gin, but so much better than that. There was citrus in his mouth and he was in Adrian's arms, with Adrian's collar around his neck. "Upstairs?"

A huff of laughter. "Yes, babe."

Adrian helped him up the stairs, as if he was in a drunken stupor, and Dom groaned in frustration, even as he got his legs back under him and he slid down from that perfect high.

"Dominic?" Adrian's voice sounded strained. They'd made it to the second floor and into Adrian's bedroom.

"You're not gonna fuck me, are you? 'Cause you think I'm too far gone to consent?" Tears pricked his eyes. "You're gonna pour me into bed, tell me you love me, and kiss my cheek, and—"

Adrian whirled him around until they were face-to-face, chests touching. Dom grappled at Adrian's shirt and met his heated gaze.

"You want me to fuck you?" Adrian growled the words.

"Yeah. Hard. Until I'm screaming."

Adrian pushed him back until he hit the side of the bed. "You sure?"

"Want all of you. Like you want all of me."

Something shifted in Adrian's expression, and he nodded. "Then I need more rope. And the cuffs."

Dom's legs gave out and he crumpled to the bed, both stunned and entirely turned on. "Yeah. Good. Get them."

A raised eyebrow. "Topping from the bottom, are you?"

Dom gave a shrug. "All those books say the submissive's the one with the true power."

Adrian laughed, and it was a pure sound. "Oh, babe. You're

completely there, all right. Quite capable of consent." He went to his dresser drawer, the one with all his toys, and pulled out the cuffs Dom had worn before. And rope. Several more bundles.

"How many of those do you have?"

"Enough," Adrian said, his teeth flashing as he grinned. He slid Dom's glasses off.

Enough, indeed. By the time Adrian was done, Dom was bound in rope, ass in the air, hands cuffed to his ankles. It was heaven. He'd moaned and rocked and squirmed while Adrian pulled and tied and ordered him still. The end was pure bliss. Open, exposed, yet covered everywhere and secure. "Oh *fuck*. Fuck me."

"That," Adrian said as he ran a warm hand over one of Dom's ass cheeks, "is the idea."

The lube was cool and slick against Dom's overheated skin as Adrian spread it up and down his crack, and he nearly lost it when Adrian pressed a finger inside him. The stretching and the pleasure of it all, on top of his senses being on fire all night long.

Adrian finger-fucked him slowly, and Dom groaned in frustration. He'd been riding the edge of pleasure for what felt like hours. "Fuck me. Please, please, please fuck me." He tried to push back on Adrian's hand, but he was too tightly bound—and that only spiked his pleasure higher.

"I *am* fucking you," Adrian said, too much amusement in his voice.

"I want it hard. This is—" Dom lost his breath when Adrian rammed several fingers in and slid over his prostate.

"You were saying?"

Dom pressed his forehead against the mattress and moaned. Another hard thrust. Same fireworks in Dom's brain and body. "Oh god."

"That's what I thought." Adrian withdrew his fingers, and there was the telltale sound of a condom wrapper.

Dom needed him. All of him. Every ounce of his focus. His hands and mouth and cock.

"You're so splendid like this, babe. Out of your mind for me." Adrian pressed against Dom's hole.

That edge of pleasure vanished, along with Dom's mind when Adrian gripped the ropes at his waist, and thrust in. All that remained was ecstasy and security and the hard, fast rhythm of being fucked into oblivion.

The room smelled of sex and rope and leather. Of Adrian. Salt and sweet clung to Dom's mouth as he moaned and shouted and begged for Adrian to never stop. Never. Never. He wanted to stretch the moment, live in the heat and safety and joy of their union.

But when Adrian slid those hands up to Dom's shoulders and kissed his spine while plowing into him, there wasn't anything left to hold on to, and he fell over that edge, screaming into bliss and fire and light.

Adrian's teeth scraped across Dom's back. "Oh fuck, baby, yeah. Come for me."

Dom could barely breathe through the intensity of it all, the way Adrian rammed in harder, the stretch of the ropes against his flesh as he shook. He'd never come without a stroke or some friction on his cock before, but he shot hard and long until tears were in his eyes and Adrian's own shout was in his ear.

Didn't really register that it was over until Adrian had him half unbound, 'cause his body sang and sang and sang like one giant guitar string that had been plucked. He was vibrating with love and life and delight and couldn't stop.

"Adrian." His voice was a scrape across broken glass.

"I'm here." Fingers on his cheeks, and Adrian's lovely eyes peering into his. "Talk to me, babe."

Worry threaded through every word. So much concern. So much love. "Can pour me into bed now."

A smile, like sunshine, like lemon. His Adrian. "Let me

finish. Get you cleaned up." He kissed Dom so softly. "I love you, Dominic."

Yeah. And Dom loved him, too. "Please stay with me." He didn't mean now. He meant longer. Didn't know how to ask for that.

A flicker in those eyes. "I'm not going anywhere."

"Good. 'Cause I love you, too." Dom closed his eyes. "Never loved anyone before you."

Lips against his forehead, then Adrian made good on his promise. The rest of the ropes were undone. The cuffs and the collar removed, and the last thing Dom was aware of was being tucked under those cool sheets he felt so safe in.

This was home.

CHAPTER
SEVENTEEN

ADRIAN WOKE SLOWLY, AND TO A SIGHT HE ABSOLUTELY LOVED—Dominic sound asleep next to him, face mashed into the pillow, his hair everywhere, and all the worries of the world gone from his body. Beautiful. Real. Whole.

Dominic Bradley was a rock star. He was also a scholar and a history geek and a book nerd. He was Adrian's, too, and that was a miracle by itself. He knelt for Adrian. Gave over his body to be bound. Loved every second of it.

The aftermath of last night's dinner had been astounding. Gratifying. Harsh. Loving.

And as much as Adrian adored every single moment he spent with Dominic, he was going to send him home. Because they both needed to recover from the events—all the events—of last night. But right now?

He would watch Dominic sleep, watch those lips that were curved into a gentle smile, and hold on. Hold on until *he* felt safe and secure. Right now, he didn't. Yes, most of last night was a wild and perfect dream. Dominic's submission. His declaration of love. The bondage and the sex. Those had been everything Adrian had wanted and more. So much more.

But the revelation about Dominic's career—this entire public life Adrian knew nothing about—that had thrown Adrian hard. And worse, his anger and Dominic's fear of discovery had cracked Dominic nearly in two.

Dominic had forgiven the anger, and Adrian believed him. It was the fear that scared Adrian. He certainly wouldn't tell anyone Dominic's secret. But he also didn't necessarily want to be a secret, too. Would he even meet the band? If he suddenly appeared as Domino Grinder's lover, well, too many people would connect the dots to Dominic.

He'd need to dwell on that. Dive deeper into the internet and see how close they already were. As much as he loved the man, Dominic was haphazard in a lot of ways. How he'd managed to pull off two separate lives for so long, Adrian had no idea. He suspected a lot of it was dumb luck.

And eventually, luck ran out.

He didn't want luck to run out for Dominic. He wanted him safe and happy. Problem was, Adrian wasn't sure how he fit into that.

Next to him, Dominic stirred and gave a soft groan, and flicked open his eyes.

"Hey, babe." Adrian brushed Dominic's messy hair from his forehead.

His reward was a sleepy smile and a drowsy reply. "Hey."

"How are you feeling?"

Dominic closed his eyes, smile widening as he stretched. "Really well-fucked."

Adrian couldn't help the chuckle, nor the heat that ran through his body.

Dominic opened his eyes again, and this time his gaze was alert—and more serious. "Thank you for last night."

"Thank you."

A little frown. "You have that look."

Confusion made Adrian shift. "What look?"

"The one you get when you've thought too much about

something." A few blinks, and Dominic's frown deepened. "You're upset."

Fuck. "I'm not." Not really. This was certainly not how he wanted to have this conversation, and seeing that spark of fear in Dominic again, sent ice into his own. "God, I love you so much."

That seemed to smooth away some of those worry lines. "Then what?"

Shit. This part was so delicate. "Well, today I want to listen to your music. Watch some videos. Find out more about this other part of you. But I think I need to do that alone."

The flicker of hurt was so hard to watch, but it vanished as Dominic sighed and nodded. "Yeah, I get that. And yeah, that's probably better."

Adrian cupped Dominic's cheek, then pulled him closer. "Babe, I'm not lying when I say I love you."

Dominic pressed his face against Adrian's chest. "I fucking know that. I just hate leaving. I always hate leaving. At least during the week, I have shit to keep me busy."

"Same." He opened space between them. "How about coffee and some breakfast?"

"Pancakes?"

"Sure, pancakes. I'd cook you eggs Benedict from scratch, if that's what you wanted."

Dominic chuckled. "Pancakes are fine." He paused. "And some bacon."

Adrian laughed. "Right. I will work for your stomach's delight." He levered himself out of bed. "But first, coffee."

Dominic smiled, though there was sadness at the edges. "Coffee with you is the best thing in the world."

They ended up eating pancakes, scrambled eggs, and bacon, and drinking copious amounts of coffee while sitting in shorts in the kitchen. Dominic squirmed a little on his chair —the same one Adrian had tied him to the night before—and that was a delight.

So was the memory of Dominic's moans, the shudders, and the taste of his mouth. Adrian sipped his coffee and pushed those thoughts away. If he kept going down that mental path, he'd be so less likely to make good on his plans.

He needed time to himself. Time to see this other Dominic. Explore the public man. The private man? He knew that one. He'd tied him up and fed him pie.

Dominic appraised him. "You're thinking again."

"Yeah, I am." He leaned over and stole a syrup-flavored kiss. "Sorry."

A huff. "I get it, though. I do. It's a lot—what happened. I should probably—" Dominic waved the hand that wasn't holding a fork. "Deal with it, too."

That Dominic wanted to—was thinking along those lines—said something. "You got anyone to talk to?"

"You mean professionally?"

Adrian nodded.

Dominic shrugged. "Nope. But I can ask around." He laughed. "Hell, I'm sure Zav or Mish know someone. They fucking know everyone, especially Zav. He—uh." Dominic snapped his mouth shut.

Well, *that* was interesting. So was the little creeping red of embarrassment sliding across Dominic's cheeks. "He what?" Adrian kept his tone light.

"I don't know how to explain Zav. He's kinda like you—he sees things. And we're friends. He takes good care of Ray and Ray is—shit." He set his fork down. "God, you don't know any of them. Ray's my best friend."

This was more than Dominic had ever spoken about his bandmates. "And Zavier is his husband, yes?" Jackson had said something about that.

Dominic nodded. "Anyway, I—kinda told him about you and me kneeling for you, and he wanted your name so he could check you out."

Adrian sat up straight. "He's kinky. In the scene."

"I guess?" Dominic toyed with his coffee cup, his cheeks so red. "I, um. Try not to think too much about that part of their life."

Made sense, since Ray was Dominic's best friend. Hell, Adrian had fooled around with Jackson, but he didn't really want to hear intimate details about his current boyfriend. "So, what did Zavier discover about me?"

Dominic's brown eye shone. "That you're a good man."

That was gratifying. He'd always been more on the periphery of the BDSM scene here, but Janelle knew him and he'd played with a few others. "I'm glad folks see me like that."

A nod. "Zav also said I should tell you about the band, way back when. Well, Ray and Mish, too. It's...a trust thing."

His throat tightened unexpectedly. "Yes, yes it is."

Dominic gripped his coffee and peered into it. "I should have trusted you sooner."

Maybe. But there were other emotions in play. He gripped Dominic's shoulder and drew him in for another kiss. "It's fine, babe. You need to trust you, too. Your needs and wants. Sometimes that takes time to work through."

"Wasn't easy on you."

"No," he admitted. "But I'm here. And you're here. And we're together. We'll make it work."

A sweet smile that begged to be kissed, and that turned into something longer and hotter, until Dominic gave one of his throaty little moans. Regretfully, Adrian pulled back.

"I should go." Soft voice and sad eyes. But the fear had vanished from Dominic.

Adrian nodded, regretting that, too.

They stretched the time out a little longer in the kitchen before Dominic headed upstairs to shower and change while Adrian cleaned up from breakfast. When he was done, he poured himself coffee and wandered out into his living room to wait.

On the coffee table, staring back, was Twisted Wishes. Holy *fuck*—Dominic, his geeky twink of a boyfriend, was a freaking *rock star*. Adrian blew out a breath and sank down onto the couch. There were songs and performances and shit to look at. A magazine to read. He pulled over his laptop, but resisted the urge to flip it open. Had a feeling Dominic would rather not see him surfing over to the Twisted Wishes website.

So he waited until Dominic returned, dressed in his button-down and slacks and bowtie, looking far from the rocker on the magazine. He gathered his shoes, then sat next to Adrian. His gaze drifted to the magazine. "The worst thing is that it feels like I'm living two lives and I don't know which one is real."

"Both."

Dominic put one shoe on. "That's what I think I want. I—" He shook his head, then put the other shoe on. "I'm not sure it's possible, sometimes."

"We'll find a way." Maybe if Adrian kept saying it, it would be true.

"I hope so."

He couldn't help pulling Dominic into another kiss, slow and sweet. The hair at the nape of his neck was damp, and he smelled of Adrian's shower gel and tasted of mint. When Adrian drew back, he met Dominic's gaze. "Call me tomorrow, and we'll talk."

A nod. Dominic rose. "We never drank that wine I brought."

Adrian pushed himself off the couch and followed Dominic to the front door. "We'll have other nights, babe."

There was that flash of fear in Dominic, and then it vanished. "Yeah."

Another kiss and murmured goodbyes, then Dominic was bounding down the steps into the streets of Brooklyn, and gone from Adrian's view.

THE HOUSE FELT EMPTY WITHOUT DOMINIC THERE WITH ADRIAN, especially up in the library. He'd wanted light and comfort, and even with the absence of the man he loved, this space still brought him joy, if somewhat muted.

He sipped a mug of coffee and flipped open the magazine to finally read the article about Twisted Wishes. It was, it turned out, a rambling interview-type piece with the author's own observations about the band's history and members interspersed between stories the band members told about themselves and answers to questions.

The whole thing made good reading. By the end, Adrian was already itching to dig deeper into the band and its members. Instead, he flipped through the photos once more, and reread the entire article. Ray had started a band in high school. Couple of iterations later, it had been him and Domino at local bars, Ray in his ripped jeans and T-shirts and Domino in his half-punk, half-goth fusion outfits. Then they'd picked up Mish, a firebrand of a redheaded base player, and their original drummer Kevin.

Their first two albums had a small following, but they'd hit their stride with the third and catapulted onto the scene— and apparently nearly crashed and burned immediately. Kevin was thrown out of the band due to his alcoholism, and they'd picked up Zavier Demos.

Zavier was a classically trained timpanist and had been a classmate of Ray's for a year. Rumor had it that they'd started off hating each other, but given that they were now *married*— that had changed.

Rocktime: And when did you realize you had feelings for Ray?

Demos: I've always had feelings for Ray. It was merely the state of those feelings that shifted.

Van Zeller: Yeah, at a certain point he stopped wanting to beat my ass.

Demos: I've never stopped wanting to beat your ass, Ray.

Yes, Adrian would probably get along with Zavier. He flipped to the photo and stared. If he hadn't known better, he'd say he met Zavier at one point or another. He shoved the thought out of his mind. Probably just had one of those faces. Movie-star looks.

The bits with Dominic—or rather, Domino—were more interesting for what they contained and what they didn't. Of course, there was all kinds of speculation about who Domino really was. And the questions asked all fell into the fishing category. Thing was—Dominic never *lied*. He'd actually told them exactly who he was, and that blew Adrian's mind.

Rocktime: So what does Domino Grinder do for fun? What are your downtimes like?

Grinder: Ya really want to know? I sneak out and go to libraries and museums. I get fucking turned on by the thought of reading a good book. Learning something new.

And underneath the makeup, hair gel, and studded leather, the man Adrian had come to love stared back from those photos. Warm brown eyes, though no glasses. That seductive mix of power, hunger, and shyness—even that came through if you knew how to look.

The article had Adrian admiring Twisted Wishes, especially their frontman, who'd been put through hell by their former label. But he and the band had come out of the whole horrible episode stronger and wiser—and with a pile of cash. Which explained how Dominic had been able to buy his place in a swankier part of Brooklyn than Adrian lived in.

And, admittedly, things here were awfully swank now. He had *such* mixed feelings about that, especially since he was technically part of the problem, even if this was his family's house. His mom wouldn't have been able to afford to live here, even if she were still alive. Nor, he bet, would she have felt comfortable. But he did, and a part of him rebelled against that.

Adrian blew out a breath and rose to head downstairs. The next step was to search the web, listen to songs, and watch some videos.

Once back in his living room, he brought up the Twisted Wishes website—and stared at it, cringing. It was a mishmash of bad design and coding. Red text on a black background. Links that didn't quite work. Too much blinking shit. If the band was popular enough to make it onto the cover of a popular magazine, then man, they needed a better web designer. He flipped through the pages and links and shook his head. They better not have paid that much for this mess. It was like something out of the early 2000s. *Holy shit.* And there weren't even any links to videos or to song downloads or...anything, really. The news was woefully out of date. At least they did have Zavier listed as a band member, so someone was updating it.

Their Twitter was okay, but not very active, and there wasn't really any other social media. No Instagram. No Snapchat. No YouTube channel.

Okay, so put those things on a list he'd have to bring up to Dominic eventually. They *really* needed a better social media person.

However, there were a bunch of fan sites that had damn good design and content. Links to high-quality concert videos, plus the official videos. Also a history of the band that was a little more in-depth than the magazine. It mentioned some of the earlier incarnations of the band and had clippings of reviews from local New Jersey freebie newspapers.

Adrian listened to a few of their songs. They were—well, exactly how Jackson had described. In between a lot of things. Not pop, though. Harder than Adrian liked his music, but the lyrics...yeah Jackson had been right about them, too.

And there was Dominic's guitar, too, screaming out of the songs at times. Simple to complex. Dizzying strings of notes. Dominic could play, which Adrian knew from the Met, but this was...he couldn't even describe it. Maybe if you mashed classical with punk or metal or something.

He hunted down some videos from their most recent tour, and by the second one, was slack-jawed. Same songs, but at a higher level, as if someone had turned up the talent of everyone in the band by three or four notches. The energy, the rhythm, and fucking *hell*, the way Dominic moved and played onstage.

Hell yes, Adrian could watch that for hours.

In retrospect, it was probably a good thing Dominic had gone home, because there were a lot of videos and he would, in fact, be watching for hours and staring at the man he loved gyrate and dance and play his guitar for screaming fans. He grabbed his remote, turned on the TV, and set it to stream from his laptop.

Domino Grinder was godlike. Walking sex. And Adrian was going to enjoy the hell out of *that* in high-definition. Better than fucking porn, his Dominic full of passion and snarl.

What would that version of Dominic taste like? The lipstick alone had Adrian hard.

Oh yes, this would be fun research, indeed.

———

SUNDAY NIGHT, DOM LAY ON HIS TOO-MODERN COUCH IN HIS too-perfect living room and stared at the ceiling, phone plastered to his ear and heart beating in his chest.

"Do you want to meet the band?" He'd have rather asked in person, but after Adrian had discovered who Dom really was—even if the results hadn't been that bad—they'd needed some time apart. Adrian to find out more and Dom to get over the shock and fear and fucking embarrassment.

Adrian had been furious, then utterly apologetic and tender. Then an exquisite Dominant and a voracious machine of a lover.

He was a fucking miracle, that's what Adrian was. But in the aftermath of fucking amazing sex, Dom had kinda forgotten to ask.

The long silence between them finally ended with an inhale of breath. "I would, yes. But only if you feel comfortable with that."

Brought fucking tears to his eyes, and he wanted to punch Adrian for being the way he was. Or kiss him. Probably the latter. "Yeah, I do. I mean, they're an important part of my life and so are you, so...yeah. I really do want you to meet them."

"Then I'd be honored to."

Of course he would. "How 'bout hearing us play? Like, come to a rehearsal?" Dom could ask him to the concert, but that was too far away. He wanted the band to know Adrian and Adrian to know the band now.

The pause was much shorter this time. "Babe, you have no idea how long I've been wanting to hear you play. That trip to the Met and that one night you played for me only made it worse."

God, he'd loved playing that Renaissance guitar. The timbre and sound. He huffed out a laugh. "I hardly played anything at the Met or at your place."

"But you played, and it was lovely and I'm selfish and want more. I want as much of you as you're willing to give me."

Dom shivered. Everything. He wanted Adrian to know everything. "Okay. How about tomorrow? We usually go from midafternoon into the evening, so you could come by after work—and I'll introduce you."

"I—Yes. I'd love that. Say between five-thirty and six?" Joy in Adrian's voice. Excitement.

"Yeah." Dom rattled off the address. "I'll leave a note at the front desk. You should be able to come up to the floor we're on, then."

"Thank you." A purr of words that made Dom shiver and slide a hand down his belly, and stop at the waistband of his boxers.

He should have been in bed, but that was empty and lonely and he never slept well there. He often slept on the couch in his living room. He could pretend he was on tour and fall asleep. Sometimes. "I miss you."

Adrian grunted. "I do, too. I think the space is good, though. I read the article. Listened to your songs. Watched videos. I don't think you'd have liked me doing that with you around."

Definitely not. Dom loved hearing Twisted Wishes songs when he was out, and it was even better if people were nodding or singing along, but to sit there and listen when Adrian heard those songs for the first time? When he decided whether he *liked* them? No.

Still, he had to know. "What did you think?"

"They're really interesting." The way he said those words, though—there was honesty there. Like Adrian actually found the songs thought-provoking or something. "I need to listen to more. You guys are amazing in concert."

Now, *that* Dom liked. "Good. Shit, I was afraid you'd think they were crap."

Adrian blew out a breath. "You know my friend Jackson from work?"

"The personal trainer dude."

"He's not *really* my trainer, but yes. Anyway, he knows

music better than I do, and he recommended your songs. Said the lyrics especially would catch my attention."

"That's because Ray's fucking brilliant."

"But so are the rest of you. I'm listening for your guitar, Dominic." There was a pause. "And I've been reading that magazine article and some of the interviews on the web. Each one might start as Ray's notes and lyrics, but it takes all of you to make those into a song."

"Fuck, you have been reading! That's like one of Ray's sayings."

Laughter. "He sounds like a good guy." Then a sigh. "But if you do want me to come to your practice tomorrow and meet everyone, I should go and get ready for bed. I have work in the morning."

"I'd rather talk to you all night."

"And I'd like to tie you up, make you beg for my cock, then drill you down into my mattress." Adrian's voice was wicked. "But we don't always get what we want."

Hard in an instant, and painfully so. "Fuck, Adrian. That's unfair!" He palmed himself through his boxers.

A laugh that was dark and delicious. "Good night, Dominic. I adore you."

"You adore teasing me." Dom slipped a hand under the waistband and stroked.

"That, too." Adrian's voice dropped in volume and tone. "You're already jacking off, aren't you?"

Dom groaned in response.

"Mmm. There's a sound I love. I'll be thinking about that all night." He whispered, "Good night, babe."

"I fucking love you." Wasn't exactly what Dom had planned to say. But he was hard and needy and he missed Adrian with all his soul.

"I know. We'll talk tomorrow."

He gritted his teeth. "Okay."

"Night," Adrian whispered, then was gone.

Dom slid his phone onto the coffee table, shoved his boxers down, and jacked off in earnest, wishing for Adrian's touch and breath and words. His heat. Those cuffs.

Should have taken it slow. Made it last. But there was too much heat and sadness and worry, so he came hard and fast, hating that he was alone, and so looking forward to tomorrow, when he wouldn't be.

CHAPTER
EIGHTEEN

WORK ON MONDAY WAS HELLISH FOR ADRIAN. WOULD HAVE been anyway with more shit from Project Brada being dumped on him, and once more having to fix William's mistakes in his own damn code. But the anticipation of experiencing the other part of Dominic's life, of meeting the people that were for all intents and purposes Dominic's family, had Adrian's mind spinning in all directions.

He really didn't need William's shit now. Not even the punishing workout Jackson had pushed him through that morning stole away Adrian's annoyance that the day would *not* go any faster.

And then Russ called Adrian into his office. Joy of fucking joys. He stopped two offices down to compose himself, because charging into the boss's domain with a huge attitude would be about as helpful as trying to shove a punchcard into a USB port. Once he'd pushed down the annoyance to a level he could hide, Adrian strode forward and knocked on the doorframe.

Russ looked up and nodded to the guest chair. "Close the door, too."

Well, *shit*. Adrian did as told and settled into the uncomfortable guest chair.

There was a look from Russ that Adrian didn't like. "We need to talk more about the problems with your work lately."

Adrian's breath caught. "*My* work?"

"There's been an increase in nightly test failures on your projects, Adrian."

Yeah, well, there was a reason for that. But it wasn't Adrian. "And if you look at the code check-ins, you'll see that those aren't caused by my coding, but someone else's 'refactoring.'" He even air-quoted the last word.

Russ frowned at him. "Are you blaming William for your mistakes?"

Adrian straightened in the chair and stared back at Russ until his boss actually flinched. "You know I'm not. I've always owned up when I've fucked up. I'm usually in here before anyone notices."

Russ looked down at his desk.

"I've been working here for six years. I know my worth. I also know when I'm being set up." Adrian paused. "If you want me out, for fuck's sake, Russ, just tell me."

Russ met his gaze again. "It's not that simple, Adrian."

Yes, it was. "Look, tell William I'm fine with cleaning up after him on Project Brada. But he needs to stay the fuck out of my code. Then you won't have to yell at me about my work."

Russ pushed a hand through his hair. "You need to learn to be a team player, Adi."

Adrian's spine went rigid. "Don't call me that." No one called him that but Jackson, and it was hard-won on both their parts. Mutual respect.

"See?" Russ waved a hand.

"It's not a nickname I'm willing to give out freely." Adrian kept his voice steady. "Please don't use it."

"This is exactly what I'm talking about."

Adrian closed his eyes briefly. "No, it's not. You're asking me to be a team player, not a friend or a lover. Hell, not even my boyfriend calls me that."

Russ shifted in his chair.

"What the hell is going on, Russ?" Because something was out of sync. "Shit has been screwy since I came back from my trip."

Nothing, just more stares, but Russ was damn uncomfortable.

Adrian sighed. "I'll double-check the sections of code I'm responsible for before I leave each night. Clean up any mistakes." He shrugged. "I can also build some automated testing other folks on the team can use to help spot issues, if you think that would help."

Russ folded his hands and seemed relieved. "That's acceptable."

This was the weirdest conversation he'd ever had. "Shall I get back to it, then?"

Russ nodded, so Adrian rose and retreated to his cube, heart in his throat. Rather than IM Jackson via the company network, he texted him on his phone.

> Just had the weirdest conversation with Russ. WTF is going on here?

Took some time, but a message came back:

> Easy. William is gunning for your job.

Adrian sat back. Sure felt like it. But his job wasn't any better than William's. They were both senior programmers. It's not like undercutting Adrian would get William anywhere, unless...

> Wait, am I up for promotion or some shit like that?

> Sometimes you're denser than a brick.

Adrian ran a hand through his hair. Well, shit.

> Beer after work?

> Any other day, yes. Can't. Meeting my catnip and getting intro'd to his friends.

> Oh ho. Getting serious. You didn't tell me this morning!

He hadn't. Mostly because he hadn't wanted to let slip who Dominic was.

> Yeah, we are. Like you and your man.

Apparently, Jackson had been at a family cookout with his jazz club boyfriend.

> Blow me, Adrian.

> Been there, done that.

The next text was an emoji of a middle finger. Adrian chuckled and set his phone aside. After all, he'd promised Russ a test. And he did need to fix all this shitty code.

SOMEHOW, ADRIAN MANAGED TO GET THE CODE FIXED, THE scripts written, and a happy little group email sent out on how to run it. He ran the unit tests on his products and sent the results to Russ, then was out the door and into the elevator when the clock ticked over to five-thirty.

Getting to the address Dominic had given him was no issue whatsoever. Like many of the brick buildings in Chelsea near the water, it had been a warehouse before renovations. There was a pile of people milling around the entrance, and after a moment, Adrian spotted the Twisted Wishes T-shirts. Fans hoping to catch a glimpse of the band?

It must have been normal, but it was also a glimpse behind the why of the fear that lurked in Dominic. He didn't know if he could cope with people peering into his life all the damn time. Thankfully, he looked like a businessman and not like a rock star's boyfriend, so he slid right through the crowd and into the lobby of the building without anyone even looking his way.

He checked in with the front desk, and as promised, the guard knew he was coming and exactly where to send him. Adrian slapped the visitor label onto his suit jacket, and the guard led him to the elevator, activated the panel with his key card, and punched the fourth floor.

The doors slid closed, and Adrian took one breath then another. God. This was it. The other side of Dominic. His friends. His colleagues. All the missing pieces.

Would they even like him? Would he say something idiotic? He'd never met anyone's family before.

The car stopped and the doors opened. There was a faint but unmistakable sound of live music coming from down the hall. He followed the sound to a door that had been propped ever so slightly open. Through the glass panel, he spied a band. *The* band—Twisted Wishes. They were in the middle of playing and holy hell, there was Dominic right *there*, his fingers flying across the strings of a bright yellow electric guitar. Jeans. One of his button-downs, but with the sleeves rolled up. Head thrown back, huge smile. Dominic moved, grooving with the rhythm, his gaze shifting to their blond lead singer, and then across the studio until those eyes snagged on Adrian's and widened.

The notes went awry with a sound that had Adrian flinching and nearly running back down the corridor—this was Dominic's domain and Adrian had just fucked it up—but Dominic's eyes lit when they met his gaze.

"Adrian!" His shout was brilliance and joy and spun Adrian's heart around in his chest.

Then everyone, all the other members of the band, were staring at him. Adrian swallowed and pushed the door open. "Hi. Sorry. I didn't want to interrupt." Heat rose to his cheeks. Fuck, this was awkward.

"Honey, we wouldn't have left it open if we didn't want you to interrupt."

He recognized Mish Sullivan, the Twisted Wishes bass player, instantly. Well, he recognized *all* the band members instantly. Adrian gave her a smile, then his gaze landed on Dominic again. He was grinning ear to ear, and that expression was infectious. Joy and light. Fucking hell. Lemons.

There was a little thump on a drum. "So, Dom, this is your gentleman friend?" Deep voice. Black hair, and a really fucking knowing grin. That was Zavier Demos, and he looked even more familiar than he had in the photo spread. Sounded familiar, too. Damn. Adrian racked his brain.

"Yeah," Dominic said. "This is Adrian."

"Adrian Doran," he said, introducing himself. "Hello."

Ray Van Zeller eyed him, his arms crossed. He still held a mic in one hand. "You're wearing a suit." Those words were almost accusatory. "Dom said you were a computer engineer."

"I am." Then it hit him. "Oh! I work for a bank. There's no such thing as business-casual, let alone jeans and T-shirts."

Ray uncrossed his arms. "Oh shit. That must be hell."

"Sometimes." Like today.

Dominic unslung his guitar and put it on a nearby stand.

"Hey. Um. Can I have a moment before you all mob him?" He closed the distance between them. "Don't mind them. They're overprotective."

"So am I." Adrian couldn't help reaching out and cupping the side of Dominic's face. Yup. Dominic was real and here. He leaned in for a quick kiss. Tasted good, too. "It's not a bad trait for friends to have."

Behind Dominic, Ray swallowed a laugh. Heat touched Adrian's cheeks.

"Nah, he's not making fun of you. He's commenting on Zav and his behavior." Dominic drew him over to a table with water and food debris and chairs.

"I'm not overprotective at all," Zavier murmured.

"Oh, bullshit," Ray said.

"Boys..." That came with an exasperated sigh from Mish.

Suddenly, the memory was there in Adrian's mind. A brief glimpse of a younger version of the Twisted Wishes drummer and that sassy deep voice. There'd been a BDSM party years ago, during one of his visits home from California, and he was sure he'd seen Zavier there, only he'd been a student at the time.

Adrian shrugged off his satchel, then took off his coat and tie, trying to figure out if he should even say anything. A touch redirected his attention to Dominic.

"What's wrong?" Soft words. "I know this isn't your element, and they're a bit much sometimes, but these are my *friends*. They're safe."

And wasn't it perfect that Dominic was looking after him? Making sure he was comfortable? Adrian laughed. "I've had a long day and I *am* off-kilter a bit." He glanced over to where the rest of the band was milling, trying not to watch them or listen in. "But it's not that. It's that I've met Zavier Demos before. I just didn't realize that until now."

"Wait, what?" He rotated toward Zavier. "You know Zav?"

Zavier had come out from behind the kit, and his smile was a small, sly thing.

Ray gave him a shove. "Wait, you know Dom's dude?"

Dom's dude. Adrian rather liked the sound of that. He cleared his throat. "We don't know each other. We crossed paths *years* ago, that's all. But I remember faces."

"Janelle's party," Zavier said.

Adrian nodded. "And you were that kid from Juilliard."

Zavier gave a little bow.

Ray's eyebrows arched. "So you're into the same stuff as Zav?"

"Will you boys just say BDSM?" Mish set her bass down and strode to the table to snag a bottle of water. "Stop being so coy. There are parental warnings on our albums, and it's not like I'm a petite and delicate fucking flower."

Adrian burst out laughing. Couldn't help it. Maybe it was the stress or the relief or just seeing Dominic so...himself...but the laughter poured out until he thumped into one of the chairs and stared back at Mish. "I like you."

She grinned. "You're gonna like us all by the time we're done here."

Dominic had that sunny smile on, and he looked light as air with buoyancy and energy.

"Hey, can I hear you play?" Adrian waved at the studio. "This time not while lurking outside a door?"

"Yeah, sure." Dominic looked over his shoulder. "Ray?"

A nod from their lead singer. "I'll even sing for your dude. Pick the song, Dom."

Tingles up Adrian's arm. He cocked a finger and beckoned. "Dominic." Like a magnet, he came, all breath and blush and perfect obedience. He framed Dominic's neck with his hands, and pulled him down into a much longer kiss. He might be *Dom's dude*, but the reverse was very much true, as well.

"Go play for me," he whispered against those sweet lips.

Dominic straightened, looked a little dazed, then gave a laugh of his own. "All right." He sauntered over to his guitar and swung it over his shoulder. "How about 'Born in Fire'?"

Ray nodded and the rest of the band got situated—and then Adrian was blown away by sound and movement and Dominic's guitar. The lyrics were something else, too, as was Ray's voice. Rhythmically, it was odd and wonderful. Mish played the perfect counterpoint to Dominic—but all Adrian could keep in his head was the way Dominic moved when he played and how absolutely free he looked. Adrian had seen a similar delight and joy in bed, but this was raw and wonderful and not erotic at all.

His heart and mind leapt. Yes. This was Dominic, in his life, with his passion.

Adrian doubted he'd ever be able to get enough of that, in bed or outside of it.

When they finished, they all looked at him, and Dominic gave a little shrug. "I know you're not really a fan."

Adrian grunted. "I just spent almost two days listening to every Twisted Wishes song I could get my hands on and watching videos and interviews." He cocked his head and held Dominic's gaze. "It's brilliant stuff. Not my usual fare, but apparently I need to branch out. Consider me a fan."

"You're not just saying that because of Dom?" Ray pinned him with a look that was pretty much *hurt my best friend and you'll be talking to me.*

Adrian shook his head. "Lying destroys trust. I meant what I said."

"Ray." Zavier spoke the other man's name like a gentle touch, and it pretty much had the same effect.

Ray softened and smiled. "Yeah, okay. I'm just looking after him."

"I'm capable of looking after myself, thank you." Dominic plucked at his guitar, cheeks red but a smile dancing on his lips.

Mish snorted. "We gonna play more?"

They picked out another song and started in on it—and stopped and started several times. Each time, Ray commented on an aspect and they corrected or tried new notes or rhythms; much of the terminology was out of Adrian's wheel-house. But when the song clicked, he felt it in his bones and sat up straighter.

Ray must have noticed, because he got a cocky-ass smile, then nodded, and that, Adrian realized, was when Ray finally accepted him.

By the end of the night, through the interactions and play-fulness they included him in on, and from just watching the band work, Mish's prediction came true. He liked all of them. Quite a lot.

He also couldn't wait to get Dominic home.

WHEN THE BAND PLAYED THE LAST SONG OF THE EVENING TO Ray's satisfaction, Dom unplugged and unslung his guitar, then grabbed his water bottle. Best practice yet. Didn't know if it was all the weeks of work or that Adrian sat enraptured on the far end of the studio. He'd seen that look from him before, that admiration, but never quite this intense outside of the bedroom.

He kinda wanted to go over there, kneel down and just— be with Adrian. Thank him for coming. For not freaking out entirely about the rock-star thing. For *liking* their music. Holy shit.

A clatter of drums shook Dom from his thoughts. Zavier spun a stick around his fingers before dropping it into the holder on the kit. "Well, that was enjoyable."

"It was fucking awesome," Mish said, and Zavier grinned.

"Yeah, I think we're almost ready." Ray clipped the mic

into the stand and glanced around at them before peering out at Adrian. "Kinda nice to have an audience, too."

Adrian straightened in his seat. "I'm grateful you let me be here."

"Sweetheart, we all wanted to meet Dom's man." Mish unplugged and set her bass down, as well. "He's only been talking about you for weeks and weeks."

Was Adrian blushing? Shit. Now Dom's cheeks were hot. "I mean, I didn't talk about you *that* much."

Ray chuckled, then his smile slipped away. "You know, I'd invite you out to dinner with us."

Ice blazed through Dom. "I'm not dressed—"

That was dismissed with a wave of a hand. "I know. But I'd like to get to know Adrian a little better."

"But even if Dominic were dressed as Domino..." Adrian left the rest hang.

Because Domino didn't have a boyfriend, and the press would be on Adrian like dogs on a fox if they saw him with the band. "I'm sorry," Dom said.

Adrian rose, and everything about his posture was relaxed, yet powerful as he made his way toward Dom. "You have nothing to apologize for. You have a public life and a private one. I'm part of the private one." He gripped Dom's shoulders, and those gold-flecked eyes held his. "I understand."

"You really did listen to all the songs and shit this weekend, didn't you?" Dom stared back. This man was a fucking wonder.

Thumbs stroked his neck, and one side of Adrian's mouth rose. "I did, yes. And read that magazine article and various things on the internet, too."

"He has to be a scientist if he's researching." Zavier's wry amusement sounded somewhere behind Dom.

He didn't bother looking, not with Adrian closing the last of this distance between them and those lips brushing, then tasting his. Fuck, he wanted out of here. Wanted to be back in Adrian's house and on his knees or in his bed or being fed dessert.

But Adrian smiled and stepped back, his gaze flicking away. Probably to Ray. "I do have to say, your website's a little...out of date. Content-wise, and stylistically."

Oh shit. Yeah, Dom knew about the content. He kept meaning to fix the links and add new shit, but he hated that. Hated the whole social media thing. Wasn't sure how it had fallen to him, except he'd been the one to say they probably should have one.

"Ah." Ray breathed the word out. "Yeah, I know. But—"

"It's me." Dom huffed a laugh. "I'm the one responsible for the social media, and I told you I only do templates and pre-built stuff."

Adrian actually pinched the bridge of his nose. "Babe." Strain there.

Zavier chuckled and Dom lobbed his water bottle at him, which he deftly caught. "I was actually laughing at your gentleman."

"Don't care," Dom said. "Fuck off, Zav."

"Guys..." Mish held up her hands.

"No, no, it's my fault, too," Ray said. "Marcella's been after me to hire a web designer and a social media handler, but I hate handing that much power over to someone outside us." He gestured at the band. "I don't trust people that much anymore. And I've no fucking clue where to even begin."

Adrian nodded. "I understand that, too." He paused, brow furrowing. "I might be able to help with the *where to begin* part of it, though. Give you a list of what you should look for."

"Really? Do you have a business card or..." Ray drew Adrian away to exchange information.

Zavier tapped Dom on the shoulder with the water bottle he'd lobbed, then handed it back. The words he spoke were quiet and serious. "He's good for you, Dom." Which was pretty much like Zavier telling him he should up and marry Adrian, 'cause he rarely made such comments about anyone. Dom stared back, and Zavier shrugged. "If you want my opinion."

"I—Thanks." Dom glanced over at Adrian's back as he and Ray exchanged numbers or emails or something in their phones. "He's magnificent."

"That's what you should hold on to." Zavier gripped his shoulder briefly, then slipped away to get his own water.

Adrian returned, somewhat chagrined. "I didn't mean to put down your work on social media."

"Well, it's been kind of crappy. If it had been anyone else, you'd have said the same thing."

"Probably. But that's not the point."

Dom took his hand. "Yeah, it is. And yeah, you're right. I don't know a damn thing about good design or managing social media. We didn't have any cash, and then when we did, we had no trust for outsiders. Hell, Ray still keeps Marcella at arm's length, and she's doing some good things for us."

Adrian's shoulders softened, and his smile returned. "If it helps, Ray did give me her contact info."

"Yeah, that's good." Dom looked around the studio at everyone getting their things to leave. "Hey, wanna get out of here? I can be the young office assistant the hot suit came here to find."

Adrian's grin sent a shiver through Dom. "A little role-play, Dominic? You are full of surprises."

"Hey, baby, I'll file your folders." He waggled his eyebrows at Adrian.

That got Dom a laugh. "I don't even know what that means." Adrian grabbed his tie, suit jacket, and messenger bag. "But yes, let's get out of here before the rest of your band leaves and you're found out."

Dom retrieved his backpack and they both said their goodbyes to Ray, Zavier, and Mish before heading out. The crowd of fans in front of the building was pretty thick, but given that he wasn't in Domino's gear, had his glasses on, and walked out with Adrian, he didn't care. Plus, Adrian was describing his weird day at work, which sounded hellish and awful.

One more reason he was grateful for being a rock star— even if he weaved through his fans undetected.

"It's hard to be a team player when you don't know the rules." Adrian twisted his face. "Three months ago, everything was great."

Interesting. "What happened?"

They made it to the subway station, and walked down to the platform in tandem, pausing only to swipe their cards. "I have no clue."

Weird. "There's gotta be something that happened. Like, did someone new come in, or like someone get a promotion or something?"

Adrian peered down at the tracks, his brows knitting. "Maybe. Jackson thinks I'm up for promotion, but the only thing that happened was that I was chosen to work at a customer site for two weeks. It went fine, though. The install was a success. The customer was as happy as customers ever get."

"So you made waves."

"I did my job, and did it well." He paused, and the silence was filled with the rumble of an approaching train. "But I suppose that might have been enough to make waves." He shook his head. "Anyway, it's just an annoyance."

Seemed like a little more, but Dom wasn't going to argue. He slipped his arm into Adrian's as the train—the one they needed, thank fuck—came to a stop. "Got dinner plans?"

Oh, that smile. Part happiness and part seduction. "How

about something simple like spaghetti, and we crack open that bottle of wine you brought the other day?"

Sounded promising. They flopped down on the plastic seats. "Can I make you late for work tomorrow?"

Adrian's eyes fluttered shut for a moment, then pinned Dom down. "Yes. I think that's very much in order, as well. We have some catching up to do."

"Anything you want, Adrian."

A nod. "And everything you need, babe."

Fuck yes. Dom leaned back in his seat, pressing against Adrian, who knew him in totality now. Perfect. Absolutely perfect. Life was grand.

CHAPTER
NINETEEN

DESPITE DOMINIC SPENDING EVERY EVENING WITH ADRIAN SINCE he'd attended Twisted Wishes' rehearsal, Adrian hadn't been late for work once. He'd even made his workout sessions with Jackson.

Hell, at this point, he really ought to give Dominic a key to his place. Watching him head back to his own place in the morning, bleary-eyed, was rough. Almost as rough as watching Dominic, sleep-and sex-mussed, lounge in bed while he picked out his suit and tie.

"This is becoming a habit," he'd murmured this morning.

Dominic's smile had been part yawn. "I like this habit."

So did Adrian.

He'd also gotten an email from Ray the day after the rehearsal, introducing Adrian to their band manager, and asking questions about the website and social media. During down times, while tests ran on his code, he started compiling a list of issues on his phone, then turned them into a return email. Hadn't heard anything after that, though.

As for *work*—well, he'd gone back over his email during the business trip he'd taken, from the correspondence with the customers to those with Russ and Russ's boss, and couldn't help but think that maybe Jackson and Dominic had been onto something. His being chosen for the customer job and having executed it well may have been seen as some kind of threat by William. An indication that Adrian might be promoted.

Part of him seethed with anger. He'd worked hard and, yes, deserved to be rewarded. But a larger part didn't care anymore. He was burning out. Too much corporate culture. Too many suits. None of it had any soul.

And there was the drop of envy for Dominic's life. Passion and love. Talent. The ability to make a difference. Turned out Twisted Wishes wasn't at all silent about equal rights, especially for queer people. Even Domino, who was usually flippant in many of his interviews, fell into serious Dominic mode when that was brought up.

It was heartening, but also came with that pang of regret. There were principles that had fallen by the wayside because of convenience and a paycheck. Maybe it was time to consider other avenues.

Once this damn project was done. Adrian fell into the rhythm of coding, so much so that he didn't pay much attention to his surroundings or whether anyone was at his cube entrance.

He flinched when Jackson rapped on the metal frame of his cube, but the quip he had in his throat died as soon as he saw the worry in Jackson's eyes and pinching at his mouth. He hadn't been that upset during their workout in the morning. "Hey, what's up?"

"You got a moment?"

The tightly whispered words made Adrian's stomach lurch. This wasn't about business. Shit. Had Jackson's job interview and potential offer fallen through? Dude had been so excited at the possibility of working on something he loved. "Of course."

Jackson stood back and nodded down the hall. Okay, so

this was a conference room chat, which meant it was serious and that Jackson didn't want the rest of the office overhearing. Adrian rose and followed him to one of the smaller rooms.

Once the door was shut, Jackson fiddled with his phone and held it out. "I thought you should see this."

Adrian took the phone and stared at the screen. It was a photo of Dominic—as Dominic, not Domino. He was obviously unaware of the photographer because he was laughing while talking on his phone. Upon closer inspection, Adrian realized it had been taken near one of their haunts—he recognized the coffee shop behind Dominic.

Cold leeched into Adrian, and he scrolled the image so he could see the gossip site—and the headline screamed out at him.

DOMINO GRINDER'S TRUE IDENTITY REVEALED.

Oh shit. Fuck. He blew out a breath...then his stomach dropped even further. Because Jackson *knew*. Somehow he knew Adrian was dating Dominic—or rather Domino. He'd never said Dominic's last name.

"How..."

Jackson twisted his face. "Apparently people noticed a twink with Domino's tattoos the other day. Creepy photographer got up a couple of floors in a nearby building with a telephoto lens and saw him playing with the rest of the band. They followed him home."

Shit. The other day. Dominic had rolled up his sleeves while playing. Adrian hadn't even thought to mention that he ought to roll them back down. Fucking heat of the summer, after all. The rest made sense, too, but that hadn't been the question he'd been asking. "No, how did you know I was involved..." He couldn't even finish his sentence.

Jackson laughed. "Oh." He rubbed the back of his head. "I

saw you and your man at the Met a couple of weeks ago, and you looked so into each other. I didn't say hello, 'cause I was out with mine, too, and well..." He gave a little shrug. "But I remembered him, 'cause he was just your type. All scholarly and cut and handsome."

Dominic was beautiful. "He *is* all that. Normally keeps his tats under his shirt."

Jackson met his gaze. "You had no idea who he was, did you? That's why you asked me about Twisted Wishes."

"No clue at first. I just sat down next to him at a local haunt, because he was reading some old gay lit about rentboys and seemed like he might enjoy some company." Seemed like ages ago. "Then I saw him on the cover of a magazine. Well, those tattoos of his."

Jackson laughed hard. "Yeah, I guess you'd know those. Jesus, Adi."

Adrian couldn't help the chuckle, but sobered quickly. "He's managed to keep his legal name out of things before now." A little more scrolling told Adrian the press had uncovered Dominic's full name...and with that, people could find out all the details associated with it, including his address. All you needed was to search through public records.

This wasn't good at all. Oh damn. He handed the phone back. "Don't say anything to anyone."

"I won't." Jackson stuffed the phone in his pocket. "But...if they've figured out who he is and where he lives..."

They'd eventually find Adrian, too. Especially since they'd been out in the neighborhood together a lot. All it took was one person to fly off at the mouth.

"This is gonna be a fucking nightmare." He clapped Jackson on the shoulder. "Thanks for the heads-up."

"No problem."

They both left the conference room, and every step back to his cube was laden with shocks of dread and worry. Dominic needed to know, if he already didn't. And if he did...god.

Adrian just hoped he was all right and with his band, who knew him and loved him.

There was no way Adrian could rush up to Chelsea and show up at their studio, not without causing more issues. By the time he entered his cube, his chest was tight and his arms tingled in precisely the wrong way. Sitting down in this state wasn't an option, so he grabbed his phone and headed toward the door. He needed air and space and somewhere quiet to call Dominic.

He got two of the three when he exited the office building into the busy streets of Wall Street. Right, so calling was out. He fired off a text message.

> Hey. I saw something on a website. They found you.

The reply came about a minute later.

> We saw. I'm okay. I'm with the band and they're keeping me calm.

Thank god for that.

> What do you need from me?

The pause was a long one. Adrian looked up and started walking toward Battery Park. Part of him still wanted to catch a train up to their studio. No one knew who he was. With his suit, they might even take him for a lawyer or...something. Someone other than the strange role he'd found himself in: Domino Grinder's secret boyfriend.

> Lie low for me. I don't want you tangled up in this shit. OMG, Adrian. I don't know what I'm gonna do.

He didn't like the sound of that. Because it almost sounded like...regret.

> We'll think of something, babe. Hang in there. When things blow over, we'll talk.

He didn't get another reply, so he strode down to the water. Halfway there, he was sweating too much and vaguely sick to his stomach. He tore off his suit jacket and swallowed the worry. Dominic was with his friends—his family.

Adrian should be there, too. Except—except he wasn't. He was in Battery Park walking with enough force that tourists parted to make way. When he reached the water, there still wasn't a reply from Dominic. He loosened his tie, sat down on a bench, and started rolling up his sleeves.

How much would it cost to walk up there? How angry would Dominic be?

His phone buzzed.

> It's not gonna blow over. Ever.

A second later another text.

> I'm sorry, Adrian.

Adrian stared at the screen, and the heat of the day vanished. His fingers flew across the screen.

> We'll work something out. Together.

There wasn't a reply. Not even after Adrian wrenched himself up and stormed up the promenade, then back down to near the subway entrance.

He tried again.

Babe, talk to me.

He took the walk back to the office slower than he'd come, mostly because his heart was beating too fast to power through the other pedestrians.

Not a word from Dominic. He cursed under his breath, and tried calling.

Come on. Pick up. But no, it clicked right over to an automated voice intoning Dominic's number. After the beep sounded, Adrian spoke. "Babe, don't do this to me. Not like this. Not now. Not after everything." He struggled to find other words, and failed. "Please call me back." There wasn't anything else he could do but hang up.

On the way back to his cube, he ducked into the bathroom to straighten out his suit and tie. Go back to looking corporate and cool and calm, even as his insides twisted and pinched and threatened to strangle every part of him.

The rest of the day passed in a blur of code and meetings. If he was quieter than normal, no one remarked on it, thank god. William was probably pleased. Jackson, though, gave him one or two worried looks. Adrian rode the train back to Brooklyn, clutching his phone in his hand, just in case it vibrated, but there was nothing—nothing.

At home, he stripped off his suit and replaced it with a T-shirt and shorts. Normal summer clothes for a day that was anything but normal.

Dominic was leaving him. Dumping him.

Fuck that. He was out the door and heading toward Dominic's place before he could even think. Didn't take him too long, given his pace, but he came to a halt a block away.

Because the sidewalk in front of Dominic's was crammed with a horde of people, and a whole bunch of them had cameras. Well, *shit*.

At least in his shorts and tee, he looked like any other gawking neighbor and not...not Dominic Bradley's boyfriend come to ream him a new one for trying to dump him. Adrian pushed out air and rolled his shoulders. He *needed* to calm down. Being an ass wasn't going to fix the situation. Last time, it had only caused Dominic pain.

Right. Maybe a beer might be a plan.

He swung back down the street and headed for Poet and Whiskey. Rather than take a table, he seated himself at the bar. Wasn't too crowded—Monday evening and all—but there were still a bunch of folks Adrian recognized as locals. The bartender, the self-same Greg who had served him and Dominic a few times, was behind the bar.

He lifted his eyebrows when he spotted Adrian and slid a coaster out. "What can I get you?" His gaze darted behind Adrian—probably checking out the crowd—then back to Adrian. "Beer, cocktail, wine?"

He'd ordered all of those at one point or another. Part of him wanted to slug back whiskey, but the more prudent part reminded him he had to work tomorrow, so he ordered one of the local microbrews they had on tap.

When Greg placed the glass on Adrian's coaster, he leaned in. "All alone tonight?"

There was something about the question that gave Adrian pause, because it wasn't *quite* flirting, but damned if he could put a finger on it. He shrugged his shoulders and kept an eye on Greg. "My boyfriend's busy. I'm just here for a beer." If Greg was feeling him out somehow, that should put an end to it.

Thankfully, Greg just nodded and moved off to serve someone else.

Granted, he might not be dating Dominic much longer. That thought felt like an ice pick to his spine. Adrian gritted his jaw, peered at his beer, then forced himself to take one sip, then another.

The cool liquid slid down his throat and loosened the knot

there. Dominic was spooked, and rightly so. But Adrian wasn't about to give up on him without a fight.

He took his phone out and typed in a text message.

> Tried stopping by your place. It's crawling with reporters. Or press. Or whatever they are.

Finally, finally, a response came.

> They're sharks. I'm not home. I'm in a hotel.

A second text came on the heels of that one.

> Ray says I'm being a fool and I should talk to you.

Adrian huffed a laugh and took another draw on his beer.

> Give Ray my thanks.

> I don't know if I should. This is a nightmare, Adrian.

He chewed on his lip, then drank. He could almost hear the panic in Dominic's voice. See the haunted expression in those wide brown eyes.

> I should call you, but I'm in a bar, so I can't. When I get home, I'll call. But Dominic, I'm serious. I want to make this work. Maybe it won't be as bad as you say...

He looked up at the TV while he waited for the reply to come. His beer was half gone, and the alcohol had done the trick of relaxing him a bit. The news was on, but it was all about the government or sports or some latest crime or another in the city.

Yeah, Dominic was famous, sure. But it wasn't like the world revolved around Twisted Wishes.

Greg the bartender came into view. "You need another?" He was still eyeing Adrian with curiosity.

This wasn't flirting, because it made his skin want to creep away. "Nah. One's enough. Just the check."

Greg nodded and moved away. The sooner Adrian got out of here, the sooner he could actually talk to Dominic.

A text had come back.

> I know you think I'm exaggerating, but I've seen what the others have gone through. Adrian, I love you. I love you too much to put you through that.

He didn't even think as his fingers typed the reply.

> Don't you think I should be the one to choose what I go through?

He finished his beer and stared at the screen. Dominic's reply was both heartening and gut-wrenching.

> Fuck. I can't do this over text. Call me when you can.

Just as soon as he paid for his beer and got out of the bar. It was too hot and too loud, even though it was hardly packed. He had to give Dominic some due, though. He was right—this whole thing was a nightmare, but not in the way Dominic meant.

> Give me a few. I'll call.

Greg came back with the slip and slid it to Adrian. "Hey, can I ask you a question?" He didn't lift his fingers from the paper.

Adrian met the man's stare. "What?"

"What's it like?" Greg smiled a bit and his eyes widened.

"What's what like?" He couldn't help the irritation slipping in. This dude was *weird*.

"Being Domino Grinder's lover."

Adrian's breath caught and his mind stuttered for a moment. Oh god. Of course. Of course someone would remember. Would know. He and Dominic came here all the damn time. People would recognize the Domino-as-Dominic now.

Holy shit.

"I mean," Greg said, and his voice took on a low tone. "You two are practically fucking by the time you leave here. Must be pretty hot."

Heat—the painful, burning kind—flared in Adrian and he fought the instinct to curl his hands into fists. Those nights had been *theirs*. His and Dominic's. Yes, they'd been pretty blatant, but he'd seen other couples that into each other. Fuck this guy. He pulled the slip out from under Greg's hand and checked the total before he drew out his wallet and placed cash on the bartop. "That's none of your damn business."

He stood and turned to head out the door.

"I know your name," Greg said. "Adrian Doran."

Fire and ice tangled in Adrian, and he rotated in place. Slowly, he stalked back over to the bar. He should just leave—walk away. But the *unfairness* of the day was finally burning through his body.

He and Dominic had been perfect. *Had been.*

"What are you going to do with it?" He returned Greg's stare, not flinching, not threatening. Steady breathing.

Greg lowered his voice. "Depends on what you're willing to give me."

Blackmail? Adrian barked out a laugh that had other people turning toward them.

The guy leaned in. "Those tabloids will pay a lot to know who you are."

Adrian followed suit, and his forehead nearly brushed Greg's. If he hadn't wanted to strangle the dude so much, it might have looked like a move. "I'm sure they will," Adrian said. He took back the dollar tip he left and straightened up. "Hope the money keeps your soul warm."

Greg's eyes widened, but that's all Adrian saw before he pushed through the bar and out the door into the warm summer evening.

Fuck. Fucking hell. Yeah, they had his name. And with that, they'd have his address and his place of work and...well, everything. He'd never really hidden much of his life. Sure, the bondage parties he'd gone to were discreet—kinda had to be when doctors and lawyers took part. But hell, these people could probably uncover his whole family history, back to immigration if they wanted to.

Maybe Dominic hadn't been so wrong after all. Only time would tell.

He did make it back to his place unscathed, though. And seemingly unnoticed, too. Good. He closed and locked the front door and drew all the blinds on every floor. Even the library. Finally, he sprawled out on the reading nook—near where he'd first tormented and teased Dominic—and eyed his cell phone.

He really did want to hear Dominic's voice. And a part of him still believed this would all blow over and they could go back to normal. Except there'd never been a normal—Dominic had always been Domino Grinder and would always be. That, too, was a part Adrian loved.

Greg's slimy question flitted through Adrian's mind. Truth was, being Domino Grinder's lover was a fucking joy because Dominic Bradley was an amazing, passionate, intelligent man, and so very compatible with Adrian's every need. He didn't want to imagine a future where he wasn't by Dominic's side.

Except neither of them really wanted their lives to be public spectacles. However, that hope seemed to be over now, so he'd manage whatever came. He indulged in a sigh, then called Dominic.

DOM FUCKING HATED HOTELS NOW. MAYBE THAT WAS FROM THE awful episode when Ray had nearly *died* on their last tour. They'd ended up stuck in a hotel for days, and they'd all been worried to the ends of the Earth about Ray.

This one was fine. A reasonably priced chain—well, reasonable for Manhattan. They'd stayed in some very sketchy places in their early days. But the white sheets and tidy room grated on Dom.

He shouldn't be here. He should either be home, bitching in his head about his own damn house, or with Adrian in the place that felt like home. But now the world had come crashing down around him.

God, when Marcella had walked in, her movements stiff and with a frown so worried that even Mish had gone still, they'd all wondered what was up. Then she'd shown them the photos.

Him. As him, not Domino. Walking around Brooklyn. The article went on to list his legal name, that he went to high school at the same time Ray and Zavier did, his college degree, and the neighborhood in which he now lived.

Including the price that his house had sold for, and a comment about how that settlement with Twisted Wishes's old label must have been quite good.

Fuck.

Everyone knew who Domino Grinder was. Now everyone

knew who Dominic Bradley was, too. He still shook and his stomach churned at the thought of his private life being torn open for all to see. How the hell was he going to walk onstage after that?

How many "I fucked Domino Grinder's ass and he liked it!" articles would now come out? Certainly some of his past one-night stands would be glad for the money a tell-all would bring in.

Ray, Zavier, and Mish had all kept him calm and they'd left the studio together, braving the sea of cameras and phones. They'd gotten into a private car Marcella had called for them, which had taken Dom to this hotel. Ray'd absconded with Dom's house keys with a promise he'd grab clothes and toiletries.

"They'll find me here," Dom had said.

"It'll take 'em a bit. You're under the name Jason Forester."

Not Domino. Not Dominic. He didn't want a third person to be. Two was one too many.

Shit. Dom rose from the bed and broke open the five-dollar bottle of water. His gut was a mess. His hands shook. All he wanted was to crawl under the covers and hope that this madness went away.

They had a concert in a couple of weeks. He didn't even know if he could get up on that stage.

Worse, he had no idea what to say to Adrian.

It wouldn't be long before the press found Adrian and hounded him. Cameras and phones and recorders would be shoved into Adrian's face while he tried to get to work.

Fuck. Adrian wouldn't want to live like that. Bet his bank job wouldn't even tolerate paparazzi floating around. Or Adrian being big news. Wasn't that some kind of security issue, or at least a PR nightmare?

Hell, he didn't want Adrian to be dragged into that awful place. The best thing would be for a clean break. Adrian would be a blip on the radar, soon eclipsed by some tell-all piece from a former lover.

Tears slid down Dom's cheeks. *Fuck.* He wiped them away. He was *not* crying. He was not.

Of course, that's exactly when Adrian finally called.

Dom attempted to school his voice, then answered. "Hey." No such luck—he sounded like a wreck.

"Hi, babe." Adrian's voice was strained, too. And soft. Sounded so far away. Dom sank to the bed again and closed his eyes. Adrian continued, "I'm not going to ask you how you're doing. Pretty good idea of that."

Dom could only grunt out a strangled half-laugh.

There was silence on the other end of the line. "I went to the Poet and Whiskey tonight after I swung by your place. Got a beer."

"Sounds nice and normal." Bitterness crept into his voice. He'd love to go sit in a bar for a few hours and lose himself with a beer and the murmur of other people, rather than the weird smell and quiet hum of this room.

This time, it was Adrian who croaked a laugh. "Except for the part where the bartender asked what it was like to be Domino Grinder's lover."

Oh shit. Everything in Dom's stomach churned. "I—Be right back." He dropped the phone on the bed and stumbled into the bathroom just in time to disgorge everything from his gut into the toilet.

He couldn't do this to Adrian. Didn't know how he was going to do this to himself. Damn, the panic hadn't been this bad in ages. Though he did feel a lot better now.

He flushed the toilet, gave his teeth a quick rinse and brush, and headed back into the room. Phone said the call was still connected.

"Adrian?"

"I'm here." His voice was paper-thin. "I'm not leaving you."

"Maybe you should."

"Knew you'd say that."

"I don't want to fuck up your life. This is gonna fuck it up so hard, Adrian. You have no idea."

A hollow laugh. "I'm learning." A pause. "Still don't want us to end."

"I don't want us to end, either." The words ripped up his throat more than chucking up his lunch. "But I can't protect you."

There was a sharp breath on the other end, then Adrian's clear voice. "You don't have to."

"But—"

"Dominic Bradley." His full name, said by Adrian in the voice that always stilled him, calmed him. "You don't need to protect me."

Maybe...maybe he didn't. A tiny weight lifted from his shoulders. "I don't know what to do about Domino."

Another pause, and Dom could almost see Adrian's confusion and the head tilt. "What do you mean?"

"Now that everyone knows who Domino really is, how am I gonna go onstage and play? I mean, I'm—" Even though he was alone in the room, he waved his hand around. "Kinda a nerd."

"You're also kind of a hard-ass rock star who plays wicked guitar and looks like a punk sex god onstage."

Oh. "That clashes rather hard with my non-Domino life."

"So?" A huff of laughter. "Before today, before all this came out, when was the last time you worried about stepping out onstage?"

God, it had been years and years. "Um. Probably some-time before Mish joined the band."

"What was it like on your last tour?"

Dom closed his eyes. The pulse of the crowd, the energy that vibrated through every venue. The thudding of his heart and the absolute certainty he had each night that they'd blow their fans away. "We were on fire. Felt like I could take over the world."

"I bet that was as much Dominic Bradley as it was Domino Grinder." Adrian's voice was as beautiful as it was soothing. "I know you. You're made of steel, babe."

The tears were back. Dom opened his eyes. "You're still not my fucking therapist."

"No. I'm still just a man who loves you with all his heart."

He took a shuddering breath. "You have no idea how much I love you."

"Well, I want to learn. I want you to tell me. But for that to happen, we need to have more time together." The slyness slipped into Adrian's voice.

Dom really hated this hotel room now. Wanted to be with Adrian in his house and in his arms. Or kneeling at his feet. "Okay. Fuck you, but okay."

A chuckle from Adrian. "I could come to you, you know. Wherever you are."

So tempting. So utterly tempting. But also dangerous. "If they know who you are..."

"They'll follow me to you." There was the bitter edge Adrian's voice had lacked before. "Makes sense."

"It's gonna be like that, Adrian. Forever."

"Maybe. Maybe not." A long pause. "But you're worth it."

Was he, though? There were other men—other people—Adrian could love. Lovers without complicated lives. But he kept those words behind his mouth.

Didn't seem to matter, because a frustrated sharpness bled into Adrian's words, as if he could see Dom, or hear those thoughts. "Listen to me. You *are* worth it. I'll take what the world throws at us."

"Adrian—"

A breath, and a voice that was layered with worry, fear, and love. "Please don't shut me out."

Dom blinked away yet more fucking wetness in his eyes.

"Okay." That came out as a whisper. This was hell. No matter which way he turned, he was going to hurt Adrian. "Then at least let me tell you what to look for?"

"You mean with photographers and shit?"

"Yeah. And like...prep for what people might ask you."

Again, it was almost as if they were in the same room. He felt Adrian's sigh. Imagined him combing fingers through that auburn hair of his. "All right. Tell me."

So he did. He listed all of the invasive questions he'd ever heard the gossip press throw at the band, all the shit he'd seen Ray and Zavier go through. All the questions he, as Domino, had refused to answer. Hell, the press had already pestered his mom and dad. "And they'll probably dig into your family, and ask them shit, too."

That got him a dark chuckle. "Is it bad if that pleases me on some level? Especially if they start asking Father Patrick about his queer little brother shacking up with a loud, tattooed rock star?"

Okay, that was kinda amusing in a weird way. "Your silver linings are interesting."

"I'm not always the nicest person," Adrian replied wryly.

Everyone had their moments of spite. This one, Dom understood. But there was another part of that whole exchange he wanted to know more about.

"Are we shacking up?" Despite everything, despite knowing the best thing to do was to let Adrian go, *this* thought warmed Dom straight to his bones. To have Adrian, to be home with him permanently was a fucking *dream*.

"If you'd like to. We'd have a lot of details to work out, but I'm serious, Dominic. I've been since the beginning. Not a fling. And I'll take what comes."

Agony ripped through Dom's heart. Everything he wanted. All that he could not ask Adrian to give. "I—need to think about that."

"I figured you might." There was that soothing tone again. "Trust what I say, though."

"I will." He believed Adrian, believed that Adrian believed what he said was true. Knew that it wasn't. "I should let you go. You have work tomorrow."

"Okay. But I want you to do something for me."

Dom pushed out a breath, his pulse kicking up. Wasn't lust—he was too damn tired and strung out—but that sense that whatever it was that Adrian offered, he would need. "What?"

"Kneel for me."

He obeyed before he even thought about it, sliding onto the hotel room floor. "Yes."

"Stay there until you find your center, Dominic."

A fresh wave of tears threatened. "I might be here a long time."

"I don't think so. You're strong. And I love you."

Dom leaned against the bed and bit back the words he wanted to say, the ones that would refute all three statements. But his heart and soul had already settled into the work Adrian had laid before him. "All right."

"Night, babe."

"Good night."

When the line went silent, Dom set the phone down on the floor, buried his head in his hands, and finally let the stress and fear and anxiety wring the tears out of him. It didn't hurt, though, and that surprised him. Felt cleansing. He took a breath, then another.

Maybe, maybe he was strong at his core. Domino was. And, as everyone kept pointing out, he *was* Domino Grinder.

So what would Domino do?

He raised his head and sat for a while, letting thoughts tumble through his head until one settled in and stayed. Domino wouldn't let go of the man of his dreams, so maybe Dom shouldn't, either.

It was so fucking hard, though. He trusted what Adrian said, but he knew he'd change Adrian's life for the worst.

Which was better? Fighting or letting go? He still didn't know.

Slowly, he rose to his feet and shook out his legs—then called room service for a burger and a beer. Tomorrow he'd sit down with the band and their manager and figure out what came next.

CHAPTER
TWENTY

THE WEEK AFTER THE REVELATION ABOUT DOMINIC BOTH FLEW BY fast and went excruciatingly slowly. Greg had made good on his threat, and a mere two days later, Adrian's own photo had been splashed across a website, along with the headline *DOMINO GRINDER'S SECRET LOVER* and some painfully intimate tidbits about their dinners. He'd wandered over to Poet and Whiskey after work, intent on giving the owner a piece of his mind, and spotted more than a few people following him.

And when he'd gotten to Poet and Whiskey, he'd pretty much killed every conversation by walking into the place. The owner found him first, and apologized profusely for the invasion of privacy. She assured him that Greg had been fired. So he'd stuck around for a beer and been surprised when the staff and patrons closed ranks around him.

The night was pleasant, and he ended up texting Dominic about it.

> Not everyone is an asshole.

Dominic had been pleased.

> Yeah, I know. My new therapist keeps pointing that out, too.

They'd been texting every day, and talking when they both knew each other was alone. It hurt to be apart. Adrian tried to keep the loneliness out of his voice, so not to add to Dominic's stress. He sounded so tired most days, but the connection helped.

None of this was easy. Watching the news about Twisted Wishes on Twitter and the gossip sites was unnerving. And so were finding people hanging out in front of his house waiting for Adrian to come out each morning.

He'd never kept a huge footprint on the internet, but there was enough public information out there. His address from real estate records. His résumé still lurked on some job-hunt sites. They'd found his gym membership, though no one there had given any reporter the time of day, thank goodness.

Work was most certainly not amused with Adrian's sudden celebrity status. But the building was secure and the front desk extra vigilant—one of the perks for working at a bank in New York City. He had suggested to Jackson that they not work out or take lunch, lest he be drawn into the fray.

Jackson waved a hand. "Adi, I am so unconcerned with this job and with those 'reporters' trying to dig into dirt on you."

The first part of that made Adrian pause. "Did you—" He lowered his voice. "You got it?"

"Of course I fucking got it." Jackson gave him a sly grin. "Just took a while for the paperwork to come through and for them to figure out my compensation. I'm turning in my notice as soon as I'm finished talking to you."

Oh. A strange mix of elation and sadness rocketed though Adrian. Jackson was leaving. Off to a job that meant something.

Dominic was up in Chelsea, passionately recording his

heart out and dodging the press, something he might not have had to do if Adrian hadn't made him—less careful? More open?

Adrian caught Jackson frowning. Shit. Head in his own problems. "Hey, I'm really glad for you."

Jackson leveled him a look. "You ain't happy, Adrian."

"I am for you. I'm just—" He shrugged. "There's a lot on my mind."

"Like your dude. And the people following him. And you." Jackson sat against the edge of Adrian's desk.

"Honestly, I think at this point Dominic's more upset that I'm being drawn into the chaos that is his life than he is that he was found out. Part of him realized it would happen eventually. And when I figured it out, I think it gave him a mental heads-up that this was coming."

"Transference," Jackson said. "He tell you that you guys should break up yet?"

Adrian didn't bother hiding his flinch. "Not in so many words."

A chuckle from Jackson. "Let me guess—doesn't want to screw up your life?"

Almost exactly the words used. "Pretty much."

Jackson grunted. "Adi. I'm gonna go in and tell Russ I'm out of here in two weeks, which you can bet means I'm being escorted out right after they do an exit interview." He stood and looked down at Adrian. "You know this office is gonna grind to a halt."

"Yeah."

"So what the fuck are you doing here when you should be talking to your man?"

The question hit Adrian hard. He hadn't even considered heading over to the studio, not when he was being tailed. Not when Dominic was in a state of panic at the chaos. "I figured once things calmed down, we'd figure shit out."

Jackson raised an eyebrow. "You're not a fool, Adrian. You

know better. He's a rising star—a rock star. This is gonna be his life."

And there was the truth. Adrian pushed away from his computer, his heart pounding. He wanted to be part of that life—part of Dominic's world. Chaos or no. If he let go of Dominic, there'd be no more quiet moments in his library. No more waking up to that smile.

Jackson stood. "Stay for the fireworks, then get out of here and go do what I know you want to do."

Adrian nodded, lips pressed tight, and watched Jackson exit and head down to Russ's office. Because cube walls didn't keep out anything, there was already murmuring around him. Whispered conversations, and this time it wasn't about Adrian's sex life with a rock star.

Domino. Dominic. Jackson was right. After the show, he needed to go to Dominic and argue that this shouldn't end. That the fame, the annoyance of the notoriety, was nothing compared to the agony of losing Dominic. His passion, his beauty, and his love.

He knew his feelings were returned. Dominic loved him—wanted him. Just didn't see a way to be together.

Adrian glanced around his cube, and thought of the email sitting in his personal account from Marcella Crane. Thought about the other from Ray Van Zeller.

Jackson was leaving this job. Maybe it was time for Adrian to, as well. There wasn't anything at all holding him here, other than a paycheck.

He stood and wandered out into the hallway. Other people were popping up over their walls, peering toward the boss's office. Five minutes later, it wasn't Jackson, but William who marched down the hall. "You." He pointed at Adrian. "You knew this was happening."

"I knew he was interviewing, yes. That he'd found some-thing that excited him in a way this place never did." Adrian cocked his head and leveled a look at William. "There's more to life than just a paycheck." He didn't honestly know whether he was talking to William—or to himself.

William shook his head. "It's only going to mean more work for you."

"Maybe." Adrian scooped up his phone. "Maybe not. We'll see." He turned his back on William and headed for the elevators.

"Where the fuck are you going?" William's voice rose shrill and hard behind him.

He waved a hand in the air. "Figure it out. You're the genius on the floor, William."

A minute later, he was on the elevator and heading to the lobby. Five minutes later, he was pounding down the steps into a subway station. Pretty sure someone was following him. Or maybe he was just paranoid. Didn't really matter at this point.

He had enough signal to fire off a text to Dominic.

> We need to talk.

When he passed through the next station, a reply came in.

> I'm sorry. I'm so sorry. I didn't want to do this to you.

> Fucking hell. You are not breaking up with me over text, Dominic Bradley!

Of course, the fucking train halted on the tracks and he no longer had signal. Adrian closed his eyes for a moment, then the train lurched forward.

When he reached the closest stop to the studio, he marched out of there and up to the street. No reply from Dominic. Maybe avoidance. Maybe panic. He didn't know, but this wasn't going to end without them speaking.

He definitely was being followed now. And

photographed. Adrian hit the call button on his phone and listened to the other end ring and ring and ring.

Finally—finally—as he got to the building that housed the recording studio, Dominic picked up.

"Adrian—"

"Don't. Just—don't. I know it's hard. I know you want to. But don't."

A hiss, as if Dominic was breathing out through his teeth. "Do you have any idea what your life will be like? The fans? The press? Nothing will be normal again."

"Sure it will." Adrian stopped in front of the building, surrounded by fans and photogs and a ton of cell phones being pointed his direction. He was vaguely aware that people were calling his name, but all he could do was crane his head up and look at the building. Count the floors. "And I have a fairly good idea what the non-normal part will be like, too."

"How could you?"

"Because I'm standing on the sidewalk in front of your studio. I'm sure if you check Twitter or something, you'll see video."

Silence.

"Dominic."

"You're *outside*?"

"I am."

"*Why?*"

He rolled his eyes. "Take a fucking guess, genius." He laughed. "You are so impossible sometimes."

"Oh my god. You are there. There's about a dozen live feeds. Ray has one up. Holy shit." On the other end, a deep rumble of a voice—probably Zavier—said something. "Yeah, but I can't just—" Dominic took a breath.

"Yes, you can," Adrian said. "You can come down here and rescue my sorry ass from this."

"I'm—not dressed." Dominic's voice was a harsh whisper.

He knew what Dominic meant, and ignored it completely. The look he wore didn't matter for this. "I'm one hundred percent certain you have clothes on, Dominic."

Silence on the other end, which only emphasized the crush and chatter of the crowd around him. He lowered his own voice, ducked his head, and closed his eyes to block out all those people staring at him. "Babe, *please*."

His next step was to fall apart on the sidewalk. It was too much to handle, the emotions. Knowing that every word, every expression was being transmitted over the internet to god knew who. Maybe even his siblings. Fuck knew what Patrick would think, him begging for his lover in public.

But he'd endure what he could for Dominic. Because Dominic had to endure so much more now that his true name was out.

An exhale on the other line. "Oh my god, Adrian. Hang on. I'll be right down."

He had no idea what had changed Dominic's mind, but relief shot through him. "Thank you." He clicked off his phone, but kept his eyes closed for a little longer. Found the calm, the center, and the control, even if his heart was trying to pound its way from his chest. His stomach was in tatters.

Maybe they would break up. There was always that possibility, even if he hated the thought. But it wouldn't be because of fear or the public or any of this shit.

He blinked his eyes open and raised his gaze to the door of the building. They fit together. In bed. Outside it. He loved the shy bookworm as much as the over-the-top rock star. Loved everything in between, too. The surrender and the steel. All of the things that made Dominic Bradley utterly himself.

The lobby door opened, and Dominic was there, pushing through the crowd of people. "Excuse me," Dominic ground out. "Can you all just...get out of my way?"

Dominic was—different—this way. But also the same. A T-shirt clung to his body, exposing his tattoos. He was wearing the faded jeans Adrian was so used to seeing on him, but with sneakers, not his dress shoes. His hair was a mess—more Domino than Dominic, but glasses perched on his nose.

When Dominic finally reached him, he grabbed Adrian by the shoulders and gave a little shake. "What are you *doing* here, Adrian?"

He peered into those wide brown eyes. "Do you remember when you asked me if I liked my job?"

Dominic slid his hands up to Adrian's neck. They were strangely cool. Soothing. Or he was overheated. "I remember everything about that night," he said.

"I fucking hate my job. It's awful. My best friend just quit and I'm going to be stuck in that corporate hell alone." After that statement blazed across the internet, he'd probably get pushed out. "I'm here because nothing in the world matters more to me than you. Not the job, not my grandparents' house, not even my library. I'd burn it all down if it meant I could be with you. I love you."

Dominic's shoulders dropped. "Fucking hell, Adrian."

There were tears lurking back in the corner of his eyes and in his mind. He missed family. Missed connections. Jackson had been a lifeline for years. So had Janelle, but they were friends—not this. Dominic was so much more than a friend. He'd become part of Adrian's life.

"I mean it."

Those hands rose to cup his face, and Dominic stepped close. Pressed his forehead to Adrian's. "I know you do. You're surprisingly, refreshingly truthful about every damn thing in the world."

Adrian met those lovely brown eyes. "Surely not everything."

A laugh, then the humor fell away. Thumbs stroked Adrian's cheeks. "You know, this is the way my life is." He nodded to the crowd rocking around them, all the people taking photos and videos and no doubt texting and tweeting all of this. "Chaos. No privacy."

Yes. And no. Adrian mirrored Dominic's hands, taking that sweet face into his own palms. "Right now, I'll admit this crowd is pretty fucking terrifying." He smoothed a thumb over Dominic's lips. "But we've had privacy. We'll have it again. Not everything is for public consumption."

A flicker in Dominic's eyes, and a curve of a smile on his lips.

"The world can have Domino. He's pretty fucking amazing. But I want *you*, Dominic Bradley. And I'm not willing to give you up without one hell of a fight."

"I hate fighting." Dominic's eyes were shining. "And I love you, too."

Adrian stepped in, until there was no space left between them at all, and whispered against his lips, "Then fucking kiss me, already." It came out as an order.

A huff of laughter, then Dominic did, and the world fell away beneath the gentle pressure of his lips and the slip of his tongue. Yes. This was right. This was theirs.

When they broke the kiss, he realized the buzzing in his head was cheers and applause, and his whole body flared with too much heat for a suit during the summer in Manhattan. "Time for you to rescue me before I pass out from the heat."

Dominic smiled, took his hand, and led him into the building and its air-conditioned splendor. When the doors closed behind them, Adrian shuddered and wrenched off his suit jacket. They headed toward the bank of elevators. "Please don't ever make me do anything like that again."

"Declare your love for me in front of the world?" Dominic's cheeks were red and his eyes a little moist. "I fucking hated that crowd, but that was the most awesome, greatest—"

Adrian grabbed the back of his neck and swallowed the

rest of the sentence in a kiss that had them both banging up against an elevator door. When he broke the kiss, he met Dominic's stare. "No. Don't you dare make me march across town with my heart in my hand to stop you from breaking up with me over something so foolish as you being a fucking rock star and trying to protect me from your life ever again."

"Oh." Dominic breathed out the word. "But it is a lot to deal with. I mean, I hid from it for years." He swallowed. "You should probably press the up button."

Adrian jabbed the arrow, but kept Dominic against the elevator door. "And I get why. People prying into your business, your personal life. Following you around. I'm not going to like that part."

Dominic grabbed his tie, pulled him in, and their mouths met in a tangle of lips and tongue. God, he felt so good, so right in Adrian's arm. His taste, his fingers digging into his arm.

The elevator dinged and the door to the left—not the one they were making out against—slid open.

With a moan, Adrian broke the kiss. "Our ride is here."

They broke apart and stumbled into the other car. There were mirrored panels in the elevator, and Adrian saw his wild reflection. Hair destroyed and moisture dripping from his hairline. His shirt was wrinkled to hell and drenched in sweat, and his tie askew. Lips red and plump from kissing. "Well, I'm a mess."

Dominic hit the button for the floor that housed the studio they'd been renting. "You're gorgeous. Stunning. I can't believe you came here for me."

"Should have come sooner. That Monday, I should have been here."

Dominic leaned back against the back of the car. "Maybe. I don't know. I was so out of it, then. To be honest, I'm still kinda terrified. But I can't change any of it...and the fans don't seem to mind. And it's not nearly as horrible as all the nightmares I've had about it." He took another breath. "I fucking walked out there as me, and saved you."

Adrian loosened his tie. "Yeah, you did."

"I was watching the feed Ray had up while we were talking and you just—you looked crushed in that crowd. Like you were gonna break open right there and then. And I realized how fucking unfair I've been to you."

That—Adrian hadn't expected those words. "You haven't been unfair to me."

Dominic straightened as the car came to a halt. "I have. I totally have."

But the door swung open and before them, in the hall, were the three other members of Twisted Wishes. And they were clapping, the fucking bastards.

"Well," Ray drawled before throwing an arm around Dominic, "for someone who hates the spotlight, that was probably your most amazing performance."

"Fuck you, Ray," Dominic said. "Wasn't a show."

Ray kissed him on the side of the head. "I know." He let Dominic go.

Mish handed Adrian a bottle of water. "You look about ready to pass out."

"That's because I am." He cracked open the bottle and drank half of it.

"The studio's cooler." Zavier gestured to the door. "And more private."

"Except for the techs," Dominic said.

Ray waved a hand. "Sent them home. No way we're recording anything else today. And Marcella's already called. She's on her way."

Because of Adrian. What he'd done. "Sorry about the sudden PR nightmare."

Zavier laughed. "Not a nightmare at all." His hand fell onto Adrian's shoulder, and slowed his entrance into the studio until they were the only ones in the hall. His eyes were bright. "What you did was astounding."

"What I did was nearly have a nervous breakdown and pass out on a sidewalk."

"You saved Dom."

"He saved me."

"Yes." Zavier grinned. "Exactly." He clapped Adrian on the back and pushed him into the studio.

He didn't understand these people—not entirely. But they felt like family.

And when he stepped into the studio and saw Dominic smiling and laughing, looking like that heady combination of Domino and Dominic, and their eyes caught—Adrian knew he was home.

———

DOM HANDED BOTTLES OF WATER TO ADRIAN TO PASS TO THE others as they all sat around the studio and waited while the furor of Adrian's well-broadcast declaration of love and Dom's "daring" rescue made the rounds on the internet. Marcella's cell phone rang off the hook for requests for interviews. She'd headed out into the hall to field the calls. After all, they would have to address what had happened.

At one point, Adrian got a text and scrunched his face in disgust at the screen of his cell phone.

Dom winced. "People bothering you?"

"No. It's Jackson. Said he was escorted out of the office after he quit. Fucking awful way to treat him." He looked up. "And apparently, I have a meeting with the boss tomorrow at 8:30 AM."

Oh. Fuck. Adrian's work. "Um. You're not gonna lose you job...?"

He shrugged, his shirt untucked, half unbuttoned, and sleeves rolled to his elbows. His tie and jacket had been thrown over a chair close to the door. "Maybe. I don't really care at the moment."

Ray ducked his head and turned away, but Dom saw the smile. He swung around to peer at Zavier. "Wait, what's going on?"

Of course, Zav raised an eyebrow. "I have no idea what you mean."

"Bullshit. You know everything Ray's got his fingers into." Dom stood and rounded on Mish. "We're supposed to do things as a band—all of us!"

Mish held up her hands. "If Ray's up to something, he hasn't let me know."

"No..." Ray faced Dom, his grin wide. "I'm just...thinking. That's all."

"You want to hire me to work on the website," Adrian deadpanned.

"I'm thinking we should hire Adrian to do the website," Ray said.

Mish rolled her eyes. Zavier spun a drumstick in his hand and said, "It's not a bad idea."

"No," Adrian said.

They all looked at him, including Dom.

"Wait, you don't want to do the website? But that list..." Ray looked lost.

Dom smacked his hand against Adrian's thigh. "And if you're gonna lose your job because of me..."

"I'm not losing my job because of you. If they don't fire me for unexpectedly walking out of the office today or for essentially saying that my position is a flaming pile of shit, I'm quitting tomorrow morning anyway. And I have more than enough vacation owed to me and a savings account built up. I can manage fine for quite some time."

"You don't want to fix our website?" Ray said again. He pulled a chair out and flopped into it.

Adrian waved a hand, his lips twisting up into a grin.

"Oh, I want to fix your website. It needs an overhaul something awful—and it's down right now thanks to the increased traffic." He held up his phone. "Funny how that works."

Zavier stilled the stick in his hand. "I'm not following this discussion correctly. You want to fix our website, but you don't want us to hire you to fix our website."

Adrian grinned at Zavier, and Dom recognized the *gotcha* in those lips. "Exactly," Adrian said.

That got a snort from Zavier.

"Is he always like is?" Ray turned to Dom.

"No. Yes." Dom sighed. "Adrian?" There was a plea in his voice.

"Sorry. I'm still a little lightheaded and giddy, so you're going to have to put up with my mood for a change." He raised a hand to silence any other outbursts. "I don't want to be hired to fix your website. I want to be hired to run your IT and your social media."

Mish strode over, dropped a water bottle into Adrian's lap, and punched him in the arm. "You're going to be just as much trouble as the rest of them, aren't you?"

Adrian got a sly grin and cracked open the bottle. "Maybe. Depends on whether the band hires me."

"We're gonna hire you," Ray said.

Adrian met Ray's gaze. "Even though I'm fucking your best friend?"

Heat shot straight to Dom's face and balls. Yeah, Adrian was starting to feel better, that was for sure.

"*Especially* since you're fucking my best friend," Ray said.

Dom buried his face in his hands. "Fuck you both. And Zavier's your best friend, too. So's Mish."

"Zavier's my *husband*," Ray said. "And I can have more than one best friend. We've had this discussion before."

Adrian snorted. "Are *they* always like this?"

Both Zavier and Mish answered, "Yes."

Dom started laughing. He couldn't help it. Everything

was wrong and everything was right. He was still Domino Grinder and he was utterly Dominic Bradley.

And Adrian Doran was gonna work for Twisted Wishes. *His* Adrian. The man who held his heart and his secrets and tied him up. The love that kept him steady and let him float above all the cares in the world.

Hands on his shoulders and then his chin, tipping his face up, and Adrian was there. "I'll give you everything I can in this world, Dominic. Just let me be with you."

"You're asking me?" Because really, if it weren't for all the other people in the room, Dom would be on his knees right now.

"I'm always going to ask." Adrian's smile was soft.

"I want your library." Dom met his gaze. "But it's gotta come with you, 'cause it's not nearly as fun without you in it."

Adrian's grin was wicked.

Somewhere behind Adrian, Ray murmured, "They're fucking perfect for each other."

"Mmmhmm," Zavier said. "And I believe this is where the three of us should go and find out what interviews Marcella's booking us for."

There was shuffling, and Mish laughing, and a door opening and closing, then silence. Dom hadn't once looked away from Adrian. Couldn't. Not from those eyes or that smile.

"Just the library and me?" Adrian whispered. "Nothing else?" He stroked fingers over Dom's cheek.

"How about the whole house and the rest of our lives? Shacking up?"

A nod, then Adrian pulled him up into his arms, and took Dom's breath away with a kiss that was hot and deep and utterly claiming. Dom dug his fingers into Adrian's hair and kissed back hard, fighting for every inch of control, until they were both hard and breathless.

When Dom came up for air, he laughed. "Did I just propose to you?"

Adrian nipped his ear. "Yup."

"So you're fine with being Mr. Grinder?"

Adrian's breath caught, then he huffed out a laugh before kissing Dom's neck. "Adrian Grinder sounds ridiculous."

"Yeah, nearly as bad as Domino Grinder."

Adrian softened at that and pulled back, hands gliding down to Dom's shoulders. "Domino Grinder is a fucking amazing man. So's Dominic Bradley. And you're the love of my life. My strength and my home."

The mirror of his own thoughts. "You're my shelter and my refuge. You're right. We can have our privacy. The public can have Domino. The rest of the band can have Dom. But you're the only one who'll ever have all of me."

Adrian's smile was joy incarnate and his kiss feather-soft. "Deal?"

"Deal." He pulled Adrian into his arms.

"You know, I'm kinda looking forward to eventually sending a wedding invite to sanctimonious Father Patrick." Adrian grinned.

Dom chuckled. "When we set a date." He sobered. "Maybe your other siblings will be kinder."

"I hope so."

He kissed Adrian's neck. "Let's get out of here. Dodge the press, buy some pie, and go home so you can tie me up and feed me."

Adrian lifted him off the ground and swung him around completely. "I fucking love my job," he said.

So did Dom.

They didn't even bother with Adrian's coat or tie, just took the fire stairwell down to the ground floor, snuck out hand-in-hand, and took off for the nearest subway stop, laughing the entire way.

CHAPTER
TWENTY-ONE

SIX MONTHS LATER

"Where the hell is my black lipstick?" Dom dug around in his makeup kit, but fuck if the damn tube showed up. All the other colors were there, including the bright orange he'd been missing since San Francisco. Huh. One vanished, the other appeared.

None of his bandmates replied, too intent on putting their own selves together.

"Try looking with your eyeshadow." Adrian leaned against the wall near Dom's makeup station in the band's dressing room, tapping away on his phone. Hadn't even looked up, as far as Dom could tell, intent on doing the social media rounds before the show.

A thrill to see him here, with the band. A dream. Some nights after concerts, when they'd piled into the bus, Dom wrapped his arms around Adrian and didn't let go. In return, he'd get loving murmurs and gentle, soothing touches.

It was better than beer. Maybe better than sex, but he wasn't quite sure of that. He'd need much more of both with Adrian before he made up his mind.

He checked the section of his kit with the eyeshadow and

the missing tube was there, just as predicted. "How did you know?"

Adrian did look up then, his grin perfect. "You tossed it there last show, after Ray argued with you about your high school science teacher's favorite color."

"How the fuck do you remember shit like that? On the road, I can barely remember what I ate for breakfast two days ago."

Adrian's eyes danced. "You didn't eat breakfast. You never do when we're on the bus. You just drink your coffee."

"And annoy the fuck out of me," Ray said, though there was laughter there.

Yeah, he did like prodding Ray, sometimes. "You still didn't tell me how you remembered where this was." He waved the tube around, then took off the cap, and applied it.

Was a little different to see Adrian in ripped jeans and a Twisted Wishes crew shirt. He'd taken to wearing one of Domino's leather cuffs, too, and didn't that pour heat through Dom when his eyes landed on Adrian's wrist.

Adrian pocketed his phone. "Good spatial memory. Weird brain thing, I guess." He gave a little shrug. "Plus, it's kind of my job to remember what you guys do."

"Pretty sure you're not going to put 'Domino lost his lipstick, what color will he choose?' onto Twitter," Zavier said.

Oh, the gleam in Adrian's eyes. "That would make a *great* poll."

Mish laughed. "Don't give him any more ideas. Insta-gramming our dangerous midnight highway eating was bad enough."

"Everyone *loves* those, though," Ray said.

"Except my stomach." Dom patted his midsection.

The slice-of-famous-life shit Adrian had been posting had been a huge hit with fans. It made them feel like they were a part of the tour, too. And, in some odd way, preserved the band's privacy. Why hunt down tabloid shit when you could hit the Twisted Wishes media accounts and see photos of the band on the bus?

Of course, Adrian cleared everything with them before posting. But fuck, did he have an eye for what fans might like. He'd also rebuilt the website from the ground up and instituted a fan club with its own forums and exclusive perks. Shit was humming along now. Hiring Adrian had been a smart move. Even Marcella agreed.

And Adrian seemed happy. Said he was. Laughed and joked. He wasn't afraid to be by Dom's side, even inviting his former co-worker and workout partner, Jackson, to their New York City show. Nice guy. Cute boyfriend. Big fans, both of them, especially of Domino Grinder. It was good meeting one of Adrian's friends, especially now.

Dom stared at his reflection—at Domino—in the mirror. He was with Adrian, both as Domino and Dominic, and that was pure magic. He swiveled in his chair. "How do I look?"

"Awesome as always," Mish said. "I envy your eyeshadow."

That was pink tonight, and there was glitter in his hair. Black leather pants and a red tank that wouldn't last the first two songs completed the outfit, along with his cuffs and collar.

Zavier nodded his approval, as did Ray.

"You look stunning, babe." Adrian's comment was soft. "Always do, no matter what you wear."

Sometimes all he wore was Adrian's ropes, in all the new and interesting ways they'd learned from Janelle. Not as much on the road, but at every hotel stop, Dom asked to be tied up, and Adrian happily obliged. That was Dom's true privacy. Those moments when it was only them and their skin and rope and kisses and moans. Dominic and Adrian.

In public on tour, the line between Dom and Domino had blended somewhat. He always dressed up to the teeth onstage, but he'd let more of his twink self come through otherwise. Less makeup sometimes. Wearing his glasses rather than his contacts from time to time, or short-sleeved shirts and tanks to showed off his ink.

Therapy had given him new ways to handle the fear and anxiety that still lingered, that horrible imposter syndrome voice that lurked in his mind. But nothing bad had come from fans or even critics since his legal name had been spilled out all over the media. Plus, Adrian was here, and while he wasn't a therapist, he did create the calm Dom so needed for his whirling mind sometimes.

His gaze slid to the cuff on Adrian's wrist. Rumor among fans was that it signified how Domino had claimed Adrian, except in so many ways, it was the other way around. Adrian had sat down next to him, all those months ago. Had made his wishes known and respected Dom's, too, and had never given up on Dom, even when Dom had just about given up on himself.

Marcella marched into the dressing rooms. "Are we ready?"

Beyond the open door, the sound of the audience pulsed.

Ray got that look, the one that meant they would fucking eat this show alive. "Yeah, we're ready."

Yeah. They would take over that stage and make it theirs. Give the audience exactly what they came here for: the best concert of their lives.

"Let's go fucking do it," Dom said.

Adrian caught his arm before he marched out after the rest of the band, and that sexy grin flipped Dom's insides out. He kissed Dom's cheek. "You're so fucking beautiful. Go rock them dead."

Every night. Each night. Same words. "I love you."

Adrian's smile widened. "You know, it's fucking awesome being Domino Grinder's lover."

"And being yours." He grabbed Adrian's hand, gave it a squeeze, then followed his bandmates out to the stage.

With a crowd in front of him, the band around him, a guitar in his hands, and Adrian waiting in the wings, there wasn't anywhere else Dominic Bradley wanted to be.

Twisted Wishes was his life, Adrian was his heart, and he was himself, at long last.

Want more Twisted Wishes? Check out the next book, REVERB!

ACKNOWLEDGMENTS

Second Edition: Again, much thanks to Layla Reyne for her support and help while I worked to bring this new edition out.

First Edition: I owe a good bit of thanks to Layla Reyne for all the writing sprints during the final push to complete this book. Also, as always, thanks to Mackenzie Walton for doing a yeoman's work with her editing and making me work hard to write the best book I can. Thanks as well to my agent, Jennifer Udden, for all her advice, and to Judith at A Novel Take for her help.

My eternal gratitude to readers and reviewers for taking a chance on my books and giving my characters a few hours of your life. I hope you enjoy reading these books as much as I enjoy writing them.

And once more, I want to thank Lori Witt for her constant love, support, and friendship.

Weave the Dark, Weave the Light

Cinnamon Roll

Love of the Game

ALSO BY ANNA ZABO

TAKEOVER

Takeover

Just Business

Due Diligence

Daily Grind

ON THE BOARD (WRITTEN WITH L.A. WITT)

Rookie Mistake

Scoreless Game

Shift Change (coming soon)

TWISTED WISHES

Syncopation

Counterpoint

Reverb

CLOSE QUARTER

Close Quarter

Slow Waltz (a Close Quarter short story)

STANDALONE WORKS

CTRL Me

Outside the Lines

ABOUT THE AUTHOR

Anna Zabo writes contemporary and paranormal romance for all colors of the rainbow. They live and work in Pittsburgh, Pennsylvania, which isn't nearly as boring as most people think.

They can be easily plied with coffee or a chance to see the Pittsburgh Penguins.

Anna has an MFA in Writing Popular Fiction from Seton Hill University, where they fell in with a roving band of romance writers and never looked back. They also have a BA in Creative Writing from Carnegie Mellon University.

Anna uses they/them pronouns and prefers Mx. Zabo as an honorific. They can be found online at annazabo.com.